40-Day Journey
to the
Heart of God:
AN
Adventure
IN PRAYER

Tammy M. Price

VMI Publishers
Sisters, OR

All Scripture taken from "Today's Parallel Bible," Copyright 2000 by Zondervan.

Unless otherwise indicated, Scripture quotations are taken from the Holy Bible, New Living Translation, copyright 1996. Used by permission of Tyndale House Publishers, Inc., Wheaton, IL 60189

Scripture taken from the Holy Bible, New International Version. Copyright 1973,1978,1984 by International Bible Society. Used by permission of Zondervan. All rights reserved.

Scripture taken from the New American Standard Bible, Copyright 1960, 1962,1968,1971,1972,1973,1975,1977,19995 by The Lockman Foundation. Used by permission.

King James Version Cambridge Paragraph of 1873 also used.

Webster's Dictionary was used for all dictionary references. Copyright 1979 MCMLVI, MCMLIX, MCMLXI, MCMLXII, MCMLXVI by Ottenheimer Publisher, Inc.

Hebrew/ Greek References taken from: *The Strongest Strong's Exhaustive Concordance of the Bible.* Copyright 2001 by Zondervan.

DeepRiver Books

a division of VMI Publishers
Sisters, Oregon
www.vmipublishers.com

ISBN: 1-933204-16-8
Library of Congress Control Number: 2006922961

Author Contact:
HOPministries03@aol.com
www.heartsofprayer.com

For the One Who gave me His all, I give mine.

I DEDICATE THIS BOOK TO:

My joy, strength, & peace
my hero, best friend, & comforter,
The lover of my soul,
healer of my heart,
& my salvation:
My Lord and Savior, Jesus Christ
With the prayer
that many more will find and know Him.

SPECIAL THANKS TO:

My precious gifts from God: my husband, Donnie Price,
our children, CJ, JD, Ali, DJ, & MJ, my family, and all the friends
and prayer-warriors who prayed this journey into print!

My thanks also go out to Bill and Nancy Carmichael, Lacey,
Colleen, and all those behind the scenes at VMI Publishing—for all of their
hard work, encouragement and prayers. I thank God for their help and
faith in me and my message!

Table of Contents

Filled with love and awe
of Your great and mighty ways,
You are our greatest desire.
Bless us with pure hearts
Oh, God, that Your dwelling place
our hearts shall be.
As You fill us with Your Holy Spirit...
for You, set our hearts on holy fire.
Sharing Your love with others
and winning souls through us,
with spiritual eyes, let us see.
Keep us safe from the devil, his demons
and all his evil, the eternal liar.
May we desire Your Word above even life itself;
tasting it daily on our lips,
Sweet as ever anything could be.
Oh, Lord, teach us to pray,
that we may know and love
You for all eternity.
Fill us with the power of Your love,
that to Your Name all glory shall be.
Bless us we pray,
As we seek Your heart and holiness,
Our heavenly Father,
from Your throne of grace above
with passion, power, honor and glory
That we may praise and bless Your holy name.

Introduction

Do you long to pray and be filled with the passion of Christ, have access to the power of the Holy Spirit, and experience the persevering Presence of God's holiness? Moses gave God forty days on the mountain, Noah gave God forty days on the sea, and Jesus gave God forty days in the desert; will you give God forty days in your heart and closet of prayer? Let us ask that He may give; seek, that we may find. Let us knock that He may open the door, on our journey of prayer to His Heart of holiness.

It is my prayer this book will be just the beginning of a passionate, powerful, and purposeful life of prayer. Whether you are a new Christian just starting to pray or a seasoned veteran, there is much to be studied on prayer; Christ desires to teach us to pray. As we learn and grow together over the next forty days, remember this is just a stepping stone to greater faith and intimacy with our heavenly Father, seeking His Heart and holiness in prayer. The art of prayer calls upon the mighty power of God to work in our hearts that we may better know Him, love Him, and serve Him. A powerful, Spirit-led life of prayer is our highest and holiest calling. One of God's deepest desires is for us to pray to Him, that our hearts may, anew, be set on holy fire for an Almighty God. The Christian life is not to be drudgery, or boring-where flames and passions die out, halting us along God's perfect path; our lives are to be an adventure-walked in prayer! Our Creator eagerly and joyfully awaits us with His Presence.

It is also my prayer that this book will help teach you that our greatest need, as God's children, is to live holy "lives of prayer." As a man lives, so shall he pray and as he prays, so shall he live. Prayer is a way of life! Thus we learn in prayer to love and worship God with all our strength, hearts, souls and minds, that our lights will shine before men and glorify our Father in heaven. We absolutely cannot fulfill His greatest commission, obey His greatest commandment or find and receive His very best promises and blessings for our lives without experiencing our adventure—without "living prayer."

God is just waiting to bless you and those you pray for! God's Heart desires to bless, heal, restore, free, love and make His children holy. Let His holiness consume our hearts. All blessings are channeled through prayer! Whether you, like me, love adventure and simply desire a greater intimacy with God, or have struggled in obeying, finding, being blessed by Him or finding His very best will for your life, if you desire these things—then this book is for you!

Prayer is an art that needs to be learned, studied, and practiced; prayer is a life of fun and excitement, which needs to be lived. Prayer is a journey that takes us to the very Heart and holiness of God, where He desires us to worship Him in this life and the next. This book is not meant to simply be enjoyed as pleasure reading, though you may; it is primarily a tool to help you reach for God's holiest, greatest and most blessed desires for you, His child. You will be filled with new joy and power as you seek God's Heart, His Presence, and His will. You will be rewarded with all this as you learn to pray, studying His Word as your personal love letter, giving you new passion, power and purpose in prayer. This journey will allow Him to remove the obstacles that have been standing in the way of a powerful, prayer-driven life. A holy life is waiting to be yours, lived for and personally blessed by God's passion, power and Presence!

Prayerfully read and study one chapter of this book each day, allowing sufficient time for the subject matter to truly sink deep into your heart. This will allow you to best concentrate and meditate on the verses God will speak to you about, and it will allow the Holy Spirit sufficient time to show you how to effectively apply each truth to your life. If you are tempted to read ahead, follow these simple guidelines:

On a calendar, write one number each day from 1–40. Read and meditate on that chapter on its corresponding day during your quiet reading time. After you've reflected and answered the questions for that day, then feel free to read ahead during any additional free time you have that day.

Growth is a slow process, which takes time and determination, but you will be rewarded with the fruit of the Spirit which is a great blessing. Your journey cannot be accomplished in just two days. And even our forty-day journey is only the very beginning start of living a life of prayer, a lifetime that serves God, seeks God and knows God intimately; a life that is driven by prayer, finding its purpose and being fulfilled in its journey.

Let us be discontent each day with our prayer lives as they are now, and always seek to grow, always seek to know God more and become more like Jesus each day. Surrendering to our heavenly Father our hearts and our time allows Him to grow within us. Let us strive for the prayer life of Christ who prayed and lived in total submission and in total dependence upon the Father. Even at this very moment, Christ sits at the right hand of the Father, interceding for the saints. Yes, right at this very moment, He is praying for you! I also am praying for you each day. You have this book in your hand because Christ prayed for it to be given to you at the exact moment you came upon it. Remember, He will empower and teach you as you read this book. As you seek God's Heart, as you seek Christ adventuring in prayer, it is He who will draw you to Himself as you draw near. He awaits us with open arms and love as we seek to be like Him and pray as He does. He waits to fill us with a passion for prayer, bless us with power in prayer, and fulfill in each of us His purpose for prayer.

There is a reason and divine purpose you desire to know God better, and you seek to learn to pray. I am not the one leading you on this journey, it is God Himself. Let us turn to Him, and Him alone, remembering this book is not a secret card we hold in our hands. Instead, is only a tool, a "tour guide" God desires us to use to get us started on our journey, leading us to Him. He desires to empower and draw us into the school of prayer with Christ. He desires that we know His Presence, experience His holiness, and lead a God-centered, exciting, fun, purposeful life, and for this, He created prayer; we must pray!

PREPARE

Prepare a quiet place and time to open the Scriptures and bow before our Almighty God in prayer. Remember not to just open this book, read it and set it down, but to bring your Bible and a prayerful heart with you as you read a chapter a day. A journal will be most helpful and a pen necessary to record your thoughts and comments right in the book. Highlight meaningful verses and phrases for further review, and make this book your very own. Old, worn sneakers are the most comfortable and useful; I pray this book will be for you as well! Let us now leave the world behind, enter into the holiest of places, learning to be humble students and servants of our loving heavenly Father in prayer.

Before you get started, it is important to make a commitment as we begin our journey in the school of prayer. Commit to read and search out how God would speak to you through the chapters of this book as you seek to learn how His Holy Spirit will empower you, transform you, and change you to live a life of prayer:

1. Commit to a daily time of prayer, Scripture study, and reading one chapter of this book.

2. Commit to finding an accountability/prayer partner to embark on this journey of prayer with you; God created pairs for a reason!

3. Commit to use what you are learning!

Whether your goals are for a victorious Christian life, weight loss, financial gain, academic gain, or physical competition, preparation is usually where battles are won and lost. Prayer is an essential preparation for a victorious, purpose-filled and fruitful, Christian life. We will also need to pray for a hedge of protection around ourselves, our family, and those journeying through this book because satan will do his very best to keep us from praying and learning to pray. He will do all he can to keep you from reading this book. He knows that the minute you put these truths to use, he has met his defeat in your life, and all those you pray for! Let the obstacles he tries to throw up only encourage you, that you are getting closer to the holiness of God!

As a runner prepares for a marathon by devoting his/her time, staying away from unhealthy habits, and preparing with his/her entire heart, so must we. Gaining passion for something requires time and energy. As a weightlifter requires stretching and straining of muscles in order to build them, so must we stretch and strain our prayers (spiritual muscles) as we must stretch and strain our hearts and surrender them to God, so that He can prepare us to pray with His passion, His power, and for His purposes. As we devote and surrender our time and energy to Him, we must willingly sacrifice all things to Christ in prayer. Are you willing?

COMMITMENT:

I am committing to spend time alone daily with God in prayer with the Bible along with quiet time for meditation and reading this book. I ask the Holy Spirit if there is something during these forty days I need to give up to be able to give the appropriate amount of time for this book:

I also commit during this time to pray for and encourage my partner:

If one person falls, the other can reach out and help. But people who are alone when they fall are in real trouble (Ecclesiastes 4:10).

Signature:

Date:

LET US PRAY

Gracious, wonderful, holy, powerful, heavenly Father God. Sanctify us by Your Spirit, teach us to pray, and I thank You, that it has been Your good pleasing and perfect will to place this book into my hands and into the lives of each of Your children's lives at just the right moment, empowering us to seek You. In Jesus' Name we pray, Amen.

Day 1

GOD's PROMISE
of PRAYER
||||||||||||||||||||||||||||||||||||||||||||||||||||

Devote yourselves to prayer, being watchful and thankful.
— Colossians 4:2 NIV —

What is prayer and why should we not only do it, but study it? Prayer is a commanded communication and response. Prayer in its simplest form is a child asking God for something and knowing he will receive it. In its most beautiful form, prayer is a child of God seeking his or her heavenly Father in worship with praise, confession, thanksgiving, and petitions with a listening and watchful heart. God created prayer as a means of two-way communication with Him, bringing forth our needs and granting them. Scripture promises, *The LORD will hear when I call* and refers to God as *you who hear my prayer;* another version says *He will answer when I call* and says of God, *you answer our prayers* (Psalm 4:3/65:2 NIV/NLT). When we become Christians, God keeps us here on earth to continue His work, and prayer is how He enables us to ask Him for the things He desires to give to us. He not only hears our prayers, but Scripture promises that He faithfully *answers our prayers with awesome deeds* (Psalm 65:5). God also desires us to pray to Him, that He may answer and we see the things only He can do!

Prayer does not begin with us, as many would believe. Prayer actually starts with God. He communicates to us our needs first so that we may ask Him in prayer for the responses He desires to fulfill. When we notice the need He has placed before us, He wants us to ask Him through prayer. This is so we will continually be brought into fellowship with Him and rely upon Him. He desires a relationship with each one of His children, and prayer is our way of communication with Him. Scripture says, *O LORD you have heard the desire of the humble; You will strengthen their heart, You will incline Your ear* (Psalm 10:17 NASB). Just picture, our heavenly Father, is "inclining" His ear down to hear our very prayers! He delights in the desires of the humble, because they are desires He has placed within us. He wants to answer and bring us into His holy presence.

God has chosen prayer as our way to desire, know, and do His will. It is our means of power, might, and victory. It is our only way to remain humble and have our hearts strengthened to remain in His will, being empowered to lead the prayer-driven life He created us for. To know it, ask for it, and be brought into it requires humility, desire, and strength. Notice He *hears the desire of the humble.* Humility conveys dependence upon God instead of self; desire brings us into the action of prayer, obedience, and surrender. It is only with His reinforcement through prayer that we are able to rely and wait upon Him.

Prayer is our only way of accomplishing all He desires us to do. Prayer is our dependence upon Him, our obedience, surrender to Him, and our friendship with Him. Scripture says, He *delights in the prayers of the upright* (Proverbs 15:8). God not only waits for us to pray, but when we do, it delights Him! We may ask, "Who is upright?" God answers in Proverbs 15:9, *He loves those who pursue godliness.* We are able to approach the throne of grace through the righteousness of Christ and, as His Spirit works in us and through us, we shall daily pursue godliness. When your heart surrenders to Christ as Lord, remaining in prayer, this is when it truly pursues godliness and not worldliness. It is a prayerful, humble servant of God who seeks Him and His will who has an upright heart.

We shall find that our journey to find the Heart and holiness of God will be a journey of pursuing His attributes, and acquiring them. We shall then have Him, as He has us. Prayer is not just for the super-saints; it is for you and me, for every child of God. God created each of us for His purpose, and only through prayer will we find His purpose for our lives and the power to carry it to completion. God had special goals for your life when you were born, and He has planted great dreams and desires deep within your heart that only self-doubt or simple self-reliance will steal. **We cannot do His work, pursue godliness, allow Him to transform our hearts, minds and lives,**

and surrender to performing God's will, pursuing our God-given dreams, goals and purposes, without prayer!

It is equally important for us to listen to God's Word as it is to speak in prayer. So many times we miss the answers to our prayers because we are either too busy talking or trying to answer them ourselves. We must believe God created prayer for us, that He hears and is just waiting to answer us! He promised, *And it shall come to pass, that before they call, I will answer; And whiles they are yet speaking, I will hear* (Isaiah 65:24 KJV). When we doubt either of these things, rather than waiting prayerfully for God's perfect timing for Him to shower His blessings upon us, we forge ahead without waiting for His answer. Read this verse again and say it aloud until you believe what God is saying to you: *I will answer them before they even call on me. While they are still talking to me about their needs, I will go ahead and answer their prayers!* God has the answers to our prayers ready before we even ask for them. He created the need, the desire, and the prayer; our answers are ready!

God desires to answer us, speaking personally through His Spirit, His Word, and our circumstances. Most importantly, He wants to reveal something to us about Himself through His answer to our prayers, therefore drawing us unto Him. Scripture says, *How blessed is the one whom You choose and bring near to You To dwell in Your courts. We will be satisfied with the goodness of Your house, Your holy temple. By awesome deeds You answer us in righteousness, O God of our salvation* (Psalm 65:4-5 NASB). We must believe God has the answers to our prayers ready before we even ask for them. When we come before him with pure hearts, He draws us near. Let us meditate on where this exchange takes place: His holy temple, our hearts being drawn into the very heights of heaven in prayer! It is only God who can satisfy our listless, empty souls with the goodness He alone can give! It is only He who can forgive, heal, free, bless and give us the grace to remain in His courts.

Oh, how He waits to bless His children as we ask in prayer. We must confess our lack of time in prayer, praise, waiting, and our resistance to His drawing us into prayer. Scripture says, *But the LORD still waits for you to come to him so can show you his love and compassion. For the LORD is a faithful God. Blessed are those who wait for him to help them… you will weep no more. He will be gracious to you if you ask for help. He will respond instantly to the sound of your cries* (Isaiah 30:18-19). Our heavenly Father responds even more quickly than a mother to her infant's cry. How He awaits, to show us His love and compassion—to be our Helper, to gracious to us!

Are you or a loved one losing strength? On whom do you rely? Remember and believe: *He waits for us to ask for His help!* He desires to show us His love, to be compassionate with us; He waits to respond to us, instantly. Let us be still and quiet in prayer, knowing He is God and allow ourselves time to listen, wait, and watch expectantly for His answers. Notice, He teaches us here that blessed are those who wait for Him to help them. We must take every verse, promise, and blessing very literally. We must ask, and we must wait. Only by remaining in prayer and His Word can we do both of these things.

He is waiting to answer as we ask. God commands we are to be *devoted to prayer, being watchful and thankful,* so He can answer us faithfully with great and awesome deeds; in this way we will see our answers. He loves not only to bless, but does so in ways only He can. We can trust that He is faithful in moving to answer our prayers. We must also be sure to wait, watch, and thank Him for His blessings! Prayer is not about getting our way with God, but about seeking Him, finding Him and being blessed by Him. It is all about Him having His way with us as He inclines His ear, waiting for us to pray with prepared, thankful, and surrendered hearts. Scripture says, *LORD, thou hast heard the desire of the humble: Thou wilt prepare their heart, thou wilt cause thine ear to hear* (Psalm 10:17 KJV). God strengthens and prepares our hearts through prayer for His holy presence and blessings that we may join Him in His workings and purposes.

Prayer acts as preparation for proper perception and reception of divine blessing; bringing us into the Presence of His glory. He is waiting for us to rely upon Him, that He may strengthen, satisfy and bless us to do His work, and most importantly, that He may reveal Himself to us.

How is it you get to know people and build great working relationships with them, slowly learning what to expect and how to react to them? This knowledge comes only through spending time with people. When you really desire to get to know a person better, you listen to that person and watch how he or she responds in certain situations. These same guidelines hold true with God. In prayer, He gives us an ever-increasing desire and ability to know and be more like Him, to join Him in His work and understand our purposes.

We have His written Word so we can read about Him, yet He did not leave us only this. Reading His Word alone may bring only head perception and not heart perception. He has given us prayer, that we may spend time with Him, getting to know Him better in our hearts and minds, as we see Him reveal Himself to us. Through His answers to our prayers, He strengthens our hearts and faith in who He is. Scripture says God *encourages* us as He hears our prayers and *comforts*. Let us not forget, He *prepares*.

Knowing God inclines His ear to hear our prayers gives insight into how important our prayers and cries are to Him. Picture a two-year-old, too upset to talk. He has a large tear rolling down his face, and you know more are on the way. Do you not pull him close and turn your ear to hear the cries of his little heart? In this way, the Lord longs to be gracious to us; He rises to show us compassion in answer to prayer. David tells why he prays to God and what he has learned of God's reaction to our prayers. *I am praying to you because I know you will answer, O God. Bend down and listen as I pray. Show me your unfailing love in wonderful ways. You save me with your strength* (Psalm 17:6-7). David learned God saves; He is patient, loving, gracious, compassionate, faithful, just, and quick to answer. God reveals His great love for us in answer to prayer.

God tells us how, even in circumstances in which we may not be able to recognize His love right away, He still loves us, but we will not see or understand His love without prayer. *I will bring that group through the fire and make them pure, just as gold and silver are refined and purified by fire. They will call on my name, and I will answer them, I will say, 'These are my people,' and they will say, 'The LORD is our God'* (Zechariah 13:9). What fires are you going through? What, in your life, is God waiting for you to cry out to Him for help with? Where do you need His mercy and compassion? If we call upon our God in prayer, we will see how He uses the fires in our lives to refine us and make us the pure utensils He desires to use in His kingdom. We will see how He uses fires to get our attention, speak to us and get us to listen so that He may bless us and show us His Heart as we make Him our Lord, God. Are you allowing God to use prayer to allow you to see your fires as blessings? What is God revealing about Himself to you in answer to your prayers?

Sin keeps us from God while prayer brings us back and purifies us, that we may be the righteous who please Him with our prayers. Scripture promises that not only does God answer when we call on Him in prayer, but He also speaks to us, forgiving and revealing His holy love for us. David prays, *O LORD, you are so good, so ready to forgive, so full of unfailing love for all who ask your aid* (Psalm 86:5). Prayer cleanses, purifies, humbles, directs, and empowers. Prayer allows us to know who God is and understand and believe what He is doing. Prayer allows us to know Him, that we will surrender to His work in us, and may join in Him in His work through us. The Christian life cannot be lived victoriously on our strength alone. We cannot rely upon human, worldly resources to seek God, know Him, serve Him or become more like Him. We must rely upon God's holy fires of love, His mercy and compassion, and His strength we will receive only in answer to prayer.

EXERCISE

Write "He *loves* me and *delights* in my prayer" on an index card; taping it somewhere you will see it often.

- ❧ What has God revealed to you about Himself, today?
- ❧ Which verse does God want you to ask Him to apply to your life today?
- ❧ For whom does He want you to pray this verse?

LET US PRAY

Gracious, wonderful, holy, heavenly Father God. Thank you for Your promises to hear and answer us, thank you for prayer. Convict us of any self-reliance. Teach us what it is to depend upon, You, oh, Lord teach us to pray …In Jesus' Name we pray, Amen.

Day 2

GOD's PURPOSE
of PRAYER
|||||||||||||||||||||||||||||||||||||||||||||||||

And this is my prayer: that your love may abound
more and more in knowledge and depth of insight

— PHILIPPIANS 1:9 NIV —

Prayer is our access to the throne of grace wherever we are, whenever we need; it is daily fellowship with God, getting to know Him better and better. Prayer is not an option for a Christian; it is a command, and through it, we receive God's power and grace. When Jesus spoke to His disciples, He said, *When you pray...* expecting prayer to be a daily part of their lives. He did not say "if," but "*when!*" Scripture tells us how seriously God takes prayer, when Samuel referred to ending his prayers for another as a sin against God (1 Samuel 12:23).

It is through prayer that we gain insight into God's Heart and wisdom, with power for godly living. It is through prayer that we ask God's grace to flow into the lives of His saints and all those around us. Prayer allows us to become aware of His movement, to join Him and how we praise Him for all He does. It is through prayer that we receive a spirit of thankfulness, full of worship and desire to serve Him, be more like Him and know Him better. An alert mind and a thankful heart see His loving kindness and cry out for more of Him each day.

Peter exhorts us to *crave pure spiritual milk so that you can grow into the fullness of your salvation. Cry out for this nourishment as a baby cries for milk, now that you have had a taste of the Lord's kindness.* He tells us not to be those who reject prayer and God's laws. *They stumble because they do not listen to God's Word or obey it, and so they meet the fate that has been planned for them.* We are commanded, *But you are not to be like that, for you are a chosen people. You are a kingdom of priests, God's holy nation, his very own possession. This is so you can show others the goodness of God, for he called you out of the darkness into his wonderful light* (1 Peter 2:2-3,8-9). This shows also, as some mistakenly believe, prayer and godliness are not just for the super-saints, but a necessary lifeline for every child of God. We are each a part of God's kingdom of priests; He desires to bless and use every one of His children to show others His goodness! Look at what Mary, an ordinary person like you and me, the mother of Jesus, says of herself, *For he took notice of his lowly servant girl, and now generation after generation will call me blessed* (Luke 1:48).

Prayer not only blesses us, it is how we bless those around us. Prayer is where God takes the ordinary, and does the extraordinary. It is where we learn to respond, as Mary did to God's wisdom and will for her life; it is how we respond to God's Word, in full trust and obedience, as she did in Luke 1:38, *I am the Lord's servant, and I am willing to accept whatever he wants.* Prayer is where He fills us with the desires of His Heart for our lives, giving us the insight and faith to accomplish His will. It is through prayer that He takes our desires and dreams and molds them into His. Remember how He took that lowly servant girl, spoke to her, filled her with faith and blessed her to be filled with His Spirit? We learn to praise Him through prayer, regardless of our circumstances, and we allow Him to do His work, regardless of the personal costs. Mary was willing to sacrifice her reputation, her husband, and even her life to accept the Words of the Lord; let us be so willing.

Prayer is the work God has made in His Kingdom now, and the coming of Christ's eternal Kingdom dependent upon. Prayer keeps us dependent upon God and rids us of our natural tendency to be self-reliant and independent. It rids us of the decision-making from eyes of flesh and turns us to making decisions from the will of the heart. Prayer opens our eyes to faith and God's wisdom and spiritual discernment. Prayer is where Jesus, *the author and perfector of our faith* fills us with courage, hope, and endurance (Hebrews 12:2). *What is faith? It is the confident assurance that what we hope for is going to happen. It is the evidence of things we cannot yet see. So, you see, it is impossible to please God without faith. Anyone who comes to him must believe that there is a God and that he rewards those who sincerely seek him* (Hebrews 11:1,6). Do you believe? Are you ready and willing to earnestly seek and receive your rewards?

God desires us to live a life of faith and obedience, but does not expect us to do it on our own. Many new Christians struggle, falter and even backslide more into their old ways by trying to live as a Christian without the power of the Holy Spirit. As we reach for our Bibles, it is important to remember we need to pray before opening the Scriptures. Christians need to develop the habit of asking for the filling of the indwelling Spirit each day in order to grow in the knowledge of God and develop the ability to obey. We must continually ask for and receive the spirit of grace, wisdom and revelation to give us divine understanding of God's truths and their application to our lives. My favorite verses for this say, *...I will put my law in their minds and write it on their hearts. I will be their God and they will be my people. No longer will a man teach his neighbor, or a man his brother, saying 'Know the LORD,' because they will all know me, from the least of them to the greatest, declares the LORD. This is what the LORD says, he who made the earth, the LORD who formed it and established it—the LORD is his name: 'Call to me and I will answer you and tell you great and unsearchable things you do not know.'* (Jeremiah 31:33-34/33:2-3 NIV). The Maker of heaven and earth wants to reveal Himself to each of us, great or small, new Christian or old. He wants us to know Him as *LORD!* He wants to answer us; we just need to ask, to *call out to Him.* He is not only our Savior, but our Sustainer, our Lord, listener, revealer, and Teacher.

Reading and studying the Bible are important, however, applying its teachings to our lives is what is most critical to our spiritual health. If we are physically thirsty and have a glass of water in front of us, it does us no good just to look at it. We must pick it up and drink it in order to satisfy our thirst. So it is with the Bible. Not only do we need to pick it up and prayerfully read it, but apply it faithfully to our lives; letting it nourish and fill within. If we read and study the Bible independent of prayer, we may gain head knowledge, but no heart knowledge. Prayer is essential in growing our faith that our hearts may understand and respond to what we read.

It is through prayer and His Word that the Holy Spirit opens the eyes of our hearts so that we may be filled with the love, knowledge, and the depth of insight God desires us to have to know Him better.

When God saves us, He also wants us to grow, but we can no more grow ourselves, than we were capable of saving ourselves. Satan believed he could grow independent of God, and we exert that very same pride if we live in prayerlessness. Paul emphasized the importance of his converts receiving the work of the Spirit in their hearts, in answer to prayer, *I have never stopped thanking God for you, I pray for you constantly, asking God, the glorious father of our Lord Jesus Christ, to give you spiritual wisdom and understanding, so that you may grow in your knowledge of God. I pray that your hearts will be flooded with light so that you can understand the wonderful future he has promised to those he called. I want you to realize what a rich and glorious inheritance he has given to his people* (Ephesians 1:16-18). We will find, as prayer opens up the Scriptures to us, Scriptures' truths will lead us back into prayer. Prayer is the access we require to enable us to understand and live out the truths in the Bible. It is in answer to prayer that we truly begin to understand the divine inheritance we have been given as children of God. It is in God's Presence in prayer that He floods our hearts with His Light, and how we receive our rich and wonderful promises and gifts from the King.

Jesus promises, *But even more blessed are all who hear the Word of God and put it into practice.* **Prayer gives us head knowledge, heart understanding and the grace, faith, and courage we need to internalize and apply His Word to our lives as He commands. Only through prayer can we see His work in our lives, and receive the necessary tools and faith to put it into practice, joining Him in His work.**

God does not want us to rely upon ourselves to serve Him, know Him, and be more like Him. God says, *Who among you fears the LORD and obeys his servant? If you are walking in darkness, without a ray of light, trust in the LORD and rely upon your God. But watch out, you who live in your own light and warm yourselves by your own fires. This is the reward you will receive from me. You will soon lie down in great torment* (Isaiah 50:10-11). God does not want us to walk about in darkness, but rather to walk in and work in His Light. It is in prayer we show our trust and reliance upon God's light. If we are prayerless, and not relying upon Him, but on ourselves and possibly others He tells us our promised outcome is torment.

God desires to bless us, reveal Himself to us, and give us all we need to perform His work and know Him better. Think of the person you love most in this world; if you had unlimited resources and power, would you not do all you could to bless that person with every possible joy he or she could possibly experience each and every day? Would you withhold your presence for a single moment to the one you love who was crying out to spend time talking to and loving you? Would you withhold a single thing he or she may ask for as long as it was not harmful to them, if it were in your power to act and to give? Our heavenly Father's wisdom, resources, and love are limitless. If you feel you have not what another needs, if you are limited in your ability to give of your time, love, resources or prayer, then turn to God Almighty, who is not limited by time, space, finances, or lack of wisdom or strength. It is through prayer that we receive all we need if we give all we have. Jesus says, *If you sinful people know how to give good gifts to your children, how much more will your heavenly Father give the Holy Spirit to those who ask him* (Luke 11:13). All you need to do is ask!

Prayer is the oxygen tank for the soul; it is the Light needed for our growth. Prayer is the lifeline for the Christian life and the only way we will gain the insight, understanding, and power to do God's work. Through prayer, we receive His blessing and protection, as we put our hope and faith in Him. *I wait for the LORD, my soul doth wait, and in his Word do I hope. My soul waiteth for the LORD more than they that watch for the morning: I say, more than they that watch for the morning* (Psalm 130:5-6 KJV). Out of our darkness, we seek light and wisdom, waiting with great expectations as those who awake on a cold, dark night wait for the warmth and brightness of the morning sun's glory. It is through prayer that we shall receive Him shining brightly upon us, in us, and through us. Scripture says that God, *who commanded the light to shine out of darkness, hath shined in our hearts, to give the light of the knowledge of the glory of God in the face of Jesus Christ* (2 Corinthians 4:6 KJV).

Proverbs 2:9 promises, after we have cried out for and received insight from God, *Then you will understand what is right, just and fair, and you will know how to find the right course of action every time.* God does not intend His children to go through life lost and confused; He not only wants to reveal Himself to us, but also what He desires for us in our lives as He gives us the power to do so.

Wisdom will enter our hearts and knowledge will fill us with joy (Proverbs 2:10). If you are not filled with joy as you handle a situation, take it back in prayer again and again until God has filled your heart with wisdom and joy. God will show you the right course of action through prayer and His Word every time, and you will be filled with joy as you carry out His plan of action for your situation. Prayer helps you to stand on His promise. *Trust in the LORD with all your heart; do not depend on your own understanding. Seek his will in all you do, and he will direct your paths* (Proverbs 3:5-6). It is only through prayer that you will find the courage to trust in Him with all your heart as you find His Heart, His purpose, and His will in all you do as well as the power to follow Him wherever He directs your path!

Remember, true prayers are born out of God's own holy Heart, flowing through us by His Spirit. When we truly experience the Presence of God, discovering the depth of the love in His Heart for us, it is impossible to keep it contained! It is like a balloon being filled with air until it can be contained no more. Such is the love of Christ that we are filled with through prayer. We are filled and filled and filled until we can no longer contain it, and we become a blessing to others.

Through prayer, we not only become more like Him, but we see where He wants us to join Him in His work. We see all those around us with eyes and hearts full of compassion and mercy and we begin, anew, to see those in need of the Light of God's love to flood their hearts, freeing them from the traps of this dark world and the enemy who has taken them captive. Paul tells us in his second letter to the Corinthians 5:18,20, *And God has given us the task of reconciling people to him. We are Christ's ambassadors, and God is using us to speak to you. We urge you, as though Christ himself were pleading with you, 'Be reconciled to God!'* There is no greater blessing once you have experienced the love of Christ and have been set free by His grace, than to pass on the mercy you have been given and share the love and power of Christ flowing through your heart.

EXERCISE

Is there anything God brings to your mind you may have been trying to accomplish on your own power instead of His? Is there anything in your life you have not bothered to pray about because you haven't believed how much He cares for you and wants to care about your needs? Is there anything you may have simply thought He couldn't possibly do? Is there anyone whose heart needs to be prepared for reconciliation to Him in answer to prayer? Ask for the faith to ask and to wait upon His mighty answer.

- What has God revealed to you about Himself, today?
- Which verse does God want you to ask Him to apply to your life today?
- For whom does He want you to pray this verse?

LET US PRAY

Gracious, wonderful, holy, heavenly Father God. Fill us with Your Holy Spirit who enables us to pray and wait in great expectation with thanksgiving for all You are doing in Your perfect answers to all our prayers. Oh, Lord, teach us what it is to depend upon You, oh, Lord teach us to pray...In Jesus' precious, powerful and beautiful Name we pray, Amen.

Day 3

OUR ALMIGHTY CREATOR GOD

||||||||||||||||||||||||||||||||||||||||||||||||||||||||||||||||||||||||

The heavens are yours, and yours also the earth;
you founded the world and all that is in it.

— PSALM 89:11 NIV —

So, to whom do we pray? The Creator of the universe. Scripture says, *In the beginning God created the heavens and the earth.* We read throughout Genesis chapter 1; our all-powerful and Almighty God **said**, *And it was so, and it was excellent..* God spoke and created. Scripture tells us, *The earth was empty* when He created it, *a formless mass cloaked in darkness. And that the Spirit of God was hovering over its surface* (Genesis 1:1-2). God's Spirit is His Spirit of power, His Spirit of creation, His Spirit of love and prayer. This same, mighty power, His Holy Spirit, is indwelling every believer.

It seems so odd we would limit Him in our prayers. How is it we doubt the One who created the universe, sent His Son to die for our sins, raised Him from the dead, and saved us from eternal damnation to be able to sustain His children? How can we doubt the truth of the Spirit who created the heaven and earth and everything in it? How could we not believe He can save and bring new life into an unsaved loved one or new life into a marriage, ministry, or wounded soul? Paul asks, *Why does it seem incredible to any of you that God can raise the dead?* (Acts 26:8). We may not want to admit we doubt Him, but we all do, and our lack of prayer and obedience shows it. The lack of His power in our churches and ministries shows our doubt in God and lack of prayer.

Scripture says, *The Lord God Omnipotent reigneth*, and that in the new city there is no temple, because *its temple is the Lord God Almighty and the Lamb* (Revelation 19:6/21:22 KJV). He is all powerful, all knowing and is everywhere. God reigns over heaven and earth and wants us to live in His power and Presence, that we will reign with Him, walking forth in His almighty victory. *God holds victory in store for the upright, he is a shield to those whose walk is blameless* (Proverbs 2:7). The Lord appeared to Abraham and Job, referring to Himself as "The Almighty-El-Shaddai;" the God who is self-sufficient, all sufficient—Who nourishes and sustains completely! God desires to appear to His children and tell us who He is, then show us God Almighty in answer to prayer. When Abraham responded with doubt to all God wanted to do in his life, He asked Abraham in Genesis 17:14, *Is anything too hard for the LORD?* God would ask us this same question. What obstacles has He chosen in your life recently that you feel you can do nothing about? He chose to bless Abraham and Sarah with a child when they were well past childbearing age. God banked His entire promise to Abraham on doing what only He could do in their lives: the seemingly impossible.

Jesus stated this same truth, *Humanly speaking this is impossible. But with God all things are possible* (Matthew 19:26). Let us respond and believe, *I know that You can do all things, And that no purpose of Yours can be thwarted* (Job 42:2). Do you believe that *He can do all things?* Do you live out the belief that nothing is impossible with God? Do you want to know He can and will do all things? When He tells you He will do something, do you believe that no purpose of God's can be thwarted, not by man, demon or nature? Notice what the first part of the verse indicates as well, with man alone, this is impossible!

Too many times, our prayers are limited because we don't understand how impossible it is for man to accomplish all things alone when he does not believe all things are possible ONLY with God! If we believe in man, the devil has us right where he wants us: powerless to fight him, live in any victory or rescue any perishing souls around us. The truth of what we believe, in man or in God, will come through prayer and will manifest itself in our actions. If we believe in man, we will live in defeat; if we believe in God, we will live in His victory and blessing. Jesus tells us to *Have faith in God. Listen to me! You can pray for anything, and if you believe, you will have it* (Mark 11:22,24). If we have our faith in God, we can pray for and have anything; if we don't, we can pray for nothing.

God desires to do the impossible in the lives of His children. Let's take a look at God, to whom we are told to pray, and some of His attributes that we may better understand and be drawn unto Him. He is all-knowing, all-powerful and always present. Let us begin to allow Him to reveal Himself to us as He did to David, who wrote, *For the LORD is a great God, the great King above all gods. He owns the depths of the earth, and even the mightiest mountains are his. The sea belongs to him, for he made it. His hands formed the dry land, too. Come, let us worship and bow down. Let us kneel before the LORD, our maker* (Psalm 95:3-6). This is the One who desires to have fellowship with us, to love us and to meet our every need. It is as we are drawn unto Him that we will be drawn away from the physical world in which we reside and closer to the spiritual world of God Almighty, clinging tightly and ever so humbly unto Him. Let the One who created the heavens and the earth fill your spirit and life with His energy, allowing His Spirit to breathe new life into your heart from His, in prayer.

It is through prayer that we are able to practice the Presence and knowledge of our most holy, Almighty God and His work in our lives. Without prayer we can be totally ignorant of His presence, His will, and totally unable to appropriate His power. We read in Genesis 28:16, *Surely the LORD is in this place and I wasn't even aware of it*. Only when we remain in prayer, are we able to see and experience His Presence on a daily basis. Solomon gives us an idea just how big and how majestic, yet how close God is to us when we pray in 1 Kings 8:27-28 (NIV), *But will God really dwell on earth? The heavens, even the highest heavens cannot contain you. How much less this temple I have built! Yet give attention to your servant's prayer and his plea for mercy, O LORD my God. Hear the cry and the prayer that your servant is praying before your presence this day*. All the heavens cannot contain our Almighty Creator, God. Acts 7:49-50 (KJV) says, *Heaven is my throne, and earth is my footstool. Hath not my hand made all things?* All things belong to God, were created by Him and for Him; this is why we pray to Him.

Job asks, giving us some understanding of prayer and why we must rely upon Him and not on the ways of man, *Can you fathom the mysteries of God? Can you probe the limits of the Almighty? They are higher than the heavens— what can you do? They are deeper than the depths of the grave—what can you know? Their measure is longer than the earth and wider than the sea* (Job 11:7-9). Yet, when we pray, we are drawn into His very Presence. He is waiting to pour His mercy, His power and wisdom, upon our lives, if we would only ask and remain in His Presence through prayer.

In Psalm 5:2, David tells us, *Listen to my cry for help, my King and my God, for I will never pray to anyone but you.* There are no gods or saints worthy of God's glory; He alone is holy. He alone is King. 1 Timothy 2:5 says *there is only one God and one Mediator who can reconcile God and people. He is the man Christ Jesus.* The mother of Jesus, Mary or any other saint is no different than you or I in God's eyes. None of them created anything, none deserve worship and none but God the Father, God the Son, and the Holy Spirit have the power and authority to answer prayer. Job confirms this notion, *To God belong wisdom and power; counsel and understanding are his. What he tears down cannot be rebuilt; the man he imprisons cannot be released. If he holds back the waters, there is drought; if he lets them loose, they devastate the land. To him belong strength and victory; both deceived and deceiver are his* (Job 12:13-16 NIV). This is the God to whom we pray, this is the Lord Almighty who is waiting for us to humbly approach His throne of grace!

God wants us to pray for the things we think are impossible because, as the Bible tells us, nothing is impossible for God. Though He is the Provider of all things, it brings much glory to His Name to perform acts far beyond human ability. God desires to use His children to do big things. He seems to love those who appear incapable of being saved (like me in my before-Jesus days), and that could include every one of us! He receives the most glory when He does the impossible because we notice it could only have been His doing. This is the God to whom we pray, the Sovereign, all-powerful, Almighty God. It is His perfect love that reaches out, into and through our hearts. He desires to spend time with us and care for our every need, revealing Himself to us in the most caring and loving of ways.

Our all-knowing, all-seeing, majestic God has His untold blessing and power at our disposal. Read aloud what Psalm 147:3-5,8 tells us about the One we can trust in prayer with our hearts' desires, our hurts and fears, and Who will rightly and powerfully answer our every prayer and take care of our every need. *He heals the brokenhearted, binding up their wounds. He counts the stars and calls them all by name. How great is our LORD! His power is absolute! His understanding is beyond our comprehension! He covers the heavens with clouds, provides rain for the earth, and makes the grass grow in mountain pastures.* It is this God whose Heart desires to save those who may appear impossible of salvation. It is this God to whom we pray, who wants to bandage our wounds and heal us. He alone provides us rain as well as love and power.

David gives us further evidence of God's almighty power and yet, too, His tender-hearted caring for His children, *The voice of the LORD is upon the waters; The God of glory thunders, The LORD is over many waters. The voice of the LORD is powerful, The voice of the LORD is majestic. The voice of the LORD hews out flames of fire. The voice of the LORD shakes the wilderness. The LORD shakes the wilderness of Kadesh. The LORD sat as King at the flood; Yes, the LORD sits as King forever. The LORD will give strength to His people; The LORD will bless His people with peace* (Psalm 29:3-4,7-8,10-11 NASB). How little we believe, much less ask for and expect to receive that which He wants to bestow upon us through prayer. How little we try to grasp understanding of His Heart, His wisdom, His power and His purposes. How we falter for lack of His strength, while we suffer for lack of His peace. Let us learn to trust, to cry out to, and to wait upon-The One who formed you and I in our mother's wombs, and knows the number of hairs on our heads, and Who calls the stars by their names as He sets them in place. He alone has almighty power, love, and grace at our disposal. His glorious gifts, His grace, His strength, His peace, and all we need to find and do His will are just waiting to be prayed down from heaven!

EXERCISE

Prayerfully read David's prayer and outcome in 1 Chronicles 17:23-18:6 and consider any parallels you are experiencing. Remember the Scriptures are a lamp unto our feet, lighting the path of righteousness for us to walk in by faith. They are your personal Love Letter from God, your Father!

- ➳ What has God revealed to you about Himself, today?
- ➳ Which verse does God want you to ask Him to apply to your life today?
- ➳ For whom does He want you to pray this verse?

LET US PRAY

Gracious, holy, heavenly Father, full of incomprehensible power, wisdom and love. How majestic Your Name and perfect Your ways. Forgive our lack of belief that You created us to enjoy You, and that You delight in our prayers. Fill us with Your Spirit, sanctifying unto Your holiness, teaching us to pray. In Jesus' powerful Name we pray, Amen.

Day 4

OUR SUSTAINER
in PRAYER
IIIIIIIIIIIIIIIIIIIIIIIIIIIIIIIIIIIIIIIIIIIIIIIIIIIIIII

*The LORD, the God of heaven, has given
me all the kingdoms of the earth and he
has appointed me to build a temple...*

— 2 Chronicles 36:23 NIV —

Our God, the Creator of heaven and earth, the Ruler, Sustainer and King of all of creation, is a compassionate, loving God who provides us with all good things. He has a plan for each of us to carry out, and He alone enables us. He cares for our every physical, spiritual and emotional need. He is the only One who is able to know and to give us each precisely what we need. He, alone, knows when we are ready to receive the answers to our prayers. Scripture says, *Every good and perfect gift is from above, coming down from the Father of the heavenly lights, who does not change like the shifting shadows* (James 1:17 NIV). All we need spiritually, emotionally, mentally and materially comes down to us from our Father God, the very same Father who created all of heaven's lights is waiting to bestow us with all good gifts.

Jesus tells us, *The thief cometh not, but for to steal, and to kill, and to destroy; I am come that they might have life, and that they might have it more abundantly* (John 10:10 KJV). Our God the Creator, the Giver of life, is a Giver in abundance. Prayer counteracts the work of the enemy who wants to destroy, kill, and steal. We must be aware the enemy watches us. He watches for just the right time, trying to push our buttons to steal, destroy, and eventually kill our relationships, our emotions, our minds, our ministries, our homes, our families, our finances, and more. All good things from heaven from our Almighty God, in answer to prayer, will bring life into all that may have been affected by the enemy. God builds, and what He asks us to do and to be, can only be built and sustained by Him and for Him.

Prayers to our all-loving, all-powerful, Almighty Father are the only ones that will be heard and answered. Our all-powerful, Almighty God is the only One who knows the heart and can build and bring life and His purposes in accordance with His good, pleasing and perfect will. We are told His gifts to us are *"good and perfect."* He knows exactly what we need and when we need it. Our God, to whom we pray, has a storehouse of bountiful, good and perfect blessings waiting to be showered down upon us from heaven. If we only understood how much He desires to bless His people. James says, *In his goodness he chose to make us his own children by giving us his true word. And we, out of all creation, became his choice possession* (James 1:18). In His goodness, He created us, chose us, and sustains us. Each of us are His chosen, loved possession. He tells us, *Ye have not chosen me, but I have chosen you* (John 15:16 KJV). He desires to care for us for He has chosen each one of us, and He desires us to know Him and love Him in return.

Peter tells us, *As we know Jesus better, his divine power gives us everything we need for living a godly life. He has called us to receive his own glory and goodness* (2 Peter 1:3). God loves us with perfect love and wants to provide for us, but we hinder Him when we fail to pray. Psalm 84:11 (NIV) says *the LORD bestows favor and honor; no good thing does he withhold from those whose walk is blameless.* He desires, even more than we, to give us His love, blessing us with all His glory and goodness, withholding no good thing! Too many are willing to give up a pursuit of holiness and righteousness. Alone these blessings are unattainable; human legs alone cannot walk a blameless walk. Rather than crying out for help and surrendering to Him, so many throw in the towel before even beginning the race. Yet, we must not give up, but surrender to our heavenly Father in prayer, letting Him do the impossible in us and through us. Let us cry out, *O LORD, you alone can heal me; you alone can save* (Jeremiah 17:14). Scripture promises as we know Him better, Jesus' divine power will give us everything we need to live a godly life. Philippians 2:13 says, *For God is working in you, giving you the desire to obey him and the power to do what pleases him.* **Where God calls us, it is He, alone, Who enables us.**

Many times, our hindrance to His powerful plan for us is a lack of surrender, which requires complete obedience and trust in Him. What keeps us from surrendering and trusting Him? Fear is one of the devil's greatest traps, rendering many Christians powerless and frozen, incapable of growing with God. Lacking surrender shows a lack of trust in God's holy love. Scripture says, *There is no fear in love; but perfect love casteth out fear: because fear has torment. He that feareth is not made perfect in love* (1 John 4:18 KJV). Many of us are truly paralyzed by fear of what God might do or ask us to do in answer to prayer; we are filled with questions instead of faith. We should not fear, but instead, allow God's love to permeate and heal our hearts, giving us the courage and knowledge we need to surrender to Him. Psalm 84:12 (NIV) says, *O LORD Almighty, blessed is the man who trusts in you.* Let us remember there is an opposite to every blessing; for the man who does not trust—will not be blessed. Many of us allow our lack of trust in Him, to keep us from being used and blessed—for fear of failing to perform God's work. We will, if we allow fear to control us, lose out on countless blessings for others and ourselves.

Scripture promises, *But blessed are those who trust in the LORD and have made the LORD their hope and confidence.* In prayer, we throw all trust and confidence toward our Creator and away from man. In trusting and resting in God, alone, we shall be blessed, that we may be a blessing. *They are like trees planted along a riverbank, with roots that reach deep into the water. Such trees are not bothered by the heat or worried by long months of drought. Their leaves stay green, and they go right on producing delicious fruit* (Jeremiah 17:7-8). Regardless of the weather, circumstance, or season of our life, prayer will push our roots deep into the living soil of our Sustainer's Heart. Worries, fears and cares aside, He shall go right on producing delicious fruit through us. Heat or circumstances shall not bring fear, but only draw us nearer and into a deeper reliance upon our only source of life.

Let us rely on God's promises, *I will never fail you. I will never forsake you.* And *that is why we can say with confidence, "The Lord is my helper, so I will not be afraid. What can mere mortals do to me?"* (Hebrews 13:5-6). Prayer keeps us relying on Him as He nourishes, cleanses, teaches and enables us to love, trust with confidence, obey and be used by Him. *Wherefore, we receiving a kingdom which cannot be moved, let us have grace, whereby we may serve God acceptably with reverence and godly fear* (Hebrews 12:28 KJV). In prayer, becoming *given* to His Kingdom, we shall receive all the grace we need to serve Him acceptably and worship Him acceptably, totally trusting Him to give us the ability to ask for and receive all His precious promises. Yes, let us learn and live, *Let us go right into the presence of God, with true hearts fully trusting him. For our evil consciences have been sprinkled with Christ's blood to make us clean, and our bodies have been washed with pure water* (Hebrews 10:22). It is the blood of Christ that prepares our hearts and bodies to go into God's Presence, to trust Him, and to receive all that God desires to bless us with. Scripture promises that, *From the fullness of his grace we have all received one blessing after another* (John 1:16). God's grace is plentiful and it is ours; let us ask in prayer and we shall all receive one blessing after another!

God says, *Ask me whatever you want me to give you* (1 Kings 3:5 NIV). If someone asked you this question right now, would you not suspect a possible ulterior motive and possibly respond with a question? Something like, "Well, what do I have to do to earn this thing that I want?" or maybe "So, what do you get out of it?" All God gives is a free gift; we must learn not to respond humanly to our heavenly Father, but spiritually. Accept His grace given through prayer. Many of us still feel we need to **do** something in order to earn salvation and God's love and blessing, therefore ignoring His grace. Many grown adults are still struggling with trying to earn the love and acceptance of parents and find it difficult to see themselves through the unconditionally loving and accepting eyes of our heavenly Father whose love is perfect and pure. **He even gives us the grace to love Him back!**

Let us no longer allow insecurities, fear, or doubt to keep us from His grace! Remember, He alone can remove these, as we ask. Only He can prepare and transform hearts. Ezekiel 11:19 says, *And I will give them singleness of heart and put a new spirit within them. I will take their hearts of stone and give them tender hearts instead, so they will obey my laws and regulations.* It is in answer to prayer that our God creates newness in our hearts so that we can obey Him. Left to ourselves, we could not obey His laws. As we continually surrender and totally rely upon our Creator in prayer, we avail ourselves to Him, allowing His love to be lavished upon us, in us and through us. Even on the days we sleep in, only pray for 5 minutes and yell at the kids, He continues to love us and sees us covered in the blood of Christ. As well, those great mornings we're up early to spend time alone worshipping, praising and praying to Him, the rest of the day, we feel His love flowing unhindered through us. However, He loves us the same on all those days, and loves each one of His children equally. Though we are equally loved on these different days; let us know we are very differently able to experience Him and receive our blessings, dependant upon prayer!

We cannot ever obtain the joy, peace, patience, kindness, gentleness, self-control and holiness God desires for our lives without Him. He desires us to seek Him and His will in every situation, enabling us to understand what to do to receive and reveal His glory. And we can be assured He desires us to find Him. As He cares for our every need, He reveals to us His Heart, His ways, and He reveals Himself. Scripture says, *God is awesome in his sanctuary. The God of Israel gives power and strength to his people. He gives us grace and glory. No good thing will the LORD withhold from those who do what is right. He grants a treasure of good sense to the godly. Then you will understand what is right, just, and fair, and you will know how to find the right course of action every time* (Psalm 68:35/84:11/ Proverbs 2:7,9). God is just waiting to teach us what to ask for, how we should use it for His glory, and He yearns for us to have the faith to act upon and receive it.

Even Paul, a very successful preacher, teacher, and missionary of over twenty years, in the Scriptures, did not rely upon self, others or study alone, but upon prayer. We read his prayer: *May our Lord Jesus Christ and God our Father, who loved us and in his special favor gave us everlasting comfort and good hope, comfort your hearts and give you strength in every good thing you do and say. May the Lord bring you into an even deeper understanding of the love of God and the endurance that comes from Christ* (2 Thessalonians 2:16-17/3:5). All understanding and endurance, all comfort, hope and strength comes from our heavenly Father. God's Spirit and the prayers of Christ strengthen our hearts to do all He has desired and ordained us to do, in answer to our humble prayers. Through prayer, we begin to understand His incomprehensible, eternal love and receive the ability to endure any obstacles we may encounter as we remain in Christ, and He in us.

Jeremiah, the prophet, tells us, *The LORD, the fountain of living water. O, LORD, you alone can heal me; you alone can save. My praises are for you alone!* (Jeremiah 17:13-14). He alone can heal. He alone can save. He promises us, while never failing or leaving us, that He will be our Strength, giving us courage and victory. *No one will be able to stand their ground against you as long as you live. For I will be with you as I was with Moses. I will not fail you or abandon you. I command you—be strong and courageous! Do not be afraid or discouraged. For the LORD your God is with you wherever you go* (Joshua 1:5,9).

He will not ever abuse us, leave us, or forsake us, and it is only He who can help us obey these commands to be strong and courageous in our battles against flesh, our enemy and sin. For victory, we must only ask, trust and obey! Ask God right now, to remove any negative emotions or scars that may hinder you from total trust in the God who loves you and wants to heal you, save you, and provide for you. God promises us: *For I know the plans I have for you, says the LORD. They are plans for good and not for disaster, to give you a future and a hope.* How do we find our hope and future? *In those days when you pray I will listen. If you look for me in earnest you will find me when you seek me* (Jeremiah 29:11-12). As He hears and answers your prayers, seek His holy heart *earnestly,* listening and watching. Notice how He wants to reveal Himself to you that you will grow totally to rely upon, trust, and love Him. Bring your deepest needs and hurts to Him now in order that He may lavish His love upon you, and fill you with His joy and peace.

EXERCISE

Write down your plans and dreams; your future and hope that God has planted deep within your heart, that He has been training you for. Ask Him for them, and thank Him for preparing you for His purposes, watching for the timing of His fulfilling them!

- What has God revealed to you about Himself, today?
- Which verse does God want you to ask Him to apply to your life today?
- For whom does He want you to pray this verse?

LET US PRAY

Gracious, holy, heavenly Father, full of incomprehensible power, wisdom, and love. Fill us with Your Holy Spirit to overflowing, that our prayers will be filled with Your power and love for Your Kingdom. We thank and praise You in advance for Your wonderful answers to our prayers, laying them before Your throne and waiting in great expectation. In Jesus' Name, Amen.

Day 5

BECAUSE of JESUS in PRAYER
||||||||||||||||||||||||||||||||||||||||||||||||||||

Therefore he is able to save completely those who come to God through him, because he always lives to intercede for them.

— HEBREWS 7:25 NIV —

Who will teach us to pray? Jesus Christ, our Savior, and Mediator, the One through whom we have access to God in prayer. Scripture tells us that Jesus has given us access to prayer, and that He ever lives to pray. *For Christ also hath suffered for sins, the just for the unjust, that he might bring us to God, being put to death in the flesh, but quickened by the Spirit* (1 Peter 3:18 KJV). His Spirit teaches and leads us in prayer. It is the very Spirit of Christ, the Spirit of prayer, which brings us to God. Paul tells us, *We have depended upon God's grace, not on our own earthly wisdom.* If he did not rely upon earthly wisdom to serve God, then how could we? *Now glory be to God! By his mighty power at work within us, he is able to accomplish infinitely more than we would ever dare to ask or hope* (2 Corinthians 1:12/Ephesians 3:20). Christ's Spirit, His mighty power working within, accomplishes, as we learn to pray. It is not in doing or trying to pray, but in learning to wait upon God's power working within our hearts that truly allows His work to come through. May He give us the grace to grow in knowing He Who hears us and prays for us, will work within and through us!

Micah 7:7 tells us, *Therefore I will look unto the LORD; I will wait for the God of my salvation: My God will hear me.* Let us look to our Lord to teach.

Let us be found looking heavenward and inward, waiting to receive our daily grace to learn and pray. The mighty Spirit that raised Christ from the dead shall bring new life into all who need it for their lack of surrender to God. Paul tells us, *Even God, who quickeneth the dead, and calleth those things which be not as though they were* (Romans 4:17 KJV). It is Christ's teaching and God's power that fills us with His prayers, bringing forth power and life. Let us look heavenward for Him that quickeneth the dead, to breathe new life into our prayers, hearts, and minds. Christ promises He is able to save us completely; let us completely surrender to Him that we may be completely filled.

As Abraham believed God could bring life and keep His promise out of a *body that was as good as dead* (Romans 4:19 NIV), let us, too, trust in the Lord to pour into our weak and feeble hearts, the faith of Abraham. Let us rise to the call of *being fully persuaded that God had* (has) *the power to do what he had promised* (Romans 4:21). **Let us call out to our heavenly Teacher, and let us know as assuredly as we ask, we are heard. As assuredly as we are heard, we shall wait until we have received. Let us not feel lacking in our waiting, as we will be left lacking without waiting.**

Before Jesus' complete sacrifice, His children did not have the same access to God we do now. The inner veil in the Tabernacle allowed only the chosen High Priest, on the Day of Atonement, to enter into the holy of holies. We read of the veil that separated the holy place from the most holy place, the inner Tabernacle. The innermost area of the Tabernacle represents the Presence of God and His holiness. His throne, represented by the ark of the testimony, was of special distinction, *Hang the curtain from the clasps and place the ark of the Testimony behind the curtain. The curtain will separate the holy place from the most holy place* (Exodus 26:33 NIV). There are fifty chapters in the Bible devoted to the Tabernacle, where Israel experienced God's dwelling. It has always been God's heart's desire to dwell with His people and for them to experience His Presence. Our Teacher's sacrifice now makes our bodies that Temple!

Adam and Eve were visited by God. *They heard the LORD God walking about in the garden. The LORD God called to Adam, where are you?* (Genesis 3:8-9). After His own creation, His children were separated from Him by sin, but as He still desired to be with us, He made the way. *And let them make me a sanctuary; that I may dwell among them* (Exodus 25:8 NKJV). Yet, let us not forget that only the priest entered once yearly to sprinkle a blood sacrifice, to ask forgiveness for Israel's sins, unto the lid of the ark.

The Hebrew word for sanctuary, "miqdosh," means "be holy." As sin separates from holiness, God in His great love for us, made a way for us to be holy, remaining in His Presence. Through our Teacher, Jesus, He sacrificed and created a way for Him to dwell with and within His people forever. Our Teacher was that Curtain, and it was He who removed it for us once and for all with His very own blood. Scripture says, *Therefore, brothers, since we have confidence to enter the most holy place by the blood of Jesus, by a new and living way opened for us through the curtain, that is, his body* (Hebrews 10:19-20 NIV).

God sacrificed out of His love for us and His desire to have a relationship with us. Let us believe our Teacher desires us to experience, anew, His Presence. At the very moment of Jesus' death, we learn of the destruction of the old ways of sacrifice. *And suddenly, the thick veil hanging in the Temple was torn apart. Then Jesus shouted, Father, I entrust my spirit into your hands!* (Luke 23:45) The very Spirit of our Lord and Savior was given to us by Him, that we may enter into the very heavenly place we had hitherto been unable to enter. Ephesians 2:18 promises, *Now all of us, both Jews and Gentiles, may come to the Father through the same Holy Spirit because of what Christ has done for us.* Oh, let us praise Him!

His teaching us to pray, pouring out His Holy Spirit, into and through us from His throne, brings us hope, that we may seek the holiness of heart He desires to bless us with. *We have this hope as an anchor for the soul, firm and secure. It enters the inner sanctuary behind the curtain, where Jesus, who went before us, has entered on our behalf. He has become a high priest forever, in the order of Melchizedek* (Hebrews 6:19 NIV). The hope of our souls to ascend unto heaven to pray and be taught by the Master has been secured. *And now God is building you, as living stones, into his spiritual temple. What's more, you are God's holy priests, who offer the spiritual sacrifices that please him because of Jesus Christ* (1 Peter 2:5). As our hope rests in the sacrifice of our High Priest alone, we shall enter into the school of His highest and holiest work and life of prayer with Him, by Him, and for Him. It is He who is building us up and teaching us, in prayer, to be His spiritual temple. In addition, we are told what we already are: God's holy priests!

As such, we must not take our calling or our responsibilities lightly. As God's holy priests, let us willingly be prepared and surrender ourselves to offer spiritual sacrifices in prayer because this is what pleases God. Let us approach Him with humble and willing hearts; nothing pleases Him more. Because of Jesus and His sacrifice we may enter into God's Presence. Because of Jesus' sacrifice, we have been blessed with eternal life in heaven. Because of Jesus, we are God's holy priesthood. Because of Jesus, we are able to enter into prayer and offer ourselves as spiritual sacrifices to please God. Because of Jesus, the very love that created us is able to dwell within us!

The teaching of man will not suffice. We must not be content with educational degrees or seminary teaching, for the even the most brilliant scholars and ministers shall be humbled in the school of prayer. Do not be content to read this book without the teaching of the Spirit of Christ. Spiritual truths must be taught by the Spirit and be accepted spiritually with humble faith. Jesus stated, *I praise you, Father, Lord of heaven and earth, because you have hidden these things from the wise and learned, and revealed them to little children* (Matthew 11:25 NIV). Let us look unto our great Intercessor as little children in our classroom. Our heavenly Teacher is waiting, not for those who feel themselves wise and learned, but for those who are humble and eager to learn. Young children not only believe everything they are taught by their teacher, but are eager and willing to learn. Let us, as children, eagerly seek those things hidden from the wise, as He loves to reveal them to those who humbly seek to know and join Him.

Jesus entered heaven and lives at the right hand of the Father, ever interceding for us, God's children. He lives to pray, and He will teach and enable us to live as God's disciples, the co-heirs of His kingdom and His co-workers in the priesthood. It is our Teacher who is ever filling us with Himself and drawing us into His Presence. *And because you gentiles have become his children, God has sent the Spirit of his son into your hearts* (Galatians 4:6). From His almighty love and power, God sends the Spirit of our holy Intercessor, our great High Priest, into our hearts. Let us be strengthened and encouraged that we may carry out our priestly duties and find great favor with God— through the Intercessor dwelling within our hearts. Let us learn from Him, who went before us, intercedes always for us and within us, so we too will live to pray and pray to live.

We must leave our earthly classroom and prayer closets, with all preconceived ideas and man-made ways of prayer behind and look heavenward, ascending into the very Presence of our heavenly Intercessor. It is here we are to enter into His classroom of prayer. His death brought

us, not only access to heaven when we die, but access to heavenly places during our lives. *Then Jesus shouted out again, and he gave up his spirit. At that moment the curtain in the Temple was torn in two, from top to bottom* (Matthew 27:50-51). His death destroyed the spiritual and physical veil, allowing our hearts to enter into the very Presence of our Holy Father. As He resides at His right hand in prayer, so shall we.

Galatians 2:20 now becomes our strength in prayer, drawing always into His heavenly teachings. *I myself no longer live, but Christ lives in me.* He sacrificed and entered into the place of honor and power, at the right hand of His Father in prayer, that we may enter, too. Scripture promises, *For by that one offering he perfected forever all those whom he is making holy* (Hebrews 10:14). The word "perfect" does not mean we are at once perfect acting Christians; it means He is maturing us—we are *those whom He is making holy*. We are perfection, in process. Jesus has been given the honor of High Priest over us as He teaches and perfects us. It is His work that makes us holy, giving us the ability and desire to worship, praise, and enter the very Presence of our holy God. He gave up His Spirit, entering into a life of prayer and intercession to gain access to the power to mature us into His holiness.

Hebrews 10:19 (KJV) says, *Having therefore, brethren, boldness to enter into the holiest by the blood of Jesus.* The One who opened the way shall be the very One to take us boldly along that way. It was by the very blood of Jesus we were saved and by His blood we are able to pray. What He accomplished once and for all, He still oversees and carries out as God's will. *Now the God of peace, that brought again from the dead our Lord Jesus, that great shepherd of the sheep, through the blood of the everlasting covenant, make you perfect in every good work to do his will, working in you that which is well-pleasing in his sight* (Hebrews 13:20-21 NKJV). It is His work in our hearts and through our prayers, with which He continually cleanses, teaches, and does His good will, drawing us ever deeper into the Presence and Heart of God.

Hebrews 5:7 tells us that *while Jesus was here on earth, he offered prayers and pleadings with a loud cry and tears, to the one who could save him out of death. And God heard his prayers because of his reverence for God.* Because of His reverence for God, Jesus' prayers were heard, and He hears ours. Entering into the heavenly classroom of our Teacher, we enter into His life, His death, and His surrender. Scripture exhorts, *your attitude should be the same that Jesus Christ had. Though he was God, he did not demand and cling to his rights as God*

(Philippians 2:5,6). Let us beware the danger of pride, the very opposite of the attitude of Christ. Pride will cause us to cling to human "self-rights" we may believe we have, demanding time for earthly pleasures over the privilege of joining Christ in prayer and obedience. Throughout the Bible, we are shown story after story concerning the sin of pride, sowing idol worship, and self-reliance which brings prayerlessness, complacency, ignorance, curses, death and destruction. We are commanded, *Instead, we will hold to the truth in love, becoming more and more in every way like Christ* (Ephesians 4:15). **Surrendering to our Teacher in prayer holds us to His truth, that we may become more and more like Him!**

Ephesians 2:21 says, *We who believe are carefully joined together, becoming a holy temple for the Lord.* Prayer allows us to remain united with Christ and His church, filled with His power over sin, continually becoming holier. Let us remember to focus on the Heart of prayer, which is becoming a holy Temple for the Lord. Prayer is not for self-gratification or for self-glorification. God's Heart desires each of us to become a holy Temple for Him! Prayers draw us into God's Heart and into His Kingdom reality. Jesus teaches our hearts as He works out holiness in our lives and all those for whom we pray. *For the Kingdom of God is not just fancy talk; it is living by God's power* (1 Corinthians 4:20). Those continually being filled with Jesus and who are united with Him in prayer are set free to experience all of God's grace and power, to find His Heart and become His Temple as they seek holiness—let it be so with us!

EXERCISE

Close your eyes and picture Gethsemane—where our Great High Priest prays sacrificing His will, His life…His prayers wringing out drops of blood; that He may experience Calvary—His blood covering you and cleansing away your sins—defeating the devil and all his works in your life; then picture the Victory over death and demons—as He is lifted unto the heavens—His Light and Life pouring down from the Throne upon you—feel the radiance and power of His Love! Thank and praise Him!

- ❖ What has God revealed to you about Himself, today?
- ❖ Which verse does God want you to ask Him to apply to your life today?
- ❖ For whom does He want you to pray this verse?

LET US PRAY

We praise and worship You and bless Your precious Name. Create in us pure hearts and willing spirits. Oh, Lord teach us who You are and how You pray. Lord, make us more like You. Oh, Lord teach us to pray...In Jesus' precious and powerful Name, Amen.

Day 6

OUR TEACHER in PRAYER

||||||||||||||||||||||||||||||||||||||||||||||||||||

I will give you a new heart and put a new spirit in you;
I will remove from you your heart of stone
and give you a heart of flesh.

— Ezekiel 36:26 NIV —

When Christ ascended to heaven, He left His earthly ministry in the care of His disciples. Now, He intercedes from heaven, carrying on His high-priestly duty to pray for us and teach us to pray so that we may fulfill God's will and give our loving hearts to Him. Let us believe He did not leave us to carry on His ministry ourselves. He knows this cannot be carried on in the flesh, but by His Spirit alone. When He speaks of a heart of flesh, He does not refer to the flesh of self, but a softened heart. Any occupation with the flesh, its desires, wills or efforts, must be repented and removed. Sin causes a heart of stone, which needs to be broken, removed and made a heart of flesh. It is He who removes, just as it is He who shall give.

Our Mediator and Giver waits for us to call out to Him; He yearns for our hearts to be obedient, desiring to learn, living prayer and praise. Let us wait upon Him as we are encouraged, *I waited patiently for the LORD; he turned to me and heard my cry. He put a new song in my mouth, a hymn of praise to our God. Blessed is the man who makes the LORD his trust* (Psalm 40:1,3-4 NIV). It is the Lord who will put a new song in our hearts. As we remain patiently in the school of prayer, crying out to God to teach us and free us from our sins, He shall always respond, filling our hearts with praise. We shall be blessed when we learn to depend upon the Lord alone to do all He desires.

Read aloud, Ezekiel 36:26 from the NLT version, *And I will give you a new heart with new and right desires, and I will put a new spirit in you. I will take out your stony heart of sin and give you a new, obedient heart.* First we must confess our sins of pride and prayerlessness that have been built within our heart of stone. He tells us, *Cursed is the one who trusts in man, who depends on flesh for his strength and whose heart turns away from the LORD* (Jeremiah 17:5 NIV). Each time we lack prayer, we rely on flesh, or man. This reliance brings us God's curses instead of blessings and teachings, because it always turns us from God. A cold, hard, prideful, unbelieving heart cannot pray. In prayer, let us first confess and seek full repentance. Praying and relying upon God; His cleansing removes the curse of the flesh!

Let us not, as so many do, give up due to disbelief or dwelling on past experiences. Let us rejoice in our newfound wisdom that God desires us to pray and will teach all we need to learn. Relinquishing to Him our stony hearts, it is He who shall pour out His Spirit and blessing into our new hearts. He promises, *If you repent, I will restore you that you may serve me* (Jeremiah 15:19 NIV). Notice that with our true repentance, God always brings restoration or reconciliation. However our restoration and reconciliation with God is not for our benefit alone, but so that we may serve Him!

Romans 5:11 says, *So now we can rejoice in our wonderful new relationship with God—all because of what our Lord Jesus Christ has done for us in making us friends of God.* The NIV version uses the words, *"through whom we have now received reconciliation."* Repentance is not only asking for forgiveness, but it also means "to turn away" from sins and being reconciled with God. In repentance and reconciliation, we will think and, therefore, behave differently.

Ask God to reveal any areas in your life where you may be depending on flesh and not on Him, because this will keep you from true prayer. Let us leave behind all disbelief and step forth into a blessed life filled with the faith that depends upon God alone and receives all from Him for which we ask!

Fully restored, let us now allow Galatians 2:20 to embody us, mind, body, soul and spirit, *I myself no longer live, but Christ lives in me.* The very God who removes our hearts of stone and restores us, also fills us with Himself. Romans 6:22 commands us, *But now you are free from the power of sin and have become slaves to God. Now you do those things that lead to holiness and result in eternal life.* Because Christ lives within us, we are able to learn to pray and live lives free from the power of sin. God freed us from the power of sin because we did not have the power to do it ourselves. Yet, He has now given us the power to do those things that lead to holiness! Through prayer and seeking holiness, we find the Heart of God, because we now will find Him dwelling as Christ within us.

Ephesians 2:6 now promises, *For he raised us from the dead along with Christ, and we are seated with him in the heavenly realms—all because we are one with Christ Jesus.* We are united with Christ when we relinquish our worldly selves. All self-effort, self-appeasement, self-absorption, self-reliance and self-worthiness must die before we can become repentant, seeking Jesus, our Teacher and Savior to fill us. Christ, our Teacher, did not only die on the Cross, He was also raised in power! Dying with Him, He promises we are raised in power with Him.

United with our Teacher, we find the Heart of God revealed in prayer. Jesus tells us, *And I have revealed you to them and will keep on revealing you. I will do this so that your love for me may be in them and I in them* (John 17:26). As our Teacher reveals God's Heart to us, we are filled with His very own love and desires for us, bringing forth praise with our every breath. Prayer shall become as natural as breathing, being filled with Him. Psalm 104:33 says, *I will sing to the Lord as long as I live. I will praise my God to my last breath!* It is only now, filled with Christ, that He enables us to obey His command to pray! Ezekiel 36:27 says, *And I will pour out my Spirit in you so you will obey my laws and do whatever I command.* God's will is always for us to obey His laws and do what He commands.

Living a life of prayer, obedience, and holiness seems impossible to the carnal mind. Let us, as we are given the power by the Spirit of Christ, surrender to the mind and attitude of Him. Paul exhorts, *Then make my joy complete by being like minded, having the same love, being one in spirit and purpose* (Philippians 2:2). Yes, this is impossible with man, but Christ promises, *What is impossible with men is possible with God* (Luke 18:27 NIV). Scripture also promises, *God will meet all your needs according to his glorious riches in Christ Jesus* (Philippians 4:19 NIV). God meets all our spiritual, mental, and physical needs necessary in the school of prayer, not according to our abilities, intelligence, or experience—but according to His glorious riches, in our Teacher and great Intercessor, Christ Jesus.

Ephesians 2:20 says, *We are his house, and the cornerstone is Christ Jesus himself.* In prayer, He shares with us, His disciples, all His glorious riches we are ready to receive. It is He who builds us. It is He who joins us to the body of Christ, His church, with our fellow believers, in prayer. When was the last time you woke up and said to yourself, "I am being built today, becoming a holy temple for the Lord?" Say it out loud right now, and each morning from this moment on. "I am being built today, becoming a holy temple for the Lord!"

No more were we capable of saving ourselves from eternal damnation, than are we able to build ourselves. Our Teacher, our Builder, the One by whom we are being built, is the very One whom we are built upon, and built by. Christ's Spirit is the very spirit of humility, obedience, building and prayer, giving us access to our Almighty, heavenly Father. Let us be humble, that we may be led and built by Him. Let us be led that we may learn all that is right. Let us trust, that we may be taught, that He may bring us along His Way.

Jesus, by His obedience, was appointed High Priest forever. He showed His ultimate love to His Father and received His Kingdom in return. As priests and co-heirs with our Teacher, He left us to rule this world and do His work, obtaining all we require through knowing Him and remaining in obedience to Him. Priests must take their holy calling as ultimate priority. **Priests have favor and power with God, living to serve God by worshipping Him and serving those around them, always in obedience to His commands. Let us be encouraged, remembering and believing each day, we are His priests!**

As His righteous priesthood, along with our great favor to receive power from God, comes our responsibly and ultimate priority to serve Him. Jesus teaches us in Matthew 5:3, *God blesses those who realize their need for him, for the Kingdom of Heaven is given to them.* We shall pray as our Teacher does, to receive blessings and power from heaven and share them with our fellow men here on earth. Man's greatest need is realizing their need for God. Our first response, enabling us to uphold and grow in our priestly duties, is simply trusting Christ, *I no longer count on my own goodness or my ability to obey God's law, but I trust Christ to save me. As a result I can really know Christ and experience the mighty power that raised him from the dead* (Philippians 3:9-10). We no longer count on ourselves, but upon our heavenly Teacher, which allows us to know Him and experience His power as He teaches us what it is to pray.

The more we know and experience His power, the more like Him we become, pure in heart, knowing God and serving man. Matthew 5:8 says, *God blesses those whose hearts are pure, for they will see God.* Not only must we totally rely upon Jesus, but we must also keep our relationship with the Father our top priority before we can share it with others through prayer and deed. Those who do not see God themselves are of little value in telling others about Him. Once we do see God, however, we must not keep this new power for ourselves, but unselfishly share it with others.

Our investments in His Kingdom are really the only ones that matter. Let us give ourselves, that we may be filled! Ecclesiastes 11:1 promises, *Cast your bread upon the waters, for after many days you will find it again.* We must humbly give ourselves to be taught by our great High Priest, to learn what it is to pray as He does. Let us cast our daily bread, all that we have, all that we are, and all we have been given, in order that we may find all being sown for His Kingdom, to be watered and blessed by Him. Isaiah 32:20 promises, *God will greatly bless his people. Wherever they plant seed, bountiful crops will spring up.* The KJV says, *Blessed are ye that sow beside all waters.* To pray with His passion, in obedience, to the Father who has saved us from eternal death and damnation, we must come with willing and surrendered hearts. It must be Jesus, who by His suffering to learn perfect obedience, who will teach us, sowing God's seeds through us. As Jesus' prayers were heard because of His reverent submission, He must be the One who teaches us to pray. He shall teach us our priestly duties as He carries them out Himself.

EXERCISE

Write Galatians 2:20 on an index card for your bedside and bathroom mirror—repeat aloud each morning and evening. Even as you move to a new verse; always wake up with a verse to quote and go to sleep thinking upon a Scripture!

- What has God revealed to you about Himself, today?
- Which verse does God want you to ask Him to apply to your life today?
- For whom does He want you to pray this verse?

LET US PRAY

We praise, worship, and bless Your precious Name. As Your Son's priesthood dwells within our hearts teach us to serve and love You by loving those around us through prayer. Oh, Lord teach us who You are and how You pray. Oh Lord, make us more like You, teaching us to pray ...In Jesus' precious, perfect and holy Name we pray, Amen.

Day 7

BEING HEARD
in PRAYER

||||||||||||||||||||||||||||||||||||||||||||||||||||||||

Today, if you hear his voice, do not harden your hearts.

— HEBREWS 4:7 NIV —

Who may pray and to whom does God listen? Followers of Jesus Christ, His children. The Bible tells us God listens only to His children, those who have received Jesus Christ as their Savior. Jesus says, *I assure you, unless you are born again, you can never see the Kingdom of God* (John 3:3). There is only one way to get to heaven, in prayer and eternity, and that is through the blood and Spirit of Christ. He continues, *Except a man be born of water and of the Spirit, he cannot enter into the Kingdom of God* (John 3:5 KJV). If you have any question concerning your eternal salvation and what it means to be born again, please take time to study the next section carefully. If you are not certain of your entrance into heaven when your time on earth is over, the rest of this study will do you no good until you make it a certainty.

Jesus tells us how to be born again, telling us also why He came from heaven to earth, *So that everyone who believes in me will have eternal life. For God so loved the world that he gave his only son, so that whoever believes in him will not perish, but have eternal life.* We will all enter into eternal life or eternal death. *God did not send his son into the world to condemn it, but to save it* (John 3:15-17). Once we accept our life in Christ, we are free from condemnation and free to approach God's throne humbly through the blood of Christ. Let us not forget, those not in Christ will not have the privileges His blood brought to His children. Jesus promises, *He who believes in Him is not judged; he who does not believe has been judged already* (John 3:18 NASB). If your prayers always remain unanswered, ask yourself if they are being heard? To whom and through whom are you truly praying?

Jesus says, *I am the way, and the truth and the life. No one comes to the Father except through me* (John 14:16). He confirms the uselessness of life and prayer not united with Him saying, *Apart from me you can do nothing* (John 15:15). Speaking of those who claim to know God, yet reject His Son, He says, *If God were your Father, ye would love me: for I proceeded forth and came from God; neither came I myself, but he sent me* (John 8:42 KJV). Scripture confirms, *I write this to you who believe in the Son of God, so that you may know you have eternal life. And we can be confident that he will listen to us whenever we ask him for anything in accordance with his will* (1 John 5:13-14). He promises those who believe in the Son of God can have confidence we will be heard as we ask His will.

We read the opposite holds true for those who are not God's children. *He does not hear when men cry out because of the arrogance of the wicked. Indeed, God does not listen to their empty plea; the Almighty pays no attention to it* (Job 35:12-13). The pleas of the wicked are empty; any prayer not empowered by His Holy Spirit contains nothing and remains unheard and unanswered. God shows us even religious festivals, as well as the prayers of the wicked, are meaningless. We are severely warned in Isaiah 1:14, *I hate all your festivals and sacrifices. I cannot stand the sight of them! From now on when you lift your hands in prayer, I will refuse to look. Even though you offer many prayers, I will not listen.* In this passage He speaks of His own favored people who refused to turn from their wickedness. *And though they shall cry unto me, I will not hearken unto them. Therefore pray not for this people, neither lift up a cry or prayer for them: for I will not hear them in the time that cry unto me for their evil* (Jeremiah 11:11,14 KJV). He had sent His prophet Jeremiah to warn them of the devastation of sin, but they refused to listen.

There will always be choices to make, and consequences for our choices. Further on, we read in the book of Jeremiah 14:12 (KJV), *When they fast, I will not hear their cry; and when they offer burnt offering and an oblation, I will not accept them: but will consume them by the sword, and by the famine, and by the pestilence.* Let us now hear the Word of the Lord and respond to it.

You may be wondering how these truths in Scripture can come from a loving God, who sent His Son Jesus to die for the world? Consider how a loving God who is holy could leave sin unpunished? He cannot for He is just. The Lord says, *I will reward you for your evil with evil; you won't be able to escape!* (Micah 2:3). If we dare consider God's justice and wrath, we must understand His holiness. Consider the words of Job 27:8-10, *For what hope do the godless have when God cuts them off and takes away their life? Will God listen to their cry when trouble comes upon them? Can they take delight in the Almighty? Can they call to God at any time?* Scripture tells us we cannot continue to refuse Him, walking in evil, and use Him as so many—who try when they encounter emergencies, then will immediately return to sin. Micah 3:4 says, *Then you beg the LORD for help in times of trouble! Do you really expect him to listen? After all the evil you have done, he won't even look at you!* **The great law of God's kingdom is that of sowing and reaping,** *I called to you so often, but you didn't come. I reached out to you, but you paid no attention. I will not answer when they cry for help. Even though they anxiously search for me they will not find me. For they hated knowledge and chose not to fear the LORD. That is why they must eat the bitter fruit of living their own way. They must experience the full terror of the path they have chosen. For they are simpletons who turn away from me to death* (Proverbs 1:24,28-29,31-32).

Do your life and prayers show you are set apart for Him, His work, His service and His holy presence? Are you the simpleton who suffers for the decisions you have sown? Does your heart believe He will answer you when you call? Or do you feel more like the enemies of God and His children that David speaks of in Psalm 18:41, *They called for help, but no one came to rescue them. They cried to the LORD, but he refused to answer them.* May we all consider this and each day what our prayers and actions show about our hearts.

Paul tells us in Romans 2:7, *He will give eternal life to those who persist in doing what is good, seeking after the glory and honor and immortality that God offers,* but this is not the whole story. Let me emphasize again what most will not tell you, nor will you hear about it in most church sermons, *But he will pour out his anger and wrath on those who live for themselves, who refuse to obey the truth and practice evil deeds* (Romans 2:8). Is this to say good deeds can get you into heaven and bad deeds into hell?

Absolutely not! God's Word teaches that only Christ can and will change our actions. Paul teaches us that only those filled with the Spirit of Christ are delivered from continuing to do evil. Most importantly, those who refuse to obey the truth will receive God's wrath and anger. Galatians 1:4 says, *He died for our sins, just as God the Father planned, in order to rescue us from this evil world in which we live.*

We cannot rescue ourselves; if we could, Christ would have died in vain. Let us not take lightly the words in Galatians 6:7 (NIV), *Do not be deceived: God cannot be mocked. A man reaps what he sows.* "What goes around, comes around," originated with our Creator!

Paul teaches about God's wrath and of His great love and mercy, *The one who sows to please his sinful nature, from that nature will reap destruction; the one who sows to please the Spirit, from the Spirit will reap eternal life* (Galatians 6:8 NIV). Eternal life cannot be earned, borrowed or bought, only given from the Spirit of Christ. Let us no longer be fooled that all good people will go to heaven, or that it is okay to sin a little. Scripture says, *The acts of the sinful nature are obvious: sexual immorality, impurity and debauchery; idolatry and witchcraft; hatred, discord, jealousy, fits of rage, selfish ambition, dissensions, factions and envy; drunkenness, orgies, and the like. I warn you, as I did before, that those who live like this will not inherit the kingdom of God* (Galatians 6:20-21). **Reread this Scripture aloud until you truly internalize the truth it contains.** Matthew 12:30 (KJV) promises, *He that is not with me is against me.* Are you friend or foe? ***Those who live this way will not inherit the kingdom of heaven!***

How would you live today if you knew it was your last day on earth? Heed God's warning in Jeremiah 13:16, *Give glory to the LORD your God before it is too late. Acknowledge him before he brings darkness upon you, causing you to stumble and fall on the dark mountains. For then, when you look for light, you will find only terrible darkness.* There is no such thing as making no choice at all; not saying yes to Christ is saying no to God. The longer you wait, the greater the risk you take of an eternity in hell. No one knows when it will be too late. If you reject God, He will reject you. Jeremiah 6:19 says, *Listen, all the earth! I will bring disaster on my people. It is the fruit of their own sin because they refuse to listen to me. They have rejected all my instructions.* No one likes to talk or think about hell, but it is real. Each of us will either go to heaven or to hell. Everyone we know will either go to heaven or hell. How will this fact impact your prayers and life from this day forward?

Do not be alarmed about all your wrong choices in the past; God is waiting to forgive you, waiting to cleanse you of your sins! Do not feel hopelessness or despair at the reality of hell and justice. Isaiah 5:16 says, *But the LORD Almighty is exalted by his justice. The holiness of God is displayed by his righteousness.* God is exalted, and we find in the display of His judgments and of His demand for righteousness, the holiness of God. Let the demand for His justice and the righteousness given to His children through Christ give us hope. He promises, *No matter how deep the stain of your sins, I can remove it. I can make you clean as freshly fallen snow. Even if you are stained as red as crimson, I can make you as white as wool. If you will only obey me and let me help you* (Isaiah 1:18-19). Are you willing to be cleansed? Will you ask Him to help you so that you may find Him in prayer and be redeemed by His Son?

We must make no assumption as to the salvation of others until we hear and see fruit; pray for salvation! Let us remember the chosen, who have not yet been invited, and be wary of those among us who have been invited and are not chosen. **Let us ask God that He pour out His spirit of judgment, righteousness, burning, repentance as well as intercession, grace, prayer and supplication so we will impact our families, friends, coworkers, neighbors and even our enemies for Christ in sacrificial prayer first, then in Spirit-empowered deed.**

Everyone loves to remember the verses in Matthew when Jesus said He would be with us always, but let us not neglect the fact that He was talking to His disciples, whom He was sending out to do His work. He gave us a command, and with it, a promise, true for all His disciples, then and now, *Therefore, go and make disciples of all the nations, baptizing them in the name of the Father and the Son and the Holy Spirit. Teach these new disciples to obey all the commands I have given you. And be sure of this: I am with you always, even to the end of the age* (Matthew 28:19-20).

Jesus gives us the heavenly reason and divine drive for our commission in John 15:12 (NIV), *My command is this: Love each other as I have loved you.* No greater thought could be conceived, no greater deed could be expressed through love than giving your life sacrificially, in prayer, as Christ Himself. He says in John 15:13, *Greater love has no one than this, that he lay down his life for his friends.* As He laid down His life, empowered by the Holy Spirit in prayer, so shall we. The selfishness of our human nature must be laid down, nailed to the Cross of Calvary, or it will keep us from our mission. It is only by abiding in Him and allowing Him to fill and control our lives, removing our human nature, that we will care about those perishing souls around us. One not filled and empowered by His Spirit shall always be unwilling and unable to carry out God's commands.

EXERCISE

Ask God to reveal to you two people (at least) that you commit to pray for daily for their salvation, and then sanctification. Write them down!

- What has God revealed to you about Himself, today?
- Which verse does God want you to ask Him to apply to your life today?
- For whom does He want you to pray this verse?

If you need to claim God's free gift of eternal salvation through Jesus you may pray this prayer aloud and find a church in your area that preaches from the Holy Bible alone and believes upon Jesus Christ alone as the Savior:

Dear God, I confess I am a sinner and ask You to forgive my sins. I believe in You and thank You for sending Your one and only Son, Jesus Christ, to die for my sins that I can have eternal life. I believe You raised Him from the dead by Your power on the third day, paving my way to heaven to be with You for eternity. Please come into my heart now; as I confess You, Jesus as LORD, and drive out anything not of You. Help me to love You so I may joyfully serve You. Thank you for answering this prayer. In Jesus' Name I pray this prayer, Amen.

LET US PRAY

Gracious, wonderful, holy, loving, heavenly Father God. Thank you for Your precious gift to us of eternal life and prayer through Your Son. Forgive us for not taking the eternity of souls with more seriousness. Oh, Lord, teach us to live as holy priests. Oh, Lord, teach us to pray…In Jesus' powerful Name we pray, Amen.

Day 8

HIS CHILDREN in PRAYER

||||||||||||||||||||||||||||||||||||||||||||||||||

Therefore, brothers, since we have confidence to enter
the Most Holy Place by the blood of Jesus.

— HEBREWS 10:19 NIV —

When we are confident in our acceptance of God's gift of eternal salvation, we can be confident He will hear our prayers and be pleased with them. As we call Him LORD, He calls us to prayer, and we may enter into the very Presence of our God Most High, bringing our praises and supplications before His very throne. David asked, *LORD, who shall abide in thy tabernacle? Who shall dwell in thy holy hill?* He answers, *He who walks with integrity, and works righteousness, And speaks truth in his heart* (Psalm 15:1,2 KJV/NASB). These are all workings of the Spirit of the Son, which allow us to abide in the holy Presence of God.

Truth speaks to our hearts in prayer. Through prayer, we receive all we need, receiving Him! Jesus is the Life, the Truth, and the Way! It is Jesus who speaks Truth in our hearts through prayer, drawing us continually to heaven and holiness. Psalm 14:5 (NIV) promises, *God is present in the company of the righteous.* Do you awaken each morning and believe God is in your company? As filled with Him as we get in our prayer closets, so shall He remain with us throughout the day. As we dwell in His sanctuary, so He dwells with us. Covered with the blood of Jesus, we do not enter His most holy place with fear or ignorance, but with confidence! As He breathes His very prayers into our hearts by the Spirit of His Son, He awaits to bless us as His children.

How many times do we have wonderful things waiting for our loved ones, and we are just waiting for them to ask? How we delight to please our children! This is even more true of God. Psalm 31:19 (NIV) says, *How great is your goodness, which you have stored up for those who fear you.* Do we really believe and ask God for those good things He has stored up for us and those for whom we pray? Are we responding to Him in prayer, as a child should to a loving, caring parent? He promises in Proverbs 1:23 (NIV), *If you had responded to my rebuke, I would have poured out my heart to you and made my thoughts known to you.* Read this again; He is just waiting to pour His Heart out to us and to make His thoughts known as we respond! Do you have fond memories of your childhood "heart to heart" talks when you felt that close bond with the parent involved? With your repentance comes a freedom as you and your parent share deep from your hearts, bringing restoration and a deeper trust and intimacy. This is the same relationship into which we may now enter with our heavenly Father.

To those whom haven't experienced loving parents or a secure childhood—please ask God to heal your heart. My heart goes out to you, as I love many close to me who struggle with this; and I am praying for you all daily! Allow Him to heal the cries of your heart; every broken bit and piece of you—to make you whole again, the way He created you, before the enemy tried to destroy you. I have seen countless persons, including Christians, bound in depression, fear, anxiety, shame, unforgiveness, bitterness and fear of rejection—being totally disabled in adulthood from experiencing love and intimate relationships with God and others, from abusive childhoods. Ask God to remove the lies and fear, the insecurities and any distrust you feel as a result of abuse, indifference and/or neglect from your childhood. Proclaim Him now; "God thank you for being my Healer, Redeemer, Friend, Savior, Comforter, and faithful loving Father." Close your eyes now—asking Him to set your heart free to experience His true love and faithful care. Feel HIS LOVE warm your heart, HIS HAND holding you close. Ask God to help you forgive your offenders, to pray for them; freeing you! Please do not let the enemy keep you bound in chains of disparity, or cloaked in the darkness of secrets and shame one moment longer—share your story with a trusted friend who will pray for both of you. I highly recommend using Beth Moore's book, *Praying God's Word* (there is nothing more powerful than His

Proclaimed Word; more about this in another chapter) and if necessary, seek Godly counseling with a certified Christian therapist or Pastor . Ask the Holy Spirit to help you find and believe the Truth about God—THAT WILL SET YOU FREE; His love is perfect and kind, it is holy and pure!

Not only may we enter His sanctuary and experience His Presence, but He is waiting to pour out His Heart to us! He just waits to bless His children! Scripture promises, *The LORD is nigh unto all that call upon him, To all that call upon him in truth* (Psalm 145:18 KJV). Not all who call on Him will receive His blessings, only those who call upon Him in Truth—in Jesus! Scripture promises also, *He will fulfill the desire of them that fear him: He also will hear their cry and save them* (Psalm 145:19 KJV). As children of our powerful, mighty God, we have great privilege in prayer. He desires to fulfill our desires! He waits to hear our cries and save! For all those hurting around us, we will receive the answer in prayer! Our Father waits to bless; He desires to heal. Psalm 147:3 says, *He heals the brokenhearted, binding up their wounds.*

Children have access to things of their Father's homes and hearts. **We have access to unlimited power and divine resources in prayer.** Let us cry out that He may heal the cries of all the hurting hearts! No sin is too great to be forgiven, no hurt too large or old to be healed. There is nothing too impossible for us to bring to Him in prayer. Let us remember always whom it is we are abiding with. Psalm 147:4-5 says, *He counts the stars and calls them all by name. How great is our LORD! His power is absolute! His understanding is beyond comprehension!* Let us remember in great humility the One to whom Jesus has given us access in prayer has unlimited resources! Psalm 24:1-2 (NIV) says, *The earth is the LORD's and everything in it, the world and all who live in it; for he founded it upon the seas and established it upon the waters.*

Let us also remember that children must be about their Father's business; our access to God is not simply for our own benefit. Instead, it is about Him being first in our lives, hearts, and prayers! The passion of the Father's house and Kingdom, must rule our hearts, that we may find His unlimited resources available to us in prayer. Again, we see David questioning those entering into God's holy Presence, into His Heart, *Who may ascend the hill of the LORD? Who may stand in his holy place?* (Psalm 24:3 NIV). Notice the use of the word "stand." This person belongs here and stands with honor and privilege. This person is ruling the land and earth for the King, with His resources and power. Children of God, given this honor are found in Psalm 24:4-6 (NIV),

He who has a clean hands and a pure heart, who does not lift up his soul to an idol or swear by what is false. He will receive blessing from the LORD. Such is the generation of those who seek him, who seek your face, O God of Jacob. As the blood of Christ purifies our hearts, we are able to seek God's face and receive His blessing in answer to prayer.

Prayer is the vital link to God's holy Presence and our gifts of power, through which we receive the ability to live a life pleasing to God and to draw others to Him. Let us understand the words of the Lord in Jeremiah 15:19 (NIV) *If you repent, I will restore you that you may serve me.* God restores us and has given us prayer, in order that we may serve Him! As Christians, our main focus needs to be on God's Kingdom and saving souls, not as our young children who desire every toy they see. My children's prayers do include praying for other people, but like us they also spend a lot of time praying to get every thing they see! As we grow in prayer and spiritual maturity, our priority must not be for every**thing** we see, but every**one** we see!

Where we invest our time, energy, prayers and money will proclaim everything about our hearts and whom we worship. We are told by Jesus, *For where your treasure is, there is your heart also* (Matthew 6:21). Let the Spirit speak to our hearts, whether they are heaven-bound, or earth-bound. For our hearts to enter the throne in prayer, they must enter wholeheartedly! We cannot have our heart's treasures here on earth and send our hearts forth to heaven in prayer at the same time. We cannot serve our own kingdom, and the Kingdom of God as well. He says, *No one can serve two masters. You cannot serve both God and money* (Matthew 6:24 NIV). As children of the Almighty God, we must serve Him in heart, deed and prayer. Everything else becomes secondary to praying for eternal security in Jesus for those who are perishing around us.

We can be confident as children of God who can now pray in the Name of Christ that we will be heard. Scripture speaks of us in Hebrews 2:11, *So now Jesus and the ones he makes holy have the same Father.* As we enter into prayer by the holiness of Christ, we shall find the holiness of God purifying us for His work. We are exhorted to continually remain faithful in prayer. *Therefore, holy brothers, who share in the heavenly calling, fix your thoughts on Jesus, the apostle and high priest we confess* (Hebrews 3:1 NIV). Prayer will bring our thoughts consistently upon Jesus, sharing in His divine nature and enabling us to participate in our heavenly calling. Let us be diligent in our work and remain in the prayer closet until we have the nature and thoughts of our Holy Savior and God. Let disbelief no longer keep God from filling our hearts and minds with Him.

God delights to hear His children and bless them; He just waits to heal and to save. David reveals to us the saving power, and Heart of our mighty God in Psalm 20:6 (NIV). *Now I know the Lord saves his anointed; he answers them from his holy heaven with the saving power of his right hand.* Scripture always tells us God answers our prayers. God has given us, His children, the power to rule the earth and everything in it, as He sends forth His power from His holy heaven in answer to the prayers of His anointed! When we read of the saving power of His right hand, we read of Christ's Holy Spirit of power and prayer. In Ephesians 4:10,12 Christ ascends to heaven to receive and pour out His gifts unto the church. *He that descended is the same also that ascended up far above all heavens, that he might fulfill all things.* By the mighty power of His Spirit, He pours out His gifts from heaven. We read also that His purpose is *To prepare God's people for works of service, so that the body of Christ may be built up.* All things are built up and brought to life and power; all things are fulfilled through Christ in prayer.

We are commanded as God's children, to be holy. *What holy and godly lives you should be living!* (2 Peter 3:11). Let us take our calling and inheritance of God's blessings with all seriousness. We must live in holiness and godliness for the Spirit to do His work in us, to build and sanctify us. As God may have His way with us in prayer, we may also have our way with Him. We must take literally, *Seeing that ye look for such things, be diligent that ye may be found of him in peace, without spot, and blameless* (2 Peter 3:14 KJV). A blameless heart has diligence with God's work, is filled with the Spirit of God and has its ways in prayer with God. Do you have peace with God? Do you even know where to receive it? Do you seek it daily? Peace is a place, an experience of God's Heart; it is a place for trust and confidence resting in the holy, powerful Heart of God where we are given the secret to peace with God.

Read this Scripture aloud, repeating every word slowly, until you have accepted into your heart: *Rejoice in the Lord always. I will say it again: Rejoice! Let your gentleness be evident to all. The Lord is near.* The Lord is near to all rejoicing in Him. Let this calm and give gentleness to your heart for the Lord is near to you! Then, we are commanded, *Do not be anxious about anything, but in everything, by prayer and petition, with thanksgiving, present your requests to God.* Let us, as His children, bring Him all things with a spirit of thanksgiving! What do we receive in the heavenly realms when we meet with

God? *And the peace of God, which transcends all understands, will guard your hearts and your minds in Christ Jesus* (Philippians 4:4-6 NIV). As His children, we should always rejoice and pray with thanksgiving, allowing ourselves to be filled with His peace for it is our gift; it is our right. It is His peace with which He protects our minds and our hearts, keeping them in Christ Jesus. With God's Presence in prayer, in the Spirit of His Son, is God's peace.

Let us read Scripture prayerfully, as children reading a letter from a loving Father, as if every Word is directed toward our hearts; let us accept our calling. *To those sanctified in Christ Jesus and called to be holy, together with all those everywhere who call on the name of our Lord Jesus Christ—their Lord and ours* (1 Corinthians 1:2). Each one of is called to holiness, a holiness that brings peace to the heart and unity to the church, returning the powerful working of the Spirit to its ministers, missionaries and members. Why must His holiness, His power establish us as a sanctified church? *So that all nations might believe and obey him—to the only wise God be glory forever through Jesus Christ!* (Romans 16:26-27 NIV).

Let us be convicted of the division, jealousy, hatred, hypocrisy and sin that the world—all nations, see and think about the church. All indications show most Christians are still controlled by their own sinful desires. The church is supposed to exemplify it's Head, Jesus Christ—to be holy and sanctified; yet divorce, lies, adultery, drinking, slander, gossip, division, hatred, jealousy, greed, and other numerous sins are just as prevalent in the Church as out! **Let us cry out to God to make us the anointed intercessors He desires us to be. Let us pray for repentance in the church, that we may be able to receive again God's power and be the shining light into the darkness, reaching out to the perishing souls around us as our hearts are healed within.** Let us consider all those we know who may not have another to pray for them. May we live and pray as children of the Almighty!

There are no coincidences. Everything, every moment and everyone in our lives, has a God-given purpose. There is no such word in the life of a Christian as coincidence; think of all opportunities eternally, considering them prayer-opportunities. Remember, we are to have an eternal purpose in the lives of others. Prayer is our access to the throne of grace wherever we are whenever we need for whomever we need it. If you have children, be sure to get them involved as well. You will probably find, as I have, children have much to teach us about prayer. Their complete, unconditional trust in God and faith in prayer is to be admired and what we, as adults, should strive to attain.

Let us join the angels, living beings and elders forever around His throne, confessing, in Revelation 5:12, *"The Lamb is worthy—the Lamb who was killed. He is worthy to receive power and riches and wisdom and strength and honor, glory and blessing."* Jesus has received all, and He may pour out all to us who bring glory to our Father, in prayer! **Prayer is a spiritual life of sacrifice to God that pleases Him from His children, bringing Him glory.** Holy prayers must be received with a holy heart, to be sent forth with power back to heaven—being received at the very throne of God.

Revelations 5:8 says, *and they held gold bowls filled with incense—the prayers of God's people!* Let us praise God that our prayers are received into heaven in golden bowls, showing us they are kept dear to His Heart, not as unimportant or useless, but they are given a glorious and rich place in heaven. Thank God right now for the eternity we will spend with Him in heaven. Thank Him for the blood of His Son that has washed our sins away, and pray that the blood of Christ will wash those clean that you know as well. Let us fill His golden bowls with much incense, let us fill His Heart with the names of those in our lives, as He fills our hearts, and prayers with His passion, with His power, and with His purpose—with His love that prays!

EXERCISE

Close your eyes, ask Him to open the spiritual eyes of your heart—allowing your heavenly Father's love and Presence to envelope you, hug you, love you, and fill you!

- ❖ What has God revealed to you about Himself, today?
- ❖ Which verse does God want you to ask Him to apply to your life today?
- ❖ For whom does He want you to pray this verse?

LET US PRAY

Gracious, wonderful, heavenly, holy, loving Father God. Forgive our lack of concern for the souls perishing around us. Fill up our hearts, entering into Your Presence with confidence, with Your will and godly desires that we will pray to please You. Lord teach us to pray…In the glorious, precious Name of Jesus our perfect Savior, Amen.

Day 9

POWER of PRAISING PRAYER

||||||||||||||||||||||||||||||||||||||

This, then, is how you should pray: Our Father
in heaven, hallowed be your name.

— MATTHEW 6:9 NIV —

Now that we know who can pray, how do we pray? As Jesus teaches in His Word! Jesus answered this same question brought by His disciples when they said, *Lord, teach us to pray.* As we ask, He answers, *This then is how you should pray: Father may your name be honored* (Luke 11:1-2). The Lord's command that we pray begins with the adoration and worship of our heavenly Father; we are able to come forth in prayer, firstly because He is our Father. *I will proclaim the name of the LORD. Oh, praise the greatness of our God! Is he not your Father, your Creator, who made you and formed you?* (Deuteronomy 32:3,6 NIV).

I love the prayers in the Old Testament, that begin reminding us Whom it is we come before, as they begin with…God, Creator of heaven and earth, the One who gives life to everything in the earth, Whose Hands stretched out the heavens! We must begin all prayer with praise of our Father, proclaiming who He is and what He has done, glorifying His Name. When we do this, we shall be filled with the proper attitude, which will prepare us to receive His Spirit of prayer, faith, humility, thanksgiving and worship.

It is through Christ's blood sacrifice that we are able to approach Him in the relationship of a child praising His Father, glorying in His Name and worshipping the Creator. In His Name, as Father, we shall realize His power and be consumed with His passions. We are encouraged, *each day proclaim the good news that He saves. Great is the LORD! He is most worthy of praise! He is to be revered above all gods. Recognize that the LORD is glorious and strong. Give to the LORD the glory he deserves! Bring your offering and come to worship him. Worship the LORD in all his holy splendor* (1 Chronicles 16:23,25,28-29). Jesus teaches us, as does David, that prayer is all about God! God is worthy, and we are to give Him the reverence and glory He deserves. Focusing first on the spirit of praise, filling our hearts in prayer, we are lifted from this world, and our hearts are lifted to His throne in praise. The proper heart of worship gives us hearts filled with His Holy Spirit and splendor for prayer. Focusing on the holiness of God in prayer as our priority, He puts to death all that is not proper, breathing life into prayers that bring glory to His Name. He says, *See now that I myself am He! There is no god besides me. I put to death and I bring to life* (Deuteronomy 32:39 NIV).

How do we know how to bring Him proper worship in prayer? The Father we come before in heaven appeared to Abraham in the Old Testament and said, *I am God Almighty; serve me faithfully and live a blameless life* (Genesis 17:1). Not only must we honor God with our mouths, but with our service in our daily lives. Let our hearts prayerfully reflect on whose heavenly Presence we are drawn into in prayer. We read of the God who is our Father, whose Name we are to revere. With the mighty seraphim before His throne, in His heavenly temple shall we begin our prayers, *Holy, holy, holy, is the LORD Almighty! The whole earth is filled with his glory!* (Isaiah 6:3). Let us shake the foundations of our prayers with the praise of God; let us see the earth through praising eyes, filled with glory.

We read of the power of prayer and praise as, *The glorious singing shook the Temple to its foundations, and the entire sanctuary was filled with smoke* (Isaiah 6:4). We read of the power of God brought forth again through praise and prayer, shown on earth when, *At midnight Paul and Silas prayed, and sang praises unto God: and the prisoners heard them. And suddenly there was a great earthquake, so that the foundations of the prison were shaken: and immediately all the doors were opened, and everyone's bands were loosed* (Acts 16:25-26). Praises brought to a holy God shall be heard, experienced and seen by all. When we praise God, we are freed from whatever chains, whatever circumstances are binding us, as God shakes us free to pray, honor and serve Him.

Worship takes us from all we are and all we are bound to, freeing us and bringing all unto Him for His service and glory. *"Holy, holy, holy, is the LORD God Almighty—the one who always was, who is to come, and who is still to come."* Let us ponder even the result in heaven, *Whenever the living beings give glory and honor and thanks to the one sitting on the throne, the one who lives forever and forever, the twenty four elders fall down and worship...And they lay their crowns before the throne and say, "You are worthy, O LORD our God, to receive glory and honor and power. For you created everything, and it is for your pleasure that they exist and were created"* (Revelation 4:8-11). What a way to start and be filled with the passion and power of Christ in our prayers! Will we not find our divine purpose as we cry out, "All for you! Holy, holy, holy, our Almighty Father, God! I am yours; I exist for your pleasure!" And we will give all our crowns, all our thanksgiving, all of our hearts before His throne in worship. Our neighbors, family and friends will be shaken as we are filled in prayer with the glory of God!

We receive great, untold blessing as we begin all prayer by hallowing the Name of the Lord. It reminds us we are His children, and that He is listening; it draws us up to His throne. Malachi 3:16 says, *Then those who feared the LORD talked with each other, and the LORD listened and heard.* Whether in corporate or private prayer, God is present when His children praise Him. He listens and He hears; He accepts our humbled praises as we are ushered in prayer unto His heavenly Presence. *Then a scroll of remembrance was written in his presence concerning those who feared the LORD and honored his name.* Let us be faithful to bring before Him our brothers and sisters in Christ, those who have honored His Name. Let us bring with us, those who have fallen, in a prayer of remembrance, that they may receive His mercy, compassion and blessing. Let us praise, that the very foundations of their disbelief, pride and bondage will be shaken and fall away.

As His children, we are commanded to serve Him, to honor Him, and to worship Him. *And do not forget the things I have done throughout history. For I am God—I alone! I am God, and there is no one else like me.* Our Father is God Almighty, our Creator, Holy One, Savior, and the mighty God who has filled pages of history and hearts of the present with His miracles. *Our Redeemer, whose name is the LORD Almighty, is the Holy One of Israel* (Isaiah 46:9/47:4). May we be encouraged in prayer as we come before our Father in worship, praising His Name, and let us remember all He has done. He says, *It was my hand that laid the foundations of the earth. The palm of my right hand spread out the heavens above. I spoke and they came into being. The LORD, your Redeemer, the Holy One of Israel, says: I am the LORD your God, who teaches you what is good and leads you along the paths you should follow.*(Isaiah 48:13,17).

It is as Father that He desires to teach us what is good and right. It is as we honor His Name in prayer and praise that He leads us along the paths He means for us to follow. Our Father brings us into His Presence, not only that we may bless and revere His Name, but that He may bless our lives.

Isaiah 51:11 promises, *Those who have been ransomed by the LORD will return, singing songs of everlasting joy. Sorrow and mourning will disappear, and they will be overcome with joy and gladness.* Would you not love to be overcome by joy and gladness every day? He promises this is exactly what we will receive in Psalm 16:11 (NIV), *You have made known to me the path of life; you fill me with joy in your presence, with eternal pleasures at your right hand.* Here, again, we learn of our heavenly Father's desire to bring us into His Presence, to show us the right path for our lives and to fill us with His joy and eternal pleasures.

How is it that we, as His children, are not filled with joy? Why do we look as dejected as our neighbors and as fearful as those with no Protector? God says, *Yet you have forgotten the LORD, your Creator, the One who put the stars in the sky and established the earth.* And He asks us, *Will you remain in constant dread of human oppression? Will you continue to fear the anger of your enemies from morning till night?* (Isaiah 51:13). **Let us remember it is our heavenly Father who is in control of our lives, health, jobs, finances, and all circumstances. Fear will only keep us from obeying and praising God, from honoring His Name and receiving His blessings. Prayer and praise of God, release us from this fear.**

Psalm 139:5 says, *You both precede and follow me. You place your hand of blessing on my head.* Picture the powerful, yet tender touch of the blessing Father's hand on a child's head, His loving arms and Presence totally surrounding, totally protecting. As if we were a toddler crossing the street, with a loving parent hovering beside and protecting us, almost saying, "I will die before anyone touches one hair on your head, my coveted child." Think how much more our heavenly Father protects and cares for us! Psalm 139:7,9 *I can never get away from your spirit! I can never get away from your presence!* As parents, we can not always be there, but God can and is. *If I ride the wings of the morning, if I dwell by the farthest oceans, even there your hand will guide me, and your strength will support me.* Our heavenly Father is heavenly! He is constantly available wherever we are for guidance, strength, or whatever we need! His supplies are unlimited, and His resources divinely fitted individually to our hearts.

Now, as our hearts address God as "Father," we acknowledge our humbleness, and claim our dependence upon Him. It is always into God's glory that our prayers begin by worshipping and adoring Him as Father and lifting His Name on high. We must remember what a great sacrifice He paid for us to call Him, "Father, dear Father." This was not done in the Old Testament; this new intimacy was brought through the blood of Jesus. John 1:12-13 says, *But to all who believed him and accepted him, he gave the right to become children of God. They are reborn! This is not a physical birth resulting from human passion or plan—this rebirth comes from God.*

Acknowledging that He is the Almighty God let our hearts be filled with awe and wonder, that He has given us the right to call Him Father. Galatians 4:6 says, *And because you Gentiles have become his children, God has sent the Spirit of His son into your hearts, and now you can call God your dear Father.* The KJV says, *God has sent forth the Spirit of his son into your hearts, crying Abba, Father.* Abba is the Aramaic term for "father." Do you see the wonder of it all? He sends forth His Spirit into our heart that cries out, bringing forth all heavenly blessings for blessed worship and praise.

As we are united in Christ in our rebirth, we are filled with all we need to have this intimate relationship with our Father. 1 Corinthians 1:7-8 (NIV) says, *Therefore you do not lack any spiritual gift. God, who has called you into fellowship with his son Jesus Christ our Lord, is faithful.* Let our faith be renewed and strengthened, lacking no spiritual gift in worship or prayer! He is faithful; He will cry out from our hearts, calling us into fellowship through Christ unto Himself. Rejoice my sisters in Christ, we lack nothing! All the spiritual graces we need to pray are available to us in fellowship with Christ! Scripture reminds us to keep our faith where our praise draws us, *So that your faith might not rest on men's wisdom, but on God's power* (Isaiah 51:13).

Christ teaches us prayer begins with worship pouring from our hearts. *God's purpose was that we who were first to trust in Christ should praise our glorious God* (Ephesians 1:12). Trusting in Christ brings us to praise God. Let us no longer struggle against His will; let us be filled with praise for the

Father who created and loves us. *How we praise God, the Father of our Lord Jesus Christ, who has blessed us with every spiritual blessing in the heavenly realms because we belong to Christ. Long ago, even before he made the world, God loved us and chose us in Christ to be holy and without fault in his eyes* (Ephesians 1:3-4). The Father of Jesus Christ is your Father and mine. Every spiritual blessing He lavished upon His Son is lavished upon us. It is only our unwillingness that keeps us on earth, unable to receive every spiritual blessing awaiting us in the heavenly realms.

Let us remember to rejoice; it will show we are God's chosen. It is the call of every child of God, as Scripture exhorts, *Rejoice in the Lord always; again I will say, rejoice! Let your gentle spirit be known to all men. The Lord is at hand* (Philippians 4:4-5 NASB). The joy of the Lord quiets and makes our spirits gentle; it makes our hearts aware of the joys and blessings of the children of God. Our prayers should focus first on praising our heavenly Father, our relationship with Him as Father, and the coming of His Kingdom. Let us pray that His desires will be our desires, enabling our worship to be pleasing and glorifying to Him. In humility, love, and faith we come into prayer seeking above all else, His holy Presence. Our heart's greatest desires will become those to remain in His Presence, doing His will, and bringing Him glory. The spreading of His message of love, hope, and salvation, the continuing redemption of His people, and the coming of God's Kingdom depend upon the prayers of His children. **God's sovereign will shall prevail from heaven, here on earth as He prevails in praise in the hearts and prayers of His children!**

EXERCISE

Ask God to fill you, anointing you afresh in prayer. Praise Him aloud for being your: Father, Freedom, faithful Friend, Provider, Protector, Redeemer, Savior, Deliverer, Sustainer, Healer, Helper, Hope, Comforter, Leader, Giver of all wisdom and revelation, Peace, Prosperity, Passion, Power, and Purpose; your King, Husband, Creator, Powerful Holy Spirit, Victory, and Glory.

- What has God revealed to you about Himself, today?
- Which verse does God want you to ask Him to apply to your life today?
- For whom does He want you to pray this verse?

LET US PRAY

Wonderful, glorious, holy, heavenly Father, we bless Your Name and lift You on high. Thank you, Father God, for our precious and glorious inheritance in Christ Jesus. Convict us to give ourselves to living prayer as Your highest and holiest calling for Your children. In Jesus' powerful and holy Name we pray, Amen.

Day 10

SEEKING HIS
KINGDOM in PRAYER

||||||||||||||||||||||||||||||||||||||||||||||||||||||||||||||||||||||||||||||||||||||

Your kingdom come, your will be done
on earth as it is in heaven.

— MATTHEW 6:10 NIV —

Following adoration of our heavenly Father; Jesus teaches us to keep God's Kingdom and His will as priorities in prayer. Hearts thankful and humbled by His awesome power, love, care and sacrifice for us as His children, we shall naturally seek His Kingdom and will above all else. Paul testifies of God, *For in him we live and move and have our being* (Acts 17:28 NIV). Jesus teaches us to live and pray as He, living, moving and being in Him. Those who pray for His Kingdom and His will shall be honored by God and answered in glory. His will seeks His holiness to reign within and without into the world.

We shall desire to remain with surrendered hearts to His ruling as we bask in the wisdom, splendor and holiness of our Lord God Almighty. By the love of Christ dwelling within us, we shall desire in prayer for the total removal of self-will, freeing us to seek our Father's Kingdom and will with all of our hearts. As Jesus was obedient to the will of the Father regardless the cost, so shall we be and our labors will not be in vain.

Let us be convinced of the worthlessness of this world and of the evil of any will not brought forth from the Father's throne. Scripture says, *You adulterous people, don't you know that friendship with the world is hatred towards*

God? Anyone who chooses to become a friend of the world becomes an enemy of God (James 4:4 NIV). If we refuse to put God's Kingdom before our own, we will make ourselves God's enemies. What weighs heaviest in our hearts must come first in our prayers. Let us first confess His power, glory, Kingdom, and will from our hearts that have been filled with praise for Him. **What we pray first, becomes what we seek first; it is what we believe and experience. Let our hearts be free to serve God as we choose for His Kingdom to rule our hearts and wills.**

It was the blood of Christ, which enables us not only to understand God's will and make His Kingdom our priority, but also to obey it. As the love of our Father fills our hearts, we shall be convinced of the urgency of redeeming His people; being able to set them free to worship and serve the God we so humbly love and serve. We are told in Scripture that Jesus did our Father's will that we may also. *Jesus came into Galilee preaching the gospel of the kingdom of God and saying, the kingdom of God is at hand.* (The Biblical meaning of *"at hand"* or *"near"* is not only in the immediate spiritual, but also the physical "imminence" of God's kingdom.) *Repent ye, and believe the gospel* (Mark 1:14-15 KJV). The NIV says, *proclaiming the good news.* The Good News is the gospel of the Kingdom. We are praying for all the prophetic writings of Scripture to be done here on earth—as they have already been done spiritually. Jesus teaches us to pray as He lived. We must pray for the spreading of the Gospel to be a priority, and we must live it out and proclaim it. We must pray for others to repent and believe, as we also must stay repentant in believing. How He desires us to live, He prays through us.

The NLT of Mark 1:15 says, *Turn from your sins and believe this good news!* Let us pray for hearts to turn from sin, that we may truly believe. Our actions and motives always show what we believe. If we spend little time in prayer and in seeking God's Kingdom, it shows we do not truly believe in it. Let the church be the first to repent how little it believes in the Good News or the power and love of God! How little it believes in doing or even knowing God's will. Once repentant, we are free to believe and to pray. We will believe, living Scripture's truth, *Oh Sovereign Lord! You have made the heavens and the earth by your great power. Nothing is too hard for you!* We must believe He, alone, is able to sustain the Kingdom He created. He who formed the heavens and earth is most certainly able to give us all we need to do His will. He most certainly can bring new life to a cold heart, broken marriage, and shattered dreams. *You are loving and kind to thousands. You are the great and powerful God, the LORD Almighty. You have all wisdom and do great and mighty miracles* (Jeremiah 32:17-18).

Jesus commands us to ask for God's will to be done here on earth. First, we must know this is possible; asking for and believing His will is loving and kind. Scripture promises God is very aware of the conduct of all people and will reward us according to our deeds. The way we live truly matters; nothing is hidden from Him. As we live, so shall we pray, and so shall our eternal reward be! We shall see anew, the world and all the perishing souls from our Father's eyes and be given an eternal perspective regarding all we know and all He desires to give. Jesus speaks to us and to His disciples, *The secret of the Kingdom of God has been given to you. But to those on the outside everything is said in parables* (Mark 4:11 NIV). God has given us understanding of the secrets of His Kingdom, yet those hearts clouded in disbelief, cannot see and, therefore, cannot obey. Prayer gives us the eternal eyes of faith, allowing us to see all the heavenly realities of our lives and those around us. God promises in Jeremiah 33:3 (NIV), *Call to me and I will answer you and tell you great and unsearchable things you do not know.* This is the very verse by which I have written all my books. I cry to God, and He answers, showing me and teaching me great things I never knew! Prayer is the channel through which all blessings of the Kingdom flow. Desire, passion and will pour from heaven and into our hearts and prayers. Revealed need, praise and desire raise back to the throne, opening the very gates to God's holy Heart.

As God's priorities fill our hearts and prayers, we shall gain untold power in prayer and passion for His Kingdom that we may find the very purpose for our lives. Jesus says, *Anyone who does God's will is my brother and sister and mother* (Mark 3:35). **Prayers for His Kingdom shall transform us, inform us, and conform us to His will.** God says in Jeremiah 32:40-41, *I will put a desire in their hearts to worship me, and they will never leave me. I will rejoice in doing good to them.* He will put the desire in our hearts for worship and He will rejoice in doing good to us! He just waits to bless His children and rejoices when He does!

Let us return again to the sermon on the mount, drawing unto our heavenly Teacher. *God blesses those who realize their need for him, for the Kingdom of heaven is given to them* (Mark 5:3). The KJV says, *Blessed are the poor in spirit.* When we know He is our Father and realize our need for Him and ask for Him, we are given His Kingdom in return! Should this not be our priority in prayer? Notice this is Jesus' first teaching on the mountainside.

Let us examine the spirit in which we come into God's Presence, receiving His perfect will. *Blessed are-they that mourn, are-the meek, are-they which do hunger and thirst after righteousness, are-the merciful, are-the pure in heart, are-the peacemakers, are-they which are persecuted for righteousness sake.* Let these be the verses we seek, for which we pray! For what shall be our blessings? We read of His great blessings as we seek first His kingdom and His will, that we shall receive, *For they shall: be comforted, inherit the earth, be filled, obtain mercy, see God, be called the children of God, for theirs is the kingdom of heaven!* (Mark 5:4-10a/b KJV paraphrased). Jesus teaches us to bring our prayers regarding the Kingdom first to God, not only because it is His, but also because it ours.

Seeking first His Kingdom lifts us out of our earthly, self-kingdom and into His holy, heavenly one! Seeking first His righteousness cleanses us from all unrighteousness. Seeking first His holiness purges from all sin. Seeking first the blessings of eternal life, delivers us from the ways of death. Seeking first all through the Cross, delivers us from the weakness of the flesh, drawing us up in the power of the Spirit. Paul states in his letter, *Written to God's holy people in the city of Colosse, who are faithful brothers and sisters in Christ* (Colossians 1:2). Do we not desire to be faithful in Christ? What was their power for living for God's will and Kingdom? Much prayer! *So we have continued praying for you ever since we heard about you. We ask God to give you a complete understanding of what he wants to do in your lives, and we ask him to make you wise with spiritual wisdom* (Colossians 1:9-10). Love for the saints shows through in their continuing prayer. His will is to give a complete understanding of Himself and what He wants us to do, as we ask.

Let our faith be reignited, as we are established in this truth of His Kingdom. His promises for those who do His will and seek His Kingdom should amaze us. Jesus teaches, *So don't worry about having enough food or drink or clothing. Your heavenly Father already knows your needs, and he will give you all you need from day to day if you live for him and make the Kingdom of God your primary concern* (Matthew 6:31-33). Our heavenly Father gives us all we need from day to day! If we live for Him, and His Kingdom is our priority, we shall know Him as Provider. The NASB version of the Bible says, *But continually seek first His kingdom and His righteousness, and all these things will be added to you.* I can testify to this, for I have literally lived this truth for years. When I take the focus off doing things "my way" and "getting things"; instead seeking Him—He gives and brings; whatever I need literally shows up on my doorstep!

Prayer will become the joy it was meant to be, when we take the focus off us, and return it to Him. As we turn from self to God, we will have all of our needs—spiritual, mental, emotional, and physical, met! God promises, *Then if my people who are called by my name will humble themselves and pray and seek my face and turn from their wicked ways, I will hear from heaven and will forgive their sins and heal their land* (2 Chronicles 7:14). Why, then, do we not do this? Why has having our basic needs met become so difficult? Why do we look everywhere but to God for our healing? Why do we not even feel we have the time to seek His Kingdom? Why do we find such little time for prayer for others? There is but one reason: pride; we do not believe His Promises, His Word, or His Will. As we remain continually before our Father in prayer, we shall be nourished and refined by His fires of holiness, delivering us from the disbelief and disobedience that keep us from His Will and His Kingdom.

If we let Him, He will divinely transform our hearts into the image of His Son, who lived and sacrificed His life for the will of our Father. He was filled and controlled by God's Spirit of power, and gave it all for God's will and glory. Let us remember Paul's words, *For everything comes from him; everything exists by his power and is intended for his glory. To him be glory evermore* (Romans 11:36). **Let us confess, "I am from God, exist by Him and for His glory."** Hebrews 13:15 says, *With Jesus' help, let us continually offer our sacrifice of praise to God by proclaiming the glory of his name.* With His Son's Spirit, we represent His Name. It is with Jesus' help that we may live according to God's will. His will is for us is to live for the glory of His Name. It is all about His Name, His glory! Let us, allow God to fill and control us with His Holy Spirit and bring His will and Kingdom to be done in our hearts, as in heaven.

He tells us, *If you believe, you will receive whatever you ask for in prayer* (Matthew 21:22). The KJV says, *And all things, whatsoever ye shall ask in prayer, believing, ye shall receive.* Let us prayerfully ponder this truth in Scripture. It really is this simple: to receive what we ask for in prayer, we must only believe. Spiritually, we accept, then we will have it physically. God promises, through prayer, that if we believe, we will receive. God is faithful and all His promises true. Believing and receiving in accordance with His will and His Word magnifies His Kingdom. He teaches to those whose lives worship God's Kingdom, who seek God's glory and do God's will; He promises those living for His Kingdom, *If you do these things, your salvation will come like the dawn. Yes, your healing will come quickly. Your godliness will lead you forward, and the glory of the LORD will protect you from behind. Then when you call, the LORD will answer. 'Yes, I am here,' he will quickly reply* (Isaiah 58:8-9).

We will know we have that which we seek when He replies and when we ask in accordance with His will; for God's children shall know His will, seeking it at all times with pure hearts. Jesus would not ask us to pray for something that we would not know how to ask for. With a command, He always gives the ability! Let me mention, when asking Him for something, we must be ever so careful not to limit the way we believe He should answer prayer! He loves to answer in the most unexpected ways! Being filled with desires for His will and living for His Kingdom, we will know what to ask for, as led by the Spirit of prayer. Being watchful and thankful-believing for our answer, we must keep our eyes of faith wide open so we see when it comes, that we may receive in the most amazing of ways!

EXERCISE

With His power—replace one worldly habit this week with a heavenly one. Add a new one each week or two!

- ◆ What has God revealed to you about Himself, today?
- ◆ Which verse does God want you to ask Him to apply to your life today?
- ◆ For whom does He want you to pray this verse?

LET US PRAY

We worship You Lord God Almighty, Creator of heaven and earth, our Provider, Protector, precious Father, perfector of our faith. Oh, Lord, teach us to daily live for and plead Your Will here on earth as in heaven. Oh, Lord, with heavenly hearts, teach us to pray. In Jesus' powerful and holy Name we pray, Amen.

Day 11

DAILY SPIRITUAL BREAD in PRAYER

||||||||||||||||||||||||||||||||||||||||||||||||||||||||||||||||||||||||||||||||

Give us today our daily bread

— MATTHEW 6:11 NIV —

Who is the One who provides all of our daily needs and provisions? Jehovah Jireh-God, our Provider, Redeemer, Healer, and Sustainer. Genesis 22:14 says, *Abraham named the place 'The LORD will provide.' This name has now become a proverb: 'On the mountain of the LORD it will be provided.'* When we ask God for our daily bread, we acknowledge our humble dependence upon Him to provide our spiritual and physical needs. Scripture says, *God gave Solomon great wisdom and understanding, knowledge too vast to be measured* (1 Kings 4:29). Why? To rule the kingdom God gave him. Even this wisdom was given in answer to prayer.

Why do we struggle to serve God? Why do we struggle to know God's will, and grow to know Him spiritually? James 4:2 says, *And yet the reason you don't have what you want is that you don't ask God for it.* We cannot do God's work without His wisdom! God fills us with spiritual knowledge to do His will, as we ask, using it for His honor. Paul prays, *And to desire that ye might be filled with the knowledge of his will in all wisdom and spiritual understanding; that ye might walk worthy of the LORD unto all pleasing, being fruitful in every good work.* Holiness, walking in His will, being worthy of Him, making fruitful all good work possible as we ask, is our daily bread!

Jesus teaches the priorities of daily communion with God and dependence upon Him. *For by him were all things created, that are in heaven, and that are on earth, visible and invisible, whether they be thrones, or dominions, or principalities, or powers: all things were created by him, and for him* (Colossians 1:9-10,16 KJV). All things by and for Him, including us! **The enemy of our souls tries to keep us from spiritual priorities and God, luring us away into dependence on ourselves and being concerned with worldly cares in order to trap and destroy us.**

Even Jesus was tempted to put physical needs before spiritual; both His obedience and reliance on God were tested. Matthew 4:2,4 says, *For forty days and forty nights he ate nothing and became very hungry.* The devil wanted Him to rely on Himself and turn stones into bread, apart from God's will. *But Jesus told him, No, the Scriptures say, 'People need more than bread for their life; they must feed on every Word of God.'* Let us beware satan will get us to try to feed ourselves apart from our dependence upon God. As Jesus defeated the devil by humbly applying Scripture, so shall we. Relying upon and believing in God, He overcame His physical hunger and gained spiritual victory. He did all this that we might, too.

Personally, I combat this daily, by not eating any food until after I've had time with God in prayer and His Word. I will not eat, exercise, or speak until I've been fed spiritually by God. Scripture exhorts, *spend your time and energy in training yourselves for spiritual fitness. Physical exercise has some value, but spiritual exercise is much more important, for it promises a reward in both this life and the next* (1 Timothy 4:7-8). Acting upon Scripture's truth, that spiritual needs are more important than physical ones, keeps our hearts humble, eyes heavenward, and our lives an example. Deuteronomy 8:3 says, *Yes, he humbled you by letting you go hungry and then feeding you with manna, a food previously unknown to you and your ancestors.* We see God humbling His people in hunger, teaching, feeding and testing their characters. We can count on being humbled and being tested; others are watching! *He did it to teach you that people need more than bread for their life; real life comes by feeding on every Word of the LORD.* We need not be discouraged; humility brings God's truth, strength and blessing. Humility brings hunger for His Word; bringing holiness.

David says, *Victory comes from you, O LORD. May your blessings rest on your people* (Psalm 3:8). Those who rely on God will be blessed! Daily dependence keeps us in the Presence of God, showing us His Heart as He meets our needs.

Let us learn to put our hearts first! Proverbs 17:22 (NIV) says, *A cheerful heart is good medicine, but a crushed spirit dries up the bones.* **The spiritual health or sickness of our hearts shall affect our minds and bodies.** Ecclesiastes 11:10 (NIV) commands, *So then, banish anxiety from your heart and cast off the troubles from your body, for youth and vigor are meaningless.* Physicians refer to stress as anxiety for the heart, a number-one killer causing sickness, mental illness, high blood pressure, and heart attacks among many. Proverbs 18:14 (NIV) confirms, *A man's spirit sustains him in sickness, but a crushed spirit who can bear?* A physical ailment is always bearable, but spiritual sickness is not. Let us heed Scriptures' command in Proverbs 4:23 (NIV), *Above all else, guard your heart, for it is the wellspring of life.* **The cause for spiritual illness: a crushed heart will always find its way back to an unguarded heart: a lack of prayer, a lack of God. Let us guard diligently our wellsprings of life!**

David prays, *Listen to my voice in the morning, LORD. Each morning I bring my requests to you and wait expectantly* (Psalm 5:3). It is not possible to catch up on your prayer for the week, as some try to do. God wants us to have a daily relationship with, and dependence upon Him. Asking and waiting expectantly, He is able to reveal Himself to us continually. Seeing Him meet our needs in answer to prayer, He further strengthens us in our faith. Remaining in daily prayer fills us spiritually, enabling us to do His will. Psalm 5:8 says, *Lead me in the right path, O LORD, or my enemies will conquer me. Tell me clearly what to do, and show me the way to turn.* David knew the necessity and the urgency of spiritual direction and blessing from God, realizing that, without God, he would be conquered. Psalm 5:12 says, *For you bless the godly, O LORD, surrounding them with your shield of love.* Most of us think we can get by for small increments of time without God, but we must understand the battle we face without Him and the true necessity of God's daily provisions and Presence.

Paul instructs, *Pursue a godly life, along with faith, love, perseverance, and gentleness. Fight the good fight for what we believe.* Our fights are spiritual; we must remain protected, in our fortress of God's armor and love. *Tell those who are rich in this world not to be proud and not to trust in their money, which will soon be gone. But their trust should be in the living God, who richly gives us all we need for our enjoyment* (1 Timothy 6:11-12,17). Let us pursue godliness, fleeing the world with its lusts and desires, and look for all from God, fighting the good fight of faith! We shall then humbly recognize our greatest need for

His shield of love!

Asking God daily for our bread reminds us blessings are not only for ourselves, but gifts from Him to be used for His work and in His Kingdom. We ask the Creator for all things to provide us daily nourishment that we may live and serve Him effectively. Psalm 1:2-3 says, *They delight in doing everything the LORD wants; day and night they think about his law. They are like trees along a riverbank, bearing fruit each season without fail. Their leaves never wither, and in all they do, they prosper.* Keeping spiritual bread our priority in prayer, so shall it be in life; our desires will be godly, our lives fruitful, and our hearts joyful. God fills us daily because our sinful nature wages war daily. Listening to a great sermon on Sunday will not keep our spirits fed for an entire week. Would we even think of only nourishing our bodies with food once or twice weekly? How much more important, then, is it to nourish our souls, which are so quickly filled with the misery of hunger!

We were created for Him and in Him; apart, we shall have no joy, sustenance, or delight, no wisdom-giving life. Psalm 16:11 (KJV) says, *Thou wilt shew me the path of life: In thy presence is fullness of joy; At thy right hand there are pleasures for evermore.* We must repent for filling ourselves instead with the empty, meaningless things of this world that only delude us from the joy, peace, and lasting pleasures we can only receive from Him. Scripture warns, *You adulterers! Don't you realize that friendship with this world makes you an enemy of God? I say it again, that if your aim is to enjoy this world, you can't be a friend of God* (James 4:4).

We may enjoy blessings while we are here, but our aim cannot be to simply enjoy this world. These pleasures are elusive and living for them will destroy us. How many, rather than being filled daily by God, have been deceived into the lies and distractions of this world? Remember always, friendship with the world is enmity to God, appearing to satisfy with excessive food, drugs, alcohol, business, money, power, fame, and even family or ministry can replace fellowship with God. How our flesh tries to find it's own satisfaction apart from God, while starving our spirits and soul!

Oh, we are not the first to seek other ways. The world has long suffered its souls to war against God's holiness, *For My people have committed two evils: They have forsaken Me, The fountain of living waters, To hew for themselves cisterns, Broken cisterns That can hold no water* (Jeremiah 2:13 NASB). God is the only fountain of living water for our spirits and we must daily be nourished by Him. Jeremiah 15:15 says, *Your words are what sustain me. They bring me great joy and are my hearts delight, for I bear your name, O LORD God Almighty.* Bearing His Name, He must be what sustains. He's our Fountain, endlessly supplying Living Waters to us, His children. How often we settle for little buckets in the ground that dry up, crack and leak, leaving us thirsty and disappointed. Apart from Him, we too, will be broken as our cisterns, useless and malnourished. Let us return, repent, and be restored and re-nourished!

Of drinking of God and trusting Him alone, Jeremiah says in 17:8 (KJV), *For he shall be as a tree planted by the waters, and that spreadeth out her roots by the river, and shall not see when heat cometh, but her leaf shall be green; and shall not be careful in the year of the drought, neither shall cease from yielding fruit.* Physical circumstances or resources no longer hinder. Returning unto God, He flows through hearts with His holy Rivers of Life, bringing spiritual blessings and bearing unfailing fruit. It is only flooded by the mighty holy rivers of God that our hearts shall be cleansed and healed. It is His Spirit that speaks; His Word that keeps. Psalm 19:11 promises, *They are a warning to those who hear them; there is great reward for those who keep them.* We must be in His daily Presence, asking, receiving, and hearing.

David goes on to say, *How can I know all the sins lurking in my heart? Cleanse me from these hidden faults. Keep me from deliberate sins! Don't let them control me* (Psalm 19:12-13). We are either controlled by sin or controlled by holiness; by the devil or by God. Romans 8:9,12 urges Christians, *But you are not controlled by your sinful nature. You are controlled by the Spirit if you have the Spirit of God living in you. You have no obligation whatsoever to do what your sinful nature urges you to do.* Being filled with God's Spirit gives us a new obligation, to deny sin and serve God!

Words can bring spiritual death or life. Proverbs 10:21 (NIV) says, *The lips of the righteous nourish many.* Proverbs 12:18 (NIV) says, *Reckless words pierce like a sword, but the tongue of the wise brings healing.* Proverbs 15:4 (NIV) tells us, *The tongue that brings healing is a tree of life, but a deceitful tongue crushes the spirit.* To bring life and bear fruit, we must first be filled with it in our hearts. Our lives cannot radiate health to others if we have death inside, so let us seek to be nourished by God alone. **What is in hearts, will come out of mouths—death or life, famine or nourishment.** Proverbs 4:4 (NIV) promises, *Keep my commands and you will live.*

Feeding on His Word and obeying it brings life! We need not ask or concern our prayers with enough for the next year, but enough only for life that day. He further advises in Proverbs 4:20-22 (NIV), *My son, pay close attention to what I say; listen closely to my words.* Paying close attention and listening closely to Him requires time. *Do not let them out of your sight, keep them within your heart; for they are life to those who find them and health to a whole man's body.* Keeping God's Word in our hearts requires daily nourishment, meditating upon His Word and being filled with His Spirit.

Jesus teaches, *It is the Spirit who gives eternal life. Human effort accomplishes nothing. And the very words I have spoken to you are spirit and life* (John 6:63). Let us pray for the fires of the Holy Spirit to consume, bringing His Word to life in our hearts, lives, and prayers. He tells us, *I assure you, Moses didn't give them bread from heaven. My Father did. And now he offers you the true bread from heaven. The true bread of God is the one who comes down from heaven and gives life to the world.* Responding to His teachings as they did, and receiving our daily bread, we shall have life, fulfillment, nourishment, and blessing! He says, *I am the bread of life. No one who comes to me will ever be hungry again. Those who believe in me will never thirst. Yes, I am the bread of life!* (John 6:32-35,38). Let us believe as did Simon Peter, *Lord, to whom would we go? You alone have the words that give eternal life. We believe them, and we know you are the holy one of God* (John 6:68). Oh, Jesus, we believe only you can satisfy! Teach us to eat of, drink of, and be ever filled by Your holiness; let us love You!

Filled with His Holy Spirit, our concern is more with our relationship with Him than with abundance of physical things. We will learn to daily ask first for our spiritual needs, remaining in His Presence as His will flows through us, enabling us to know and serve Him in holiness. We are promised that, as we ask, we shall be filled and empowered by Jesus' very own Spirit; He promises abundant answers to our prayers. *Let anyone who is thirsty come to me and drink. For the Scriptures declare that rivers of living water will flow from the heart of those who believe in me* (John 7:37-38).

EXERCISE

Do not eat each morning until you have prayed, praised, and proclaimed God's Word, spending time with Him in prayer, and in His Word!

- What has God revealed to you about Himself, today?
- Which verse does God want you to ask Him to apply to your life today?
- For whom does He want you to pray this verse?

LET US PRAY

We come before You with humbled and thankful hearts full of praise, lifting Your Name on high. Father, give us this day our spiritual daily bread necessary to accomplish Your purposes and will in our lives for the current and imminent reigning of Your Kingdom. Fill us to Rivers overflowing, teaching us to pray...In Jesus' precious Name, Amen.

Day 12

DAILY PHYSICAL
BREAD in PRAYER

||||||||||||||||||||||||||||||||||||||||||||||||||||||||||||||||||||||||||||||||||||||||

Give us this day our daily bread

—MATTHEW 6:11 NIV —

Depending upon Jesus, the Bread from heaven for spiritual life, God has also designed our bodies to require daily physical nourishment that we may ask and depend upon Him, our Provider. Psalm 33:7-9 says, *All humanity finds shelter in the shadow of your wings. You feed them from the abundance of your own house, letting them drink from your rivers of delight.* All humanity is dependent upon God Almighty. Sinful humanness would much rather think of itself as self-sustaining and self-dependant; however, God has created us and it is only He who blesses. Deuteronomy 8:17-18 says, *He did it so you would never think that it was you own strength and energy that made you wealthy. Always remember that it is the LORD your God who gives you power to become rich.*

When His children admit dependence, asking daily bread from our heavenly Father, we will receive; this is our promise. Scripture promises, *True humility and fear of the LORD lead to riches, honor and long life. The LORD will not the godly starve to death, but he refuses to satisfy the craving of the wicked* (Proverbs 22:4/10:3). Psalm 37:17-19 states, *But the LORD takes care of the godly. Day by day the LORD will take care of the innocent. They will survive through hard times; even in famine they will have more than enough.* Even in famine, we have more than enough to share with all. Jesus teaches, *I am come*

— 84 —

that they might have life, and that they might have it more abundantly (John 10:10 KJV). Jesus came to give life more abundantly!

Asking for daily bread keeps God our priority. Proverbs 30:8-9 (NIV) says, *Give me neither poverty nor riches, but give me only my daily bread. Otherwise, I may have too much and disown you and say, 'Who is the LORD?' Or I may become poor and steal, and so dishonor the name of my God.* As we ask for daily needs and remain in His Presence, we can focus on honoring God's Name above riches and self. Scripture says, *Wealth is worthless in the day of wrath, but righteousness delivers from death.* Prayer keeps righteousness our priority, filling our hearts with generosity. *One man gives freely, yet gains even more; another withholds unduly, but comes to poverty. A generous man will prosper; he who refreshes others will himself be refreshed* (Proverbs 11:4,24-25 NIV). As we give, God gives to us, bringing thanksgiving from many hearts. Deuteronomy 8:10 says, *When you have eaten your fill, praise the LORD your God for the land he has given you.* Asking and thanking reminds us that all is *given* to us. The next verses warn us, however, to beware, lest we forget God, become proud and disobey Him. Prayer keeps hearts grateful and humble, our blessings flowing, and lives obedient.

Remember the rules of sowing and reaping? When we ask, we receive, and we must thank and give in return; God multiplies all by returning even more. He promises when we are faithful with little, we shall be given more. **Daily bread keeps our treasures in heaven, not on earth.** *Don't store up treasures here on earth, where they can be eaten by moths and get rusty, and where thieves break in and steal. No one can serve two masters. For you will hate one and love the other, or be devoted to one and despise the other. You cannot serve both God and money* (Matthew 6:19,25). Serving God, we will not serve money; it will serve us, as we use it to serve God's will. Allowing love for money always replaces love for God and His people. As He provides abundantly for our daily needs, He gives us the opportunity to show Him obedience in giving and not storing, choosing eternal treasure over physical, and in return, we will receive spiritual blessings beyond measure. Obedience always brings power in prayer and brings blessing.

We show our trust in Him by living daily and giving away our excess. Greed brings a curse, showing trust in money instead of in God. Proverbs 11:26,28 (NIV) says, *People curse the man who hordes grain, but blessings crown him who is willing to sell. Whoever trusts in his riches will fall, but the righteous will thrive like a green leaf.* We daily make our choice in life and prayer; cursing or blessing. Trust and thrive- or fear and fall?

Freeing us from the trap of fear, greed and worry, Matthew 6:25-26,32 command, *Don't worry about every day life—whether you have enough food, drink and clothes. Doesn't life consist of more than food and clothing? Look at the birds. They don't need to plant or harvest or put food in barns because your heavenly Father feeds them. And you are far more valuable to him than they are.* Do we ask and receive our daily bread, or trust in stored riches, falling into the trap of worry and poverty? Christians are exhorted, *Why be like the pagans who are so deeply concerned about these things?* Do you see? He is just waiting to bless, honor, and set you free! Take time to be alone with Him outside today. Watch the birds, the flowers, and His creation around you. He cares for you, His child even more; will He then not so much more take care of your daily needs? Remember again, His promise in Matthew 6:33 (KJV) and stand firm in it, *But seek ye first the kingdom of God, and his righteousness; and all these things shall be added unto you.* Do you believe? Holiness seeks and lives for His kingdom, receiving His all from heaven. He will faithfully give, that in prayer, we receive blessings for all.

He promises, as we are faithful with what He gives us, to increase it that we may continually join in the work of His Kingdom, bringing glory to His Name. As we ask, we do so for the benefit of others. We see a key to God's Heart in 2 Corinthians 12:19, *Everything we do, dear friends, is for your benefit.* As holy servants of God, all we have, all we receive and all we do is for the benefit of others. As God's Heart is to bless, so must ours be. His holy Word having its way in our hearts, so our words will have their way in His. Praying and living to give, we will bless others—not in the weakness of the flesh, but by receiving, giving and living in the power of the Cross. *Although he died on the cross in weakness, he now lives by the mighty power of God. We, too, are weak, but we live in him and have God's power—the power we use in dealing with you.* He further instructs, *Rejoice. Change your ways. Encourage each other. Live in harmony and peace. Then the God of love and peace will be with you* (2 Corinthians 13:4,11). Glorying in Him, casting all He gives at the foot of the Cross, we know He is with us, changing our ways.

Scripture commands us to use physical resources to care for the needs of others, beginning in our homes. Children show godliness at home by caring for widows, and widows show godliness by giving of their time and resources.

1 Timothy 5:4-6 says, *But if she has children, their first responsibility is to show godliness at home and repay their parents by taking care of them. This is something that pleases God very much.* We cannot let sin, doubt, our lack of time, energy, money, room, or resources ever allow disobedience. If we have not, we have asked not. God always brings what we need to obey Him! *But a woman who is a true widow, has placed her hope in God.* How do we know when our hope is in God? By our actions! *Night and day she asks God for help and spends much time in prayer.* She does not work sixty hours a week nor lounge selfishly doing nothing; she asks God for what she needs, and spends her time wisely in prayer. *But the widow who lives only for pleasure is spiritually dead.* Let us ask the Spirit to search our hearts, prayers, and lives; let us repent, for God's holy fires will fan new flames in those who are spiritually dead! We need only ask!

Hearts wholly given to God each morning in prayer receive blessings and find Him wholly willing. Abraham was wholly given to God. Genesis 12:2-4 (NIV) says, *I will make you a great nation and I will bless you; I will make your name great, and you will be a blessing. I will bless those who bless you, and whoever curses you I will curse; and all peoples on earth will be blessed through you.* Abraham's response to God's blessing: *So Abraham left, as the LORD had told him.* He showed complete, surrendered blessing and immediate obedience; he listened to God's Word, and was blessed in return; using these blessings to benefit others. Oh, the Heart of God Who brings forth, and then blesses holiness!

Romans 15:2 says, *We should please others. If we do what helps them, we will build them up in the Lord. For even Christ didn't please himself.* Pleasing others builds up—includes using all of our resources, blessings, time and talents for the benefit of others, in the Lord. **Lives given to God receive from God all things in prayer!** Jesus promises, *He that loveth his life shall lose it; and he that hateth his life in this world shall keep it unto eternal life. If any man serve me, let him follow me; and where I am, there shall also my servant be: if any man serve me, him will my Father honour* (John 12:25-26 KJV). Serving our Savior, His resources become ours, His path ours, as so His persevering Presence and honor, are ours. All those in Scripture who lived for God lived in prayer remaining in His love, obeying in faith, and being showered with His blessings.

God promises to meet all the needs of His children. He, alone, enables us to do His work as we carry His Name. Daniel prayed, *O LORD, you are a great and awesome God! You always fulfill your promises of unfailing love to those who love you and keep your commands. We do not ask because we deserve help, but because you are so merciful. O LORD, listen and act! For your own sake, O my God, do not delay, for your people and your city bear your name* (Daniel 9:4,18-19). As we continue to spend more time knowing God, His Word filling and controlling our hearts, our prayers become those of faith in who He is and what He has promised to do. Many lack the faith to remain in prayer because they know not to Whom they pray, or what He desires to give. We are only asking Him to provide those things He has promised. His Heart desires to share, not because of our worthiness, but because of His worthiness, unfailing love, and never-ending mercies. Faithfully, He fills our hearts with His holy breath of fire, that we may ask, seek and knock, that we may have, find and be free to receive all we ask in prayer. It is for Him that we pray, and it is for His namesake that He answers.

His holiness works its way through our hearts; His passion consumes, His power is released, and His purposes revealed to us. Daniel 9:21,23 reads, *As I was praying, Gabriel, came swiftly to me at the time of the evening sacrifice.* God releases His blessing angels, His power, and His love, in answer to wholehearted prayer. *The moment you started praying, a command was given. I am here to tell you what it was, for God loves you very much.* Prayer releases our hearts to receive the love and blessings from His Heart, allowing Him to love others through us. Prayer gives us the ability to serve Him in obedience.

Romans 12:9-13,21 says, *Don't just pretend to love others. Really love them. Hate what is wrong... Love each other with genuine affection, and take delight in honoring each other.* Being filled with God's love is the only true way we can love and serve others. As He delights in honoring us, we will delight in honoring others. *Never be lazy in your work, but serve the Lord enthusiastically. Be glad for all God is planning for you and always be prayerful.* Prayer allows us to be empowered to serve, seeing His purposes through His provisions and being thankful as He uses us for His work. *When God's children are in need, be the one to help them out. And get into the habit of inviting guests home for dinner or, if they need lodging, for the night. Conquer evil by doing good.* As God conquers the evil from our hearts, our good deeds and sharing shall overcome the evil in others. Hebrews 12:29 says, *For our God is a consuming fire.* Our homes, our prayers and our lives are for sharing with others. Prayer allows God's love to consume and flow through us. It burns the evil that keeps us from remaining in His love and using our physical blessings to His glory, only holiness sustains.

We should always ask for others first in prayer, and then for ourselves. The very law of God's kingdom is always giving, serving, and loving by putting others first. Hebrews 13:1-3 (NASB) says, *Let love of the brethren continue. Do not neglect to show hospitality to strangers, for by doing some have entertained angels without knowing it. Remember the prisoners, as though in prison with them, and those who are ill-treated, since you yourselves are in the body.* God tells us to look to the needs of others, and not to neglect or forget to love. The Holy Spirit reminds and unites us with our brethren in prayer. God's all-consuming holiness takes us away from ourselves and into His Heart. He consumes our hearts, that we may consume His. Hebrews 13:15-16 (NASB) says, *Through him then, let us continually offer up a sacrifice of praise to God, that is, the fruit of lips that give thanks to His name. And do not neglect doing good and sharing, for with such sacrifice God is pleased.* Hearts created to worship, to love, and to share and be united with others, must sacrifice in order to serve. Our actions will show whom we serve, God and holiness, or self and sin. Prayer—doing God's will, sharing in Christ, and sacrifices of praise all allow us to please God, as we ask Him for our daily bread.

EXERCISE

Prayerfully find, with your husband's permission, a ministry to invest your prayers, time, and money—sacrificially.

- ❖ What has God revealed to you about Himself, today?
- ❖ Which verse does God want you to ask Him to apply to your life today?
- ❖ For whom does He want you to pray this verse?

LET US PRAY

Gracious, wonderful, holy, heavenly Father. Forgive us for allowing pride and laziness to keep us from prayer, acknowledging our need for all things from You daily. Continue to teach us the true needs of our bodies and souls, and we shall hunger and thirst for You and Your righteousness, holiness, and mercy. In Jesus' precious Name, Amen.

Day 13

DAILY REPENTANCE
in PRAYER

||||||||||||||||||||||||||||||||||||||||||||||||||||||

Forgive us our debts.

— MATTHEW 6:12A NIV —

Confidently entering into the Presence of our holy God, we must have confession and repentance, receiving forgiveness of our sins. Drawing us unto the throne of grace for prayer to worship our Almighty, heavenly Father, the cleansing and healing blood of Christ removes our sins and purifies our hearts. God will not remain in the presence of sin. It must be confessed and cast out for us to live prayer. Proverbs 11:21 (NIV) says, *Be sure of this: The wicked will not go unpunished, but those who are righteous will go free.* Coming into the righteousness of Christ, we are free to worship, pray, and live. Repentance brings restoration, renewal, refreshment, revival and rejoicing! Proverbs 11:27 promises, *If you search for good, you will find favor.* God finds favor with repentant hearts. Again, in Proverbs 12:2, *The LORD approves of those who are good, but he condemns those who plan wickedness.* Any wickedness remaining in our hearts brings a divided heart, a condemned heart.

We cannot be filled with God's holy Presence and unresolved sin. 1 John 1:5-7 says, *God is light; in him there is no darkness at all. If we claim to have fellowship with him yet walk in darkness, we lie and do not live by truth.* Sin is the act of any unrighteousness or walking in darkness; interrupting our relationship with God. *But if we walk in the light as he is in the light, we have fellowship with one another, and the blood of Jesus, his son, purifies us from all sin.*

Though we are cleansed and pure once and for all by accepting and claiming salvation, we must live in a continual spirit of humility and repentance. We are promised of God's faithfulness to confession, *If we confess our sins, he is faithful and just and will forgive our sins and purify us from all unrighteousness* (1 John 1:9 NIV). Not only does He forgive, but He cleanses, washing away all impurities, leaving hearts white as snow once again.

Prayerful hearts must be confessing hearts! To confess something is to speak in agreement. Continually seeking God's forgiveness in confession, we agree with Him about sin; seeking to do good and refraining from evil. In our flesh's struggle against confession, we may believe He is unwilling, or that confession is unnecessary. Let us kneel before Jesus and ask, that we may be cleansed. We read, *And a leper came up to Him and bowed down before Him, and said, Lord, if You are willing, You can make me clean. Jesus stretched out His hand and touched him, saying, "I am willing, be cleansed"* (Matthew 8:2-3 NASB). Daily confession allows the Lord access to search, examine, and cleanse our hearts.

Do you want to bow down? Are you willing to hear what our Lord may ask of you? Jesus is always willing to cleanse; are you willing to be cleansed? Do you know why you need Jesus to cleanse you? Let us even confess the traps we've chosen of pride and unwillingness; God will gladly give us the grace for that too, as we ask. We must not forget the continual struggle of spirit against flesh and holiness against sin. Let us remember, *Temptation comes from the lure of our own evil desires. These evil desires lead to evil actions and evil actions lead to death* (James 1:14-15). **Relying on self for desire or freedom from sin, fails. Daily seeking forgiveness keeps our desires and power those God fills us with, rather than those of the flesh.**

Scripture says we must daily *refuse to let the world corrupt us* (James 1:27). Our lives are lived daily in spiritual battle. Already having victory in Christ, we must now refuse to allow ourselves to be corrupted. It is a daily choice. The enemy would like us to allow corruption by rejecting truth, by forgetting it and surrendering to the world instead of God. Daily, we must choose to accept God, for James 2:10 says, *And the person who keeps all of the laws except one is as guilty as the person who has broken all of God's laws.* Each thought, word, action, and decision either enables the enemy or enables God. Of course, the enemy always tries to deceive us; he's been doing it thousands of years. He deceives when we doubt and reject God's Word, believing satan instead and accepting sin. The devil packages sin so that even to a Christian it may not appear sinful. "Just a little won't hurt" and "nobody will ever know" are two great big lies of the enemy that lead to death and destruction. Another is, "God's Word doesn't really mean that—does it?" Eve fell for it. The enemy tells us to do what feels good and leads us to lean on our emotions and away from God.

Another way the enemy keeps us from confession is by convincing us there will be no consequences, or that it's a sin too little to matter to God. As our Pastor, Julian Riddle, taught in one of his sermons entitled, 'Seven Cold Splashes on the Spirit:' "The flesh likes to turn sin into a cuddly little pet. We fall into the trap of believing them too little to be harmful. We hold them on our laps, even getting attached to them." The enemy knows we have victory over sin, therefore, he knows it must deceitfully be brought to us in small increments, looking harmless and even playful and fun. The real truth of all sin is found in James 1:15 (NIV), *Then, after desire has conceived, it gives birth to sin; and sin when it is full grown, gives birth to death.* All sin leads to death!

Satan attempts to continue in deception; for then our "cuddly pet" appears so big and ferocious, there is nothing we can do about it. Buying into his lies, we will hide it and try to deal with it on our own. These traps give satan a stronghold in our hearts, keeping us prisoner to the very sin we allowed. We cannot accept an evil desire or thought, not even for a moment. When satan sends an evil idea into our minds and we consider it, our desire grows and grows until we have to have it, no matter how much it costs! The thoughts and lies the enemy tempts us with must immediately be rejected! Romans 6:23 promises, *The wages of sin is death.* We must guard our minds, keeping hearts repentant, that we will carefully choose our thoughts and actions, realizing the outcome. **Sin brings death—physical and spiritual; prayer keeps us pure and safe!**

Paul exhorts, *It is not that we think we can do anything of lasting value ourselves. Our only power and success comes from God. The old way ends in death; in the new way, the Holy Spirit gives life* (2 Corinthians 3:5-6). All sins root themselves back to pride, doing things apart from God. Without prayer, we, too, try to deliver ourselves from sin, resulting in deadly failure. We must believe every one of God's truths in Scripture, and take them literally. 2 Corinthians 4:4 says, *Satan, the god of this evil world, has blinded the minds of those who don't believe.* We cannot see sin, but God reveals it and frees us from it, as we believe. We have hope, *But whenever anyone turns to the Lord, then the veil is taken away. Now, the Lord is the Spirit, and wherever the Spirit of the Lord is, he gives freedom* (2 Corinthians 3:16-17). When God forgives us for our sins, He frees us to walk in holiness, hating and seeing the truth of sin.

Let us join David again in the Psalms, the perfect place for prayer, *O LORD, you are so good, so ready to forgive, so full of unfailing love for all who ask your aid.* He is so ready, we need only ask and rely on His aid! Do you believe how ready He is? *Grant me purity of heart that I may honor you.* He desires our holiness even more than we do; it honors Him and He will grant it. *For your love for me is very great, You have rescued me from the depths of death!* (Psalm 86:5,11,13). God's love delivered us from hell and will continue to deliver from sin, *the depths of death!* What is required of us in return? Prayer. Humbled hearts brought to God in prayer, bringing godly sorrow and strength.

We were created with hearts to worship; if we don't worship God, we will worship something or someone else! If we don't worship in truth and spirit by God's holy grace, we will worship in flesh, worshiping the enemy, which is just what he wants. Let us beware this great sin of prayerlessness, which leaves us at the mercy of the flesh, rather than being filled with the Spirit and all His grace, being the reason for all spiritual death and destruction. Romans 8:13 says, *For if you keep following it, you will perish. But if through the power of the Holy Spirit you turn from it and its evil deeds you will live.* Empowered by the Spirit we will turn from sins and its evil deeds—to God and live! The enemy does all he can to keep us relying on the flesh.

Paul warns further, *Be very careful, then, how you live—not as unwise but as wise. Do not get drunk on wine, which leads to debauchery. Instead, be filled with the Spirit, always giving thanks to God the Father for everything, in the name of Jesus Christ* (Ephesians 5:15,18 NIV). Wine leads to "debauchery." The root word "debauch" means "to corrupt or dissipate, to scatter, to waste." The Greek root word, "aselgeia," translates to "sensuality, lewdness, filthy." Let us strongly rephrase-"wine-not, waste-not!" BE FILLED WITH THE SPIRIT—NOT FILTH, WINE & WASTE! Prayer keeps us careful, wise, and filled with the Spirit; giving thanks for everything. Prayer fulfills God's laws to live in our hearts.

If you or another has taken any sin lightly, beware! Amos 1:3 says, *The people of Damascus have sinned again and again, and I will not forget it. I will not let them go unpunished any longer!* Punishment will come; we don't know how or when, but without repentance, it comes; the worst being the death of our daily, loving intimate relationship with God. Any sin is an act personally against a holy God. The psalmist cried out, *For I cried out to him for help, praising him as I spoke. If I had not confessed the sin in my heart, my LORD would not have listened. But God did listen! He paid attention to my prayer* (Psalm 66:17-19). God listens to praising, repentant hearts, but will not listen when confession is neglected.

We learn, again, the lesson of defeating sin, with repentance and thanksgiving, ushering in God's unfailing love, so ready to forgive and so ready to be near. We listen to David, confessing adultery and murder, *Against you, and you alone, have I sinned; I have done what is evil in your sight.* Sins are an act against God as well as man. *Purify me from my sins and I will be clean; wash me and I will be whiter than snow. Oh, give me back my joy again; you have broken me—now let me rejoice.* Sin always steals our joy, as it is only found in God's Presence. *Create in me a clean heart, O God. Renew a right spirit within me. Restore to me again the joy of your salvation, and make me willing to obey you.* David knew he needed God's cleansing forgiveness to restore him so that he could praise God again. *Unseal my lips, O LORD, that I may praise you* (Psalm 51:4,7-8,10-11,15). God has created us to praise; we are utterly brokenhearted when we are torn apart from Him by unconfessed sin.

The enemy's purposes are to steal, kill and destroy; sin is his weapon. He wants to take from us, keep from us and bring death to all God has for us. He knows Jesus has defeated his power and work, but he doesn't want us to know or believe it. What we believe, or don't, is how we will act; it is the power we will live under. 1 John 3:8 gives victory, if we will walk in it, believing, *When people keep on sinning, it shows they belong to the devil, who has been sinning since the beginning.* Are you ready for the really great news? *But the son of God came to destroy these works of the devil.* The NIV version says, *The reason the son of God appeared was to destroy the devil's work.* **Read these aloud; the devil's works were destroyed by Jesus! Jesus' work canceled and cancels satan's! With God, we have Jesus' power, victory and holiness; without God's Presence, we live in agony and defeat.**

Let us be ever so encouraged and strengthened in heart and prayer! 1 John 2:12,14 says, *I am writing to you my dear children, because your sins have been forgiven because of Jesus, because you are strong with God's Word living in your hearts, and you have won your battle with satan.* God's forgiveness through the blood brought the devil defeat. Now God's holy powerful Word lives in our hearts, and He shall not dwell with sin! Neither our great smile, nor winning prayers, only the Cross, has set us free! Christ's prayers brought forth His blood at Gethsemane that His blood would, too, pour from the Cross. God's love poured through the veins of Christ, enabling Him to sit at the right hand of the Father, clothed in glory and power, forever loving, interceding, and saving.

Holiness and righteousness bring glory, honor and power—power of the risen King! 1 John 2:28-29 promises, forgiveness brings righteousness, *Continue to live in fellowship with Christ so that when he returns, you will be full of courage and not shrink back from him in shame.* That gives thought for some sobering evaluation of our daily prayers and choices. Continue to live in fellowship with Christ! What an honor; what a responsibility. Have you ever taken a day to act like you knew Jesus was right there with you? Set Him a place at your table, a seat in your car, a place with you as you teach and play with the kids, talk on the phone, watch television. Since we know God is always right, we also know that all who do right are His children. Confession frees us from shame, releasing us in power to do what is right again!

EXERCISE

Pray Psalm #32 aloud, inserting your name and another's.

➤ What has God revealed to you about Himself, today?

➤ Which verse does God want you to ask Him to apply to your life today?

➤ For whom does He want you to pray this verse?

LET US PRAY

May we sing joyfully to You-Lord, we who are righteous for it is fitting for the upright to praise You. We praise You for destroying the works of the devil in our lives. Forgive and restore, healing our hearts that we may praise you! Oh, Lord, teach us to pray...In Jesus' precious Name, Amen.

Day 14

DAILY FORGIVENESS
in PRAYER
||||||||||||||||||||||||||||||||||||||||||||||||||

Forgive us our debts, as we also have forgiven our debtors.

— MATTHEW 6:12 NIV —

Jesus teaches us that out of God's divine mercy and forgiveness towards us, we are to forgive others. Accepting God's forgiveness, we are commanded and able to completely forgive those who have sinned against us. As we forgive—we shall be forgiven. Let us join the disciples behind locked doors, listening to Jesus, *Suddenly, Jesus was standing there among them! "Peace be with you!" he said. As he spoke, he held out his hands for them to see, and he showed them his side. They were filled with joy when they saw their Lord!* (John 20:19-20). When we are called to forgive, let us look at our Savior's pierced hands and side. The very hands we pierced, He holds out to us. Realizing our great sins that brought the need for God to sacrifice His only begotten Son on the Cross, we will find it impossible to allow the spirit of unforgiveness to remain in our hearts.

Let us remember ourselves with honesty. Deuteronomy 9:6-7 says, *The LORD your God is not giving you this good land because you are righteous, for you are not—you are a stubborn people. Remember how angry you made the LORD your God out in the wilderness. From the day you left Egypt until now, you have constantly rebelled against him.* Praise God, we don't get what we deserve, which would be hell. We don't deserve forgiveness, yet in God's mercy we have received it and must share it! Let us praise, for *He has not punished us for* all our sins, nor does he deal with us as we deserve. For his unfailing love toward those who fear him is as great as the height of the heavens above the earth. He has removed our rebellious acts as far away as the east is from the west. The LORD is like a father to his children, tender and compassionate to those who fear him (Psalm 103:10-13).

To whomever pierces our hearts, we shall still hold out our hands of sacrifice, compassion and prayer. Anyone who has hurt us, no matter how badly, must be forgiven, and we must pray for that person! What did Jesus do as He was being crucified for our sins? **He forgave in prayer! He gave up His rights as God, and we are commanded to give up our rights and forgive as well.**

The devil's job is to try to steal God's love and blessings. He sets deep traps when we allow an unforgiving spirit to take root into our hearts. Romans 2:1-2 warns *When you say they are wicked and should be punished, you are condemning yourself, for you do these very same things. And we know that God, in his justice, will punish anyone who does such things.* With forgiveness, we relinquish all rights for revenge, letting our hearts go and keeping free from the enemy's traps; we let God be in charge of the situation. Romans 12:17-19 commands we, *Never pay back evil for evil to anyone. Do things in such a way that everyone will see that you are honorable. Do your part to live at peace with everyone, as much as possible.* Not everyone will respond in peace, but we must. *Never avenge yourselves. Leave that to God. For it is written: "I will take vengeance; I will repay those who deserve it," says the Lord.* Remember, we either let God, or we let the devil!

Within prayer and forgiveness of sin dwells Jesus, His peace and His joy, freely given and freely shared. Obedience floods our hearts with peace because He is there. Jesus teaches, *Peace be with you. As the Father has sent me, so I send you. Then he breathed on them and said to them, "Receive the Holy Spirit. If you forgive anyone's sins, they are forgiven. If you refuse to forgive them, they are unforgiven"* (John 20:21-23). Receiving Jesus' peace and joy with which our hearts ache to be filled comes through forgiveness!

Not only must we release ourselves to be forgiven, but we must release others as well. 2 Corinthians 2:7-8 says, *Now it is time to forgive him and comfort him. Otherwise he may become so discouraged that he won't be able to recover. Now show him that you still love him.* Complete forgiveness, including comforting others with God's love, brings encouragement, recovery and restoration. Romans 13:10 (KJV) says, *Love worketh no ill to his neighbor: therefore love is the fulfilling of the law.* The power of love is enormous, and we must allow it to flow unhindered through our hearts and prayers.

Our experience as Christians is to be shared, allowing Christ to speak and live through us. As we hear, so shall we speak. We must live, eat, breathe, pray and live His Word that we may truly be a living testimony of God's love and Presence. Scripture says, *You are to take this message everywhere, telling the whole world what you have seen and heard.* Then, we are asked, *And now, why delay?* When God commands, we must not delay! Delay is sin, as sin keeps us in delay. *Get up and be baptized, and have your sins washed away, calling on the name of the Lord* (Acts 22:15-16). His command that we ask forgiveness, as we forgive others, keeps God's honor before ours, that He may use us to love and to teach others.

Responding with revenge and anger at a wrong against us only represents our flesh, not God's glory. *For you are still controlled by your own sinful desires. You are jealous of one another and quarrel with each other. Doesn't that prove you are controlled by your own desires? You are acting like people who don't belong to the Lord* (1 Corinthians 3:3). The spiritual outcome of being controlled by the flesh and reacting as the unsaved is that we are rendered unable to grow, allowing emotions like anger, jealousy, and unforgiveness to control and destroy us.

Unforgiveness binds us to the situation and keeps God from it, bringing pain, as with all sin, and death of spiritual growth, relationships, and health, among others. Scripture warns that lack of faith, and taking matters into our own hands will, in turn, take it out of God's hands. Romans 14:23 says, *The man who doubts is condemned if he eats, because his eating is not from faith; and everything that does not come from faith is sin.* Daily, let us forgive, choosing to believe God can be trusted, and allow His forgiveness to work through and free us from sin!

Right before Jesus' teaching on effective prayer, we learn of the danger of an unforgiving, critical spirit. John 7:1-2 (NIV) warns, *Do not judge, or you too will be judged. For in the same way you judge others, you will be judged, and with the measure you use, it will be measured to you.* To be heard in prayer, we are to have humble spirits. Let us not hold others to perfection, lest we, also, be held to that humanly unattainable measure! Unforgiveness judges the sins of others, from pride in our hearts. Judging others brings condemnation to our hearts and hinders our relationship with God.

He then exhorts, *Why do you look at the speck of sawdust in your brother's eye and pay no attention to the plank in your own eye?* An unforgiving spirit overlooks our own sins and judges those of others. *You hypocrite, first take the plank out of your own eye, and then you will see clearly to remove the speck from your brother's eye* (John 7:3,5 NIV). Unforgiveness keeps us focused on our hurts and others' sins, because the enemy doesn't want us to recognize or deal with our own. Only repentance allows us to see ourselves and others, even when they hurt us, through the holy eyes of God.

Let us forgive and confess that our eyes and hearts may stay peering heavenward and be blessed! Jesus prayed for us many years ago, *Make them pure and holy by teaching them your words of truth* (John 17:17). God does not teach us to wait to forgive others until our "time of prayer" or even for them to ask forgiveness. Instead, when we draw before Him, living as He does and being taught by Him; it will be in purity and holiness with continually repentant, humble, and forgiving hearts. Living humbly with teachable hearts in prayer allows His Spirit to continually teach, speaking to our listening hearts of any unresolved sins, any unresolved unforgiveness; allowing us to immediately choose forgiveness, choosing obedience.

Paul speaks of our freedom in Christ to forgive, becoming holy, *Once you were slaves to sin, but now you have obeyed with all your heart the new teaching God has given you. Now you are free from sin. Before, you let yourselves be slaves of impurity and lawlessness. Now you must choose to be slaves of righteousness so that you will become holy* (Romans 6:17-19). God's unconditional love flows through purified hearts, bringing forgiveness and prayer and leaving room for God's holiness, judgment and punishment, not ours. Needing daily purification and love, asking will remind us in order to receive it, we must first give it away.

Experiencing even extreme pain in some situations, we will have faith, not in the experience of the flesh, but in God working His purposes, glory and will through it. Jesus responded to the message of his friend's sickness, *Lazarus's sickness will not end in death. No, it is for the glory of God. I, the son of God will receive glory from this. Although Jesus loved Martha and Mary and Lazarus, he stayed where he was for the next two days and did not go to them.* Whatever we go through, however grave the situation may seem, prayer will give faith and hearts that think eternally, looking past the grave. Anything in our lives God allows to die, will either be consumed for our good, or raised to life with His power, for His glory. Holiness must come through faith alone!

Let our flesh be crucified, as we wait on God—allowing time in prayer for the flesh to die! John 11:9 says, *There are twelve ours of daylight every day. As long as it is light, people can walk safely. They can see because they have the light of this world.* Let us not tarry to trust or forgive. Our time here is limited and it is time now to respond, to forgive, and to obey. God requires the whole heart; half-hearted, delayed surrender is no surrender at all. Mary responded by falling at Jesus' feet, *Lord, if you would have been here, my brother would not have died* (John 11:32). Let us repent of hearts crying out, "Where were you, *if you would have been here*-how could you allow this to happen?" Let not fear, doubt, grief or dissension breed disobedience and anger. Let us remember my girlfriend Missy's favorite saying, "You are God, I am not!" Let us trust, in God's Will, God's Way, and God's When! Do not "blame" God; if you are distressed because He is waiting to respond—trust Him, it is for a good reason!

Giving forgiveness includes accepting it for self and releasing any anger or bitterness towards God. Scripture warns, *Don't sin by letting anger gain control over you. Don't let the sun go down while you are still angry, for anger gives a mighty foothold to the devil.* While the emotion of anger isn't sin, letting it control us is! But we can combat this immediately! Some may count to ten; we must pray! **Break out into praise and prayer, releasing the power and purpose of God immediately into the situation. Reject the flesh, emotion, sin, and the devil who wants to control you and don't let him!** *Don't let the sun go down, it gives him a mighty foothold. Get rid of all bitterness, rage, anger, harsh words, and slander, as well as all types of malicious behavior. Instead, be kind to each other, tenderhearted, forgiving one another, just as God through Christ has forgiven you* (Ephesians 4:26-27,31-32).

It needs to be forgiven and forgotten that very day. Don't believe the enemy of our souls that tells us we don't have any control over a situation, or that it can wait! We are to forgive others as God forgives us: immediately, unconditionally, and compassionately. He knows in waiting, unforgiveness will simmer in us like poison, eating us away from the inside out. We give the devil a mighty foothold when we hesitate to turn to God, rather than allowing the Holy Spirit to have control when we harbor or ignore any sin. And let Proverbs 22:24 be taken to heart, *Keep away from angry, short-tempered people, or you will learn to be like them and endanger your soul.* Anger endangers our souls! Daily bread, daily repentance, and daily forgiveness is letting God have daily control!

Unforgiveness, anger and bitterness are traps of the devil, which keep us from worshipping God. All things God allows into our lives were preordained for us to become more like Jesus. Let us repent and rejoice. Isaiah 48:18,20 says, *Oh, that you had listened to my commands! Then you would have had peace flowing like a gentle river and righteousness rolling like waves.* Peace like a river, righteousness like waves! God did not create sin. Sin is a lack of God's holiness. He has redeemed us; His Heart yearns to fill us with peace and righteousness. Let us listen to His commands! *Yet, even now, be free from your captivity! Leave...singing as you go! Shout to the ends of the earth that the Lord has redeemed His servants.* Praise God; He does not leave us trapped. He tells us to be free! It is then that God can use us to free others as we leave, singing and shouting to the ends of the earth! We get a glimpse at the heart of God's purposes in Isaiah 42:6-7, *I, the LORD, have called you to demonstrate my righteousness, I will guard and support you, for I have given you to my people as the personal confirmation of my covenant with them. And you will be a light to guide all nations to me. You will open the eyes of the blind and free the captives from prison. You will release those who sit in dark dungeons.* Are you trapped in a dark dungeon? Is your spirit, your heart crying to be freed? It is God's will that you demonstrate His righteousness, that you be a light to others, freeing them and being freed! Cry out to Him; He will help you forgive.

Love forgives—for forgiveness frees our entire hearts and those for whom we pray to love, worship and serve. Bringing our anger, pain and those who have hurt us to God for forgiveness, gives glory to God as He releases His passion into our hearts, His power into our prayers; His purposes restoring and drawing us into His Heart of holiness.

EXERCISE

Prayerfully write down who you need to forgive, with God's help—forgive and pray for them. Renounce any pride, anger, bitterness, and disbelief; walking forth free in Truth, repentance, and restoration—singing as you go!

- ◆ What has God revealed to you about Himself, today?
- ◆ Which verse does God want you to ask Him to apply to your life today?
- ◆ For whom does He want you to pray this verse?

LET US PRAY

Sing joyfully to the Lord for it is fitting for the upright to praise Him. Create in us pure hearts and willing spirits that forgive. Oh, God, love others through us, freeing us all from the bondage of sin. May we always let You-God, denying the enemy. Oh, Lord, teach us to pray.. In Jesus' precious Name we pray, Amen.

Day 15

OUR PROTECTOR in PRAYER

||||||||||||||||||||||||||||||||||||||||||||||||

And lead us not into temptation.

— MATTHEW 6:13 NIV —

Jesus teaches us to ask daily and acknowledge and rely upon God to keep us away from temptation. This acknowledges our old fleshly nature, left to its own desires and weaknesses, will be enticed by temptation and lead us to sin. The word "tempt" means "to persuade, to lure." The devil brings different means, according to our individual flesh, to persuade us to sin, lure us away from God and towards him. David cried out, *Come with great power, O God, and rescue me! Defend me with your might* (Psalm 54:1). We rely on God's power, not our own when we recognize satan's cunning and deceitfulness, appealing to the weakness of our flesh. Alone, we are no match for satan's lies and deceptive ways; to fight them we must turn to God.

David continues to cry, *I am overwhelmed by my troubles. My heart is in anguish. The terror of death overpowers me.* Drawing upon God's grace, power and strength within keeps us from being enticed, overwhelmed and overpowered by fear, sin, and death. He confesses, *But God is my helper. The LORD is the one who keeps me alive! For you will rescue me from my troubles and help me to triumph over my enemies* (Psalm 55:2/54:4,7). Acknowledging our need for holy power, spiritual eyes and discernment from our heavenly Helper, Redeemer and Rescuer from temptation and sin, brings triumph! Allow the Spirit, our Teacher, to direct you to a Psalm each day, praying your name into it aloud and allow His passions, power and purposes to lead you in a whole new way.

Glory ye in his holy name; Let the heart of them rejoice that seek the LORD. Seek the LORD and his strength, Seek his face continually. David teaches us the power of praise, seeking and glorifying God's holy name, bringing deliverance from temptation and sin. *Be ye mindful always of his covenant; The Word which he commanded to a thousand generations* (1 Chronicles 16:10-11,15 KJV). Living in prayer keeps us mindful of His covenant to deliver, protect and care for us. His Word brings power as we face daily temptations and attacks from the enemy. A victorious, God-purposed, holy, prayer-driven life can only be lived by the power of God Almighty, remaining in His Presence.

1 Chronicles 16:27,35 (NIV) reminds, *Splendor and majesty are before him; strength and joy in his dwelling place. Cry out, Save us, O God, our Savior; gather us and deliver us from the nations, that we may give thanks to your holy name, that we may glory in your praise.* We were born to worship and praise our Creator; His Heart's desire is to deliver, that we can! We agree with Him that we want to be delivered, and we ask for change, for sin and demons to be cast out, unlike the people in Matthew 8:34, *The entire town came out to meet Jesus, but they begged him to go away and leave them alone.* Hard to imagine? That is what we do when we don't ask for God's help against temptation. Jesus tells us to ask in prayer, to acknowledge our need, desire and willingness by God's power not be led away into temptation.

Temptation isn't from God, nor would He ever lead us there. James 1:13 says, *No one who wants to do wrong should ever say, "God is tempting me." God is never tempted to do wrong, and he never tempts anyone else either.* He teaches us He is our only means of living in victory. Scripture says, *but every man is tempted, when he is drawn away of his own lust, and enticed* (James 1:14 KJV). Our old natures run and lust after temptations, instead of seeking God. Prayer keeps us mindful of His Kingdom, bringing the power of God's Word to deny the flesh and save souls.

James further instructs, *So get rid of all the filth and evil in your lives, and humbly accept the message God has planted in your hearts, for it is strong enough to save your souls* (James 1:21). Temptation is from satan, brightly packaged and appealing to the fleshly eye, yet with devastating consequences hidden for the soul. Prayer-driven, holy lives give us spiritual eyes to see and defeat these evil ways by God's almighty power. 1 Peter 1:5 promises, *And God, in his mighty power, will protect you until you receive this salvation, because you are trusting him.* Because we trust in Him! Daily asking reminds us we trust in Him.

1 Peter 1:2 commends us, *God the Father chose you long ago, and the Spirit has made you holy. As a result, you have obeyed Jesus Christ and are cleansed by his blood. May you have more and more of God's special favor and wonderful peace.* Daily asking God to keep delivering us from temptation, we receive His favor as we're kept in His peace, reminding us what He has done and who we are in Him. Our hearts are sanctified by His Spirit, His Word and prayer and when we see temptation, we are able to resist and overcome it. In daily prayer and holiness, we receive more and more of His grace with godly, holy desires and living, bearing fruit through our prayers. Commanded to resist temptation, the way we live and pray allows God to keep us from it. 1 Peter 1:13-16 (NIV) says, *Prepare your minds for action; be self-controlled; set your hope fully on the grace to be given you when Jesus Christ is revealed.* His Word and prayer prepare us, setting our hope upon Jesus and living in accordance with His grace. *As obedient children, do not conform to the evil desires you had when you lived in ignorance. But just as he who called you is holy, so be holy in all you do; for it is written: "Be holy, because I am holy."* As His holy children, we cannot live in ignorance, for doing so would conform us to our old, evil desires. With new minds and spirits come new desires. He calls us to be holy, and He is faithful!

Through his deception and cunning, satan seeks us to follow the lusty desires of our old flesh, always making the rewards of following temptation look great and the consequences minimal. Ezekiel 13:7 (KJV) says, *Have you not seen a vain vision, and have ye not spoken a lying divination, whereas ye say, The LORD saith it, albeit I have not spoken?* He warns that we can be easily seduced into seeing things as the enemy would like us to, and not how God sees them. *These evil prophets deceive my people by saying 'All is peaceful!' when there is no peace at all!* The traps and temptations of the enemy will always appear as though things are fine when they are not! *It's as if the people have built a flimsy wall, and these prophets are trying to hold it together by covering it with whitewash!* (Ezekiel 13:10) "Whitewash" is a wall whitener that glosses over the faults in walls, making them appear pure when they are really not. Pleading daily, we ask for His spiritual eyes, that He may remove the whitewash and reveal our impurities and sin. In prayer, God reveals the attempts of the enemy to discourage, to disgrace, and dissuade us from holiness.

God responds to prayer, *I will tear off the magic veils and save my people from your grasp. They will no longer be your victims. Then you will know that I am the LORD.* A "victim" is one harmed or destroyed by another. This is the devil's goal in the life of a Christian. Our Lord keeps us from the grasp of the devil, remaining at the throne of grace, power and glory. God's Heart's desire is that we not fall or remain victim to the enemy. Oh, let us cry out and be victors of His holy grace! *You have discouraged the righteous with your lies, when I didn't want them to suffer to grief.* When suffering at the hands of sin, this is the enemy's will, not God's. The enemy desires to trick and trap us with his lies, discouraging and destroying us. *And you have encouraged the wicked by promising them life, even though they continue in their sins. For I will rescue my people from your grasp. Then you will know that I am the LORD* (Ezekiel 13:21-22). The devil always encourages sin, promising life or some other thing he cannot deliver. He only brings destruction, defeat, and death. Yet, when we ask, God will rescue! *"Then you will know that I am the LORD."* God responds, that we know Him as Lord!

The enemy always tempts us to doubt God and His Word. He tries to convince the world God doesn't listen, care or respond. His tactics keep us from asking for deliverance because he knows God is waiting to respond to prayer. Psalm 56:8-9,13 says, *You keep track of all my sorrows. You have collected all my tears in your bottle. You have recorded each one in your book.* God cares for every tear, pain, and sorrow. His Heart longs for the joy of His children and our deliverance, victory over and freedom from sin. *On the very day I call to you for help, my enemies will retreat.* The very day we call on Him! The enemy and all his demons and evil authorities tremble and flee as we call upon the name of Jesus! *This I know: God is on my side. For you have rescued me from death; you have kept my foot from slipping. So now I can walk in your presence, O God, in your life-giving light.*

God rescued our very souls from death with the blood of His Son. Oh, how He desires us to remain in His protective, loving, persevering Presence and care! Psalm 57:1,3 tells us to ask, that we may receive. *Have mercy on me, O God, have mercy! I look to you for protection, I will hide beneath the shadow of your wings until this violent storm is past.* The NASB says, *Until destruction passes by. He will send help from heaven to save me, rescuing me from those who are out to get me. My God will send forth his unfailing love and faithfulness.* We pray and He sends forth! We ask and He keeps us safe from destruction. We cry out, and from heaven, He sends forth His angels to guard, deliver and save us. Jeremiah 15:20 promises, *They will fight against you like an attacking army, but I will make you as secure as a fortified wall. They will not conquer you, for I will protect and deliver you. I, the LORD, have spoken!* Once we have surrendered to God, living in His holy Presence, though the enemy may come at us like an army, we are as secure as a fortified wall! **His holy fires pour from His throne in prayer and keep us living in His Light, in His Power, Grace & Mercy—with certain victory over sin!**

Prayer brings victory, keeping evil desires and the continual temptation to serve and worship other gods denied. Jeremiah was sent with a message of destruction to Judah, unless they repented. Jeremiah 26:13 says, *But if you stop your sinning and begin to obey the LORD your God, he will cancel this disaster that he has announced against you.* Only the Holy Spirit has power over the flesh. It is our own evil desires to be, possess and have gods and idols to serve that we battle with; flesh will not defeat flesh. Thus, the job of the Spirit, wrought from a holy heart and devoted to God, alone, in living prayer.

Daily asking for God to keep us will help us be alert to the enemy's schemes and prepare us for his attacks. 1 Peter 5:8 (NIV) says, *Be self-controlled and alert. Your enemy the devil prowls around like a lion looking for someone to devour.* He tries to scare us with his growl and hide in the bushes so as to sneak up on us, but prayer gives us eyes to see through the bushes, immediately disarming his attacks. We know God's power over the lions Daniel safely spent the night with. Remaining self-controlled and alert takes away the enemy's advantage.

It seems the advantage in any type of battle goes to the side that can effectively surprise the enemy and who best knows the territory. Realize, the devil looks for someone to devour; he is not omniscient or omnipresent like God, but does watch for the opportune time to attack; he watches to discover our weaknesses of the flesh. He knows he must sneak in, so he watches and waits, learning our territory, so we must know too! The more we know the Word of God and surrender to a life of prayer, the better prepared we are for his attack.

2 Peter 1:3 (NIV) says, *His divine power has given us everything we need for life and godliness through our knowledge of him who called us by his own glory and goodness!* We must know Him, to have His divine power, realizing all He

has given us. When trouble strikes, we may be tempted to call on everyone else for help. Oh, how the enemy loves this. Friends, family, even the church may let us down when we struggle with temptation, but God will not. Any battle plan not empowered by Him fails. 2 Timothy 4:17-18 says, *But the Lord stood with me and gave me strength, he saved me from certain death. Yes, and the Lord will deliver me from every evil attack and will bring me safely to his heavenly Kingdom.* So many Christians fail and live ungodly lives, unable to resist temptation because they do not even know they are in a battle. We're commanded, *Resist him, standing firm in the faith.* We only need to resist— standing firm. God even gives grace for this! *And the God of all grace, who has called you to his eternal glory, after you have suffered a little while, will himself restore you and make you strong, firm and steadfast* (1 Peter 5:9-10 NIV). God has a purpose for each of us. Let the enemy no longer steal your passion, purposes, dreams, and power! The Lord is here to save and keep.

EXERCISE

Prayerfully find a Bible verse that pertains to your particular battle with the flesh; proclaim that Truth into your life by speaking it, memorizing it, and living it! Always ask God to make His Word fruitful in your heart and life, letting Him know you are willing for His power to be made perfect in your weakness.

- ❖ What has God revealed to you about Himself, today?
- ❖ Which verse does God want you to ask Him to apply to your life today?
- ❖ For whom does He want you to pray this verse?

LET US PRAY

Our Strength and our Shield we sing praise to You and lift Your Name on High. Free all those we pray for including ourselves from the strongholds we've allowed the evil one to have upon us, freeing us by Your Truth. Keep us continually in Your Presence, learning to love You that we may hate the ways and passions of this world as You do…In Jesus' precious and powerful Name above all names we pray, Amen.

Day 16

OUR DELIVERER
in PRAYER

||||||||||||||||||||||||||||||||||||||||||||||||||

But deliver us from the evil one.

— Matthew 6:13 NIV —

It is the Lord who rescues us from evil attacks and brings us safely into His Kingdom. Jesus tells us to pray for our deliverance from evil and to allow the eyes of our hearts to be filled with faith so we can see the realities of the spiritual realms we pray and live in. It is not the physical world wherein our battles lie; it is in the heart and mind, our spirits are what the enemy wishes to conquer. Jesus teaches, *You are not defiled by what you eat; you are defiled by what you say and do. But evil words come from an evil heart and defile the person who says them. For from the heart come evil thoughts, murder, adultery, all other sexual immorality, theft, lying, and slander* (Matthew 15:11). Our battlefield is in the heart in prayer! We speak in prayer in the faith of God, not in the enemy, as the psalmist said, *I believed (in God); and therefore I have spoken. With that same spirit of faith we also believe and therefore speak* (2 Corinthians 4:13 NIV). We speak, believing in God's Hearts desires and in His abilities.

Philippians 3:2-3 warns, *Watch out for those dogs, those wicked men and their evil deeds, those mutilators who say you must be circumcised to be saved.* Prayer watches. *For we who worship God in the Spirit are the only ones who are truly circumcised.* Many claim to worship God, but only the Spirit is able; flesh always worships the flesh. We cannot believe in human attempts to earn salvation, nor to be delivered from the enemy. *Instead, we boast about what*

Christ Jesus has done for us. We are no match for satan on our own; Christ brought, and brings us victory.

Yes, even a Christian heart cannot be trusted to tend to itself! Jesus warns, *Watch out that you are not deceived. Watch out! Don't let me find you living in careless ease and drunkenness, and filled with the worries of this life. Don't let that day catch you unaware, as in a trap.* Dissipation, drunkenness, and anxieties of life are all, among others, traps of the enemy. *Keep constant watch. And pray* (Luke 21:8,34-36). The NIV says, *Be always on the watch, and pray that you may escape.* Imagine ignoring bombs blowing up, or walking through a field full of landmines and covered traps, giving no thought to protection. The enemy has traps laid out for all of us that can only be avoided or escaped with the help of God's Hand.

Proverbs 16:17 warns, *Violent people deceive their companions, leading them down a harmful path.* Maintaining godly company is one way God keeps us safe. Scripture tells us anyone who is not working with God is working against Him. Paul warns, too, *Watch out for those who cause divisions and put obstacles in your way, Keep away from such people, By smooth talk and flattery they deceive the minds of naïve people; I want you to be wise about what is good, and innocent about what is evil* (Romans 16:17-19 NIV). We are to keep away from and watch out for those who come in with flattery, attempting to cover their intended destruction.

Proverbs 17:4 tells us, *Wrongdoers listen to wicked talk, liars pay attention to destructive words.* Let us beware our thoughts, talk, what we listen to, watch, and where we go with whom! Proverbs 11:5-6,9 also exhorts, *The godly are directed by their honesty; the wicked fall beneath their load of sin. The godliness of good people rescues them; the ambition of treacherous people traps them. Evil works destroy one's friends; wise discernment rescues the godly.* Let the blessings and Spirit of God continue to protect, uphold, rescue and lead us in prayer along His path of life as He fills us with joy! Psalm 41:1-3 promises, *Oh, the joys of those who are kind to the poor, The LORD rescues them in times of trouble. The LORD protects them and keeps them alive. He gives them prosperity and rescues them from their enemies. The LORD nurses them when they are sick and eases their pain and discomfort.* Troubles and discomfort come, but we have a Comforter, Rescuer, Giver of prosperity; One who eases pain for those who have been kind to the poor.

Meanwhile, my enemies lay traps for me; they make plans to ruin me. I choose to hear nothing, and I make no reply. We must not defend an argument with the enemy; this is where Eve fell into rebellion. *For I am waiting for you, O LORD. You must answer for me, O LORD, my God. But I confess my sins; I am deeply sorry for what I have done* (Psalm 38:12,14-15,18). Wait upon God, for His Presence brings godly sorrow and repentance, and He delivers! Let us glory in God's deliverance; let us praise Him! Psalm 3:1-8 (NIV) states, *O LORD, how many are my foes! How many rise up against me! Many are saying of me, 'God will not deliver him.'* There may be times when we wait upon God that others may scoff at us, but we must praise, knowing our Deliverer is only a prayer away! *But you are a shield around me, O LORD; you bestow glory on me and lift up my head. To the LORD I cry aloud, and he answers me on his holy hill. I lie down and sleep; I wake again because the LORD sustains me. I will not fear the tens of thousands drawn up against me on every side. Arise, O LORD! Deliver me, O my God! Strike all my enemies on the jaw; break the teeth of the wicked. From the LORD comes deliverance. May your blessing be on all your people.*

Not many go into battle or even into a competition without learning about the opposition. It is always beneficial to know your enemy. Like it or not, we have enemies, the devil and his workers, the world and our flesh. Satan answers to God, telling Him where he spends his time in Job 1:7 (NIV), '*Roaming through the earth and going back and forth in it.*' Like it or not, he is roaming here and knowing his character will help us to be watchful and alert to recognize his work. Scriptures call him the father of lies, the god of this world, and the prince of the demons and of the powers of the air. He is a slanderer and accuser of the brethren; he is presumptuous, proud, wicked, subtle, deceitful, fierce and cruel. He perverts the Scriptures, hinders the spread of the gospel and is the adversary of God and man. He is cursed by God, appears as an angel of light, was cast down from heaven, is the source of apostasy and has an everlasting fire prepared for him and his workers. He desires an army on his side warring against God and sets traps to hinder God's children. More importantly—he is NOT all powerful, every where at once, nor does he create or have divine unlimited resources. Most importantly -- he IS our already-defeated adversary!

Fear not, Jesus says, *I saw satan falling from heaven as a flash of lightening! And I have given you authority over all the power of the enemy, and you can walk among snakes and scorpions and crush them. Nothing will injure you. But don't rejoice just because evil spirits obey you; rejoice because your names are registered as citizens of heaven* (Luke 10:18-20). In prayer, we go forth with the authority and power of Jesus' mighty Name; best of all, we are already citizens of heaven! Whatever the enemy brings against us will not sting or destroy us. Filled with the life of Christ, He gives His ultimate authority over all spirits even the ruler of this dark world and the of heavenly realms. Nothing that happens to us is out of God's power, reach or control. Saints of the Old Testament give us glimpses of spiritual battles in the physical world. Constantly in battles against their enemies; with God, they received victory, and without Him, defeat. *Then the spirit of God came upon Azariah, and he went out to meet King Asa as he was returning from battle. Listen to me, Asa! he shouted. Listen all you people of Judah and Benjamin!* He shouted-to every one-not just the battle leaders, the entire community. *The LORD will stay with you as long as you stay with him! Whenever you seek him, you will find him. But if you abandon him, he will abandon you. For a long time, Israel was without the one true God.* When we are not with God, we are in trouble! *During those dark times, it was not safe to travel. Problems troubled the nation on every hand* (2 Chronicles 15:1-3,5). Let us not leave the protective Hand and Presence of the Almighty!

God's holy children, Christ's ambassadors and students of prayer are no longer ruled by sin. In the movie *The Big Fish,* the main character is grabbed and held by a big tree trying to keep him in darkness—from his destiny. He, however doesn't believe in its power—so he refuses it, and the tree drops him and shrinks away. It is the same way with the enemy; he tries to appear big and dark and scary with the power to hold and keep us, but we only need to say no! Let us believe he has no power! If he knows he can deceive our hearts and minds to hold onto us, he will. It is our hearts the enemy is after, as the rest will follow; keeping us from God's very best—our divine destiny!

We may wonder why so many are in bondage to the enemy, why so many warriors and their families are captives to the plunder of tyrants? Where is God's power? Did God let them go or lose them? Why are there so many Christian families living in abuse, alcoholism, divorce and every other kind of evil? The Lord answers in Isaiah 50:1-2 *No, you went away as captives because of your sins. Was I too weak to save you? Is that why the house is silent and empty when I come home? Is it because I have no power to rescue? No, that is not the reason! For I can speak to the sea and make it dry!* **If we have lost the power of God in prayer, we have not God, for He dwells in the light, but the evil**

one tries to keep us in darkness.

Satan cannot steal our salvation, but if we let him—he can keep us from the revealed and experienced Presence of God and from having an eternal impact for Christ in the lives of others. Hebrews 12:20 says, *Now may the God of peace*, also in John 20:19-22 *"Peace be with you…" he said. They were filled with joy when they saw their Lord! He spoke to them again and said, "Peace be with you." Then he breathed on them and said to them, "Receive the Holy Spirit."* God gives peace and joy, His energy, and excitement; the enemy is out to steal these from us. Even in service, if joy or peace is lost, our service is no longer for or empowered by God. God wants all of us, so He can powerfully fill us increasingly with Himself, His Holy Spirit. Hearts set upon Him in prayer will receive Him, breathing His very life into them.

God Almighty is in the business of setting His children free! Our holy Savior, Redeemer, Protector, and Friend, Lord, God Almighty waits with a loving Heart to pour out His power, His perfect, infinite and inescapable love and grace. Would you leave your child, or any child, in the hands of a kidnapper, or personal enemy if that child may have wandered into his trap? Certainly not! Yes, a Christian can be trapped by the devil; who else does he care about trapping? Would you not do everything in your power, holding back nothing to save and to return safely home a beloved child? Let us not find Him wanting for workers willing to pray! Thus the battle for our hearts, to keep us from prayer, that the enemy can restrain us, constraining God from sending, teaching and being sent to free the captives and save souls.

2 Timothy 2:11-12 promises, *If we die with him, we will also live with him. If we endure hardship, we will reign with him. If we deny him, he will deny us.* Let us receive His power to die, to live, to endure, to reign, and to not be denied. There is only one place to receive God's joy, peace, protection, and Jesus' passion. His power flows through and His purposes are found only in our heart's home—His Presence!

Jude 20-23 (NKJV) exhorts, *But ye, beloved, building up yourselves on your most holy faith. Praying in the Holy Ghost, Keep yourselves in the love of God,* God's love keeps, we must choose to remain, abiding in prayer and His Word, strengthening for spiritual warfare. *Looking for the mercy of our Lord Jesus Christ unto eternal life. And of some have compassion, making a difference: And others save with fear, pulling them out of the fire; hating even the garment spotted by the flesh.* God doesn't just keep us, He uses us, built up and empowered by

His spirit of prayer, reaching right into the flames of hell, and pulling out, sharing the gospel unto salvation of souls.

Our battles are spiritual, our power divine, our enemy unseen, and our resource to victory the very Presence and Heart of God, in prayer! God has left us here with a job and all the resources we need to perform it victoriously. Eternity of those souls we need to pray for are at stake; let us mimic our Master, our Teacher, who, in Mark 6:46, *Went up into the hills by himself to pray.* One person at a time, one heart at a time, one church at a time, one prayer at a time, God desires to return His power through His Presence back to His people and thus we must pray!

Prayer is our access to the throne of grace wherever we are and whenever we need. Pray for the Spirit to ignite new passion for prayer that we may realize and experience His mighty and divine power at our disposal; His Kingdom here before we get to heaven. As we give ourselves to living prayer, may we desire and pray, "Your kingdom come...Your will be done...ON EARTH— IN OUR HEARTS, AS IT IS IN HEAVEN, for Yours is the Kingdom, the power, and the glory forever and ever...Amen."

EXERCISE

Read aloud Psalm 62-63.

- What has God revealed to you about Himself, today?
- Which verse does God want you to ask Him to apply to your life today?
- For whom does He want you to pray this verse?

LET US PRAY

Our Strength and our Shield, we sing praise to You and lift Your Name on high. Fill us with Your Holy Spirit, humbly resisting the devil in every way at the very moment of his approach. Oh, Father God, teach us to pray. In Jesus' Name, Amen.

Day 17

OUR POWER
in PRAYER

||||||||||||||||||||||||||||||||||||||||||||||||||||

*But you will receive power when the
Holy Spirit comes on you.*

— ACTS 1:8 NIV —

God's mighty power received in and through prayer is the power of His Holy Spirit. Christ prayed and ministered here on earth in the power of the Holy Spirit, as must we. God says, *I will pour out the Spirit of grace and supplication* (Zechariah 12:10 NASB). God's very own Spirit is poured into our hearts and enables us to pray! This same Spirit that dwelt within Christ now dwells within you and me. The Holy Spirit holds, within His power, all the wisdom and purpose we need for prayer. Ephesians 6:18 and Jude 20 command, (NASB). *With all prayer and petition pray at all times in the Spirit, and with this in view, be on the alert with all perseverance and petition for all the saints.* He is the Spirit of prayer, petition, alertness, perseverance, and unity for all saints. *Beloved, building yourselves up on your most holy faith, praying in the Holy Spirit.* He is the Spirit of love, salvation, faith, humility and holiness with which we are to pray.

We are told in Jude 21, *Keep yourselves in the love of God.* Spirit-filled prayer keeps us living in God's love. Scripture explains, we are able to pray in the Spirit, *Because you are sons, God has sent forth the Spirit of His son into our hearts, crying, "Abba! Father!" I have been crucified with Christ; and it is no longer I who live, but Christ lives in me; For all of you who were baptized into*

Christ have clothed yourselves with Christ (Galatians 4:6/2:20/3:27 NASB). The NLT says, *All who have been united with Christ in baptism have been made like him.* We pray in the Spirit in our unity with His baptism, clothed with His Spirit, as He prays, living within each of us.

As we live, so shall we pray. Paul says, *Because of Christ and our faith in him, we can now come fearlessly into God's presence, assured of his glad welcome* (Ephesians 3:12). The Holy Spirit of prayer draws us boldly into God's Presence; He cannot reject Himself! Thus the necessity of a wholly surrendered heart desiring for and giving its all for God. His holiness fills our hearts with the very desire and power to live out prayer. Truly living a holy life and praying with passion and power begins, first, with a heart filled with the desire for it.

The Holy Spirit pours out all this desire and sanctification through prayer; the Father desires to pour out His Spirit into our hearts, *If you sinful people know how to give good gifts to your children, how much more will your heavenly Father give the Holy Spirit to those who ask him* (Luke 11:13). How much more—to those who ask Him! We are each sealed with the Spirit when we accept God's gift of salvation, as Ephesians 1:13 (KJV) states, *Ye were sealed with that Holy Spirit of promise*-but it does not end there! His Heart's desire is daily to continually fill and quicken us further with Him.

Paul prays for the manifestation of the Spirit in Ephesians 3:16-17 (KJV), *that He would grant you, according to the riches of his glory, to be strengthened with might by his Spirit in the inner man; that Christ may dwell in your hearts by faith.* The Holy Spirit of prayer strengthens us, giving the spirit of faith that Christ increasingly dwells and prays within. Let us pray, experiencing His spirit of power, resurrection, and authority, *That you will begin to understand the incredible greatness of his power for us who believe him* (Ephesians 1:19). The Spirit is that of wisdom and understanding, enabling us to pray with spiritual wisdom and authority over the rulers of this world. This is the same mighty power that raised Christ from the dead and seated Him in the place of honor at God's right hand in the heavenly realms. Let us not despair and fail as a result of thinking things cannot change in our prayer-lives. The Holy Spirit brings back life from the dead and raises up to heaven with power and honor. His Spirit poured within breathes through us heavenly lives of prayer!

Remaining at the throne of the Lamb lets our hearts be ignited by the holy fires of God pouring forth as we journey to His Heart. Remember the disciples who couldn't watch and pray even an hour in Christ's time of need, the same who argued over who would be greater in heaven? Upon His resurrection, Jesus gave His disciples the Holy Spirit and instructed them in the Kingdom, strengthening them to spiritually understand, persevering in united prayer for ten days before bringing the promised Gift of the mighty Spirit outpouring for all believers! Acts 1:2-3,14 (NASB) says, *Until the day when he was taken up to heaven, after He had by the Holy Spirit given orders to the apostles whom He had chosen. Appearing to them over a period of forty days and speaking of the things concerning the kingdom of God.* Though they had stumbled on the way, having been crucified in Spirit with Him at the Cross, He was now able to give them fully His Spirit, for new understanding, conviction and power. *These all with one mind were continually devoting themselves to prayer.* The spirit of prayer enabled them to fully receive the outpouring of more of the Spirit at the day of Pentecost. "Come—Holy Spirit, crucify us with Christ, raise us in hope of new and united prayer—giving us this day our daily bread!"

The Holy Spirit is the spirit of patience, love, and obedience, giving faith that fills us with power and desires from God's Heart. Many lack the desire and ability to witness, as churches and ministries lack divine fruit from lack of Spirit-empowered ministering, praying and waiting. Jesus commands us only to act and witness in His power. He says, *Do not leave until the Father sends what he promised.* God has promised to give, as we ask—let us wait with thankful hearts devoted to prayer! *John baptized with water, but in a few days you will be baptized with the Holy Spirit.* The indwelling seal is different from the Spirit's baptism, clothing and empowering for special service. Those called must be baptized and clothed! *When the Holy Spirit has come upon you, you will receive power and will tell people about me everywhere, in the ends of the earth* (Acts 1:4-5,8). As we are willing to give up self, and truly receive Him, He is more than ready and able to pour out, fill, and empower us.

Ephesians 2:18,22 (NASB) says, *For through Him we both have our access in one Spirit to the Father.* Being in the Spirit is our access; flesh cannot worship before the throne. *In whom the whole building being built together, is growing into a holy temple in the Lord, in whom you also are being built together into a dwelling of God in the Spirit.* The Spirit builds us into God's dwelling place. Being crucified with Christ, His Spirit through united prayers, ever increases His inheritance within us. Seeking to be filled with God in the Spirit, our end is to love the brethren and suffer for them, that they, too, will know Him, sharing with us, in His inheritance.

I cannot overstate the importance of the Holy Spirit empowering all we do in life and prayer! What must we do to receive fully all He has to give? Ask and obey! Jesus promises, *If ye love me, keep my commandments. And I will pray the Father, and he shall give you another Comforter, that he may abide with you forever. At that day ye shall know that I am in my Father, and you in me, and I in you* (John 14:15-16,20 KJV). The spirit of obedience and love, the Comforter who keeps, is in Christ's love, and in us! Let us cry out, to be filled with the Spirit and obey! The Greek Word "parakletos," or counselor means, *"one called along aside to help, also: an advocate, one who talks to the Father in our defense."* Jesus sends forth the promised Spirit to help us in all our needs of obedience, love, prayer, and service. He gives wisdom and leads in prayer, bringing us into, empowering and preparing us for God's will.

He promises, *"But when the Father sends the Counselor as my representative—and by the Counselor I mean the Holy Spirit—he will teach you everything and will remind you of everything I myself have told you. I am leaving you with a gift—peace of mind and heart. And the peace I give isn't like the peace the world gives. So don't be troubled or afraid"* (John 14:26-27). **A prayerful heart receives the spirit of peace, in heart and mind; what a wonderful Gift!** Stormy weather, unknown futures, finances, health, families, decisions- all with a peaceful heart and mind!

Praise God for His Holy Spirit, our Teacher, and let us pray for His outpouring of truth, wisdom and power upon churches and its members' hearts! Our Teacher, Jesus, baptizes with Spirit, pouring out from heaven. *I saw the Holy Spirit descending like a dove from heaven and resting upon him. I didn't know he was the one, but when God sent me to baptize with water, he told me, 'When you see the Holy Spirit descending and resting upon someone, he is the one you are looking for. He is the one who baptizes with the Holy Spirit.' I saw this happen to Jesus* (John 1:32-33). The pouring out of the Spirit prepares hearts, gives us watchful eyes, listening ears and understanding minds able to live in prayer.

We not only worship God in Spirit, but in the spirit of truth and revelation. Jesus promises, *I will send you the Counselor—the spirit of truth. He will come to you from the Father and will tell you all about me. It is actually best for you that I go away, because if I don't the Counselor won't come. If I do go away, he will come because I will send Him to you.* All knowledge of

Christ, power, and wisdom pour out from the very Heart of Christ, through the spirit of prayer. *When the Spirit of truth comes, he will guide you into all truth. He will not be presenting his own ideas; he will be telling you what he has heard. He will bring me glory by revealing to you whatever he receives from me* (John 15:26/16:7,13-14). He no longer walks only with His disciples; He walks within, fills, empowers, teaches, transforms, loves, sanctifies, counsels, comforts, restores, guides, reveals, sends, and prays through us!

The Spirit knows, agreeing, continually united with the Heart, Mind, and will of God, giving all power and divine purposes to our prayers. As Jesus did only what He was commanded by the Father, empowered by the spirit of prayer, so must we. Jesus says, *I am not alone—I have with me the Father who sent me. Your own law says that if two people agree about something, their witness is accepted as fact. I am one witness, and my Father who sent me is the other* (John 8:16-18). Praying in this Spirit, we are agreeing with and praying for the very will of God, sanctifying hearts and lives in every circumstance, empowering and uniting every purpose for His Kingdom and glory.

Godly desires pouring from His holy rivers wash all that is self-will, cleansing and preparing for His divine will. The Spirit gives new life to God-given dreams and aspirations, casting out all that remains of the old, which hinders and holds us back from achieving all the very best God desires to give and to do in, through and for us! He gives us hearts and minds that pray in heavenly ways, *For those who are according to the flesh set their minds on the things of the flesh, but those who are according to the Spirit, the things of the Spirit.* Spirit-filled hearts and holy minds pray after the spiritual, not the physical. *For the mind set on the flesh is death, but the mind set on the Spirit is life and peace and those who are in the flesh cannot please God* (Romans 8:5-6,8 NASB). For our hearts and lives to please God, we must be given totally to the Spirit through prayer.

Seeking after God's will; the Spirit leads and direct our paths divinely. Paul encourages, *He who did not spare his own son, but delivered Him over for us all, how will He not also with Him freely give us all things?* Be encouraged, God spares nothing as we are filled with His Holy Spirit and empowered for His work in prayer! *But in all these things we overwhelmingly conquer through Him who loved us* (Romans 8:32,37 NASB). The Spirit brings us to the Cross, raising us to conquer in prayer, passionately and powerfully, *in all these things!* Daily filling attunes to the leading of the Holy Spirit. Knowing His Holy

Spirit in prayer gives assurance of receiving His answer, having been directed straight from God's Heart, flowing by the mighty rivers of the Holy Spirit through us and back to His throne of power, mercy and grace.

EXERCISE

Ask God to baptize and anoint you with the Holy Spirit, for His glory and service. Ask Him daily to fill you with His Holy Spirit; always asking Him to enable you to Pray in the Spirit on all occasions with all requests, thanksgiving and petitions for all the saints.

- ❖ What has God revealed to you about Himself, today?
- ❖ Which verse does God want you to ask Him to apply to your life today?
- ❖ For whom does He want you to pray this verse?

LET US PRAY

Gracious, wonderful, holy, perfect, heavenly Father, we praise and ask You to fill us with Your Holy Spirit. We confess all areas of self-reliance and sins grieving Your Spirit. Lead, guide and protect us we pray. Teach us to pray, living guided by the Spirit, Oh, Lord, teach us to pray. In Jesus' precious and powerful Name, Amen.

Day 18

LISTENING
in PRAYER
|||||||||||||||||||||||||||||||||||||||||||||||||||||

*Call to me and I will answer you and tell you great
and unsearchable things you do not know.*

— JEREMIAH 33:3 NIV —

From the Heart of God, the Holy Spirit brings prayer into our hearts that we will call out to God, receiving that which He desires us to know, pray, and live. This is only attainable through spiritual revelation by His divine power. Let us remember, to whom we are praying, with His own power. Jeremiah 33:2 (KJV) says, *Thus saith the LORD the maker thereof, the LORD that formed it, to establish it; the LORD is his name.* We enter the presence of the Lord who formed and established the earth by His power and receive His power in prayer. Entering the heart of Moses, called the man of God, may we be strengthened as he blesses his people, knowing His Holy Spirit, *The LORD came from Sinai, And dawned (rose to) them from Seir; And he came from the midst (myriads of holiness) of ten thousand holy ones; At his right hand there was a flash (a fiery law) of lightening for them. Indeed, He loves the people; All Your (His) holy ones are in Your hand, And they follow Your steps (or lie down at your feet); Everyone receives of Your words* (Deuteronomy 33:2-3 NASB). The Holy Spirit brings life and holy desires into our hearts. Let us accept and understand His instructions, as they will enable us to fall down at His feet in worship, ignited by IIis holy fires of praise.

Vainly will we try to seek or receive without the power of the mighty,

Holy Spirit. God says, *Between the city walls you build a reservoir for water from the old pool.* God's Spirit is all we need, let us not revert to depending upon this world, or our old ways of doing and thinking about things! Let the old pools dry up, calling out to our Maker as He fills us with His Spirit, that we may depend upon the new way. *But all your feverish plans are to no avail because you never ask God for help* (Isaiah 22:11). The NASB version says, *You did not depend on Him who made it. Nor did you take into consideration Him who planned it long ago.*

God has mighty plans for each of our lives, only brought forth with His power as we consider Him. Holy Spirit-inspired plans and steps, prayerfully taken, will prevail. We are warned against making our own plans and going our own way. Isaiah 28:11-12 says, *Since they refuse to listen, God will speak to them through foreign oppressors who speak an unknown language! God's people could have rest in their own land if they would only obey him, but they will not listen.* Oh, the saying "listen and obey, there's no other way!" It is true. Ecclesiastes 10:20 warns us, *Never make light of the king, even in your thoughts.* Praying in the Holy Spirit allows Him control of our prayers, thoughts, actions and listening skills!

Allowing His Holy Spirit reign within our hearts, we will listen more than talk in prayer! Amos 4:13 (NIV) says, *He who forms the mountains, creates the winds and reveals his thoughts to man.* We cannot know and seek His will and holiness for our lives if we excuse ourselves from prayer. He who reveals His thoughts to man is to whom we cry out and ask! *He who turns the darkness and treads the high places of the earth—the LORD God Almighty is his name.* If we need to know something, or need help, He is just the One to ask, He who treads the high places of earth! They do say to get something done right the first time, it is always best to go straight to the top! We, as children do—often, tend to try to ignore what we don't want to hear, so we refrain from asking or listening. If it doesn't make sense for us to do or pray exactly what God has said, we try to figure it out ourselves before we pray and obey. This sin occurs too often. "Well, God, I know you spoke to me about this, but it doesn't make sense, so maybe I'll pray about it a few more weeks, or try my way first!" Sound familiar? Me, too.

Ecclesiastes 11:5 (KJV) says, *Even so though knowest not the works of God who maketh all.* Faith by the Spirit overcomes when we "*knowest not*" where our prayers and actions take us, letting us throw our all upon His waters, receiving the grace to obey. Let our prayers always begin at the throne, poured out through holy hearts, keeping us in His loving, divine, powerful, omniscient Hand! Let us remember, His Holy Spirit knows the very best for us.

'For I know the plans that I have [am planning] for you,' declares the LORD, 'plans for welfare and not for calamity to give you a future and a hope. Then you will call upon Me and come and pray to Me, and I will listen to you. You will seek Me and find Me when you search for Me with all of your heart. I will be found by you,' declares the LORD. 'and I will restore your fortunes and will gather you from all the nations and from all the places where I have driven you,' declares the LORD, 'and I will bring you back' (Jeremiah 29:11-14 NASB). His Spirit inspires us to seek Him with all our hearts! He wants to *"bring us back"*!

Our God is a God of restoration. His Holy Spirit doesn't let us die out in the desert; He draws us home, to the holy Heart of God. My beloved sisters in Christ, God has mighty plans and purposes for your life! The (NIV) version of Jeremiah 29:11 says, *Plans to prosper you.* He created us, He planned our lives, our holiness, our redemption and healing. We are exhorted to *Live a life worthy of the calling you have received* (Ephesians 4:1). We each have His calling in our lives; let us surrender wholeheartedly to be empowered and worthy to walk in that calling — finding our prosperity. His Son, Jesus, ever intercedes for us only for these very best purposes, filling our prayers with His power and glory and testifying to God on our behalf so that He may answer with His authority and power. What does He want? The Holy Spirit wants whole hearts!

Growing, being filled, and walking, empowered, by the Spirit on our journey, are you beginning to see your lives in view of God's purposes and not only your own? Are you yet finding in prayer and life that your priorities and actions are changing? The past unsurity, drudgery and stumbling of prayer is becoming an exciting adventure filled with anticipation and renewed passion? Don't be surprised if these changes bring struggle. Remember, the daily battle of the flesh and Spirit means you and me! We will not all have the same purposes, yet we are all meant to find our own, letting God accomplish them through us as He moves us from boredom and complacency to power.

God wants to listen and speak, so that He may empower each of us. Jeremiah 1:5-9 says, *I knew you before I formed you in your mother's womb. Before you were born I set you apart and appointed you as my spokesman to the world.* His Spirit allows us to see His mighty love; He formed us! He has divine plans and purposes for our existence! How many first respond to God's calling, as I did, agreeing with Jeremiah, *Oh, Sovereign LORD, I can't speak for you I'm too young!* Excuses are lies from the devil, where God calls; He will empower-in prayer! The Lord's reply to us? *Don't say that, for you must go wherever I send you and say whatever I tell you. And don't be afraid of the people, for I will be with you and take care of you, I, the LORD, have spoken!* Let us have humbled, listening ears, bringing out empowered hearts with "marching orders" received in prayer. *Then the LORD touched my mouth and said, See, I have put my words in your mouth! Today I appoint you to stand up against nations and kingdoms.* The Holy Spirit appoints, anoints for service, and gives gifts so we may serve Him, speak to Him, listen to, obey and love Him.

Let us learn from another obedient servant, who says of God, *The Sovereign LORD has given me his words of wisdom, so that I know what to say to all these weary ones.* There are so many weary hearts, how can we not cry out for Him to cleanse, use, take and empower us? *Morning by morning he wakens me and opens my understanding to his will. The Sovereign LORD has spoken to me, and I have listened, I do not rebel or turn away* (Isaiah 50:4-5). Let us repent of allowing the sin of rebellion into our hearts, keeping us from listening; being teachable and empowerable.

We are commanded, *Don't be fooled by those who try to excuse these sins, for the terrible anger of God comes upon all those who disobey him.* His spirit of holiness filling our hearts and prayers will convict us of sin, giving heavenly insight into the actions of light and darkness. *Don't participate in the things these people do. For though your hearts were once full of darkness, now you are full of light from the Lord, and your behavior should show it!* We were once, but must be no longer. Are your words and actions showing you who is empowering your heart? *For this light produces only what is good and right and true* (Ephesians 5:6-9). His Spirit is the spirit of light, conviction, wisdom, obedience, humility, courage, faith, and determination; let us cry out with all our hearts, "Shine your Light into every bit of our hearts; removing all darkness, filling, changing and empowering us to seek, know, do, and surrender our all to Your will!"

His prophet continues to encourage our hearts, *Because the Sovereign LORD helps me, I will not be dismayed. Therefore, I have set my face like a stone, determined to do his will. And I know that I will triumph* (Isaiah 50:7). Letting the Spirit fill-gives faith and determination! Ask for the courage to step into

His will, His triumph—His Promised Land; He is drawing, and only waits for us to listen and ask, are we willing? Will we obey when He speaks?

Surrendering to the Holy Spirit's supreme control over our will, lives and hearts, we find our calling, empowering, and satisfaction in Him alone. **His holy waters quench our thirst for righteousness, His Word fills our appetite for truth, and His spirit of prayer fills our needy hearts with His persevering Presence, bringing us into His power, passion, and purposes through prayer.** Being filled in abundance with the spirit of power, truth, grace and supplication, our prayers are filled with God's love, energy, direction, courage and protection.

Jeremiah 1:17-19 says, *Get up and get dressed. Go out, and tell them whatever I tell you to say. Today, I will make you immune to their attacks. You are strong like a fortified city that cannot be captured, like an iron pillar or a bronze wall.* We are told to get up, go out and tell! The Holy Spirit is God's voice, strength and power, His creating energy, spirit of victory and fortification. *None will be able to stand against you. They will try, but they will fail. For I am with you, and I will take care of you. I, the LORD, have spoken!* He is the spirit of caring, comforting and abiding.

Isaiah 59:21 (NASB) promises, *As for Me, this is My covenant with them, says the LORD: My Spirit which is upon you, and My words which I have put in your mouth shall not depart from your mouth, nor from the mouth of your offspring, nor from the mouth of your offspring's offspring, says the LORD, from now and forever.* His Spirit and Words shall not depart. He not only promises to dwell within, He wants to fill, as we are commanded in Ephesians 5:18 (KJV), *but be filled with the Spirit.* Filled daily with His spirit of prayer, wisdom and power, our prayers bring blessing upon generations to come for God's divine purposes.

Relying upon the Holy Spirit in prayer and life enables us to live a spiritual existence as residents of the Kingdom. It is through prayer we are equipped and trained and how our struggles become God's victories. The Holy Spirit arms with the whole armor of God. We cannot use any apart from the other; the entire armor is necessary for victory, being held together and empowered with the Holy Spirit of prayer. Read aloud, and put into practice, daily Ephesians 6:10-17. Paul says, *Be strong with the Lord's mighty power.* Prayer brings the power of His mighty Spirit. *Put on all of God's armor so that you will be able to stand firm against all strategies and tricks of the devil.*

All of God's armor is necessary for it to work effectively. *For we are not fighting against people made of flesh and blood, but against the evil rulers and authorities of the unseen world, against those mighty powers of darkness who rule this world, and against wicked spirits in the heavenly realms.* Though we will see physical manifestations, the realities are spiritual. Spirit-empowered prayer takes us into the unseen realities where our hearts dwell.

Use every piece of God's armor to resist the enemy in the time of evil, so that after the battle you will still be standing firm. Stand your ground, putting on the sturdy belt of truth and the body of armor of God's righteousness. We need the power of God to resist and be protected. *For shoes, put on the peace that comes from the Good News, so that you will be fully prepared. In every battle you will need faith as your shield to stop the fiery arrows aimed at you by satan. Put on salvation as your helmet, and take the sword of the Spirit, which is the Word of God.* Everything is "put on," except the things of the Spirit, which we are to take and to use! We will cover, extensively, in another chapter, the power of the Sword (Word) of the Spirit, which is the Word of God in prayer. The Spirit of prayer is an offensive and defensive weapon; all the others are defensive only. *Pray at all times and on every occasion in the power of the Holy Spirit. Stay alert and be persistent in your prayers for all Christians everywhere.*

What is done in the physical is from the spiritual first. We need to claim Christ's victory and power, living spiritually by these realities that we will physically see them. **Praying in the Spirit is a vital necessity to reaching for God's very best in the lives of those for whom we pray.** He waits for us to join Him in His spiritual work by prayer to bring about the saving of souls, blessing our lives and others with His Great power, opening His floodgates of heaven for blessings to be poured upon each of the lives for which we pray, the outpouring of His Spirit and power upon His church universal and the coming of His Kingdom. These are spiritual battles and realities first and foremost—we must prepare for them by allowing the working of His Holy Spirit in our lives and the lives of others through Spirit-empowered, listening and reacting prayer.

EXERCISE

Practice listening in prayer. Praise God, and come before Him with a pure, silent heart; trusting what He says to you and obeying. He will bring confirmation in His Word and your life.

- ➥ What has God revealed to you about Himself, today?
- ➥ Which verse does God want you to ask Him to apply to your life today?
- ➥ For whom does He want you to pray this verse?

LET US PRAY

We praise You, holy, Father God, asking You to fill us with Your Holy Spirit. Oh, Lord, teach us what it is to be led and empowered as You were here on earth by the Spirit. Teach us to pray and live in holiness. Lord, teach us to pray. In Jesus' precious and powerful Name, Amen

Day 19

HIS SPIRIT LIVING
within PRAYER

||||||||||||||||||||||||||||||||||||||||||||||||||||||||||||||||||||||||||

What the righteous desire will be granted.

— Proverbs 10:24 NIV —

As the Holy Spirit fills us, empowering and leading our lives and desires through prayer, let us learn more of Him, that our surrender may be whole-hearted, opening the floodgates of heaven through holy hearts. Many grow up with some understanding of God and Jesus Christ, whether brought up in a Christian or secular environment. **However, even as Christians, many remain unclear as to the Holy Spirit and His importance regarding righteousness and all necessary work in God's Kingdom, including our own hearts.** Zechariah 13:9 (NIV) says, *This third I will bring into the fire; I will refine them like silver and test them like gold. They will call on my name and I will answer them; I will say, 'they are my people,' and they will say, 'The LORD is our God.'* He is the spirit of burning, convicting and cleansing of sin. Isaiah 4:4 says, *the LORD will wash the moral filth from the daughters of Zion. He will cleanse Zion of its stains by a spirit of judgment that burns like fire.* He pours out judgment, bringing godly sorrow to our hearts, then calls upon the Name of God and brings the Spirit of righteousness and restoration. His spirit of repentance and the holy refining fires of God's Presence test and approve through prayer. A heart continuing in the holy fires of God is purified and made holy.

The Holy Spirit draws us into a righteous relationship with God in prayer, bringing surrender, and making Him Lord of all. He is the very spirit of adoption, assurance, and baptism, filling and enabling God to call us "His," and for us to call our God, "LORD." Paul writes, *We know that God loves you, and that he chose you to be his own people. For when we brought you the Good News, it was not only with words but also with power, for the Holy Spirit gave you full assurance that what we said was true. So you received the message with joy from the Holy Spirit in spite of the severe suffering it brought you. In this way you imitated both us and the Lord* (1 Thessalonians 1:4-6). Many hear the message and say they believe, but do not receive. His Spirit allows those He has chosen to be His to accept Truth, with power, assurance and joy, transforming and baptizing hearts with power into the Kingdom and image of Christ.

Isaiah 11:2-3,5 says, *And the Spirit of the LORD will rest on him—the Spirit of wisdom and understanding, the Spirit of counsel and might, the Spirit of knowledge and the fear of the LORD. He will delight in obeying the LORD…He will be clothed with fairness and truth.* Knowing God, receiving Him in power and might, and growing in the fear of the Lord are all manifestations of the Spirit. Let us receive all that is Christ—that He may have all of us; praying and living through holy hearts with His passion, power and purposes! As He is our great delight, we realize how we are His delight. Clothed in fairness and truth; hearts delight in obeying the Lord!

He promises, *But when you pray, go into your room, close the door and pray to your Father, who is unseen. Then your Father, who sees what is done in secret, will reward you* (Matthew 6:6 NIV). Even as the Spirit draws us to God, He draws God to us, seeing and pouring out blessing from what is done in secret. Are you learning to pray to God as your Father? Do you allow the Spirit to spill out all that is your heart, as a child in need of your heavenly Father, grabbing His Heart and holding tight until you have all you can grasp? The closet of prayer, behind closed doors, is a place in which to build a relationship of intimacy with God that requires devotion of time. The Spirit of this intimate relationship with our Father holds the keys to prayer, the heart, and the Kingdom; bringing forth God's Presence and blessing sought after in the closet of prayer. Little of the prayer closet is always an indication of little of His Spirit. Little of the Spirit brings little prayer, righteousness, holiness, blessing, or change.

The transforming Spirit is necessary to bring into our hearts the desire for the Kingdom and bring forth all promises and blessings as children of the King. Matthew 6:33 (NIV) promises, *But seek first his kingdom and his righteousness, and all these things will be given to you as well.* God's Holy Spirit brings forth the Kingdom into the hearts of men with the desire to seek and experience His righteousness and Presence above the temptations of this worldly kingdom. Jesus responded to His disciples' lack of power. *He replied, Because you have so little faith. I tell you the truth, if you have faith as small as a mustard seed, you can say to this mountain, 'Move from here to there' and it will move. Nothing will be impossible for you* (Matthew 17:20 NIV). They lacked ability because they lacked the Spirit of faith, speaking to the mountain to move, and have it done as spoken. Had they focused so much on their doing, they forgot to receive first? The Holy Spirit is the Voice of God speaking through hearts and moving mountains, casting them into the sea.

Jesus promises, *I tell you the truth, what ever you bind on earth will be bound in heaven, and whatever you loose on earth will be loosed in heaven* (Matthew 18:18 NIV). This truth is unfathomable to the human heart, yet the heart empowered by the anointing and enlightenment of the Spirit- knows and acts upon His truth. In prayer, God asks us to loosen the spirits of oppression and sickness as He binds the wounds of His children.

These same things that Jesus did, show us the Holy Spirit's jobs, and God's tender Heart. Isaiah 61:1 (NASB) says, *The Spirit of the LORD God is upon me. Because the LORD has anointed me to bring good news to the afflicted; He has sent me to bind up the brokenhearted, to proclaim liberty to the captives and freedom to the prisoners.* Let us loosen the chains of sin that bind and send in prayer, the Spirit of life, freedom, and healing, binding the wounds of the brokenhearted! God's Holy Spirit gives us the keys to the Kingdom of heaven, unlocking the power of God wrought in persevering prayer.

His spirit of righteousness must dwell in hearts unrestrictedly for our desires to be surrendered totally to His, bringing us into His will and great power. Jesus' Spirit, as He called the tax collector, calls us, *Follow me. And he arose and followed him* (Mark 2:14 KJV). His Holy Spirit enables us to "arise and follow." Our lives given up for Him, desires united as His, we shall have all we ask in prayer. Psalm 37:4 (KJV) contains a powerful promise, *Delight thyself in the LORD; and he shall give thee the desires of thine heart.* What are your heart's greatest desires? Write them down and pray them aloud with confidence each morning. As we delight in Him—our hearts are prepared to receive His very best, the desires of His Heart for us! Our greatest desires are those God has placed there; He is waiting for you to ask, speak and believe in them, prayerfully acting upon them to receive!

He promises in the very next verse, *Commit everything you do to the LORD, Trust him, and he will help you* (Psalm 37:5). The Holy Spirit is the spirit of promises and commitment; God's commitment to us and ours to Him. Psalm 3:8 (KJV) promises, *Thy blessing is upon thy people.* His blessing is upon us; let us receive it with faith! He commands, *Trust in the LORD with all your heart and lean not in your own understanding.* With each command, let us accept His blessing. *And he will make your paths straight* (Proverbs 3:5-6 NIV). Be encouraged to pray and obey beyond your wildest imagination; He commits His Heart and heavenly Helper to us in prayer as we delight in, commit to, and trust Him with all our hearts.

We are commanded many times in Scripture to *trust in the Lord*, God, our heavenly Father. For complete surrender to His leading in prayers and working in our lives we must know, by His spirit of grace, to whom we are surrendering. Job 32:8 says, *Surely it is God's Spirit within people, the breath of the Almighty within them, that makes them intelligent.* A deeper understanding of the Spirit of God and Christ living within, breathing life and prayers into our hearts, allows us to yield ourselves with full assurance and whole-hearted trust.

As Jesus revealed God to us here on earth, the Spirit reveals Them to us in our hearts. To know Him is to receive the spirit of wisdom and revelation, bringing the fear of the Lord and allowing the spirit of humility. Proverbs 3:7-8 says, *Do not be wise in your own eyes; Fear the LORD and turn away from evil. It will be healing to your body and refreshment to your bones.* The Holy Spirit is the spirit of healing and refreshment, even to the deepest, inner parts. Prayer brings healing, binding God's Word, love and wisdom to hearts. We are told of His Spirit as the spirit of wisdom, long life and peace, *Long life is in her right hand; in her left hand riches and honor. All her paths lead to peace. She is a tree of life to all who hold her fast. The LORD by wisdom founded the earth, by understanding He established the heavens. My son, let them not vanish from your sight; keep sound wisdom and discretion, so they will be life to your soul. Then you will walk in your way securely and your foot will not stumble. For the LORD will be your confidence and will keep your foot from being caught* (Proverbs 3:15-19,21-23,26 NASB). God's spirit of power and wisdom is our safety, bringing life to our souls and allowing us to walk in the Spirit, confidently along His paths of peace and prosperity.

As God moves our hearts in line with Himself, by His spirit of righteousness, we move His Heart too. We read the success the Holy Spirit brings in 2 Chronicles 26:5, to a humble heart seeking God, *Uzziah sought God during the days of Zechariah, who instructed him in the fear of God. And as long as the king sought the LORD, God gave him success.* Our Instructor brings success into our lives, seeking Him. God's Holy Spirit is the spirit of success, humility, repentance, restoration, healing and renewal. He does God's desires, filling us with holiness and driving out sin and failure. Amos 5:14-15 says, *To do what is good and run from evil—that you may live! Then the LORD God Almighty will truly be your helper, just as you have claimed he is. Hate evil and love what is good, remodel your courts into true halls of justice.* The Holy Spirit we surrender to, allowing more and more of His filling, is our heavenly Helper, allowing us to do good as He fills us with godly desires and with God's hatred for evil. The New King James Version uses the words, *And the LORD, the God of hosts, shall be with you, as ye have spoken.* **The reference to speaking is a reference to prayer, God's forerunner to His Presence, Helper, and blessing; allowing us to seek and speak life into all God desires to bring forth.**

How can we be assured we are receiving the Spirit in prayer? Accept in faith all that you ask for, and it will surely come! God promises, *When the Holy Spirit controls our lives, he will produce this kind of fruit in us: love, joy, peace, patience, kindness, goodness, faithfulness, gentleness, and self-control. Here there is no conflict with the law* (Galatians 5:22-23). He produces fruits of righteousness! We cannot earn it, find it elsewhere, or do the growing ourselves; we do the allowing by abiding in His Word and praying. Memorize and daily ask for this verse, seeking with your whole heart, surrendering to the Spirit's working. Let us cry out, "Spirit, come fill and control us, bearing Your fruit in our hearts!"

He promises, encouraging hearts, *The one who sows to please the Spirit, from the Spirit will reap eternal life. Let us not become weary in doing good, for at the proper time we will reap a harvest if we do not give up* (Galatians 6:8-9 NIV). Sowing to please the Spirit, we reap a harvest; let us not grow weary! By prayer, His Spirit pours out, His spirit of strength, perseverance, repentance, righteousness, restoration, salvation, supplication, purification, sanctification, holiness and refining. God's Spirit brings wisdom and perseverance in answer to prayer, of Christ Himself, refining us and making His Heart and mind become ours.

God's greatest desire is that we be like His Son, loving Him with all our heart, and loving others as ourselves. He says, *God wants you to be holy. God has called us to be holy, not to live impure lives. Anyone who refuses to live by these rules is not disobeying human rules but is rejecting God, who gives his Holy Spirit to you* (1 Thessalonians 4:3,7-8). God calls each, to give His Holy Spirit! Impure lives come from impure hearts and pure lives from pure hearts. We are able to obey His rules by receiving His holy pure Heart first.

Do not be discouraged, He pours out His purification through hearts as we ask, thank and believe. Paul encourages**,** *And so we keep praying for you, that our God will make you worthy of the life to which he has called you. And we pray that God, by his power, will fulfill all your good intentions and faithful deeds* (2 Thessalonians 1:11). We read also**,** *And now this good news has been announced by those who preached to you in the power of the Holy Spirit sent from heaven* (1 Peter 1:12). All prayer, preaching, and acceptance of God's Word must be through the power of the Spirit. We must not be concerned with what we can do about righteousness, but with what God sends from heaven, as we ask!

EXERCISE

Write down your heart's desires—ask God for them in prayer, believing and receiving them; thanking Him for them in advance of His fulfilling them. Make your plans, prayerfully preparing for His answers!

- ❧ What has God revealed to you about Himself, today?
- ❧ Which verse does God want you to ask Him to apply to your life today?
- ❧ For whom does He want you to pray this verse?

LET US PRAY

We praise You Father God, asking You to fill us with Your Holy Spirit. Lead, guide, forgive, cleanse and protect us we pray. We confess all our impurities. Fill us with Your love and knowledge of Your righteous, wonderful power and blessed Holy Spirit. Oh, Lord, teach us to pray. In Jesus' Name, Amen.

Day 20

OUR KEY in PRAYER

||||||||||||||||||||||||||||||||||||||||||||||||||||||||||||||||||||||||||||||||||||||||||||||||||||||

And if we know that he hears us—whatever we ask—
we know that we have what we asked of him.

— 1 JOHN 5:15 NIV —

God's work which He wishes us to join Him in by prayer and deed comes from faith. Repeat the above verse out loud inserting your name. Hebrews 11:1 asks, *What is faith? It is the confident assurance that what we hope for is going to happen. It is the evidence of things we cannot yet see.* Scripture says, *without faith it is impossible to please Him, for he who comes to God must believe that He is and that He is a rewarder of those who seek Him* (Hebrews 11:6 NASB). **We must believe that He *is* and also that He rewards His children that seek Him.**

Focusing on Him alone, praising Him for who He is and what He does, allows the spirit of faith to pour into our heart. To pray with His power, we must accept and grow in His Spirit and gifts of faith. There is the faith for salvation, yet we must not be content with only that! Paul says in Philippians 1:25, *I will continue with you so that you will grow and experience the joy of your faith.* A faith which does not grow is a spiritually sick, prayerless life. Prayer brings and receives an ever-growing, believing faith, which pours health, life, and joy into holy hearts.

Paul says, *The life which I now live in the flesh I live by faith in the Son of God, who loved me and gave Himself up for me* (Galatians 2:20). We live by faith, in Jesus, Who allows us to obey and please God. Peter tells us the great worth of our faith—saying, *your faith is far more precious to God than mere gold* (1 Peter 1:7). Our faith is precious to God; let us have hearts filled with faith! Many struggle with the concept of faith, and therefore lack the ability to act upon it. Action is only possible when it is a manifestation of the Spirit living within and through us. The Spirit brings faith; being in God, not self. We are incapable of pleasing or accepting God apart from the Spirit.

Galatians 3:14 says, *He redeemed us in order that the blessing given to Abraham might come to the gentiles through Christ Jesus, so that by faith we might receive the promise of the Spirit.* All heavenly blessings, graces and gifts are received through Christ, in faith, by the works of the Spirit. Paul reprimands us for trying to receive spiritual blessings and please God through the flesh. He asks, *Have you lost your senses? After starting your Christian lives in the Spirit, why are you now trying to become perfect by your own human effort?* We must remain with all focus on Christ, not self to receive the faith required to truly pray and obey. *I ask you again, does God give you the Holy Spirit and work miracles among you because you obey the law of Moses? Of course not! It is because you believe the message you heard about Christ* (Galatians 3:3-4). The Holy Spirit comes with His power, not our efforts or programs, because we believe. Failure always leads back to human effort. All from heaven is spiritually sent and spiritually accepted.

Faith allows us to live in heaven, and heaven in us. Paul describes those growing and living by faith, in Philippians 1:27. He says, *You must live in a manner worthy of the Good News about Christ, as citizens of heaven. I will know that you are standing side by side, fighting together for the Good News.* Are we living, acting, and praying as citizens of heaven? The NASB says, *Standing firm in one spirit, with one mind striving together for the faith of the gospel.* Do we stand united with all God's children, fighting for the Good News? Oh, how the devil loves to keep the church busy arguing about inconsequential issues such as music and dress, keeping it busy and dividing it with politics, programs and activities. He will do anything to keep us from unity, prayer, and faith in God.

His spirit of humility keeps the spirit of faith growing. Paul encourages humility, encouragement, love, compassion, and the unity brought by faith. Philippians 2:1-2 (NASB) says, *If there is any encouragement in Christ, if there is any consolation of love, if there is any fellowship of the Spirit, if any affection and compassion, make my joy complete by being of the same mind, maintaining the same love, united in spirit, intent on one purpose.* The spirit of faith brings us united with our Father, His Son, and Holy Spirit intent on His heavenly purposes. Where there is lack of struggle in prayer for others, desiring to suffer for the Gospel, there is lack of faith.

Where there is lack of joy in prayer and service, there is lack of the Spirit and God's divine purposes. Paul states, *For to you it has been granted for Christ's sake, not only to believe in Him, but also to suffer for His sake, experiencing the same conflict which you saw in me, and now hear to be in me* (Philippians 1:29 NASB). Christ struggled; He suffered and was persecuted. He gave His life for the gospel. How can we deny His right to use us for the same? His Spirit brings us into struggle and suffering, enabling us to count it all joy in faith, knowing the outcome is for the sake of others to God's glory.

David teaches us that in faith, we trust God and wait in prayer in the midst of troubles, knowing deliverance will come! Psalm 13:2-6 says, *How long shall I take counsel in my soul, Having sorrow in my heart all the day? Consider and answer me, O LORD my God; Enlighten my eyes, or I will sleep the sleep of death, and my enemy will say, I have overcome him, but I have trusted in Your loving kindness; my heart shall rejoice in Your salvation. I will sing to the LORD, because he has dealt bountifully with me.* Regardless of how bleak, long-lasting, or impossible our circumstances seem, even when the enemy appears to have the upper hand, faith turns us to God, bringing praise and deliverance. Faith knows suffering, even while waiting upon God, to be a great and precious privilege with the assured outcome of deliverance, blessing and victory! Waiting prayer allows the Spirit to rush faith increasingly into our hearts, lifting us into the heavenly places, enlightening our eyes and restoring our power, joy and peace, seeing through the eyes and holy Heart of God.

Sometimes, we admit we are even unsure for what we ask and for what we wait; these moments require even greater faith. We are always called upon to trust in and react in our faith in God, only finding this determination, faith, grace and power as He pours it out from His throne in prevailing prayer. God says, *Listen to me, all who hope for deliverance—all who seek the LORD! Consider the quarry from which you were mined, the rock from which you were cut! The LORD will comfort Zion again and make her deserts blossom. Her barren wilderness will become as beautiful as Eden—the garden of the LORD. Joy and gladness will be found there. Lovely songs of thanksgiving will fill the air* (Isaiah 51:1-2). Let our hearts be comforted and filled with joy!

We are cut from the rock of the King, our faith worth more than precious gold! Seeking deliverance from lack of prayer and faith, He fills us with His holy breath of living waters, nourishing the desert with prayer, joy, thanksgiving and faith; breaking free hearts from bareness to beauty. God promises, *For the mountains may depart and the hills disappear, but even then I will remain loyal to you. My covenant of blessing will never be broken, says the LORD, who has mercy on you* (Isaiah 54:10). Drawing our hearts and the hearts of those for whom we pray to God's throne of mercy, our spirits cling to His faithfulness and promises of blessing.

Let us be faithful with all He blesses us with that we may receive more, walking forth always in the faith of His Word, power and covenant of love and blessing. He promises, *All your sons will be disciples of the LORD; and the well-being of your sons will be great. In righteousness you will be established; you will be far from oppression, for you will not fear; and from terror, for it will not come near you, If anyone fiercely assails you it will not be from Me. Whoever assails you will fall because of you. No weapon that is formed against you will prosper; and every tongue that accuses you in judgment you will condemn. This is the heritage of the servants of the LORD, and their vindication is from ME, declares the LORD* (Isaiah 54:13-15,17 NASB). Write each of these separately in the front of this book; speak them aloud, and believe!

What we believe is always evident in how we act, how we pray and how we shall receive. The Spirit brought forth in prayer fills us with the faith that knows Who God is, and who we are in Him. Knowing and believing, we walk forth in His covenant blessing, asking and receiving with the faith of glory. Faith poured out in prayer ushers in the life, power and blessing of heaven to accomplish the seemingly impossible. His outcome, in Isaiah 55:13 says, *Where once there were thorns, cypress trees will grow. Where briers grew, myrtles will sprout up. This miracle will bring great honor to the LORD's name; it will be an everlasting sign of his power and love.* Accepting His spirit of love and faith to fill our hearts and empower our prayers brings great honor to His Name, showing His power and love truly brings forth life from death, all only He can do in answer to prayer.

Faith brings love into action; knowing and doing because God has said it! Only in continued intimate connection with Jesus will we grow and obey in faith. God formed the earth to be subject to man, yet we must receive the proper heavenly tools, His gifts, to join in our Father's work and appropriate all His authority and blessings. Hebrews 2:10-11 (NASB) says, *It was fitting for Him, for whom are all things, and through whom are all things, in bringing many sons to glory, to perfect the author of their salvation through sufferings. For both He who sanctifies and those who are sanctified are all from one Father; for which reason He is not ashamed to call them brethren.* Faith enables us to be transformed and united with Christ, bringing forth our sanctification.

Faith is being led of the Spirit to a verse and accepting His instruction and teaching. Faith is action in our lives brought from prayer and the Holy Spirit speaking to us in God's Word. Faith hears God's Word and Voice and believes. Hebrews 2:1,4 (NASB) warns, *For this reason we must pay much closer attention to what we have heard, so that we do not drift away from it. God also testifying with them, both by signs and wonders and by various miracles and by gifts of the Holy Spirit according to His own will.* The spirit of faith in God allows us to pay close attention to His commands, and Voice, receiving His power and enabling and desiring reception of all gifts He pours out from the Holy Spirit. We shall be prepared, in Spirit-led prayer, to understand His working power in our hearts, ready to receive the dispensations of His Spirit poured out through prayer for the sake of His work for the Kingdom.

Faith looks at a situation not as "bad" or "good," but as an "opportunity" for God's grace and glory, sifted through the Sovereign Hand of God. All situations in your life are heavenly, God-ordained situations. For God promises, *And we know that all things work together for good to them that love God, to them who are called according to his purpose* (Romans 8:28 KJV). Praise springs forth from our hearts of faith, even in pain, knowing each circumstance is permitted by God for our good, controlled by His loving Heart to transform ours.

Romans 5:1,3-5 (NASB) promises, *Having been justified by faith, we have peace with God through our Lord Jesus Christ. And not only this, but we also exult in our tribulations, knowing that tribulation brings about perseverance; and perseverance, proven character; and proven character, hope; and hope does not disappoint, because the love of God has been poured out within our hearts through the Holy Spirit who was given to us.* Faith knows and experiences God's love daily and intimately with joy in trials and blessings. All faith comes from and is based on Him, in His Word. 1 Corinthians 15:1 says, *For your faith is built on this wonderful message.* We believe He is who He says He is and He does all He promises He will. Jesus says, *Anyone whose Father is God listens gladly to the words of God. I know Him and obey Him* (John 8:47,55)**.** Faith hopes, waits, listens, perseveres, knows, and obeys! We are commanded, *Today you must listen to his voice. Don't harden your hearts against him* (Hebrews 4:7). Faith receives direction, decision, determination and definitive answered prayer!

As the dews of heaven fall upon hearts in prayer, soaking in the glory, holiness and faith of God, He grows His love and Spirit in our hearts. Hebrews 6:7 says, *When the ground soaks up the rain that falls on it and bears a good crop for the farmer, it has the blessing of God.* Faith grows our knowledge and understanding of God, allowing His rain of righteousness and faith to soak Him up into our hearts, that He bears good crops through our growth and prayers. It assures us He hears and rewards, waiting with praise and thanksgiving in holy hearts. Hebrews 6:12 promises, *Then you will not become spiritually dull and indifferent. Instead you will follow the example of those who are going to inherit God's promises because of their faith and patience.* The spirit of faith allows us to walk in the heavenlies and not by sight, believing and receiving all we ask in prayer as we hope in the spiritual, not the physical world.

Oh, let us be filled with the faith that tells us in Hebrews 10:35-36, *Do not throw away this confident trust in the Lord, no matter what happens. Remember the great reward it brings you! Patient endurance is what you need now, so you will continue to do God's will. Then you will receive all that he has promised.* Let us receive faith, believing all His precious promises, in His mighty keeping power, that we may receive them!

EXERCISE

Each morning, pray a Psalm out loud, inserting your name to make it personal. Faith comes by hearing the Word of God; **begin speaking it in your prayers!**

- What has God revealed to you about Himself, today?
- Which verse does God want you to ask Him to apply to your life today?
- For whom does He want you to pray this verse?

LET US PRAY

Author and Perfector of our faith, Father, Creator of all things, forgive us all of our sins especially those of not believing and receiving Your spiritual gifts and our answers to prayer. Oh, Lord, teach us what it is to pray and live by faith. Oh, Lord, teach us to pray with unswerving faith as You did, Oh, Lord teach us to pray. In Jesus' powerful and precious Name, Amen.

Day 21

LOVE OF CHRIST in PRAYER

||||||||||||||||||||||||||||||||||||||||||||||||||

He answered, "Yes, Lord, you know that I love you."
Jesus said, "Take care of my sheep."

— JOHN 21:16 NIV —

Seeking God with hearts filled with His Spirit, Christ's love purifies and brings wholehearted surrender and sacrifice, preparing hearts to care for His sheep. All powerful prayer is born out of His love. As His love and life grows in our hearts, we desire to share not only in His prayers and blessings, but also in His sufferings and sacrifices for God and others. Let us remember, each day, *Since Christ lives in you...if we are to share his glory, we must also share his suffering* (Romans 8:10,17).

Jesus' entire life was surrendered out of love for His disciples. Jesus asks us to love Him by caring for His sheep; His children. We hear His prayer for us in John 17:19, *And I give myself entirely to you so they also might be entirely yours.* Christ gave himself entirely, that we might also. *And I have declared unto them thy name, and will declare it: that the love wherewith thou hast loved me may be in them, and I in them* (John 17:26 KJV). His powerful, almighty love, living and praying within, leads and empowers us to live prayer—surrendered and sacrificing for His Name, for His Kingdom.

His love, living in our hearts, enables us to do unto others through unlimited services of prayer and deed. *Morning, noon and night I plead aloud, and the LORD hears my voice...give your burdens to the LORD, and he will take care of you* (Psalm 55:17-18). The burdens of God's children fall upon our hearts, as they do on Jesus. We join Him in prayer by the power of His love. The Spirit of the Son's love draws us nearer to God, humbly purifying our hearts that we may love and care for others through prayer and sacrifice.

Jesus' love is our example and power of complete and total surrender to God. Paul says, *For the Kingdom of God is not a matter of what we eat or drink, but of living a life of goodness and peace and joy in the Holy Spirit. If you serve Christ with this attitude, you will please God* (Romans 14:17-18). Serving others by Christ's love, He fills hearts with His attitude of goodness, peace and joy. For the joy we know is before us, let us please God—sacrificing, being purified, and caring for His sheep!

Romans 14:19 commands, *So then, let us aim for harmony in the church and try to build each other up.* Christ's love brings harmony, peace, and building. Loving within the church body allows His love to flow out into our communities and nations, yet it must begin within! As He gave His entire life through love, dying for its cause, we must die to ourselves that we may live for others in love. Romans 15:1-3 (NIV) says, *We who are strong ought to bear with the failings of the weak and not to please ourselves. Each of us should please his neighbor for his good, to build him up. For even Christ did not live to please himself.* He teaches how total surrender in obedience to God is to love Him by pleasing others, that He may love them through us.

We are commanded to *Accept one another, then, just as Christ accepted you, in order to bring praise to God* (Romans 15:7 NIV). Total surrender by love in obedience brings praise to God! Hearts and motives in prayer are kept pure; He teaches us to put others before ourselves in prayer. Paul gives this example, *I urge you, brethren, by our Lord Jesus Christ and by the love of the Spirit, to strive together with me in your prayers to God for me* (Romans 15:30 NASB). Our action of prayer follows His command to love others, taking care of His sheep by His power and spirit of love.

Continually looking to Christ as our example for all, *We know what real love is because Christ gave up his life for us. And so we ought to give up our lives for our Christian brothers and sisters* (1 John 3:16,18). Christ waits to take us from selfishness to sacrifice; God's will conforming us to the image of His Son. The power of Christ's love gives the willingness and desire to put self aside, by encouraging and taking others to the throne in prayer. Scripture tells us to stop just saying we love each other; but to also show it by our actions.

What do your actions show about whom you love? How we spend our money and, more importantly, on what we focus our time, prayers, and energies, shows what fills our hearts. Humbly, thankfully and joyfully serving Him in prayer and deed, we shall grow to be more filled with and become more like Him. Giving ourselves to others as Christ did, we give ourselves totally to God and to prayer!

Praying and living united and empowered by Christ's love, we bring peace and harmony to His Kingdom. Romans 12:9,16 encourages, *Let love be without hypocrisy. Live in harmony with each other. Don't try to act important, but enjoy the company of ordinary people.* The Spirit of Christ brings unity, change and great power in prayer. Many would agree the world does not see the church as a place of love and unity, but as those whose lives are full of hypocrisy, bickering and division. 1 Timothy 1:4-5 (NIV) says, *These promote controversies rather than God's work—which is by faith. The goal of this command is love, which comes from a pure heart and a good conscience and sincere faith.* Humbly setting aside differences of culture, economic or religious background and denominations, we are able to reach out with purified and unified hearts.

Not only self, but the church must also **"walk the walk and talk the talk!"** Paul exhorts all Christians, *Now, dear brothers and sisters, I appeal to you by the authority of the Lord Jesus Christ to stop arguing among yourselves. Let there be real harmony so there won't be divisions in the church. I plead with you to be of one mind, united in thought and purpose* (1 Corinthians 1:10). Christ's spirit of love is the spirit of harmony, unity and peace. We are all to have the united mind and purpose of Christ. It is the devil who is causing divisions, grumbling and keeping the church busy in the pride of self, so we will not be able to reach beyond the front doors.

By the power of Christ's love, let us love man, therefore pleasing God. Romans 9:17 (NASB) says, *For this very purpose I raised you up, to demonstrate My power in you, and that My name might be proclaimed throughout the whole earth.* Being raised up by His power, we live and pray for His purposes—proclaiming His Name. Whom has He sent you to love? Where in your family, in your church body, can you pray for His love to flow in and heal? Where has He shown you His Name is going to be great through you? Filled with love in our hearts and by our action of prayer, we know Christ lives in us. Romans 13:9,14 says, *The commandments against adultery and murder and stealing and coveting—and any other commandment—are all summed up in this one commandment: 'love you neighbor as yourself.'* Christ living within loves others; born out of love from the very Heart of God. *But let the Lord Jesus Christ take control of you, and don't think of ways to indulge your evil desires.* **Because God first loved us, we are able to love those for whom we pray.** *Love leads us to pray and prayer leads us to love.* **Our time should not be spent on pleasing self, but on pleasing God by loving and caring for His sheep.**

Many may argue lack of time is the only restriction to praying for others—it is a lack of love, a lack of Christ within. However, where there is Christ's powerful love, there will be time! He, many times, went upon the mountain to pray all night. Ephesians 4:23 says, *There is to be a spiritual renewal of your thoughts and attitudes.* Our new attitude of Christ, one of love, faith, and sacrifice will no longer say, "I can't, I need or I want," but will say instead, "With God, I can, I will, and as He wants." Ephesians 5:2 commands us to *Live a life of life filled with love for others, following the example of Christ, who loved you and gave himself as a sacrifice to take away your sins. And God was pleased, because that sacrifice was like sweet perfume to him.* As God sacrificed His one and only Son out of love, we also sacrifice out of love for those we know and for those we don't because God loves them. God met our greatest need out of His love for us; let us pass it—and pray it on!

Galatians 6:2 (NASB) commands us to *Bear one another's burdens, and thereby fulfill the law of Christ.* The law of Christ is the law of love. Whether we know of another's physical or spiritual burdens, we are to help always in prayer and sometimes in deed. Living in the power of His love frees us to serve and love others rather than self and sin. Galatians 5:1 (NASB) says that, *It was for freedom that Christ set us free; therefore keep standing firm and do not be subject again to a yoke of slavery.* The love of Christ frees us to stand firm on God's foundation, doing His work and fulfilling His purposes of love in prayer.

Galatians 5:6 says, *What is important is faith expressing itself through love.* This world teaches expressing power, prestige, and independence, exalting self, sacrificing everything to gain it all and then finding you really have gained nothing. Scripture teaches our faith in Him expresses itself in humble love and dependence. Faith frees us to love where there is hurt and hate. Faith frees us to pray instead of slander. Faith frees us to leave our worldly desires behind to sacrifice all for the sake of love. The undying spirit of love for Christ comes as we ask, flowing through—as we surrender.

The powerful love of Christ enables us to commit every situation, every loved one, every cry of our own hearts to the Father. As did Jesus, in Luke 23:46 (NASB), *crying out with a loud voice, said, "Father, INTO YOUR HANDS, I COMMIT MY SPIRIT." Having said this, He breathed His last.* Let us breathe our last on our own, that our prayers will be the very breath of the Almighty, empowered by His love. John 3:16 reminds us that love gives all; it sacrifices even when it hurts, and only then it brings life and power, *For God so loved the world that he gave his one and only Son.* One willing to sacrifice little in prayer receives little power in return. We must ask, is His love flowing through? Are we ready and are we willing? James 2:13 says, *There will be no mercy for you if you have not been merciful to others. But if you have been merciful, then God's mercy towards you will win out over his judgment against you.* Again, we are taught of the sowing and reaping. Wanting to receive more love, more mercy and more of God, we must give it away!

A heart willing to be totally filled with the love of Christ, surrendering all, receives His all and will do His all, through passionate prayer; good deeds can only spring forth in love-empowered prayer. As our hearts are filled there, we shall be poured out, as was Christ. We need to try to comprehend how much He desires to continue to meet our needs out of His great and incomprehensible love. He calls out of love, *Come to Me, all who are weary and heavy-laden, and I will give you rest. Take My yoke upon you and learn from Me, for I am gentle and humble in heart, and YOU WILL FIND REST FOR YOUR SOULS* (Matthew 11:28-29 NASB). Jesus walked as we do. God loves us so deeply, He gave up His rights, humbling Himself as a man, to come and save us, giving rest to our souls. He loves us too much to leave us destroyed and wearied by the sin and darkness of this world.

As His love fills us, we have a humbled heart that cries out for the lost. We must take His yoke upon us so that the burdens of this world don't weigh us down. We shall find our strength, His love praying through our hearts as the Holy Spirit pours God's love for others into our hearts and returns them in His power to the throne. We are able to love others and be concerned for their needs above ours because the love of Jesus reigns in our hearts. The love of Christ gives us the very desire and ability to obey God's commands that He will be pleased to answer our every prayer. It's this spirit of humble sacrificial love that delivers the power to obey, pray, serve, and sacrifice at any personal cost.

EXERCISE

Get up thirty minutes earlier to pray each day. This will require setting your alarm earlier, and as you go to bed earlier, ask God to wake you up earlier, bright-eyed and chipper-tailed!

- What has God revealed to you about Himself, today?
- Which verse does God want you to ask Him to apply to your life today?
- For whom does He want you to pray this verse?

LET US PRAY

We bless Your Name and praise You, Father God, for Your sacrifice of love, for giving us all that we need for salvation and lives of godliness. May our love abound in knowledge of You. May we begin to grasp the love You have for us and for those whom we pray for. Oh, Lord, teach us to be more like You—pour out Your spirit of love and unity once again upon Your church. Oh, Lord, teach us to pray. In Jesus' powerful Name, Amen.

Day 22

FASTING for FREEDOM

||||||||||||||||||||||||||||||||||||||||||||||||||

*The time will come when the bridegroom will
be taken from them; then they will fast.*

— MATTHEW 9:15 NIV —

Striving to sacrifice ourselves in prayer, as Jesus did, we shall feel the times
when there is additional need of the Spirit's power and blessing and we
experience the need to fast. Notice, He said that *"they will" fast,* that is all of us,
not just some. Our Teacher gives us an indispensable discipline of a victorious,
holy, surrendered heart in a life of prayer—FASTING! Exactly what is fasting?
Both the Hebrew (Old Testament) *sum* and Greek (New Testament) *nestial/
nesteuo* words for fasting in Scripture, mean literally, "to voluntarily abstain
from food as dedication to deity, as a sign of mourning, going without food."
This is what Jesus spoke of as a Christian's call (Matthew 6) as well, referring
to His fasting in the desert, Moses fasting on the mountain, Ezra (Ezra 8)
calling for a national fast, and Nehemiah (Nehemiah 1:4) fasting upon the
destruction of the wall of Jerusalem, among other examples in Scripture.

As the devil has literally stolen the power of God from most Christians
by deceiving them into believing service is more important than prayer, the
enemy has deceived many Christians who do pray, into the belief that it is
better to sanctify self by giving something up, than to follow Scripture's call
to refrain from food. Fasting prepares the body and spirit for God's Presence,
being fed and nourished spiritually, rather than physically.

Yes, Scripture tells us to be sanctified and set ourselves apart, holy unto the Lord. This is a daily process of the Holy Spirit unto a willing and surrendered heart. A heart in fasting will more willingly be set apart; easily able to identify those worldly things standing in the way of listening to and obeying God's Word and Spirit. Scripture commands we sacrifice time, sleep, money, sex, clothing, and other comforts, many times in combination with and resulting from fasting for prayer and holiness to have their way in our hearts and lives. **However, these sacrifices alone must not replace our obedience to the discipline of fasting from food to seek and receive God's Presence and holiness in prayer!**

Let us remember, as with all, this must be prompted, led and sustained by the Holy Spirit of prayer working in our hearts! Scripture says, *But holy men of God spake as they were moved by the Holy Ghost.* It is God's Holy Spirit of love that moves holy men to speak in prayer and to fast. *For of whom a man is overcome, of the same is he brought in bondage* (2 Peter 1:21/2:19 KJV). Man shall worship God in love or be overwrought in sin, shall be overcome and moved by God in love or moved away by sin, shall be in bondage to God's love or enslaved to sin. Fasting removes the bondages of sin, ushering in the holy, freeing Presence of God Almighty.

There are times we will feel we are not being overcome by the spirit of love in a given situation, but by sin, and fasting must break loose this bondage. There are occasions we feel the Spirit is not moving in answer to prayer, when the situation seems desperate and there is the need for concentrated focus upon the Word, will and powers of God. Fasting shall be necessary in such times to bring the desired breakthrough of God's powerful love. The spirit of fasting, in our hearts, agrees with Christ, that we need spiritual strength. Fasting turns us from this world, unto God, loosens the grip of the world and the enemy and breaks forth God's almighty power and angels for deliverance.

We must be willing to overlook our physical needs for God's spiritual power. Jesus teaches us there are those things for which prayer, alone, is not sufficient. This doesn't mean God's power is not sufficient; it means our faith and obedience isn't. The psalmist says**,** *LORD, give to me your unfailing love, I will walk in freedom, for I have devoted myself to your commandments. LORD, you are mine! With all my heart I want your blessings. I will hurry without lingering to obey your commands* (Psalm 119:41,45,57-58). Prayer and fasting turns us to cling to God and His holy Words of love as ours, all that we need. Fasting brings godly desires springing forth in our hearts and quick obedience as our hearts are entirely devoted to seeking and finding God. The spirit of love brings us to deny food for a certain increment of time, throws itself and those prayed for at the throne to be nourished and blessed in heaven alone! Psalm 21:7 says, *The king trusts in the LORD. The unfailing love of the Most High will keep him from stumbling.* Seeking God's will, wisdom and blessing, fasting seeks His love to keep. Our trust is taken from the physical world, and any doing we could try to act only with God's Spirit and wisdom poured from the throne. Fasting will loosen the bonds of the self-will and be bound to the will of God.

David cried out for even his enemies, filled with the love of Christ. *Yet when they were ill, I put on sackcloth and humbled myself with fasting. When my prayers returned to me unanswered. I went about mourning as though for my friend or brother. I bowed my head in grief as though weeping for my mother* (Psalm 35:13-14 NIV). The Spirit fills us with the love and compassion of God that, even for our enemies, we weep. When prayers seem unanswered, we are not to give up, but to be humbled in prayer and fasting. Fasting brings sensitivity to the Spirit, revealing the need for repentance and spiritual understanding, where our prayers must change, or be newly ignited. Fasting removes all hindrances of the heart, ensuring us God will move mountains in answer to and with wholehearted devotion and love. Fasting opens our hearts to receive the spirit of humility, repentance and faith for restoration. Fasting and prayer opens our hearts and minds for receiving and renewal, opening God's Heart with the keys of holy hearts and faithful obedience.

Our obedience to the command of fasting holds untold power and blessings. Fasting gives us sensitivity to the Holy Spirit as God speaks to us through prayer, His Word our circumstances, and MULTIPLE other ways. With all sin loosened, hearts are free to walk, to listen, see spiritually, and to obey. Turning from the physical world, we now live, breathe and pray in the spiritual, preparing us to receive His power, purposes and priorities. Fasting brings us into a holy response to all circumstances. We read of Hezekiah's response to his enemy who had defeated all its adversaries, *When King Hezekiah heard their report, he tore his clothes and put on sackcloth and went into the temple of the LORD to pray* (Isaiah 37:1). He, alone, draws us to Himself, enabling us to live in surrender, holiness and sacrifice, relying wholly upon His love.

Fasting turns off human reason and intelligence, opening the gateway for the spirit of wisdom and understanding, of sacrifice and courage, leading hearts, minds and feet with eyes of faith where the human mind cannot travel: to the mighty Heart and blessings of God. Moses says, *When I was gone up into the mount to receive the tablets of stone, even the tables of the covenant which the LORD made with you, then I abode in the mount for forty days and forty nights, I neither did eat bread nor drink water: and the Lord delivered unto me two tables of stone written with the finger of God* (Deuteronomy 9:9-10, KJV). As we pray and fast, God fills us with the power of His Spirit, preparing those for whom we pray and ourselves for appropriate understanding and use of His Word in ministry and spiritual battles in prayer. Christ, Himself, fasted; how much more are we in need of fasting than He was?

Fasting takes us upon the mountaintop with Moses, into the desert with Jesus and to the Heart of holiness with David. Christ's love teaches us to sacrifice and pray for others, confronting, in prayer, spiritual battles of bondage, needing to totally turn away from anything physical that may hinder faith and holiness, distracting us from God and the power of His holy love. Fasting brings the power of God to use us to receive, appropriate, and teach His Word with the power of the Spirit and pray for those in disobedience to it. The mighty love of Christ, bringing us to fast and pray, doesn't condemn, but asks God's love and patience for those caught in sin, averting judgment and pouring out instead, His grace and mercy.

For true preparation, before being called into God's destiny for us, requires prayer and fasting. To pray and live with Christ's passion, the Holy Spirit's power, and be drawn into the persevering Presence and divine purposes of God, we must be prepared. Let us fast to be chosen, to hear our calling and to be empowered. We read in Acts 13:2-3 *One day as these men were worshipping the LORD and fasting, the Holy Spirit said, 'Dedicate Barnabas and Saul for the special work I have for them.'* The Spirit speaks clearly to those given to prayer and fasting, as well brings forth the power of praise, blessing and direction, bringing the holy rivers from within flowing through the hands of those given to God. *So after more fasting and prayer, the men laid their hands on them and sent them on their way.* It is only in prayer and fasting that children of God are sent out with the mighty power of the Spirit. We must realize our need and dependence upon God's power and love by the Holy Spirit through fasting and prayer that we may return the church and our missionaries the power of God. Let us pray and fast that holiness shall once again take over heathenism!

God waits to take broken hearts from worshipping the world or self and renew, restore and return to the worship it was made for: God, by loving and serving others. We read in Isaiah 58:6-11 (NASB), *Is this not the fast which I choose, to loosen the bonds of wickedness, to undo the bands of the yoke, and to let the oppressed go free and break every yoke? Is it not to divide your bread with the hungry and bring the homeless poor into the house?* The power of His love loosens from sin and unties all hurts and concerns that oppress. As His prayers and love pour through, God not only releases those for whom we pray, we find that, first, our hearts are freed. *Then your light will break forth like the dawn, and your recovery will speedily spring forth; and your righteousness will go before you; the glory of the LORD will be your rear guard.* Fasting always brings repentance and recovery. As the sin is burned from our hearts, He is able to flow unhindered, speedily springing forth His fruit of righteousness and salvation, healing the cries of the heart. *Then you will call, and the LORD will answer; you will cry, and He will say, 'Here I am.' If you remove the yoke from your midst, the pointing of the finger and the speaking wickedness, and if you give yourself to the hungry and satisfy the desire of the afflicted, then your light will rise in the darkness and your gloom will become like midday.* Fasting brings humility and conviction of sin, freeing us to serve and love others filled with joy and the light of Christ's love. *And the LORD will continually guide you, and satisfy your desire in scorched places, and give strength to your bones; and you will be like a watered garden, and like a spring of water whose waters do not fail.* Fasting frees God's love to flow through to others that He may bless, strengthen and fill us with Himself. Prayer and fasting frees our hearts from the bondages of this world to be filled with His living waters of powerful love to rivers overflowing!

Fasting prepares and cleanses heart, body and soul with repentance and great godly sorrow for personal sins and those of others; bringing us in line with His perfect will, removing our own rebellion and casting out all sin hindering prayer and God's work. I have yet to fast without ending up in godly, sorrowful tears cleansing my heart with repentance. Fasting also builds faith to cast out demons that otherwise could not be cast out, allowing us to hear from God clearly, willingly and powerfully; growing a hunger and thirst for God's Presence above all else, with a passionate hatred for sin. Fasting builds faith to do His will in His time, for His purposes and glory. Genuine fasting and prayer is led and enabled by the Spirit within, in humility, motivated by the desire for holiness and surrender. Our humble actions are answered by our Father in power and grace, giving us all spiritual riches and nourishment, wisdom and an even deeper revelation of Himself and His will for us and those for whom we pray. God does amazing things in us and through us when we pray and fast, things He otherwise would not do, and we would otherwise not be empowered to receive His blessings in return.

EXERCISE

Prayerfully write down a particular burden God has placed upon your heart; as led, pray and fast about it for one-three days or meals, or more. Don't just "not eat"—focus wholeheartedly on prayer—praising God for this particular area of deliverance for the person whom you pray. Focus on God, then on them—how does God want you to pray? Proclaim His Word for the person(s). Please receive medical clearance from your physician; though I know of no one who would not benefit physically and spiritually from fasting, at the very least one meal—as God leads.

- What has God revealed to you about Himself, today?
- Which verse does God want you to ask Him to apply to your life today?
- For whom does He want you to pray this verse?

LET US PRAY

Gracious, precious, holy, heavenly Father God. Oh, Lord, teach us to love as You do, teaching us to fast, that we will seek for Your power and Presence, freeing all of Your captive children in the bondages of sin. Oh, Lord, teach us to pray. In Jesus' precious Name we pray, Amen.

Day 23

PURE HEARTS
in PRAYER

||||||||||||||||||||||||||||||||||||||||||||||||||

If my people, who are called by my name,
will humble themselves and pray and seek my face and
turn from their wicked ways, then will I hear from
heaven and will forgive their sin and heal their land.

— 2 CHRONICLES 7:14 NIV —

As the Holy Spirit fills our hearts with Jesus' powerful love, He heals and purifies from all evil and unrighteousness. God desires us to pray to Him, seeking Him with all of our hearts. Seeking God in prayer and worship, He requires we come before Him with pure and humbled hearts, turning from this world to put Him first, as our one and only love. Amos 6:1,8 (NIV) says, *Woe to you who are complacent in Zion…I abhor the pride of Jacob and detest his fortresses.* The almighty love of God flowing through hearts sweeps away all pride and complacency of sin and the suffering of our brethren.

Worshipping God cannot be done with a heart that lives for self, or it is done in vain. God commands, *Let justice roll on like a river, righteousness like a never-failing stream!* (Amos 5:24 NIV). His spirits of love and righteousness humble hearts, calling to prayer, calling us to cry out to our Deliverer from complacency, oppression and sin, freeing the healing, righteous rivers to flow. His mighty love calls through hearts, not for self alone, but for His land, His people! God is waiting for us to cry out, seeking His face, and turning from our wicked ways so that He may hear, forgive and heal!

Allowing anything to dissuade or distract us from earnestly praying to God, we shall struggle in prayer. All spirits of complacency and pride must be cast off. He is willing and waiting to heal from sin; we must only ask. Many are too content to have little belief for change, or feel God's Heart is far from their situation. Complacent hearts always rest in the sin of prayerlessness, keeping God from hearing, forgiving and healing. It is a mystery He has bound His moving to our asking, yet Scripture proves it to be so.

Our God is a God of mercy and restoration; He is also a God who demands holiness and prayer! Let us be encouraged of God's mercy in answer to a pure heart calling out to Him on behalf of His people. In Amos 7, God gives him visions of devastation and judgments, *When they had stripped the land clean I cried out, "Sovereign LORD, forgive! How can Jacob survive? He is so small!" So the LORD relented. "This will not happen," the LORD said.* God brings another vision of devastation, a judgment of fire. *Then I cried out, "Sovereign LORD, I beg you, stop! How can Jacob survive? He is so small!" So the LORD relented. "This will not happen either"* (Amos 7:2-5 NIV). Let us be encouraged to cry out with purified, holy hearts for God's children. The devastation of sin can be healed, even averted, through prayer. **Passionate, powerful prayer rains down from heaven through holy hearts, earnestly seeking Him with the power and purposes of His love, righteousness, and restoration!**

God's love commands and answers a pure heart. His holiness demands we seek and love Him, not objects, self, or family first. Let us read of Job's response to losing all family and possessions**.** *He said, "I came naked from my mother's womb, and I will be stripped of everything when I die. The LORD gave me everything I had, and the LORD has taken it away. Praise the name of the LORD!"* (Job 1:21) Regardless of circumstances, a pure heart full of God's love praises Him and holds onto nothing of this world.

God speaks of him, *Have you noticed my servant Job? He is the finest man in all the earth-a man of complete integrity. He fears God and will have nothing to do with evil. And he has maintained his integrity, even though you persuaded me to harm him without cause* (Job 2:3). God's love and righteousness overpower even the worst of circumstances, bringing hearts that praise God in times of health and wealth or poverty and illness.

A pure heart holding with all its might to a holy God, praises even greater blessing from heaven. Tested and tried, even accused by his friends, he praised God, pleaded forgiveness, and brought forth blessing and healing. Scripture says, *When Job prayed for his friends, the LORD restored his fortunes. In fact, the LORD gave him twice as much as before! So the LORD blessed Job in the second half of his life even more than the first* (Job 42:10,12). Dear child of God, His love tests and refines, in preparation for His double portion of blessing; it forgives, heals and restores! Praise Him that He may shower down His love, holiness and righteousness from His storehouse bringing forth your blessings, healings, and restorations! Let us hold nothing before God from this world, that He may be pleased to answer the prayers brought from heaven from His holy heart, flowing, unhindered through ours!

We are warned of idols, *Be careful not to break the covenant the LORD your God has made with you. You will break it if you make idols of any shape or form, for the LORD your God has absolutely forbidden this. The LORD your God is a devouring fire, a jealous God* (Deuteronomy 4:23-24). Accepting Christ as Savior, we also enter a covenant for Him to be Lord. Many fall short of this understanding and teaching. Salvation is a free gift of God by grace, and not works; but we must still maintain a responsibility to our relationship with God, Who demands pure and holy hearts. He is a jealous God, an all-consuming fire; He must always remain our first love, and He has every right to be! Let us cry out for the church to repent, that He may come, that He will heal.

A holy heart has its way with a holy God. Moses speaks**,** *As I said before, I stayed on the mountain in the LORD's presence for forty days and nights, as I had done the first time. And once again the Lord yielded to my pleas and didn't destroy you* (Deuteronomy 10:10). These were whole-hearted pleas in God's Presence alone for forty days! He was totally given to God and God yielded to His pleas! Surrendering to His holy fires of righteousness, remaining in His Presence, filled with compassion for His people, let us cry out, removing any idols in our hearts, that He will yield to our prayers!

Sin always separates us from fellowship with God; repentance always restores. Yet entire hearts are required to approach the throne of grace, where He awaits with merciful love. Returning from sin, He says, *From there you will search again for the LORD your God. And if you search for him with all your heart and soul, you will find him. When those bitter days have come upon you far in the future, you will finally return to the LORD your God and listen to what he tells you. For the LORD your God is merciful-he will not abandon you or destroy you or forget the solemn covenant he made with your ancestors* (Deuteronomy 4:29-31). His holy love promises to bring better days, as well His Spirit and love causes us to search, calling upon Him with all our listening heart.

Only a heart filled with the love of Christ can seek God, drawing heart and soul to be purified with the healing rains of righteousness, holiness and prayer. If we allow anything of this world to distract us and keep us from prayer and intimate time with God, He shall be unable to answer our prayers because we will not be ready to receive them. Deuteronomy 6:5-6 commands, *You must love the LORD your God with all your heart, all your soul, and all your strength. And you must commit yourselves wholeheartedly to these commands I am giving you today.* It is a heart committed to Him, to which God commits Himself.

That which we love is that to which we are committed, what we do and live for. Christ's love died for us, that we may live for Him. Do we? Let us surrender to His power of love and rivers of righteousness, loosening all commitment to this world and self, that we may seek Him, find Him, love, know and be blessed by Him! He demands, *You must destroy all the nations the LORD your God hands over to you. Show them no mercy and do not worship their gods. If you do, they will trap you* (Deuteronomy 7:16)**.** Leaving any sin in our lives is a trap; traps are set to keep us from loving and serving God. We cannot worship anything else and God at the same time. Let us not grow complacent; the enemy is out to destroy our love and whole-hearted worship of God. We must submit to God's authority in every area of our lives and bring Him the whole heart He requires, paid for, created and deserves!

Christ's powerful, cleansing love is waiting to flow through our hearts, lives, and prayers. And in that order! Where we ask, we must be ready, first, to obey. God's love called us out from destruction, calling for pure, obedient hearts. Deuteronomy 10:12-13,15-16 says, *And now, what does the LORD your God require of you? He requires you to fear him, to live according to his will, to love and worship him with all your heart and soul, and to obey the LORD's commands and laws that I am giving you today for your own good.* He requires from us, that we may receive from Him. His requirements are not because He needs us to do them; they are from His love and are good for us. *The LORD chose your ancestors as the objects of his love. And he chose you, their descendants. Therefore, cleanse your sinful hearts and stop being stubborn.* We must choose to surrender, allowing Him to cleanse us; we are the objects of His love, let us not choose stubbornness, but choose His love!

Deuteronomy 10:20 commands, *You must fear the LORD your God and worship him and cling to him. Your oaths must be in his name alone.* Prayer is done in the spirit of the fear of God, worshipping Him alone and clinging to Him, living, dying, and praying in His Name, to bring glory to Him. Let our oath of love be to God alone that His holiness may continually cleanse. Loving Him and clinging to Him in prayer releases us from the traps of our enemy and all curses; it heals hearts. Giving Him access to our entire hearts, gives us access to His promised abundance of blessings from His storehouse in heaven in answer to our prayers.

Righteous hearts are humbled, listening, trusting and obedient hearts God blesses. Let us look at Joseph, who loved and obeyed God's voice regardless of the looks of things. We read, *And Joseph her husband being a righteous man and not wanting to disgrace her, planned to send her away.* Hearts seeking God, purified and listening, are always ready to surrender their good, well-meaning plans for His. *Joseph awoke from his sleep and did as the angel of the Lord commanded him, and he took Mary as his wife* (Matthew 1:19,24 NASB). Joseph could have called off the wedding, even having Mary stoned, for what looked like infidelity during their engagement, which, in biblical times, was as binding as marriage. Yet, to a righteous man God spoke. Joseph listened and obeyed and God blessed!

Matthew 2:13-14 (NASB) says, *When they had gone, behold, an angel of the Lord appeared to Joseph in a dream and said, "Get up! Take the Child and His mother and flee to Egypt, and remain there until I tell you; for Herod is going to search for the Child to destroy Him." So Joseph got up and took the Child and His mother while it was still night, and left for Egypt.* So Joseph got up. Not the next morning, he obeyed in the middle of the night, when it was inconvenient and he couldn't see the whole picture.

There are times when our safety and deliverance from the destroyer comes in God's moving us; let us listen and obey! Most times, blessing follows obedience that requires faith and inconvenience. Travel at night was not a customary thing; he couldn't hop into the car, flip on the headlights and turn on the radio. Joseph did not care for his comfort, nor fear the night, but God alone!

When God speaks, we must listen and act upon our faith in Him, not allowing any disbelief or doubt into our hearts or minds. Let us say, as Paul,

So take courage! For I believe God. It will be just as he said (Acts 27:25). God desires to bless obedience, holiness and surrender brought forth from a heart wholly given to, trusting and in love with Him. Matthew 5:8 promises *God blesses those whose hearts are pure, for they will see God.* **Let us praise Him; He delivers us not only *from* the enemy, but most blessedly, *into* His persevering Presence!**

Believing His great unfailing love for us, we find Him and His very best for us in prayer. We settle, no longer, to remain the way we are, or for things to remain as they are, but we are filled with an earnestness of heart. Finding and letting God have His way with us that we may have Him, He promises to bless, in prayer. We unite with David's heart, *No wonder my heart is filled with joy, and my mouth shouts his praises! My body rests in safety. For you will not leave my soul among the dead or allow your godly one to rot in the grave. You will show me the way of life, granting me the joy of your presence and the pleasures of living with you forever* (Psalm 16:9-11). Living with Him forever begins the moment we accept Christ into our hearts. He leaves us not to rot and decay in sin, but brings us forth into joy and blessing. We are to live life, being blessed in His Presence now, from His Heart of holiness, in His spirit of prayer!

EXERCISE

Allow the Holy Spirit to search and purify, that you may seek and therefore find God in prayer. Prayerfully consider, what are you unwilling to "let go of"? Allow the Holy Spirit to search and purify; to help you let go and surrender your all!

- What has God revealed to you about Himself, today?
- Which verse does God want you to ask Him to apply to your life today?
- For whom does He want you to pray this verse?

LET US PRAY

Wonderful, glorious, heavenly Father God. Convict us, Holy Spirit, when we have divided hearts, purging sin from among us. Teach us what it is to love You, know and serve You wholeheartedly in and through prayer. In Jesus' powerful, precious and holy Name, Amen.

Day 24

LOVE INTERCEDING
in PRAYER

IIIIIIIIIIIIIIIIIIIIIIIIIIIIIIIIIIIIIIIIIIIIIIIIIIII

The harvest is plentiful, but the workers are few.
Ask the Lord of the harvest, therefore,
to send out workers into his harvest.

— MATTHEW 9:37-38 NIV —

Ultimately obeying Christ, in His command to love others as He loves, we are called to His highest and holiest work of intercessory prayer. To intercede is to, "make a plea for someone else." We, for God's children, as Christ does, come before God and make pleas on behalf of the affairs of others. Philippians 2:4 (NIV) says, *Each of you should look not only to your own interests, but also to the interests of others.* His heart filling ours, His priorities, honor and Kingdom's work become ours.

As we ask, He answers. Let us ask, *Until at last the Spirit is poured down upon us from heaven. The wilderness will become a fertile field, and the fertile field will become a lush and fertile forest. Justice will rule in the wilderness and righteousness in the fertile field* (Isaiah 32:15-16). This is God's calling for lives to intercede and ask Him to pour Himself out from heaven. As He fills and bears fruit through prayers, He asks that we pray for His fields to be watered, to be fruitful and bear abundant harvest for Him. Zechariah 10:1 (NIV) commands we *Ask the LORD for the rain in the springtime; it is the LORD who makes the storm clouds. He gives showers of rain to men, and plants of field to everyone.* Intercessory prayer humbly relies upon God our Master, who makes and gives to others, as we ask. Asking releases those for whom we pray into God's hands and keeps us from trying to fix people and situations ourselves. David says, *And even though I am the anointed king, these two sons are too strong for me to control. So may the LORD repay* (2 Samuel 3:39). Intercessory prayer agrees with God, saying, "I cannot, but you can, and you know best."

Jesus says, *For the Father himself loves you dearly because you love me and believe that I came from God. Yes, I came from the Father into the world, and I will leave the world and return to the Father.* We ask, in agreement with His love and Word, that He blesses Christ at His right hand, to exercise His authority and power in accordance with God's will. *I have told you all this so that you may have peace in me. Here on earth you will have many trials and sorrows. But take heart, because I have overcome the world* (John 16:27-28,33). Christ's love, peace, and authority in prayer overcome the world, as His powerful amazing love in us, draws others by prayer. Our very souls were purchased by the blood of Jesus. The deepest desire and need of our souls is complete surrender to the very calling Jesus has for us to join Him in intercessory prayer.

Intercessory prayer for others is born out of sacrificial love from God's Heart waiting to pour out as promised, to those who ask, and will receive. His love for others fills us with the faith and desire necessary in prayer to see ministers and members empowered and hurting hearts healed. Acts 3:16 says, *Faith in Jesus' name has caused this healing before your very eyes.* God's love for His children and His desire to bring them to Himself is brought through intercessory prayer.

Christ, our Teacher and enabler, began His ministry of intercession here on earth, now continuing at the right hand of the Father, continuing His redemptive work through us. Acts 4:8,10 says, *Peter, filled with the Holy Spirit, said to them, "Let me clearly state to you and to all the people of Israel that he was healed in the name and power of Jesus Christ from Nazareth, the man you crucified, but whom God raised from the dead."* In prayer for others, for God's Kingdom, we pray in Jesus' Name and power. Let us remember the Cross was not the only part of His mighty work. Sacrificing His flesh, following His blood wringing prayer in the Garden; He was raised to the heavenliest by God's mighty power. This is the power we must pray in, preach and witness in, that hearts must be healed by. Sacrificing Himself in prayer, and then on the Cross He released the great, divine power necessary in intercessory prayer.

Now, interceding for us, His saints, His kingdom of priests, He draws, asking us to join Him in His highest and holiest work. Let us study His prayer for Himself and us before He left His earthly ministry. This prayer was for our benefit, not His; let us learn as Jesus gives us the keys to His Heart's desires and goal of His ministry. *Jesus spoke these things; and lifting up His eyes to heaven He said, Father, the hour has come; glorify Your Son, that the Son may glorify You, even as You gave Him authority over all flesh, that to all whom You have given Him, He may give eternal life. This is eternal life, that they may know You, the only true God, and Jesus Christ whom You have sent* (John 17:1-3 NASB). Christ's prayer and heart's desire is to give all glory to His Father and give eternal life to us. He only receives from the Father that He may glorify Him, by fulfilling His purposes. Intercessory prayer brings us to this calling united with the Heart and mind of Christ's love. The holy cry of God's Heart is that we receive eternal life, that we may know Him! We don't stop at knowing Who He is, but He wants us to experience Him, God the Father, the Son, and the Holy Spirit.

Jesus prays further in His priestly prayer, for us to be kept in His Name, guarded, kept safe from the evil one. He prays also for our unity, empowerment, joy, holiness, purity, being taught God's Word, and wholeheartedness; He desires we be united with Him, that we may see His glory. He prays further, *Holy Father, keep them in Your name, the name which You have given Me, that they may be one even as We are. And I have revealed you to them and will keep on revealing you. I will do this so that your love for me may be in them and I in them* (John 17:11,26 NASB). Even as the Father and Son are united, so prayer unites us, keeping in Their love and power. Christ's prayers and sacrifice becoming ours, others' needs becoming our needs. All we do and pray are for His sake, united in His Name. He teaches, *If any of you wants to be my follower, you must put aside your selfish ambition, shoulder your cross daily, and follow me* (Luke 9:23). Ask today for His holy love and desire to consume your daily life of prayer.

Those He calls, He prays for and empowers. Let the enemy not discourage this holy, priestly work as he has for so long. Let us confess, *As for me, I will certainly not sin against the LORD by ending my prayers for you* (1 Samuel 12:23). **Lack of prayer is a sin against God.** Let us be hindered no longer as His children in the work to which He calls us! Let us be encouraged, seeing some of whom He called with Him to preach the Good News. Luke tells us He took the twelve disciples, *Along with some women he had healed and from* *whom he had cast out evil spirits. Among them was Mary Magdalene, from whom he had cast out seven demons* (Luke 8:2). It is not that we are unworthy of self, but healed! Christ's healing prepares our hearts for His Presence, teaching, and service, for His love, His grace and passion in intercessory prayer.

Mary prayed, served and loved with passion. Upon His crucifixion, she followed Him from the cross to the grave, leaving only to serve Him in preparing ointments and spices. Early Sunday morning when the rest of the disciples were locked fearfully behind closed doors, she and the other women were first to the tomb, receiving the news of His resurrection, and then they told the others.

Whatever possessed us in the past, His passion must possess us now, His passion for prayer and His Presence, for God's glory and for telling others of the salvation of souls. Where we struggle, let us pray, "Heal us that we may know you, be possessed entirely by You, pray effectively for Your glory, seeking You with our whole heart, that we may find Your Presence, the risen Christ, and be empowered to tell others."

Let our faith remain in His work in and through us, not in our work for Him. Romans 1:4 reminds God raises up only that which comes from heaven, *And Jesus Christ our Lord was shown to be the Son of God when God powerfully raised him from the dead by means of the Holy Spirit.* Living and praying by His powerful Spirit brought forth from heaven, and returning shows we are indeed His children. We do not need doctoral degrees to be used by Jesus in this highest and holiest work, bringing saint and sinner to Christ; we just need Him!

God's supply of seed and workers sent into the harvest waits upon prayer, as does the softening of hearts to receive God's gift of Christ. God waits upon the prayers of His saints to empower His church and servants. Though feeling yet unworthy, even unable, regardless of feeling, receiving His spirit of prayer and supplication, it is He praying within! Remember, obedience first; feeling follows the action. 2 Corinthians 12:9 (NIV), *But he said to me, My grace* is *sufficient for you, for my power is made perfect in weakness.* Bow in silent adoration and praise; take time to receive in weakness and humility, believing He will answer according to His power.

Zechariah 2:13 says, *Be silent before the LORD, all humanity, for he is springing into action from his holy dwelling.* Our praises, prayers and even silent adorations arouse Him to action. When we know not what to pray, let faith take control of our hearts, allowing His Spirit to pray from within. Remember His promise of hope, blessing us, *For I know the thoughts I think towards you...of peace, and not of evil, to give you an expected end; and I will be found by you and turn away your captivity.* Every blessing and all of His Kingdom depends upon the earnest prayers of His people. *And ye shall seek me, and find me, when ye shall search for me with all your heart* (Jeremiah 29:11,14,13). God's almighty, amazing love consumes hearts with His passions in life and prayer, bringing freedom and unlimited power from the throne of God; turning away from captivity. Lives given entirely surrendered to Christ's life allow nothing of self to be desired, but for His Kingdom's reigning, restoration and glory.

Let us learn from another surrendered to God. Lives touched by heaven must remain to live and receive from there. A Jewish missionary to the Gentiles, Paul lived focused on the Cross and went forth in the Spirit's power for God's business. He says, *I came to you in weakness—timid and trembling. And my message and preaching were very plain. I did not use wise and persuasive speeches, but the Holy Spirit was powerful among you. I did this so that you might trust the power of God rather than human wisdom* (1 Corinthians 2:3-5). Human weakness and power in prayer is for the benefit of God's children who rely upon the Spirit and teach others to do the same. In each epistle, His great love for His brethren and knowledge of His dependence upon God led to prayer. Romans 1:9,11-12 says, *God knows how often I pray for you. Day and night I bring you and your needs in prayer to God, whom I serve with all my heart by telling others the Good News about his Son.* He expresses His love in prayers and desires to visit them, sharing His reason, *So I can share a spiritual blessing with you that will help you grow strong in the Lord. I'm eager to encourage you in your faith, but I also want to be encouraged by yours. In this way, each of us will be a blessing to the other.* Paul learned the power of God's love was a blessing for the mutual benefit and encouragement of the church.

Have you noticed hope and light spring back into a wearied one's heart when you share what God is doing in your life, how He answers prayers? When we pray for others, the power of His love draws us to them many times. I have, very unexpectedly, met people I have prayed for from around the world, just at the time we each needed encouragement. God's love pouring out through prayer breaks us out of our comfort zones and takes us into "God zones" in both spiritual and physical realms.

Paul, spending much time in prayer for those whom he loved, also requested and relied upon much prayer from them. Even after twenty years, he wouldn't move, speak or minister on his own power. Ephesians 6:18-19 (NASB) exhorts, *Be on the alert with all perseverance and petition for all the saints, and pray on my behalf, that utterance may be given to me in the opening of my mouth, to make known with boldness the mystery of the gospel.* His whole heart given for the gospel relied upon the Holy Spirit's ministry for Himself and those for whom he prayed, divine power and understanding of the merciful love and saving power of Jesus.

John 1:23 says, *I am a voice shouting in the wilderness, 'Prepare a straight pathway for the Lord's coming!'* Love paved the way for intercessory prayer and intercessory prayer paves the way for love. Powerful ministry comes forth only from powerful prayer by the love of Jesus, flowing from heaven into our hearts and out through our prayers. It is the very power and passion the New Testament churches experienced and the very need of the church today.

The church worldwide, pastors, evangelists and missionaries are in much need of powerful, persevering prayer. Daily, ask God to fill hearts with His love for His people and work, relying upon His promise in Matthew 6:33, that seeking first His kingdom and His righteousness, all these things will be given to us. We cannot out-give God, even in prayer. As His Kingdom's desires replace our earthly ones; we ask, thank and receive! Pay very careful attention as you pray for others to see how God brings those blessings into your very own life in abundance as well. True love gives, and when given, it is blessed and returned in abundance.

EXERCISE

Pray Matthew 9:38 daily; pray for the workers that He sends by name. Find out the names of the missionaries that your church supports, or a large church near you; let them know that you are praying—it is very encouraging to them and will bless you as well.

- What has God revealed to you about Himself, today?
- Which verse does God want you to ask Him to apply to your life today?
- For whom does He want you to pray this verse?

LET US PRAY

We bless and praise You by the almighty love and power of Jesus working within our hearts. Build mighty armies of intercessors and missionaries, empowered by prayer. Lord, teach us what it is to love others by interceding in prayer, surrendering ourselves wholly to Your work. Oh, Lord teach us to pray...In Jesus' Name, Amen.

Day 25

IN HIS NAME
WE PRAY

||||||||||||||||||||||||||||||||||||||||||||||

Until now you have not asked for anything in my name.
Ask and you will receive, and your joy will be complete.

— JOHN 16:24 NIV —

Divine power in prayer comes in believing prayer, in the Name of Jesus. Before the crucifixion of Jesus, the disciples' power, faith and joy were not complete. He told His disciples, *You too have grief now; but I will see you again, and your heart will rejoice, and no one will take your joy away from you* (John 16:22 NASB). We know through all their misunderstandings, arguments, faulty faith, lack of prayer and denial of Jesus, even hiding behind locked doors in the upper room after His death, they needed help! Their joy, actions, faith and understanding depended upon what they saw and He explained; they did not yet have full faith and understanding of who He was.

He says, *I have spoken of these matters in parables, but the day will come when this will not be necessary, and I will tell you plainly all about the Father.* They lived and ministered with Him, yet they needed to be in Him, and He in them. *The truth is, anyone who believes in me will do the same works I have done, and even greater works, because I am going to be with the Father* (John 16:25/14:12). His sacrifice was that we could come in His Name and know the Father. They needed, as we need, the indwelling Spirit of Christ in order to live, pray and witness in His power—doing *even greater works*! His blood on the Cross purchased our lives, uniting us with the Trinity in His Name.

His resurrection brought us into His full inheritance and divine resources by His love, power and Presence.

Jesus promises, *In that day you will not question Me about anything. Truly, truly, I say to you, if you ask the Father for anything in My name, He will give it to you* (John 16:23 NASB). One of the secrets to empowered prayer, reaching the Heart of holiness, is the Name of Jesus. Acts 2:21 says, *And anyone who calls on the name of the Lord will be saved.* Let us believe, as He has saved by His Name and fills, we can ask for anything. Romans 6:6 (NIV) says, *For we know that our old self was crucified with him so that the body of sin might be done away with, that we should no longer be slaves to sin.* We reject sin, accepting the indwelling of Jesus as Savior and Lord with a new name, His Name.

Jesus repeats at the beginning of this promise the word "truly" twice. He means what He says; it is all truth and relates to all of His children, and He emphasized this truth. He repeats this promise, *And I will do what ever you ask in my name, so that the Son may bring glory to the Father. You may ask me for anything in my name, and I will do it* (John 14:13-14 NIV). Again, saying, *If you remain in me and my words remain in you, ask whatever you wish, and it will be given you* (John 15:7 NIV). John 16:23 (NIV) says, *I tell you the truth, my Father will give you what ever you ask in my name.* When Jesus learned total submission to His Father, surrendering His will in prayer, He gave us the power of His blood shed at the Cross and asked, in His Name, allowing us to be filled with the Holy Spirit for God's work and glory.

Read with the promise of answered prayer again, John 14:13-14, *Because the work of the Son brings glory to the Father. Yes, ask anything in my name, and I will do it!* In His Name we receive all He has been given. Paul says, *I pray that you will begin to understand the incredible greatness of his power for us who believe him. This is the same mighty power that raised Christ from the dead and seated him in the place of honor at God's right hand in the heavenly realms. Now he is far above any ruler or authority or power or leader or anything else in this world or the world to come. And God has put all things under the authority of Christ, and he gave him this authority for the benefit of the church* (Ephesians 1:19-22). His authority and power is for our benefit, as we come in His Name for the church! We must begin to use it; let the church again experience the Name, Love and power of Jesus. Let us pray!

He gave His life to prayer, glorifying the Father, and now He gives us His Name, power, authority and holiness to complete His work and

bring His Father continued glory. Speaking of His ascension, He says, *I will ask the Father, and He will give you another Helper, that He may be with you forever* (John 14:16 NASB). His love desired, and we need Him to dwell within, unhindered. Let us, too, have the faith and courage, in His Name to say, "I will ask, and He will give." Prayer in Jesus' Name is that simple, that profound, that wonderful and powerful! He gave His all in prayer, that He could give us our heavenly Helper, Himself and the Father, revealing His glory in prayer.

Remember, in biblical times, a person's name represented his or her title, character, attributes, or career. A person's name was the source of one's pride or shame, their power and authority, or their downfall. Frequently, in the Scripture, when God changed a person from heathen to heavenly, He changed his or her name. Jesus was born from heaven, deriving His Name from there, and giving it to us as we exchange a heathen heart for a heavenly one.

An angel of the Lord speaks of Mary and God's Son to Joseph, *For the Child who has been conceived in her is of the Holy Spirit. She will bear a Son; and you shall call His name Jesus, for He will save His people from their sins.* He was conceived by the very power of the Holy Spirit brought forth from God's holy Heart of love to be with us. *Behold, the virgin shall be with child and shall bear a Son, and they shall call His name Immanuel, which translated means, God with us* (Matthew 1:20,23 NASB). He sends forth, too, not only the child to save, but His angel to name Him. The Greek form of "Jesus" is the name "Joshua," which means, "the Lord saves." His Name came from heaven to be with and save us from our sins. In His Name, we pray as those saved and on behalf of those He desires to save. We are born again of the Spirit, drawing to His holiness, clothed in Jesus' Name, to save and serve His Kingdom, bringing Him glory.

John proclaims in 1:29, *Look, there is the Lamb of God who takes away the sins of the world!* Drawing the world to the throne of grace, we say of our hearts, here is the Lamb of God who takes away the sins of the world. We, united in His Name, come in prayer, covered and empowered, holy in the blood of the Lamb. The mighty blood of the Lamb, flowing throughout veins, hearts, minds and prayers make us all His! As a bride takes the name of her bridegroom out of love for him, our devotion to God is similar; what we will do now represents "us" instead of "me" and we become His. This ownership not only means serving out of obligation, but with a deeper love that respects and obeys, bringing joy and not burdens. Our greatest joy becomes the simple, loving relationship, and life of prayer, out of which all else joyfully flows.

As Jesus fills, so too He builds within the desires to do that which we were created to do. John 2:17 says, *Passion for God's house burns within me.* When our passion dwindles, we have lost the relationship and drive to live for whose Name has given us a new nature. New Christians are sometimes said to be "on fire for the Lord." Remaining in prayer, we are always on fire for Him! His holy fires of love shall keep us in love with and passionate about all that consumes Him in an ever-increasing measure.

Let us be encouraged, just as the union with our husband obligates them to care for our every need, using all his resources; so we have an even greater union and commitment from Christ by our spiritual union with Him. When we accept Him as Lord, receiving His Name—He commits now to love, care for and avail to us all we need. We share in His glorious heavenly inheritance and power! Philippians 2:9 says, *God raised him up to the heights of the heaven and gave him a name that is above every other name.* He shares all He has, including the honor and positions, the financial, emotional and spiritual resources His Name holds; and Christ's Name holds all! It is His joyful responsibility and desire to meet every one of our needs as we now worship and serve Him in love.

Our grasping of His power in prayer is done by His Name; by and for His work, and because of His love and sacrifice for us. In His Name, He brings the grace to pray, to love, to serve. John 1:16 (NASB) promises, *For of His fullness we have all received, and grace upon grace. For the Law was given through Moses; grace and truth were realized through Jesus Christ.* Jesus denied Himself and surrendered to the Father's will to bring His love and power, realized and fulfilled into our hearts, lives, and prayers. The NIV uses the words, *we have received one blessing after another.* God's Heart's desire is to bless in His Son's Name. The Name He sent forth from heaven is that which must bring us back, receiving from heaven, its blessings. Let us hold in front of us daily, "all to be blessed by heaven must first and foremost be from heaven!" Coming from any other name means we would use those resources to serve another. In Jesus' Name, we are blessed to bless His Name. David says, *Every day I will bless thee; And I will praise thy name forever and ever* (Psalm 145:2 KJV). Jesus' Name, love, power, and passion poured though holy hearts brings blessing and praise to the Father.

Referring to Jesus as child, God says, *I called my Son out of Egypt* (Matthew 2:15). Those God calls out of this world into holiness, come as His Son, and only in His Son's Name. "In Jesus name" is not a phrase added onto the end of prayers, to simply empower them. The entire life, heart and desire must be empowered by the graces of His Name. The life He lives through, He draws in His Name, but a life given to iniquity does not receive that which it asks in Jesus' Name, for it does not live for Him, but self. He warns those who claim work in His Name, but never bear fruit for His Kingdom, *"I will reply, 'I never knew you. Go away; the things you did were unauthorized'"* (Matthew 7:23). Even as Christians, we must be ever so careful to live according to the Name of Christ, humbly, loving and serving in holiness, never apart from, behind or before God's timing and power.

Matthew 3:16-17 says, *After his baptism, as Jesus came up out of the water, the heavens were opened and he saw the Spirit of God descending like a dove and settling on him. And a voice from heaven said, "This is my beloved Son, and I am fully pleased with him."* Jesus received His power and grace from heaven, pleasing our Father, fulfilling God's purposes in His timing. We come as the Son who said in Matthew 3:15 (NASB), *Permit it at this time, for in this way it is fitting for us to fulfill all righteousness.* Scripture tells us He depended upon His Father for every decision, including daily empowering for ministry, whole-hearted obedience and painful sacrifice, and especially in resisting temptation as He brought forth the fruits of righteousness, holiness, obedience and love. Dear Sisters, let us be like Him!

Jesus came, obeyed, and lived and died in prayer denying the favor of His Father on the Cross, that we could receive it—let us worship Him. Ephesians 2:7,10 says, *God can always point to us as examples of the incredible wealth of his favor and kindness toward us, as shown in all he has done for us through Jesus Christ.* **He has given us the favor of His Son hanging on a Cross; how can we doubt this Name will not continually bring us all favor, blessings and grace, all we need to continue His work?** He continues to tell us *We are God's masterpiece. He created us anew in Christ Jesus, so that we can do the good things he planned for us long ago.* He created each one of us as His masterpiece. We are created, anew, in the Name of Jesus to do what He created us to do!

Jesus speaks in John 12:27, *"Now my soul is deeply troubled. Should I pray, 'Father, save me from what lies ahead?' But this is the very reason why I came!"*

Do not be troubled by your life; seek God's glory! What is your purpose in God's kingdom? What likes, interests, and talents has He given you? Deep in your hearts are passions waiting to be kindled anew, dreams to be lived out and purposes to be joyfully fulfilled in His Name. Ask, and you will know! Seek, and you will find! Knock and He will open every door that needs to be opened for you to do that which He created you to do. He wants you to be in Him, everything He created you to be. Coming in His Name, we come as a delighted in daughter to her Father, receiving what we need for His—now our family business; bringing forth His holiness, power, and His glory.

EXERCISE

Write down why God has created you; what part do you play in His family business? Pray over how He wants you to play a part in the "big picture" no matter where He has placed you to serve.

- What has God revealed to you about Himself, today?
- Which verse does God want you to ask Him to apply to your life today?
- For whom does He want you to pray this verse?

LET US PRAY

We bless Your Name that is above all names having authority, power and dominion over all things. Oh, Lord Jesus, teach us to be totally united and submissive, living and praying in Your Name. Oh, Lord, teach us to pray the prayers that will be answered by the Father in Your power and Your Spirit. In Jesus' glorious, powerful and precious Name we pray, Amen.

Day 26

HIS WORD WITHIN

||||||||||||||||||||||||||||||||||||||||||||||||||||||||||||||||||||||||||||||||||||||

If you remain in me And my words remain in you,
Ask whatever you wish, And it will be given you

— JOHN 15:7 NIV —

Praying God's will in the Name of Jesus and obeying His commands in love, His Word must remain within. We must know Jesus personally in order to represent Him in our prayers and please God, for this He has given us His Spirit and indwelling Word. The insight, wisdom and faith required for praying in the Name of Jesus within God's will is powerfully accomplished by the Word of God. Each is indispensable to the other. With God's holy Word, so comes His will and inescapable, glorious, powerful Presence! Solomon prays, *That Your eyes may be open toward this house day and night, toward the place of which You have said, 'My name shall be there,' to listen to the prayer which Your servant shall pray toward this place* (1 Kings 8:29 NASB). Scripture brings us into the Presence and prayers of our Holy Father, in His Name. God created, watches over and empowers His Word; it is essential in a passionate prayer life to bring forth holiness from His Presence and into our hearts.

God's Word brings with His Presence, healing love. We read, *The LORD was furious with them, and he departed. As the cloud moved from above the Tabernacle, Miriam suddenly became white as snow with leprosy. So Moses cried out to the LORD, Heal her, O God, I beg you!* (Numbers 12:9-10,13). Moses knew the withdrawal of God's Presence brought illness only He could restore, and He did!

We now have God's indwelling Presence, which will not leave, but mustn't be stifled. His new covenant promises, *I will put my laws in their minds, and I will write them on their hearts. I will be their God, and they will be my people. For everyone from the least to the greatest will already know me...and I will forgive their wickedness and will never again remember their sins* (Jeremiah 31:33-34). His Spirit reigning within heals hearts, freeing us from sin as we pray, allowing us to know Him through His Word.

God's love and judgments, His righteousness and holiness, His Presence and will for us are found in His Word. **For the Spirit to dwell and fill increasingly within, we must spend quality and quantity time in His Word; not only knowing it but living by it.** He uses Scripture to speak to us, guide, teach, transform, heal, and pray through us. *The Spirit came into me as he spoke and set me on my feet. I listened carefully to his words* (Ezekiel 2:2). The NASB says, *And I heard Him speaking to me.* God uses His Word and Spirit to speak personally, and as we carefully listen, we will hear.

Ezekiel 3:1-2 says, *The voice said to me, "Son of man, eat what I am giving you—eat this scroll! Then go and give its message to the people..." So I opened my mouth, and he fed me the scroll. "Eat it all", he said. And when I ate it, it tasted as sweet as honey.* As our bodies need nourishment; our souls need to eat of His Word. His Word, as honey, is not only pleasant, bringing joy to those who read and pray in it, but it is also beneficial in every way to us. Honey is full of carbohydrates and good vitamins as His Word is full of energy, health, and is an offensive against spiritual illness. We must maintain spiritual health to be ready to give, pray and to tell. Telling His message and sharing His love, we live, desire, are filled with and are in love with His Word.

With His Holy Spirit, He pours out understanding and obedience with His cleansing Word, bringing glory and holiness. He says, *'I will show the holiness of my great name...Then the nations will know that I am the LORD... when I show myself holy through you before their eyes...I will gather you...and bring you back into your own land. I will sprinkle clean water on you, and you will be clean; I will cleanse you from all your impurities and from all your idols. I will give you a new heart and put a new spirit in you...And I will put my Spirit in you and move you to follow my decrees and be careful to keep my laws* (Ezekiel 36:23-27 NIV). God's holy heart cleanses ours, showing His name great through us, His people. He waits to restore, to cleanse and to give. Receiving His Spirit, it is His desire to move us to obey His Word. His Spirit and Word cleanse, heal and restore. Let us pray He will continually pour out

His Spirit that we may draw continually to His cleansing, holy, restoring and powerful Word.

His Word brings movement, to Him and to us. Spoken words bring the entire body, mind, soul and heart springing forth into action. Spoken words draw forth emotion, grabbing hold of heart and being. His Word promises, creates, cleanses and achieves, bringing us into His holiness and His holiness within us. His holiness says, *I will…I, the LORD have spoken…the Sovereign LORD has sworn this by his holiness* (Amos 3:15/4:2). His Word moving Him, moves us. Created by the Word, we are commanded to be as He, to live, breathe, listen, eat and speak of, memorize, act and walk by that which formed and sustains us. 1 Peter 1:16 says, *He himself has said, You must be holy because I am holy.* He said, He is and we must be. What He has said, He does and we are. Therefore, what we say, He will do.

As we draw nearer to our Teacher, seeking Him further, we find His Word necessary to our hearts and lives. Psalm 1:2-3 (NIV) says**,** *His delight is the law of the LORD, and on his law he meditates day and night. He is like a tree planted by streams of water, which yields its fruit in season and whose leaf does not wither. Whatever he does prospers.* We may think of the meditation as a quiet, inner thought. However, the original Hebrew word used here is "haga" meaning " to utter a sound, moan, to mutter." Scripture calls us to speak His Word aloud to ourselves in meditation.

Psalm 2:8 (NIV) says of Christ and us, *'Ask of me, and I will."* Also, Psalm 3:4 (NIV)**,** *'To the LORD, I cry aloud, and he answers me.'* His Word and prayer spoken bring God into action. The spoken Word cleanses, fills, nourishes and empowers, bearing fruit through holy hearts. Nourished by His streams of living waters, we do not have seasons of drought, instead we are trees whose leaves never fall. As Jesus teaches the power of Scripture, praying it into our lives, praying with doubt or praying amiss in our own words will be a thing of the past. We will know, by meditating on His Word, reflecting on and agreeing with it aloud, that we are praying within God's will, by His power and for His purpose for those for whom we pray. Our prayers, as our lives, will prosper and bear fruit in everything we do and pray.

God's Word contains every promise He has made and has waiting for us—every promise He desires to fulfill for us. His Word is where our hope, restoration, and comfort are contained; Scripture is where we find Him. Reading Scripture aloud, *Happy are those who obey his decrees and search for him with all their hearts.* His Word increasingly living within draws us nearer and trustfully deeper into His holy Heart. *Help me abandon my shameful ways; your laws are all I want in my life. Do not snatch your Word of truth from me, for my only hope is in your laws. Your promise revives me; it comforts me in all my troubles. I meditate on your age-old laws; O LORD, they comfort me. I reflect on who you are, O LORD, and I obey your laws because of this.* Through God's Word, we come to know Him intimately, bringing prayer in the Name of Jesus, claiming Him for our very own as our only desire, our only hope. Each command and directive of God is given within the Scriptures—that we may know Him, how to live in obedience to Him and be blessed by Him, praying in accordance with His will. *I pondered the direction of my life, and I turned to follow your statutes* (Psalm 119:2,39,43,50-51,55,59). Being able to pray in faith and reach for the blessings of which He awaits to abundantly shower upon those for whom we pray, we must know how to ask appropriately! Knowing Him in His Word brings the ability and desire to ask and live in obedience to His commands, blessing us and those for whom we pray.

God's Word is living and active and He promises it doesn't return to Him void of the purpose for which He sends it forth. Therefore, His living and active Word living within is our absolute key necessity to passionate, powerful, purposeful, lives of prayer. Psalm 119:93,105 inspire the power of His Word; *I will never forget your commandments, for you have used them to restore my joy and health. Your Word is a lamp for my feet and a light for my path.* Knowing and praying His Word brings joy, health and restoration because it always draws us into His persevering Presence, where His good, pleasing and perfect will lays. The Word reminds, *The LORD keeps watch over you as you come and go, both now and forever more* (Psalm 121:8). Read this again, aloud. Does that not comfort, empower and build your desire to know more of the One who does not sleep, but is always watching over?

Isaiah 34:16 says, *Search the book of the LORD, and see what he will do. He will not miss a single detail. For the LORD has promised this, His Spirit will make it all come true.* His Spirit is the Spirit of the Word, of which it was written and of which He sends to teach, speak through and to fulfill. Within His Word and our intimate relationship, we find not only why He created us, but our power in praying in the Name of Jesus; claiming His abundant love and blessings that are realized fully. As the Holy Spirit teaches and leads us to specific verses during prayer and Scripture study, we will grow to know God and hear Him speak personally to us through His Word; which He is waiting to make come to pass in our lives.

He says, regarding Jonah's whining over a withering plant that sheltered him, *You feel sorry about that plant, though you did nothing to put it there. And a plant is only, at best, short lived. But Nineveh has more than 120,000 people living in spiritual darkness. Shouldn't I feel sorry for such a great city?* (Jonah 4:10) Growing to know Him, we understand how His Heart's desire is to free, heal, redeem, restore, and bless those willing to pray and be used for His work. We are encouraged to stop whining about physical circumstances and, instead, see the greater need—God's bigger picture and have His Heart and compassion for those living in spiritual darkness and oppression. His Word enables us to see circumstances through His eyes, thus, finding how to pray about them in His Word.

Hebrews 4:12 (NASB) promises, *The Word of God is living and active.* Let us remember our call to the full armor of God, completed in Ephesians 6:17 (NASB) *and take THE HELMET OF SALVATION, and the sword of the Spirit, which is the Word of God;* putting all into action in verse 18, *praying at all times in the Spirit.* Praying in the Spirit, for the love and sake of Christ, we must use His weapon—the *living and active* tool of the Spirit in prayer, His powerful Word.

His powerful Word, voice and breath bring us faith and joy, and our enemy defeat. Isaiah 30:30-31/31:8 says, *The LORD will make his majestic voice heard. With angry indignation he will bring down his mighty arm on his enemies. It will descend with devouring flames, with cloudbursts, thunderstorms, and huge hailstones, bringing their destruction. At the LORD's command, the Assyrians will be shattered. He will strike them down with his rod. The Assyrians will be destroyed, but not by the swords of men. The Word of God will strike them, and they will panic and flee.* Claiming His promises, power, and protection for His purposes, He abundantly blesses these prayers filled with faith by His love and His powerful, striking Word. Each time we speak His Word, it strikes a blow to the enemy—picture striking the devil or his workers with a double-edged long sword every time God's Word is proclaimed, spoken, and/or prayed—he panics and flees!

David says, *Here I am, I have come as it is written about me in the scroll. I desire to do your will, O my God; your law is within my heart* (Psalm 40:7-8 NIV). His Word brings us into His will, giving us the desire and power to obey. Scriptures take root in our hearts and bring forth the fruit of the Spirit, making us His, and He ours. He promises, *'My purpose will be established, And I will accomplish all My good pleasure; truly I have spoken; truly I will bring it to pass. I have planned it, surely I will do it* (Isaiah 46:10-11 NASB). Prayerfully opening His Word, He speaks, giving direction, blessing, and faith. Knowing exactly what He wants us to ask of Him, we are able to patiently and watchfully wait for our answers with thanksgiving and praise, being empowered by the Spirit to acknowledge His will according to His Word which promises we will receive that which we have asked.

God promises time in memorization of and prayer using His Word will never be in vain. His Word bears fruit, always according to His will. His Word is essential in our hearts and prayers because He is much bigger than our thoughts and words. Isaiah 55:8-11 (NASB) says, *For My thoughts are not your thoughts, nor are your ways My ways. For as the heavens are higher than the earth, so are My ways higher than your ways and My thoughts higher than your thoughts.* Neither He nor His Word will ever fail us. *For as the rain and snow come down from heaven, and do not return without watering the earth and making it bear and sprout, and furnishing seed to the sower and bread to the eater; so will My Word be which goes forth from My mouth; it will not return to me empty, without accomplishing what I desire, and without succeeding in the matter for which I sent it.* God is the furnisher of seed for sowing. Praying by His Spirit and using His Word bears and sprouts amazing and powerful results! He pours out His seeds of salvation, sending forth His rains of righteousness and cleansing holy rivers, making us white as snow. His powerful Word will accomplish His holy purposes sent forth in prayer.

EXERCISE

Ask God to reveal to you in His Word a personal promise. Memorize, pray and proclaim it, live it!

- ➡ What has God revealed to you about Himself, today?
- ➡ Which verse does God want you to ask Him to apply to your life today?
- ➡ For whom does He want you to pray this verse?

LET US PRAY

Fill us with Your Spirit oh King of Kings. May Your Word live, breathing through our hearts and prayers, that we may speak Your promises of divine protection, healing, salvation and abundant blessings. Sanctify our hearts and those for whom we pray. Oh, Lord teach us to pray in Jesus' powerful holy Name we pray, Amen.

Day 27

WORDS OF LIFE
in PRAYER

IIIIIIIIIIIIIIIIIIIIIIIIIIIIIIIIIIIIIIIIIIIIIIIIIIIII

*Through these he has given us his very
great and precious promises.*

— 2 PETER 1:4 NIV —

Scripture contains the Wisdom and Power we need to know Jesus and become holy like Him, defeating satan and breaking through to God's abundant promises. The apostle Peter writes; *Grace and peace be multiplied to you in the knowledge of God and of Jesus our Lord; seeing that His divine power has granted us everything pertaining to life and godliness, through the true knowledge of Him who called us by His own glory and excellence.* Knowing God in His Word better and better brings abundant divine power, with all His grace and peace needed for life and godliness! Knowing Him, He gives Himself to us, allowing us to use His Word to speak, live, and pray with power and authority! *For by these He has granted us His precious and magnificent promises, so that by them you may become partakers of the divine nature, having escaped the corruption that is in the world by lust* (2 Peter 1:2-4 NASB). The divine power of creation, life and His glory, brings us His powerful Word, that we may partake His divine nature and glory. He grants, and we partake.

There is no greater joy, no greater power, and no greater glory than **knowing God, Jesus; our Savior, Teacher, Healer, Promise, King, and Friend.** Our hearts being His, we speak on His behalf, with His divine power and authority. His Heart and power through ours, pleads God's precious promises contained in and through Him, "The Word" into the lives of those for whom He prays. Partaking of His divine nature we know the Word, and He lives in us! His inheritance, power and Kingdom are ours; we rule with Him and for Him; as He rules His kingdom in and through us.

Jesus promises, *My true disciples produce much fruit. This brings great glory to my Father* (John 15:8). Christ gloried in His crucifixion; bringing His Father glory. His ascension brings us into His glory, allowing us to be raised into heavenly places with Him in prayer. He promises, *All that the Father has is mine; this is what I mean when I say that the Spirit will reveal to you whatever he receives from me* (John 16:15). His "true disciples" have access to the Father and all He gives through Christ and His Word. Receiving and knowing His Word, His glory flows from the throne into our hearts, drawing us to The Word, bearing fruit.

2 Peter 1:5 says we must *make every effort to apply the benefits of these promises to your life. Then your faith will produce a life of moral excellence.* Making every effort to apply His promises; applying His Word to our lives brings holiness, and God's glory. Spiritual sickness doesn't glory or benefit God, holiness does. *A life of moral excellence leads to knowing God better.* There is no greater blessing or power than the very holy Presence of God brought forth from the growing knowledge and application of His Word indwelling.

Only the power of the Holy Spirit and prayer combined with His Word bring the work and life of the Spirit. We must always ask the Spirit to reveal and teach, anointing His Word with power. His Holiness demands His empowering. Paul says, *And we will never stop thanking God that when we preached his message to you, you didn't think of the words we spoke as being just our own. You accepted what we said as the very word of God—which of course, it was. And this word continues to work in you who believe* (1 Thessalonians 2:13). Paul spent much of his time ministering to his churches through prayer. His preaching was not done by the flesh, but by the Spirit empowering God's Word into his members' hearts. **God's spoken, anointed Word brings Life!**

In the valley of the dry bones, God tells his prophet to prophecy using His Word; *Then he said to me, "Speak to these bones and say, 'Dry bones, listen to the word of the LORD! This is what the Sovereign LORD says: Look! I am going to breathe into you and make you live again!'"* His spoken Word gave instruction to be used by the prophet. It accomplished the body being formed, yet it had no breath, no power or life. Until He continues; *Then he said to me, "Speak to*

the winds and say… 'Breathe into these dead bodies so that they may live again.'"
So I spoke as he commanded me, and the wind entered the bodies, and they began
to breathe (Ezekiel 37:4-5,9-10). God tells us, too that *gentle words bring life*
and health…a person's words can be a life-giving water; words of wisdom are as
refreshing as a bubbling brook. Words satisfy the soul as food satisfies the stomach;
the right words on a person's lips bring satisfaction…for the tongue can kill or
nourish life (Proverbs 15:4/18:4,20-21). The NASB in 18:21 says, *Death*
and life are in the power of the tongue. How important the Words we speak!
Knowing and using God's Word spoken in prayer and ministering, brings
forth His mighty Spirit to nourish, bring life and health, refresh, satisfy and
breathe new life into our hearts, souls, prayers and His Word.

Prayer opens to door for the Word, and the Word opens our eyes to
pray. His Spirit sent forth by prayer opens the door for us to go forth with
His Word, imparting spiritual blessing. Spending time in His persevering
Presence, being fed by His Word- we decrease and He increases within hearts,
out into our actions. **The fuel of the Spirit—His spoken Word -- ignites**
the passions of the heart and mind, giving firm footing, grace and energy
to the feet carrying the message of the Gospel. 2 Peter 1:10 says, *work*
hard to prove that you really are among those God has called and chosen. Doing
this, you will never stumble or fall away. You will never stumble or fall away!
Surrendering to God's Word and Spirit in our hearts, He commits Himself
to keep us, bears fruit through us and we experience His mighty and precious
promises that reveal Himself; which He uses to bring forth life-to save, heal
and keep!

1 Timothy 2:1-4,8 commands, *pray for all people…plead for God's mercy*
and give thanks. Pray this way…so we can live in peace and quietness, godliness
and dignity. This is good and pleases God our Savior, for he wants everyone to be
saved and to understand the truth…I want men to pray with holy hands lifted up
to God. Praying, and physically living His Word, He saves- pouring out His
spirit of righteousness, salvation and divine understanding; bringing hearts-
Himself. Knowing Him, we're able to please Him, being blessed and bringing
Him glory. Making us holy, hearts and hands are drawn to heaven, lifted in
praise and prayer!

1 John 1:1-2 speaks of our passion, power and purpose of life and prayer,
love and holiness; *the one who existed from the beginning, He is Jesus Christ, the*
Word of life. This one who is life from God was shown to us…we now testify and

announce to you that he is the one who is eternal life. God's Word of life growing from our hearts will burst forth with thanksgiving as well as testimony. To testify of His love we must experience, pray, know and live it.

We will not fall away, for He promises; *we have an Advocate with the Father, Jesus Christ the righteous.* The NIV says He *speaks to the Father in our defense.* Christ's Words bring power, for they are the Word, His Words of life. These are those we must speak, bringing life, healing and Light to an otherwise darkened world, and many darkened hearts. *I am writing a new commandment to you, which is true in Him and in you, because the darkness is passing away and the true Light is already shining. The one who loves his brother abides in the Light and there is no cause for stumbling in him* (1 John 2:8,10 NASB). God's Word shines Light within our hearts, producing love and abiding in Christ, the Word of life, our Light.

Psalm 45:1,2 (NASB) promises a heart made holy in the Word. *My heart overflows with a good theme; I address my verses to the King; My tongue is the pen of a ready writer. Grace is poured upon Your lips; therefore God has blessed You forever.* Did your grandma, like my Grandma Clarol, remind you as a child, "garbage in, garbage out?" Let's be transformed by "God's Word in, powerful praise/prayer out!" God's Word in hearts brings His grace upon lips, blessing upon lives and hearts!

Let's not limit the power of God's Word. God's Word is heavenly, having knowledge power and authority over all. His Word's authority in our hearts gives us His authority in prayer. Jesus spoke only what the Father said; He used His Word in prayer and to minister, all the more must we! His spoken words, to heal, save, keep safe, and keep from sin are the words of creation, promise, life, and sustaining of the Father. Our spoken words in prayer being those of the Father increase our faith, love and knowledge of His holy Heart. Psalm 60:6 testifies, *God has promised this by his holiness.* Discovering He is holy and "true to His Word," we trust His promises to be fulfilled- becoming our hope, truth and power for life and prayer. This is His power, as much as we allow and seek, that receives of His Word and promises in prayer.

Speaking of His covenant promises in prayer gives nourishment to the soul, bringing joy and faith to the heart, renewing flames to the fires of our love for our King and Redeemer. Psalm 24:10 (NIV) says, *Who is he, this King of glory? The LORD Almighty—he is the King of glory.* It's He who promises, *If you listen carefully to the voice of the LORD your God and do what is right in his* eyes...*I will not bring on you any of the diseases I brought on the Egyptian, for I am the LORD, who heals you* (Exodus 15:26 NIV). We don't only read and speak-we are healed as we listen CAREFULLY!

He asks, *I am the LORD, the God of all mankind. Is anything too hard for me?* As He promises who we are, *I will surely gather them...I will bring them back and let them live in safety. They will be my people and I will be their God. I will give them singleness of heart and action so that they will always fear me for their own good and the good of their children. I will make an everlasting covenant with them: I will never stop doing good to them and I will inspire them to fear me* (Jeremiah 37:27,37-41 NIV). **God is waiting to bless, to restore and to heal!** His Spirit and Word inspire the heart and soul to fear and please Him; bringing us good and Him glory. The holiness and prayers of one generation will not stop, but continue for our children! Holiness of heart brings holiness of thought and action, keeping God's revealed Presence and blessing upon cities and generations.

He continues, *I will heal my people and will let them enjoy abundant peace and security. I will bring and will rebuild. I will cleanse them from all the sin they have committed against me. Then this city will bring me renown, joy, praise and honor ...they will be in awe and will tremble at the abundant prosperity and peace I provide for it* (Jeremiah 33:6-9 NIV). My dearest sisters, do you see? Do you believe? Our holy loving God is our God, we are His people. **His will is keeping His promises contained in His Word-bringing Him renown, joy, praise and honor**—returning hearts from foreign lands, healing, blessing, and giving peace and prosperity- that many nations will be in awe at the abundance of His children's inheritance!

We're not to live sickly, feeble, destroyed lives like that of the heathen who have no hope, future, true joy and no provider to answer prayer. Let's bring Him praise; *'give thanks to the LORD, Almighty, for the LORD is good; his love endures forever.'* He promises, *For I will restore their fortunes and have compassion on them. I myself make this promise, declares the LORD.* He waits to restore and to bless as we proclaim His Word and will; *Recently you repented and did what was right in my sight: Each of you proclaimed freedom to his countrymen. You even made a covenant before me in the house that bears my Name* (Jeremiah 33:11,26/34:15,5 NIV). What verse do you need to proclaim for your countrymen? Who in your life, church, and family needs to be freed from sin, returning to their Lord? What in your lives and those you pray for needs to be restored-marriages, prodigal children or mates, health, ministry, relationships, finances? Proclaim His victory aloud today!

Regarding specific prayer requests; praise God, repent for yourself and others, thank Him for the circumstances, then ask Him to lead how He would have you pray specifically. Ask the Spirit to open and reveal to you, in His Word regarding the situation and hearts for which you pray. Write them down, and proclaim them in agreement with Him, knowing His will is to proclaim His love and forgiveness, repentance, restoration, redemption, rebuilding and to revive that His children will live in obedience to His Word bringing Him glory-and in the faith that nothing is impossible for Him. Do not stop praying, until you have that which He promises!

His Word, Spirit and prayer, His holiness promises, restores and heals, bringing His Presence. His purpose to dwell in the holy city, says, *Now the dwelling of God is with men, and he will live with them. They will be his people, and God himself will be with them and be their God…he will wipe every tear…no more death, mourning, crying, or pain* (Revelation 21:3-4 NIV). Do you see God's Heart's desires are to dwell with us bringing joy, removing tears, mourning and pain? His holy Presence requires holy hearts humbled in prayer. Bring Him your tears, mourning, and pain. His Presence restores your joy and peace, bringing new life to that which was dead- to that which you mourn. Thus, we do not go before or behind, but **walk with Him**. Isaiah 40:31 also promises, *but those who wait on the LORD will find new strength. They will fly high on wings like eagles. They will run and not grow weary. They will walk and not grow faint.* Walking with Him, according to His Word and Spirit we run and walk without weariness, we mount on the wings of eagles and soar to the heights of the heavens on the mighty winds of the Lord- to dwell **with Him.**

EXERCISE

Write down anything in your life that seems impossible. Is there anything you believe is too hard for the LORD? Repent, then continue in His heavenly Strength to stand firm on His Promises to you! Remember, your answers are already accomplished spiritually in the heavenly realms; you are just waiting to experience them physically here in earth.

•❖ What has God revealed to you about Himself, today?

•❖ Which verse does God want you to ask Him to apply to your life today?

•❖ For whom does He want you to pray this verse?

LET US PRAY

Glorious, holy Father God, we bring You glory, honor praise and thanksgiving in the Name of Jesus. Oh, Lord, teach us to pray and live Your Word with all hope in Your Heart's desires to heal, restore and save. In the precious all-powerful Name of Jesus and His blood, we pray, Amen.

Day 28

POWER in PRAYING HIS WORD

||||||||||||||||||||||||||||||||||||||||||||||||||||

Rather, worship the LORD your God; it is he who
will deliver you from the hand of all your enemies.

— 2 KINGS 17:39 NIV —

God's mighty power contained in His Word delivers us and those for whom we pray from the hand of the enemy, blessing according to His will. God's Word is at work within us by the power of the Holy Spirit. His Word working within us allows Him to accomplish that which is His will. Hosea 1:7 (NIV) says, *Yet I will show love…I will save them—not by bow, sword or battle, or by horses and horsemen, but by the LORD their God.* His Word gives instruction, direction, devotion, life, wisdom and fear of the Lord, enabling us to praise through to His saving victory.

Hosea 14:2-3 (NIV) tells us to *Return to the LORD…take words with you and return to the LORD. Say to him: forgive all our sins and receive us graciously, that we may offer the fruit of our lips. Assyria cannot save us; we will not mount war-horses.* Praying His Word reveals the condition of the heart and brings repentance, preparing the way for the Lord. His Word shows His will, bringing the faith to wait, ask, and receive and going only when sent. Jesus says, *Nourishment comes from doing the will of God, who sent me, and from finishing his work* (John 4:34). Seeking God's will in His Word nourishes us so that we may find and complete that which He has sent us to do.

Praying His Word empowers and humbles; it gentles and quiets the soul, bringing us into the Heart and mind of God. Remaining in Him, His Word within our hearts, our desires and wishes will be those heaven-sent. **Our hearts and prayers begin to show His Heart's desires for us.** Our Teacher promises, *All things have been handed over to me... nor does anyone know the Father except the Son, and anyone to whom the Son wills to reveal Him...learn from Me, for I am gentle and humble in heart, and you will find rest for your souls* (Matthew 11:27,29 NASB). Relying upon Him and His Word for all things gives the strength to surrender to Him, that we become like Him. Praying Scripture gives us rest, handing our burdens to Him, with His promise to be given whatever we wish. His teaching brings forth obedience and faith, enabling God to do His work, and showing us ours, empowered and brought forth by prayer.

Praying God's Word enables our hearts to obey His greatest commandments of love, and to carry out the great commission. His mighty Word must be received as His truth, then sent forth with His Spirit to bear fruit. John 3:27 says, *God in heaven appoints each persons work.* To be blessed by heaven, must come from heaven first. Scripture reveals and sends His anointing, His Truth, Spirit, love and the power to heal and to free. Throughout the gospel of John, Jesus spoke and people were healed, sent, commissioned and God's love was revealed. John 4:23 says, *For God is Spirit, so those who worship him must worship in spirit and truth.* God's love and Truth revealed in the Word, our Teacher, and sent forth with the power of the Spirit, enables us to worship God in truth and spirit that we may know, love and serve Him.

Praying His Word prepares the heart for His passions, the mind for His wisdom and revelation, the feet to walk in His Presence, and the body and soul to live and pray for His purposes. Mark 1:2-3 (KJV) says, *Behold, I send my messenger before thy face, which shall prepare thy way before thee...Prepare ye the way of the Lord.* A missionary thanking me for Specific Scripture prayer one day said, "Prayer is the airplane that goes before us into the country, making the pathway safe before we land, and prepares the hearts to be saved." We don't go forth, asking God to bless our plans; we receive instruction and blessing that we may walk forth into His prepared hearts and plans — His victories He secured at the Cross!

For Jesus says, *No one can come to me unless the Father who sent me draws him. It is written, 'They will be taught by God.' Everyone who listens to the Father and learns from him comes to me* (John 6:44-45 NIV). Let us listen, praying and speaking God's Word, as Jesus did . He says, *I have much to say about you and much to condemn, but I won't. For I say only what I have heard from the one who sent me, and he is true* (John 8:26). Can we say our speech is not condemning, but only the words God wants us to speak? The mouth and heart that prays must also speak God's Words in communication with others. His Words of truth give freedom to hearts and lives. He promises, *If you continue in My Word, then you are truly disciples of Mine; and you will know the truth, and the truth will make you free* (John 8:31-32 NASB). We do not rely upon our words in witnessing or prayer, but on the Word and power of God, empowering, sending, preparing, drawing, teaching, judging, freeing, healing and restoring. His Word, continued in, makes free!

Praying God's Word takes us beyond the cares of, and into the praises of the day no matter the outlook. It is in His Word, knowing, speaking and doing, that we find Him, His Heart of holiness and ours. Jesus speaks of the Word in our hearts in Luke 8:15 (KJV), *But that on the good ground...an honest and good heart, having heard the Word, keep it, and bring forth fruit with patience.* God's Word brings forth the fruits of repentance, salvation, righteousness, patience and holiness. The words of the flesh bear the fruits of death, division and destruction. His Word abiding and reigning in hearts bear Kingdom fruit!

Jesus has given us these—His Words that He may complete His work in the hearts for which we pray, and ours. He prays aloud, *I come to You; and these things I speak in the world so that they may have My joy made full in themselves. I have given them Your Word...Sanctify them in the truth; Your Word is truth* (John 17:13-14). We find when we worship, live and pray in truth and spirit, the words we pray for others sanctify our hearts first, making us holy. Let us pray for the spirit of holiness to work mightily within hearts, that He may work mightily through prayers. His spirit of wisdom and revelation by the Holy Spirit who lives within, gives wisdom and understanding so that we may effectively pray His Word in our prayers. Examining the Scriptures and meditating upon them, the Holy Spirit will impress upon our hearts specific Scripture verses to claim and proclaim regarding certain needs and for specific answers to prayer into the lives of those for whom we pray. Let us be made holy, that we may proclaim, blessing the name of the Lord!

EXERCISE

Speak the following aloud and obey, as He guides your heart into His holiness:

COMMANDS: (all NIV).

♦ **Psalm 27:14** *Wait for the LORD; be strong and take heart and wait for the LORD.*

♦ **Matthew 26:41** *Watch and pray that you do not fall into temptation. The spirit is willing, but the body is weak.*

♦ **Ephesians 5:18** *Do not get drunk on wine, which leads to debauchery. Instead, be filled with the Spirit.*

♦ **Ephesians 6:10,18** *Finally, be strong in the Lord and in his mighty power. And pray in the Spirit on all occasions with all kinds of prayer and requests. With this in mind, be alert and always keep on praying for all the saints.*

♦ **Colossians 4:2** *Devote yourselves to prayer, being watchful and thankful.*

♦ **1 Thessalonians 5:16-18** *Be joyful always; pray continually; give thanks in all circumstances, for this is God's will for you in Christ Jesus.*

♦ **1 Timothy 2:8** *I want men everywhere to lift up holy hands in prayer, without anger or disputing.*

Let our hearts repent, preparing the way, so that we may seek Him, receiving His Presence and promises, in Scripture. Let us watch and wait thankfully for Him to do that which He desires. **LET US SPEAK WITH FAITH THAT WHICH HE WILL DO IN OUR HEARTS, LIVES & PRAYERS:**

PROMISES: (all NIV).

♦ **Exodus 33:17-19** *And the LORD said to Moses, "I will do the very thing you have asked, because I am pleased with you and I know you by name." Then Moses said, "Now show me your glory." And the LORD said, "I will cause my goodness to pass in front of you, and I will proclaim my name, the LORD in your presence..."*

♦ **Jeremiah 33:3** *"'Call to me and I will answer you and tell you great and unsearchable things you do not know.'"*

♦ **Isaiah 61:1** *The Spirit of the Sovereign LORD is on me, because the LORD has anointed me to preach good news to the poor. He has sent me to bind up the brokenhearted, to proclaim freedom for the captives and release from darkness for the prisoners.*

♦ **Isaiah 65:24** *"Before they call I will answer; while they are still speaking I will hear."*

♦ **Jeremiah 29:11-13** *"For I know the plans I have for you," declares the LORD, "plans to prosper you and not to harm you, plans to give you hope and a future. Then you will call upon me and come and pray to me, and I will listen to you. You will seek me and find me when you seek me with all your heart."*

♦ **Matthew 18:19-20** *"Again I tell you that if two of you agree about anything you ask for, it will be done for you by my Father in heaven. For where two or three come together in my name, there I am with them."*

♦ **Luke 11:9-10** *"So I say to you: Ask and it will be given to you; seek and you will find; knock and the door will be opened to you. For everyone who asks receives; he who seeks finds; and to him who knocks, the door will be opened."*

♦ **Luke 11:13** *"If you then, though you are evil, know how to give good gifts to your children, how much more will your Father in heaven give the Holy Spirit to those who ask him!"*

♦ **John 16:23** *"I tell you the truth, my Father will give you whatever you ask in my name."*

♦ **Romans 8:37** *No, in all these things we are more than conquerors through him who loved us.*

♦ **Romans 12:2** *Do not conform any longer to the pattern of this world, but be transformed by the renewing of your mind. Then you will be able to test and approve what God's will is—his good, pleasing, and perfect will.*

♦ **Philippians 4:4,6-7** *Rejoice in the Lord always…Do not be anxious about anything, but in everything…with thanksgiving, present your requests to God. And the peace of God, which transcends all understanding will guard your hearts and your minds in Christ Jesus.*

- **Hebrews 7:25** *Therefore he is able to save completely those who come to God through him, because he always lives to intercede for them.*

- **1 John 5:14-15** *This is the confidence we have in approaching God: that if we ask anything according to his will, he hears us. And if we know that he hears us—whatever we ask—we know that we have what we asked of him.*

➥ What has God revealed to you about Himself, today?

➥ Which verse does God want you to ask Him to apply to your life today?

➥ For whom does He want you to pray this verse?

LET US PRAY

We worship You Jesus, the Name above all names our Lord, our Savior and our Salvation. Forgive us, Oh heavenly Father, for not surrendering ourselves to the authority of Jesus. Oh, Lord, teach us to pray Your Word, allowing You to pray through us; the prayers that will be answered by the Father in Your power and Your Spirit. In Jesus' precious, perfect, glorious, holy Name we pray, Amen.

(For an entire book of powerful Scripture prayers; please see my book, **Alphabet Prayers...the Power of Praying Scripture into the Hearts You Love...for Your Husband, Children, and Pastor.**) Please also check back frequently on www.heartsofprayer.com for future publications, including that of a Personal Scripture Prayer Journal with over 1000 Scripture prayer verses compiled into 31 days of various areas of prayer-needs.

Day 29

FAITH to OBEY in PRAYER

|||||||||||||||||||||||||||||||||||||||||||||||||||||||

I call with all my heart; answer me,
O LORD, and I will obey your decrees.

— PSALM 119:145 NIV —

Our obedience to God is dependent upon our desire to call out to Him and rely upon Him to answer. Our obedience is possible, primarily, because of Christ's obedience for us, His death on the Cross. It is one of the many mysteries of God that He enables us to obey Him as we ask, yet we, too, are responsible for obediently responding to His commands and answers to our prayers. James 1:22,25 exhorts, *Remember it is a message to obey, not just to listen to…if you keep looking steadily into God's perfect law—the law that sets you free—and if you do what it says and don't forget what you heard, then God will bless you for doing it.* We not only listen to the perfect laws, we keep looking, continuing in His ways because doing so sets us free and brings Him glory. To those who obey Him, He gives the honor to serve and know Him intimately. Searching intently into His law, we search for Him, our freedom and blessing Giver. Obedience frees us from sin, heartache, fear, and failure, freeing us to be who God wants us to be in Christ, enabling us to do that which is His purpose for us. God requires obedience and always blesses it!

God's love and grace growing in our hearts brings forth our obedience and love for His laws and ways. Psalm 119:163-167 promises, *Those who love your law have great peace and do not stumble. I long for your salvation, LORD, so I have obeyed your commands. I have obeyed your decrees, and I love them very much.* The more His love flows through, controlling emotion and action, the greater obedience to and love for His laws we shall have.

Obedience to our Father keeps us under His protective care, where He promises we will not stumble! Disobedience causes pain while obedience brings blessing and sure footing. He promises, *I the LORD, will punish…who set up idols in their hearts so they fall into sin…I will do this to capture the minds and hearts of all my people who have turned away…in this way the people will learn not to stray from me, polluting themselves with sin* (Ezekiel 14:4-5,11). **God's holiness allows sin to cause pain, directing us away from it and back into blessing.**

Let us pray He will do **whatever it takes** to capture the minds and hearts of His people who have turned away, bringing forth His will and blessing. Let us cry out with David, *Remember your covenant promises, for the land is full of darkness and violence! Arise, O God and defend your cause* (Psalm 74:20,22). It is a mystery still even deeper that we are responsible to ask and obey when He moves in answer to prayer and moves us to ask and obey. But, most importantly, He defends and fulfills His cause as we, in obedience to His commands, pray and receive that we may obey!

God desires us to live in obedience to His Word that we may worship Him and remain in His Presence and blessing. *I said this so I could keep my promise…to give you a land flowing with milk and honey.* Those in disobedience lose the honor of worshipping God and the splendor of His holiness. *What right do my beloved people have to come to my temple, where they have done so many immoral things?* (Jeremiah 11:5,15). We do not lose His love when we don't obey, but the blessing of worship and His holy Presence.

Notice, too, these evil practices to which He refers are in His Temple; we are now that temple. 1 Corinthians 6:19 reminds, *Don't you know your body is the temple of the Holy Spirit, who lives in you and was given to you by God? You do not belong to yourself.* Obedience is required of His children because we are His holy Temple; He dwells within, for we are His. He does not leave as He did in Old Testament times but we can either allow Him full access to our hearts through obedience, or we stifle His Spirit by disobedience. He commands we let no sin or idols in His sanctuary of our hearts. Ezekiel 44:2-3 (NASB) says, *This gate shall be shut…and no one shall enter by it, for the LORD God has entered by it…he shall sit in it as prince to eat bread before the*

LORD. Our obedience is the bread for our King; He returns in proportion to our surrender of His reign within.

As my wonderful teacher and Pastor Julian Riddle warns, we mustn't turn God's grace, into dis-grace! We cannot believe the carefree attitude that we are human and will sin anyway, living in disobedience and taking no responsibility for our actions and choices. We are accountable for the obedience in our lives, or lack of it. We are commanded to no longer sin as the Holy Spirit of Christ lives within. We were purchased at a great sacrifice and are commanded to be holy, to love God with all our hearts, souls, minds and strength and to honor God with our bodies. Because Christ denied Himself and remained in obedience to our Father all the way to the Cross, God shall not deny us in Presence or prayer. Because Christ surrendered to God's will, so may we. **Power and favor with God, joy and praise, are born from obedience to, love for and faith in Him.**

2 Corinthians 7:1-2 commands, *Let us cleanse ourselves from all defilement of flesh and spirit, perfecting holiness in the fear of God…make room for us in your hearts.* Holy hearts living in obedience make room within for more of the abiding riches and power of Christ's love and generosity for our brethren. As Christ died, giving His all to us and lives ever interceding for man by God's grace, this, too, shall be our experience.

Paul states, *Now He who supplies seed to the sower and bread for food will supply and multiply your seed for sowing and increase the harvest of your righteousness; you will be enriched in everything for all liberality…producing thanksgiving to God…they will glorify God for your obedience* (2 Corinthians 9:10,13). Obedient hearts entrusted with the seeds of righteousness give and bring glory and praise to God when faithful with what they are given. Obedience opens the pathway for ever-increasing seeds to be sown, righteousness to be harvested through prayer and deed, and Christ's riches ever pouring out from heaven.

1 John 2:3,5-6 (NASB) says, *We know that we have come to know Him, if we keep His commandments.* Our true knowledge of the One abiding within is proved by obedience to Him. *Whoever keeps His Word, in him the love of God has truly been perfected.* To know Him is truly to have His love perfected within; obedience bearing the fruit of love. *By this we know that we are in Him: the one who says he abides in Him ought himself to walk in the same manner as He walked.* Obedience is simply walking in God's path with love, and abiding

by His will. Obedience brings our feet to spring forth to walk the prayers and love in our hearts. Many say obedience is a thing of the past—let us find the ancient way. Jeremiah 6:16 (NIV) says, *Stand at the crossroads and look; ask for the ancient paths, ask where the good way is, and walk in it, and you will find rest for your souls.* Our lives must be a continuous stream of obedience, standing, looking, asking, and walking in the way He leads, finding rest for the soul!

Living in God means living in His Truth and love and being in obedience to Him. This, not for our own benefit alone, but for that of the church. 2 John 1:1-2 says, *As does everyone else who knows God's truth—the truth that lives in us and will be in our hearts forever.* Christ's truth lives and intercedes within our hearts for the church, and so shall we in obedient lives. 2 John 1:6 commands, *Love means doing what God has commanded us, and he has commanded us to love one another.* God's greatest command of love is shown in obedience and born out of Him dwelling within. Walking in the Light of His glory in prayer, He brings us into obedience that He may bless us in accordance with His will.

Continuing to pray His Word, learning that He desires we live in His promised abundance of power, answered prayers, and blessings, our faith shall grow and our obedient, willing hearts walking in His truth and knowing His good and perfect will shall be fulfilled. Psalm 37:30-31,37 (KJV) promises, *The mouth of the righteous speaketh wisdom. The law of God is in his heart; none of his steps shall slide. Mark the perfect man, and behold the upright; for the end of that man is peace.* God blesses obedience with firm footing as we walk, our end being peace. God's Heart's desires are to bless His children with His holiness, bringing forth peace, joy and wisdom. His salvation is not to be accepted and thrown aside, but to be obediently walked in.

Trusting and obeying God, regardless of the circumstance or length of time He takes to answer us, gives Him great honor and brings us great blessing. Let our mouths confess, *Your goodness is so great! You have stored up great blessings for those who honor you. You have done so much for those who come to you for protection, blessing them before the world. You hide them in the shelter of your presence, safe from those who conspire against them. Be strong and take courage, all you who put your hope in the LORD!* (Psalm 31:19-20). We shall obey Him as much as our hope and courage are from Him and in Him. Hearts and feet in perfect obedience, sheltered in Him, open the keys to His storehouse of great blessings to poured out from His throne.

Psalm 18:16,24 says, *He reached down from heaven and rescued me; he drew me out of deep waters. The LORD rewarded me for doing right, because of the innocence of my hands in his sight. To the faithful you show yourself faithful; to those with integrity you show integrity.* Confidence in His Spirit within His law and His faithfulness allows us to obediently wait for only heaven-sent desires and movement.

As much as our hearts are ready to receive and give to heaven, He is ready to pour out and return! Psalm 19:7-9 says, *The law of the LORD is perfect, reviving the soul. The commandments of the LORD are right, bringing joy to the heart. The commands of the LORD are clear, giving insight to life. Reverence for the LORD is pure…the laws of the LORD are true.* Hearts believing His Word will joyfully and speedily obey it, bringing forth reverence for Him and blessing in the Light of His Presence. We must not lag behind or jump ahead, but wait and obey. Let us confess our lack of faithfulness and obedience and wait upon Him, that He may bless! He commands in Malachi 3:7,10, *You have scorned my laws and failed to obey them. Now return to me, and I will return to you…bring all the tithes into the storehouse so there will be enough food in my temple. If you do, says the LORD Almighty, I will open the windows of heaven for you. I will pour out a blessing so great you won't have enough room to take it in! Try it! Let me prove it to you!* Let us repent anything withheld from heaven and give it freely: our hearts, service, money, time, resources. He freely gives an abundance; we will not even have enough room for all He pours out from His storehouses in heaven in return for our devotion to Him!

EXERCISE

Ask God to increase your faith and love, your wisdom and knowledge of Jesus Christ; that you may joyfully obey His plans for you. Take a "leap of faith" today, obey His prompting to do, or begin something you can do only with His help!

- ❧ What has God revealed to you about Himself, today?
- ❧ Which verse does God want you to ask Him to apply to your life today?
- ❧ For whom does He want you to pray this verse?

LET US PRAY

Holy, wonderful, faithful Father God. Oh, Lord, teach us to obey You joyfully, giving our all in prayer, and receiving Yours! Convict our hearts of any disobedience in attitude, word, or deed—or lack thereof. Oh, Lord, teach us to pray… In Jesus' powerful and precious Name we pray, Amen.

Day 30

RECEIVING in PRAYER

||||||||||||||||||||||||||||||||||||||||||||||||

*And we receive from him anything we ask, because
we obey His commands and do what pleases him.*

— 1 John 3:22 NIV —

We overcome the evils of this world and have anything, yes anything, we ask for, obeying God and doing what pleases Him. We are to obey the Voice of God, the will and Word of God, and the Presence of God—Jesus and His Holy Spirit. We are also to obey our conscience, which is our God-given safety feature within us agreeing with His will and each and every command God has given us in His Word. As God fills to overflowing with His rivers of righteousness and love, we hear His Voice with tender consciences, receiving power, direction and blessing because He hears ours.

John 10:31 (KJV) promises, *We know that God heareth not sinners, but if any man be a worshipper of God, and doeth his will, him he heareth.* God hears those who do His will. Remembering *this is the confidence that we have in him, that if we ask any thing according to his will, he heareth us: and if we know that he hears us, whatsoever we ask, we know that we have the petitions that we desired of him* (1 John 5:14-15 KJV). Asking within obedience, we have the passion necessary to bring prayers with confidence of His hearing and our having.

His Spirit pours out the faith and patience necessary to worship Him and do His will until we receive what we have asked for. Obedience brings the persevering and praising power to release the answers waiting to be showered upon earth from heaven and the wisdom and understanding to pray for God's purposes and His will. As we obey His commands, He shall delight in showering upon us His love, grace and His blessings, especially the most precious of gifts, His Holy Spirit—leading to abundant and blessed lives of prayer.

1 John 5:18-19,21 brings courage and instruction to the heart to obey, *We know that those who have become part of God's family do not make a practice of sinning.* Not yet perfect, we are becoming holy, making it not our "practice" to sin. *For God's Son holds them securely, and the evil one cannot get his hands on them...the world around us is under the power and control of the evil one.* We must expect the world and the heathen to be rebellious and evil; they are under the devil's control but we are not! He cannot touch us, lest we allow it. *Keep away from anything that might take God's place in your hearts.* Obedience keeps us far from those things continually trying to take God's rightful place. He must remain our one and only love that we remain in His hand, favored, blessed and heard—receiving in prayer!

He says, *Loving God means keeping his commandments, and really, that isn't difficult. For every child of God defeats this evil world by trusting Christ to give the victory. And the ones who win this battle against the world are the ones who believe that Jesus is the Son of God* (1 John 5:3-5). Our victory is secure, the battle is won, in Jesus' Hand—when we walk, as He did, in perfect obedience, we walk in His victory. This promise is secure threefold, *There are three that bear record in heaven, the Father, the Word, and the Holy Ghost: and these three are one. And there are three that bear witness in earth, the Spirit, and the water, and the blood: and these three agree in one* (1 John 5:7-8 KJV). **Let us, too, speak in agreement, "every child of God overcomes evil and obeys by trusting Christ!"**

Jesus promises obedience and ushers in the indwelling of His Spirit, *All those who love me will do what I say. My Father will love them, and we will come to them and live with them. The prince of this worlds approaches. He has no power over me, but I will do what the Father requires of me, so that the world will know that I love the Father* (John 14:23,30-31). In His school of prayer, He invites us to walk daily with Him to the garden at Gethsemane, humbling our hearts and wills to the Father, receiving His grace and glory to obey; overcoming the enemy by sacrificing self, nailing our human earthly passions and desires to the Cross and walking forth empowered by the Holy Spirit in obedience to our Father's desires. In this way, we show the world our love for

Him and His power within us.

John 10:3-4,10 reminds us how our heavenly Teacher and Shepherd loves, cares for and guides us, *The gatekeeper opens the gate…the sheep hear his voice and come to him. He calls his own sheep by name and leads them out…he walks ahead of them, and they follow him because they recognize his voice.* We obey, because we know His voice; He abides within giving peace, joy and the grace to follow and obey. Prayer will open the gates only our gatekeeper can open, leading His children to Him; let us obey, let us pray!

Obedience allows hearts to be humbled and made holy, flooded with the Light of His Presence. As the bright summer sun warms the entire body, basking in His holiness our body, soul and spirit will be flooded with His holy fires. 1 John 1:5-7 promises, *God is light and there is no darkness in him at all. We are lying if we say we have fellowship with God but go on living in spiritual darkness…if we are living in the light of God's presence, just as Christ is, then we have fellowship with each other. And the blood of Jesus, his Son, cleanses from every sin.* Fellowship with God and Christ in their Light brings the fellowship of His church, blessing, love, prayer, encouragement and holiness for all. We are saved to pray, being made holy to serve, not for self, but as Christ, for all.

Scripture says**,** *When they saw him, they worshipped him…and Jesus spake unto them, saying, All power is given unto me…Go ye therefore, and teach all nations, baptizing them in the name of the Father, and of the Son, and of the Holy Ghost: teaching them to observe all things whatsoever I have commanded…I am with you always, even unto the end of the world. Amen* (Matthew 28:17-20 KJV). The obedient, serving heart receives His power to go, passion for His commission and His Presence in worship, teaching others observation and obedience to His Word and baptizing them in His Name. In obedience, He is with us always and everywhere He sends us!

Trusting and loving God sacrificially, we also joyfully obey all those over us even when we don't agree with them personally; knowing God is Sovereign and allows our circumstances in Him to His glory and our good. In prayer, we realize that He is first changing our hearts within through outer circumstances and only then can He change our outer circumstances When we find ourselves struggling to obey anyone in authority over us, we must repent and surrender, trusting God.

Philippians 2:2 commands, *Make me truly happy by agreeing wholeheartedly with each other, loving one another, and working together with one heart and one purpose.* Prayerfully submitting with thankful hearts for one purpose, we see all with an eternal perspective, letting go of the desire to get our own way and bringing forth God's ways and will. Obedience trusts God's omnipotence and sovereignty knowing in Romans 8:28 (NIV), He promises, *In all things God works for the good of those that love Him and are called according to His purposes.*

Obedience allows Him to work out His purposes and plans in our hearts, prayers and lives, for our good and His glory! He promises, *For those God foreknew he also predestined to be conformed to likeness of his Son. He who did not spare his own Son...how will he not also, along with him, graciously give us all things?* (Romans 8:29,32 NIV). Obedience to His abiding holiness and powerful love conforms us to the image of His Son. He provides the grace and desire to obey, along with all things!

EXERCISE

Let's prayerfully explore how God desires to reward obedience with His love, Presence, and blessings (all NIV):

Circle what we are commanded to do and put a box around His promised blessing:

♦ **Deuteronomy 7:9** *Know therefore that the LORD your God is God; he is the faithful God, keeping his covenant of love to a thousand generations of those who love Him and keep his commands.*

♦ **Deuteronomy 4:40** *Keep his decrees and commands, which I am giving you today, so that it may go well with you and your children after you.*

♦ **Deuteronomy 7:12-14** *If you pay close attention to these laws and are careful to follow them...He will love you and bless you and increase your numbers. He will bless the fruit of your womb, the crops of your land-your grain, new wine and oil... You will be blessed more than any other people.*

♦ **Deuteronomy 15:4-6,10** *However, there should be no poor among you, for in the land the LORD your God is giving you to posses as your inheritance, he will richly bless you, if only you fully obey the LORD your God and are careful to follow all these commands I am giving you today. For the LORD your God will bless you as he has promised, and you will lend to many nations but borrow from none. You will rule over many nations but none will rule over* you. Give generously to him and do so without a grudging heart; then because of this the LORD your God will bless you in all your work and in everything you put your hand to.

♦ **Deuteronomy 5:6-21,29** *(KJV). I am the LORD thy God which brought thee out…from the house of bondage. Thou shalt have no other gods before me. Thou shalt not make thee any graven image. Thou shalt not take the name of the LORD thy God in vain. Keep the Sabbath day and sanctify it…in it thou shalt not do any work. Honour thy father and mother…that thy days may be prolonged, and that it may go well with thee. Thou shalt not kill. Neither shalt thou commit adultery. Neither shalt thou steal…bear false witness against thy neighbor…desire thy neighbor's wife… covet thy neighbor's house. O that there were such a heart in them, that they would fear me, and keep all my commandments always, that it might be well with them, and with their children forever!*

♦ **Joshua 1:8/3:5** *Do not let this Book of the Law depart from your mouth; meditate on it day and night, so that you may be careful to do everything written in it. Then you will be prosperous and successful. Consecrate yourselves, for tomorrow the LORD will do amazing things among you.*

♦ **2 Chronicles 16:9** *For the eyes of the LORD range throughout the earth to strengthen those whose hearts are fully committed to him.*

♦ **Acts 6:4,7** *(KJV). We will give ourselves continually to prayer, and to the ministry of the Word. And the Word of God increased; and the number of disciples multiplied greatly; and a great company of the priests were obedient to the faith.*

♦ **Acts 10:44/11:15-17** *While Peter was still speaking these words, the Holy Spirit came on all who heard the message. "As I began to speak, the Holy Spirit came on them…I remembered what the Lord had said: 'John baptized with water, but you will be baptized with the Holy Spirit.' God gave them the same gift he gave to us, who believed in the Lord Jesus Christ."*

♦ **Philippians 2:8-9,12-13** *He humbled himself and became obedient to death—even death on a cross! Therefore God exalted him to the highest place and gave him the name that is above every name. Therefore…as you have always obeyed…continue to work out your salvation with fear and trembling, for it is God who works in you to will and to act according to his good purpose.*

•◦ What has God revealed to you about Himself, today?

•◦ Which verse does God want you to ask Him to apply to your life today?

•◦ For whom does He want you to pray this verse?

LET US PRAY

Gracious, holy, amazing, heavenly Father. We thank you for Your Word and our understanding of it, applying it in our prayers and desiring to apply it to our lives bringing glory to Your Name. We praise You for Your commands. Forgive where we have failed to listen, meditate upon and obey them, grieving Your Spirit. Bless us with Your courage, power, conviction, wisdom and protection as we obey You sacrificially and joyfully. In Jesus' powerful and precious Name we pray, Amen.

Day 31

ABIDING in CHRIST

||||||||||||||||||||||||||||||||||||||||||||||||||||||||||||||||||||||||||||||||||||||||||||||||

Remain in me, and I will remain in you. Neither
can you bear fruit unless you remain in me.

— JOHN 15:4 NIV —

Abiding in Christ's love, with Him in us, bears the fruitful lives of prayer God desires to bless us with. A victorious, Christian life and ministry always stems from a victorious prayer life with Christ as its strength. John 15:5 promises, *Yes, I am the vine; you are the branches. Those who remain in me, and I in them, will produce much fruit. For apart from me you can do nothing.* Lack of abiding is why there is much unanswered prayer and Christians falling away from their faith, being held captive by the enemy and appearing no different from the unsaved. Abiding in Christ is imperative for God's power and His glory.

Fruitful lives of prayer are only born out of abiding in our glorious Lord and Savior, Jesus Christ. He is our power, love and glory. Apart from Him, all we do is powerless and meaningless. Fruitful lives depend upon prayer and prayer depends upon the abiding of Christ. John 15:8 says, *My true disciples produce much fruit. This brings great glory to my Father.* Abiding, fruitful prayer lives bring glory to our Father. We ask, and He pours out His glory, nourishing with His rivers of Living water to bear much fruit through His children.

Abiding simply yields fully to His Spirit within, remaining in His powerful love. He promises, *When you obey me, you remain in my love, just as I obey the Father and remain in his love. I have told you this so that you will be filled with my joy. Yes, your joy will overflow.* Holy hearts abide in Christ and receive abundantly, overflowing with His joy! *You didn't choose me. I chose you. I appointed you to go and produce fruit that will last, so that the Father will give you whatever you ask for, using my name* (John 15:10-11,16). He has chosen and appointed each of us to go and produce heavenly, eternal fruit.

As fruit-bearers, we use His Name in prayer, living in Him and being given all we ask! Many will serve for a while on their own, bearing some fake fruit and getting discouraged. Failure is promised without the abiding in Christ; victory is secured only with His abiding power. John 16:24 promises again, *Ask, using my name, and you will receive, and you will have abundant joy.* Oh, are you seeing His desire to abundantly bless our hearts with His joy and peace, remaining in His Presence? Do you see how He intends to answer prayer for the obedient heart, abiding and growing in His love?

The ways of our world deceive, saying it is important to have a lot of stuff; be powerful and independent. Scripture says, *I am the true Vine, and my Father is the Gardner. He cuts off every branch that doesn't produce fruit, and he prunes the branches that do bear fruit so they will produce even more* (John 15:1-2). We must in prayer and dependence, be cleansed and pruned; that in growth we may become like our Teacher the Vine, who tells us, *I don't speak on my own authority. The Father who sent me gave me his own instructions as to what I should say. And I know his instructions lead to eternal life; so I say whatever the Father tells me to say!* (John 12:49-50). All that is not of God in our hearts, lives and prayers will be removed, that we will say and do only that which is our Father's will. Our prayers and desires, as Jesus', are filled with divine instruction and Word from the throne. This may be uncomfortable, and this wood (our words or actions) may even seem useful, yet our heavenly Gardener knows best what is purposeful, and what isn't, for each personally, in His Kingdom.

The job of a grapevine is to nourish the branches, bringing forth fruit from the nourishment of the sap. The branch needs only remain attached to the vine, drawing and receiving the sap flowing through, bringing forth fruit that grows naturally. Christ frees us to receive the grace to bear fruit and remain within. Paul says, *If you are trying to make yourselves right with God by keeping the law, you have been cut off from Christ! You have fallen away from God's grace. But we who live by the Spirit eagerly wait to receive everything promised to us who are right with God through faith* (Galatians 5:4-5). Faith remains abiding, not concerned with doing or earning, but with receiving. God's grace and mercy flow through His branches, receiving its blessing from the throne alone.

Any branch with resistance, even partially, to the Vine's sap, eventually hardens and dies, being unable to flourish, unless its hardness (in our case, sin) is removed for the nourishment to flow through. Then it may be mended or grafted back in. Galatians 6:9 encourages, *Don't get tired of doing what is good. Don't get discouraged and give up, for we will reap a harvest of blessing at the appropriate time.* Discouraged branches bearing no fruit are dying and useless to the Gardener; they are cut off and removed so as not to hinder the growth of the fruitful branches that reap a harvest of blessing in God's appropriate time!

Hearts abiding and waiting in the heavenly Vine delight in Him, His ways, and His Word, inheriting His blessings and becoming the channel through which He pours out unto men from heaven. Psalm 27:14/37:7/32:8 (NIV) tell us, *Wait for the LORD; be strong and take heart and wait for the LORD. Be strong and take heart, all you who hope in the LORD. You are my hiding place; you will protect me from trouble and surround me with songs of deliverance.* A branch "waiting" is nourished and filled, bearing fruit and is given all through prayer. Psalm 37:4 (NIV) promises, *Delight yourself in the LORD and he will give you the desires of your heart.* That which dwells and flows within is always worked without. Abiding hearts resting in Christ are guarded, filled, taught and blessed in waiting.

Abiding in our Vine brings strength, deliverance and praise. Here, we are protected, cleansed and made holy. Psalm 33:21/34:8,10 (NIV) says, *In him our hearts rejoice, for we trust in his holy name. Taste and see that the LORD is good; blessed is the man who takes refuge in him...those who seek the LORD lack no good thing.* Hearts rejoicing rest secure in Him, our Vine, His Spirit abiding in us. May our heavenly-sustained, nourished hearts rejoice in His holiness—lacking no good thing!

Christian strength is born out of our weakness and willing dependence upon God in His Word and His church. He created Christ and His church that we shall humble ourselves and live to His glory, unified in Christ. Christ Himself testifies, *both the one who makes men holy and those who are made holy are of the same family. He says, I will declare your name to my brothers; in the presence of the congregation I will sing your praises...Here am I, and the children*

God has given me (Hebrews 2:11-13 NIV). Living our lives apart from God or His people is not His will; we are His family, abiding and growing together. Branches do not flourish alone, but in groups. We are His children, living, walking and abiding in His holy presence, unified by our nourishment and purpose.

Revelation 21:23 says, *For the glory of God illuminates the city, and the Lamb is its light.* Looking at a vineyard full of grapes near harvest, each group of vines and branches look as though all are intertwined and connected, each holding tightly together to that which helps it reach and draw nourishment from the light of the sun. John testifies, *And the angel showed me a pure river with the water of life…flowing from the throne of God and of the Lamb, coursing down the center…On each side of the river grew a tree of life, bearing twelve crops of fruit… leaves used to heal the nations.* We need the abiding waters of Life, His Word, His city and His people. *No longer will anything be cursed. For the throne of God and the Lamb will be there, and his servants will worship Him* (Revelation 22:1-3). **Let us speak the Words of Life—flowing from within that our prayers may bring His righteous rivers flowing from the throne, bearing fruit, healing our nations and freeing His Presence to reign within!**

God created us to worship Him. In independence, we look, as we did before salvation, for other things to fill the God-worship spot in out hearts. We either find ourselves too busy with self-duties, or trying to fill our heart's need to worship with something emotional or physical to worship instead, yet, we are not abiding and being filled by God. Let us repent the sin of prideful independence and rebellion that we may humbly die to self and in Him abide, worshipping and bringing glory to God in fruitful abiding lives of prayer.

Jesus says, *"A kernel of wheat must be planted in the soil. Unless it dies it will be alone—a single seed. But its death will produce many new kernels—a plentiful harvest of new lives. Those who love their life in this world will lose it. Those who despise their life in this world will keep it for eternal life* (John 12:24-25). Do you yet feel the irresistible call to worship with all your heart, soul, mind and strength? Joy and grace are found alone at the Cross, where we throw our lives to be crucified, bearing a plentiful harvest!

Let us confess daily, aloud, Galatians 2:20-21 (NIV), *I have been crucified with Christ and I no longer live, but Christ lives in me. The life I live in the body,*

I live by faith in the Son of God, who loved me and gave himself for me. I do no set aside the grace of God, for if righteousness could be gained through the law, Christ died for nothing. Dying to self in our cause for and faith in Christ, He carries on His harvesting of many new lives through righteous hearts and empowered prayers.

We are not alone. Take the first step, though you feel weak; kneel at the throne and be filled with the rivers of Life, flowing heavenly power within. Philippians 1:30 reminds, *We are in this fight together.* We are able to throw self to the ground and abide in Christ. Though you feel unfit for this holy, heavenly life of abiding, rejoice! God brings the sufficiency not always in our surety of remaining to the task or removing entirely the burden, but in humbly drawing us deeper to His Heart! 2 Corinthians 12:8-9 says, *Three different times I begged the Lord to take it away. Each time he said, My gracious favor is all you need. My power works best in your weakness.* Some may say this prayer remained unanswered. He answered in His holiness and all-powerful, divine knowledge, pouring out His grace, drawing Paul deeper to Him, humbling and strengthening. Allow the power of Christ to work through you to be strengthened through any weaknesses you may possess; it is all for the good of Christ. Let us trust; He answers the prayers of abiding hearts, in His perfect ways and His perfect timing.

His spirit of faith now tells humbled and empowered hearts in Philippians 3:7, *I once thought all these things were important, but now I consider them worthless because of what Christ has done.* The cars, homes, money, fame, trips, and all prestige of this world become meaningless; we now live to pray and bear fruit. Using resources not to exalt or please self, but to have further opportunity to spread the Good News and glorify His Name. Christ enables as we allow, for He promises, *This same God who takes care of me will supply all your needs from his glorious riches, which have been given to us in Christ Jesus. Now glory be to God our Father* (Philippians 4:19). Our riches found in abiding in Jesus Christ will provide all we need and all we could ask for, as we bring glory to God!

EXERCISE

Prayerfully consider, what does God want removed from your life? What kernel of wheat from your life does God want thrown to the ground to die; that it may later sprout forth for His kingdom? Where does He want to be the Strength you daily rely upon in your weakness? Where can you sacrifice more time throughout your day to pray and praise—relying upon God to give you daily, even hourly grace for your circumstances?

- What has God revealed to you about Himself, today?
- Which verse does God want you to ask Him to apply to your life today?
- For whom does He want you to pray this verse?

LET US PRAY

Wonderful, gracious Father, Lord God Almighty. Come, prune us, cleanse us, cutting away anything and everything, or anyone that weighs us down and hardens us to Your Word and our growth. Oh, Lord, teach us to abide in You that every prayer will be filled with Your passion, Your power, and for Your glory; In Jesus' powerful, precious Name we pray, Amen.

Day 32

RIGHTEOUS REQUIREMENTS of PRAYER

||||||||||||||||||||||||||||||||||||||||||||||||||

Both of them were upright in the sight of God, observing
all the Lord's commandments and regulations blamelessly.

— LUKE 1:6 NIV —

God blesses those who walk in righteousness and holiness, obeying His commands and observing His regulations by answering prayer. Righteousness means to be "upright, proper, conforming to truth and in proper standing with God." God blesses the prayers and lives of the righteous because they obey His commands, fear Him and seek His will and His Kingdom above all else. The righteous and holy heart reveres God by praying and sacrifices self daily, pleasing Him and furthering His Kingdom. Proverbs 11:19-20,23,30-31 promises, *Godly people find life...he delights in those who have integrity. The godly can look forward to happiness...the godly flourish like leaves in the spring. The godly are like trees that bear life-giving fruit, and those who save lives are wise.* Abiding in Christ, His love, and Word, we live in obedience and are blessed with the spirit of righteousness and holiness, becoming a life-giving fountain blessed by the King who reigns over our hearts, prayers, lives and minds. Proverbs 10:6,9,11,20 promise, *The godly are showered with blessings. People with integrity have firm footing. The words of the godly lead to life...the words of the godly are like sterling silver.* Filled with Him, He flows into all areas of the holy life—blessing words and prayers; giving life, sure footing and light for the path of the foot and the heart.

God promises the prayer of a righteous man is powerful and effective. His obedience here and continuing intercession now gives us His eternal righteousness, enabling us to live in obedience to and utilize God's Word, which Hebrews 4:12 says *is full of living power.* The heart living in His Word lives in the power and glory of God. Living according to the Word, gives us its power in prayer!

As our bodies live Romans 15:16, *As a fragrant sacrifice to God...pure and pleasing to Him by the Holy Spirit,* so our prayers are pure and pleasing. God's Heart's desire is that *In reference to your former manner of life, you lay aside the old self, which is being corrupted...that you be renewed in the spirit of the mind, and put on the new self...created in the likeness of God...in righteousness and holiness of the truth* (Ephesians 4:22-24 NASB). He asks each morning, just as we chose to put on clothes appropriate for the day, we choose to put aside the old dirty rotten, smelly attitudes, desires and thinking of self and instead put on our new, beautiful clothes, desires and thinking necessary every day of our blessed lives!

As we follow His command in James 4:10 (NASB), *Humble yourselves in the presence of the Lord.* He promises, *He will exalt you.* We are children of the King; let us not live as paupers in rags; instead, humbly put on our majestic, beautiful robes of holiness. Psalm 58:11 (NASB) promises, *Surely there is a reward for the righteous.* The NLT uses the words, *those who live for God;* describing the righteous. He promises as we treat Him, we are treated, saying, *'By those who come near Me I will be treated as holy...I will be honored.'* (Leviticus 10:3 NASB). He lives for and through those hearts honoring Him in holy prayer, choosing daily to live for Him. He lifts righteous hearts to reign with Him in the Presence of His holiness—at the throne of His mercy, grace and glory!

God's purpose and will for our hearts and lives are revealed in Leviticus 11:44-45 (NASB), *I am the LORD your God. Consecrate yourselves therefore, and be holy, for I am holy. For I am the LORD who brought you...thus you shall be holy, for I am holy.* He is, and we must be. As we allow Him to be "MY Lord God," not a distant God who doesn't see or care, but One who has called us out and up to become holy as He.

Genesis 1:27 says, He *created people in his own image; God patterned them after Himself.* God's Heart's desire is that His creation be restored to holiness, as He is. When Adam and Eve chose to sin, He removed them from His Presence, withdrawing His breath of holiness. Genesis 3:24 reads, *After banishing them from the Garden, the LORD God stationed mighty angelic beings to the east of Eden. And a flaming sword flashed back and forth, guarding the way to the tree of life.* God created us, not to "be" Him, but to be holy like Him. The Cross took His wrath and hatred for sin and replaced it with the spirit of restoration poured and sent forth at Pentecost. **For Christ fulfilled in Himself all things, that they may be fulfilled in ourselves, yielding to His work.** John 17:19 (NIV) states, *For them I sanctify myself, that they too may be sanctified.* His Spirit, Word, and prayer sanctify; placing us back into God's image of righteousness and holiness. He breathes His life, righteousness and holiness back into us through prayer!

Are you finding as the Holy Spirit fills with His spirit of righteousness, which is a dispensation of the fruit of the Spirit—a fruit of abiding, the desire and thirst for God's Word and His Presence are above all else? Galatians 5:16 promises, *When you live according to your new life in the Holy Spirit…you won't be doing what your sinful nature craves.* Sacrificing time and the things of this world no longer seem like sacrifices, but the greatest joys of holy hearts, now born from the whole-hearted cravings and desires to know, love, and serve Him. Those who are filled with Him, crave and obey His Word at any cost and seek His favor to bless His Kingdom and bring Him glory. We move from prayer being a time set aside and a special place to be alone with God, into living a life of prayer in righteousness and holiness daily. Filled in the morning closet of prayer, we continue in Him now and throughout the day. As breathing and walking are natural, so will praying be become natural to the spiritually healthy heart and soul! For Acts 17:28 says, *In him we live and move and exist. 'We are his offspring.'* Surrendered to His Spirit, we become like Him because we are filled with Him, to rivers overflowing; living, moving, existing "in prayer."

The spirit of righteousness humbly strives for God and delights in pleasing Him above all else. Psalm 104:34 says, *May he be pleased by all these thoughts about him, for I rejoice in the LORD.* Still thrilled by His blessing, we rejoice in His Name, living to seek and please Him. Praying and living for His glory and Kingdom fills hearts with reverence for His Name, righteousness and holiness. Proverbs 15:33 says, *Fear of the LORD teaches a person to be wise, humility precedes honor.* Sin in our hearts and lives is now taken very seriously, living in continual humble repentance, seeking earnestly after the will of God and His power, pleasing Him above ourselves or anyone else. Proverbs 16:15 promises, *In the light of a king's face is life, and his favor is like a cloud with the spring rain.* Remaining in the Presence of our King, His Light transforms, bringing life and righteous rains from heaven—watering the seeds of truth and salvation upon our hearts. When we live to please God, He is able to use us to do His will and serve His holy purposes, as David, our psalmist, spoken about in Acts 13:36, *He had served the purpose of God in his own generation.* **Holy hearts seek the Heart of God; finding the will of God, fulfilling His very highest and holiest purposes for their lives!**

Hearing and living the Word increases faith -- reminding us of His power, love, and virtues. Psalm 32:8,10-11 says, *I will guide you along the best pathway for your life. Unfailing love surrounds those who trust the LORD. So rejoice in the LORD, and be glad, all you who obey him! Shout for joy, all you whose hearts are pure!* He reminds us we are those, *Who have been called by God to be his own holy people…the more you grow like this, the more you will become productive and useful in your knowledge* (1 Corinthians 1:2/2 Peter 1:8). His spirit of righteousness makes divine wisdom given to us useful in our prayers; giving productive lives, leading us along the BEST *pathway for our life.*

Remember, in Psalm 33:6,15, *The LORD merely spoke, and the heavens were created. He breathed the Word, and all the stars were born.* His Word breathing through us in prayer brings His power to create and transform, placing everything in His highest work in the heavens. *He made their hearts. So he understands everything they do.* Prayer transforms the heart, divinely inspiring the pure motivations and inspirations of the soul. Living His Word guides continually into His will and His motivations, where we are promised to find His Presence and blessing in answer to prayer.

Jesus promises, remembering from day ten, in Matthew 5:6-8 (NASB), *Blessed are those who hunger and thirst for righteousness, for they shall be satisfied. Blessed are the merciful, for they shall receive mercy. Blessed are the pure in heart, for they shall see God.* Living by Scripture and prayer prepares hearts for the fruits of righteousness and holiness to burst forth, harvesting godly desires; equipping the heart and mind for God's purposes and plans, in His Presence.

Conforming us to the image of His Son, God desires us to be holy, as He is, and to be filled with Him, for He is love! Evil is not an entity that can overtake or overpower God's children, it is a lack of growing in our faith, knowledge, grace and holiness, a lack of love—allowing evil. Growing in our knowledge of Him, we live, not for self, but for love. God blesses us to bless others, the greatest of these blessings being His love. 1 Corinthians 13:1-2,13 says, *If I could speak in any language in heaven or on earth but didn't love others, I would only be making meaningless noise…and if I had the gift of faith so that I could speak to a mountain and make it move, without love I would be no good to anybody.* Surrendering to His Holy Spirit of power released through hearts and prayer, must have its motivation in love. *There are three things that will always endure: faith, hope, and love, and the greatest of these is love.*

Acquiring His character and virtues given by His Spirit, allows us to see and love Him, receiving His love and blessing to pour out into our hearts and lives in love as He pours out His from heaven, saving souls and redeeming His children. 1 Corinthians 13:4-7 tell us of God's holy Heart, *Love is patient and kind…is not jealous or boastful or proud or rude. Love does not demand its own way…is not irritable, and it keeps no record of when it has been wronged. It is never glad about injustice but rejoices when the truth wins out. Love never gives up, never loses faith, is always hopeful, and endures through every situation.* How many Christian marriages could be saved in true love? How many wayward children could be kept from a life of sin? As we open our hearts to His holiness, we enable His love to flow through us in prayer and deeds that never give up or lose faith! We become as He, that we may be the purified channel of blessings for others through which He loves, lives, prays, and must flow.

Before we can win others for Christ, we need to pray, first, for the spirit of righteousness and holiness to be poured out among churches that we will not be known for hypocrisy, but for practicing what we preach. This is what must be preached, prayed, and lived from the pulpit; truth in God's Word. Job 33:3-4 says *I speak with all sincerity; I speak the truth, for the Spirit of God has made me, and the breath of the Almighty gives me life.* When the love of God in holy praying hearts sees brethren in sin, we shall fall to our knees and pray, not giving up or giving in, but knowing it is God's will for them to be holy! Job 33:23-26,29-30 promises, *But if a special messenger from heaven is there to intercede for a person, to declare that he is upright, God will be gracious and say, 'Set him free. Do not make him die, for I have found a ransom for his life.' Then his body will become as healthy as a child's, firm and youthful again.*

When he prays to God, he will be accepted, and God will receive him with joy and restore him to good standing. Yes, God often does these things for people. He rescues them from the grave so they may live in the light of the living. God desires His children to live abundant lives in His Light!

Let us repent the times we chose darkness, praying always for those we know are living in it now. God promises in 1 John 5:16, *if you see a Christian brother or sister sinning in a way that does not lead to death, you should pray, and God will give that person life.* Scripture tells us to pray for the unsaved, for the church, ministers, missionaries, members, leaders, ourselves, our enemies and our brothers who have fallen in sin. Psalm 85:10-13 says, *Unfailing love and truth have met together. Righteousness and peace have kissed! Truth springs up from the earth, and righteousness smiles down from heaven. Yes, the LORD pours down his blessings. Our land will yield its bountiful crops. Righteousness goes as a herald before him, preparing the way for his steps.* The righteousness and holiness of Christ, for all we know, saved and unsaved, includes the thousands of struggling, prayerless Christians and churches falling daily into the hands of the enemy must be secured in heaven by holy hearts living and heralding daily with the Righteous Hand and Heart of a holy God.

We remember, too, the blessing upon God's faithful, holy servant in Job 42:8,10 (NASB), *And My servant Job will pray for you. For I will accept him so that I may not do with you according to your folly, because you have not spoken of Me what is right, as My servant has. The LORD restored the fortunes of Job when he prayed for his friends, and the LORD increased all that Job has twofold.* Whatever the righteous might lose in this life—for His Kingdom's sake, God promises that in restoration and love it is returned twofold in prayer, furthering His Kingdom and bringing forth His glory.

EXERCISE

On your calendar mark a weekly day to pray for the fruit of Righteousness to grow and burst forth from the hearts of your own children, as well as God's children worldwide. Pray for God to bring you like-minded sisters in Christ to join you in your weekly prayer. Focus on a different country each month, having someone research specific prayer needs; spiritual, economic and political concerns. Please see my website www.heartsofprayer.com to join others in an annual worldwide Mom's Day of Prayer hosted by MDOP each

January. Let us join in ransoming the hearts of many!

- ◆ What has God revealed to you about Himself, today?
- ◆ Which verse does God want you to ask Him to apply to your life today?
- ◆ For whom does He want you to pray this verse?

LET US PRAY

Father God, pour out Your spirit of righteousness and holiness into the lives of all Your ministers, missionaries, and members. Ignite in us the desire to live holy and righteous lives, interceding for many, bringing forth the fruit of righteousness that they and we may be holy as You are holy. In Jesus' wonderful and holy Name, Amen.

Day 33

MOTIVATIONS
HINDERING PRAYER
||||||||||||||||||||||||||||||||||||||||||||||||||||||||||||||||||||||||||||||||||||||||||||

*When you ask, you do not receive because
you ask with wrong motives.*

— JAMES 4:3 NIV —

God promises to hear and answer all our prayers, promising we will receive anything we desire, so why don't we? **What is the answer to unanswered prayer? Sin.** Psalm 66:18 (NIV) says, *If I had cherished sin in my heart, the LORD would not have listened.* Human pride believes "it must not have been God's will" and gives up immediately. Pride and this world tell us not to look at ourselves, but to blame others for our problems, shortcomings, or sins; most make an unfortunate habit of the same thing with failure in prayer.

Scripture repeatedly tells us that hearts holding unto sin, have unheard prayers. Each blessing and virtue has an opposite. For every "have," there is a "have not." Evil or sin is the lack of holiness in the heart. For each broken command, the Word promises lack. So, we can look at Scripture's promises regarding prayer like this: If we ask…we shall receive. If we ask not…we shall have not. If we believe…we shall receive. If we believe not…we shall receive not. If we seek…we shall find. If we seek not…we shall find not. If we knock…the door is opened. If we knock not…the door remains unopened. If we yield…we are filled. If we yield not…we are filled not! Hearts living in sin cannot live in prayer; this yields only fruit from this worldly kingdom; as

Romans 6:23 promises *the wages of sin is death.*

Scripture tells us the motivations of the heart determine the weight of our words in prayer. A heart living in the world, for the ways of the world will be motivated only by worldly desires. Jesus tells His disciples, *I chose you to come out of this world, and so it hates you* (John 15:19). Christians who have not come out of the world's ways have improper motivations in prayer; for we either "let" God have and motivate, or "let not", "letting" the devil have and motivate.

James 3:15-16 warns, *Jealousy and selfishness are not God's kind of wisdom. Such things are earthly, unspiritual, and motivated by the devil. For wherever there is jealousy and selfish ambition, there you will find disorder and every kind of evil.* When a prayer remains "unanswered," we must ask the Spirit to search our hearts for its origin and motivation. James 4:3 says, *Even when you do ask, you don't get it because your whole motive is wrong—you only want what will give you pleasure.* The NIV uses the words, *that you may spend what you get on your pleasures.* One problem that hinders our prayers is based on the selfishness of them. Psalm 37:33 says, God *will not let the wicked succeed.* Allowing wickedness in the heart brings unanswered prayer.

Colossians 3:2,5-6 demands, *Let heaven fill your thoughts. Do not think only about things down here on earth.* Heavenly thoughts bring heavenly prayers and blessings. Earthly thoughts bring forth only words of the lust of the heart, which brings death and cursing; which may seem a "blessing" received in the earthly world, but will perish and bring destruction. *So put to death the sinful, earthly desires lurking within you. Have nothing to do with sexual sin, impurity, lust, and shameful desires. Do not be greedy for the good things of this life, for that is idolatry. God's terrible anger will come upon those who do such things.* The definition of lust is a "strong craving." What we feed our bodies, souls, minds and hearts is that which it craves. Though seemingly earthbound, our hearts, minds and prayers filled with His Word and Spirit are loosed from this world, remaining heaven–bound, that we may crave more and more of Him.

Matthew 6:22-23 says, *Your eye is a lamp for your body. A pure eye lets sunshine into your soul. But an evil eye shuts out the light and plunges you into darkness. If the light you think you have is really darkness, how deep that darkness will be!* Any space in the heart and mind not occupied by and looking to God will be occupied by and look upon the lust of the flesh that lurks and lies in wait to fill those dark voids where God's Spirit is missing. Living and praying for and in His Kingdom, we invest, bearing fruit. Living and praying for the world and flesh, we invest also, but bear death. Matthew 6:21 (NASB) says, *Where your treasure is, there your heart will be also.* Asking for blessing for selfish gain brings, not blessing, but God's wrath; let hearts repent for He promises that He means and brings what He says!

This is not to say He does not bless us here on earth; He does! Those He blesses are those who worship Him even in the enjoyment of abundant finances, a beautiful home, car or vacation, seeking always to use what He gives spiritually and financially to bless His Name and Kingdom, bringing glory to Him. Scripture says a man is known by his heart, with man's natural heart and desires being sinful. 2 Corinthians 13:5,8 (NASB) says, *Test yourselves to see if you are in the faith; examine yourselves!* Fruitless prayers reveal a spiritually sick heart, with improper motivation. *For we can do nothing against the truth, but only for the truth.* Whatever motives and desires we hold in our hearts will come out into our words and prayers.

Truthful, divinely motivated hearts and prayers reveal Christ within, bearing fruit. Hearts motivated against the truth lack fruit in prayer, revealing the need for repentance and restoration to the truth. He knows our motives behind all service and prayers; they must be for the Kingdom, not for reward. Isaiah 45:7,13 (NASB) says, *The One forming light and creating darkness, causing well-being and creating calamity; I am the LORD…I have aroused him in righteousness and I will make all his ways smooth; He will build My city and will let My exiles go free, without any payment or reward.* Scripture tells us to look at our heart's motivations and our relationship to God when we encounter unanswered prayer.

This does not mean prayers we don't perceive as answered immediately should be considered "unanswered." Prayers from the throne through holy hearts may require persevering prayer, though they have already been answered in the spiritual realms. They are answered because they come from God-through pure hearts just waiting to receive. God may though, be hindered in answering prayers we do not persevere in; not receiving blessing through disbelief and impatience.

True "unanswered" prayers are those God does not hear nor bring blessing through for they are not truly prayers, or are cut short by sin. When the heart has been sanctified and prayer truly stems from the heavens, it is always answered. Those remaining unanswered are desires of the flesh, not really true prayers at all. Isaiah 59:1-2 warns *Listen! The LORD is not too weak to save you, and he is not becoming deaf. He can hear you when you call. But there is one problem—your sins have cut you off from God. Because of your sin, he has turned away and will not listen any more.*

The heart's motivations cannot be to please the world or self, and God at the same time. The mouth cannot worship the world or flesh profaning God's Name, then think in the time of need to be able to come into prayer to bless and receive from His Name too. Proverbs 16:2/15:28 warns, *People may be pure in their own eyes, but the LORD examines their motives...the godly think before speaking; the wicked spout evil words.* Let us be careful and thoughtful with what our lips profess during the day, and in our prayers, which honestly reveal the desires and condition of our hearts.

True prayer is divinely inspired, poured from heaven preparing the heart and the way for the Presence, blessing and work of God. True prayer tells us we know we shall receive what we have asked, because we are filled with His desires and know God hears us. Solomon warns in Ecclesiastes 11:9-10 (NASB), *Rejoice...let your heart be pleasant...follow the impulses of your heart and the desires of your eyes. Yet know that God will bring you to judgment for all these things. So, remove grief and anger from your heart and put away pain from your body.* Scripture tells us the heart prays as the life is lived and the life lives as the heart prays. Many say this Scripture teaches God's will is whatever we desire-not necessarily, as all desires aren't holy; it warns that we will give an account to God for all done. Not all allowed is beneficial, nor is it necessarily God's will, as Scripture speaks of those taken captive to do the devil's will.

Paul exhorts, *Another reason for right living is that you know how late it is...the coming of our salvation is near* (Romans 13:11). A heart living for the Kingdom has the urgency and passion of Christ and the need for God's blessing and power to be poured out for the work of the church. The selfish heart knows no urgency nor perseverance, only the passion of the flesh. Romans 13:12-13 commands, *So don't live in darkness. Get rid of your evil deeds. Shed them like dirty clothes. We should be decent and true in everything we do, so that everyone can approve of our behavior. Don't participate in wild parties and getting drunk, or in adultery and immoral living, or in fighting and jealousy.* Participation in the world and its sinful, ungodly pleasures separate us from living and desiring to be in the Presence of our holy God.

Let us always look to Christ, who teaches what it is to live, pray and minister with the right motives. He did all to glorify God, not Himself. If our lives are to be lived as His, and our prayers answered as His were, they must be for God's glory and not our own. Paul says, *We are not our own masters when we live or when we die. While we live, we live to please the Lord...so in life and death we belong to the Lord. Christ died and rose again for this very purpose, so that he might be Lord* (Romans 14:7). Lives motivated to please God are blessed by Him, filled with joy and peace in His service, in prayer. Hearts living for self find prayer and service frustrating and futile, living in constant fear of rejection, in frustration and with unanswered prayer.

Romans 14:17-18 (NIV) says, *The Kingdom of God is not a matter of eating and drinking, but of righteousness, peace and joy in the Holy Spirit, because anyone who serves Christ in this way is pleasing to God and approved by men.* Prayers in the Spirit are for the advancement of God's Kingdom and not our own. *For I am by God's grace...so it is right for me to be enthusiastic about all Christ Jesus has done through me in my service to God. My ambition has always been to preach the Good News* (Romans 15:15,17,20). Let us search our ambitions, desires and motives in prayer. Our service must be for His Kingdom and glory to receive His blessing, where God lives in power through hearts given to Him. By grace, He blesses, sustains, and fulfills the godly ambitions, desires and motives of the pure heart.

Consider some prayers that you have questioned if God is going to answer or whether you have even been praying according to His will, because they appear unanswered? Are you experiencing peace or frustration with these prayers? What is your true motive behind these prayers? Ask and allow God to search your hearts and reveal any impure motives—filling you with godly desires and motives. Do you live your life for your own pleasures, or to serve God and others? Are even good deeds in ministry and towards others for your glory or God's? It is very easy to be misled and do great things for all the wrong reasons—and these will fail. Being selfish is a part of our old human nature, and we must continually turn away to overcome it. The more we do, though, claiming our victory through the blood of Christ, the more naturally serving God out of a joyful heart to glorify Him becomes!

EXERCISE

Prayerfully consider the following, circling any known sins you need to repent, and ask God to reveal any unknown to you. Do not postpone repentance; ask forgiveness now by seeking a pertinent verse to pray into your heart-until you receive freedom:

♦ *Gluttony *Unwholesome talk *Adultery *Stealing *Coveting *Lust *Gossip

♦ *Rage *Anger *Brawling *Slander *Malice *Unkindness *Unforgiveness

♦ *Lacking Joy *Vanity *Pride *Laziness *Judgmental *Doubt *Lack of Confession

♦ *Loving the "world" *Not Honoring parents *Bitterness *Murder/Hate *Fear

♦ *Lacking Faith *Selfishness *Lacking peace *Not doing good *Wrong motives *Idolatry

♦ *Lying *Deceitfulness *Discontent *Swearing *Rebellion *Lack prayer/ worship/serving God

♦ *Complaining *Not tithing or giving *Ungrateful/unthankful *Jealousy *Disrespectful *Arguing

♦ *Unloving attitudes *Not attending church *Not resting—working on Sabbath *Condemning—Includes dishonoring any authority figure or law. Yes, this includes arguing with your husbands, parents or bosses, breaking the speed limit and cheating on your taxes!

PSALM 51

(Insert your name and pray aloud).

Have mercy on me, O God, according to your unfailing love; according to your great compassion blot out my transgressions. Wash away all my iniquity and cleanse me from my sin. Against you, you only have I sinned and done what is evil in your sight, so you are proved right when you speak and justified when you judge. Surely I was sinful at birth, sinful from the time my mother conceived me. Surely you desire truth in the inner parts; you teach me wisdom in the inmost place. Cleanse me with hyssop, and I will be clean; wash me, and I will be whiter than snow. Let *me* hear joy and gladness; let the bones you have crushed rejoice. Hide your face from *my* sins and blot out all *my* iniquity. Create in *me* a pure heart, O God, and renew a steadfast spirit within *me*. Do not cast *me* from your presence or take your Holy Spirit from *me*. Restore to *me* the joy of your salvation and grant *me* a willing spirit, to sustain *me*. Then *I* will teach transgressors your ways, and sinners will turn back to you. Save *me* from bloodguilt, O God, the God who saves *me*, and *my* tongue will sing of your righteousness. O Lord, open *my* lips, and *my* mouth will declare your praise. You do not delight in sacrifice, or *I* would bring it; you do not take pleasure in burnt offerings. The sacrifices of God are (<u>my</u>) broken spirit; (<u>my</u>) broken and contrite heart, O God, you will not despise. In your good pleasure make (<u>me</u>) prosper; build up (<u>my</u>) walls. Then there will be righteous sacrifices, whole burnt offerings to delight you; then bulls will be offered on your altar.

- ◆ What has God revealed to you about Himself, today?
- ◆ Which verse does God want you to ask Him to apply to your life today?
- ◆ For whom does He want you to pray this verse?

LET US PRAY

Wonderful, glorious, heavenly Father full of love compassion and mercy. We, again, confess our own unworthiness and unwillingness to be in full submission to Your will and for Your glory. Oh, Lord fill us with godly desires and proper motives; teach us to surrender, live and pray like You. In Jesus' Name we pray, Amen.

Day 34

GOD's GLORY
in PRAYER

|||||||||||||||||||||||||||||||||||||||||||||||||||||||

Ascribe to the LORD the glory due his name;
Bring an offering and come before him; worship
the LORD in the splendor of his holiness.

— 1 Chronicles 16:29 NIV —

Presenting ourselves before God in prayer, we must come with hearts full
of worship, having motives to bring glory to Him. Job 8:20 says, *God*
will not reject a person of integrity, nor will he make evildoer's prosper. He will
fill your mouth with laughter and your lips with shouts of joy. Many come to
prayer in order to try to control God, rather than to worship, being filled and
controlled by Him. Yes, He wants us to ask and receive; He created prayer
especially for this. He also wants us to listen and become motivated by the
desire to find, hear from, and receive the ability to obey Him in prayer.

Ezekiel 1:11-12 reads, *Each had two pairs of outstretched wings—one pair*
stretched out to touch the living beings on either side of it, and the other pair
covered its body. Living in prayer gives us the wings of eagles to soar to the
highest heavens, uniting us with the body of Christ and taking us from self
and fleshly living, humbly to the heights of worship and glory in the holiness
of God in life and prayer. *They went in whatever direction the spirit chose, and*
they moved straight forward in all directions without having to turn. Prayer
keeps us going God's way, whichever way that may be. Improper motivations
allow the heart to fall and turn away quickly when faith falters.

Prayer must have its motives in obedience to His Word and Spirit, bringing the church its needed power for God's work. Many, in prayer, will ask and then demand the answer; how and when. Ezekiel 1:4 says, *I saw a great storm coming…driving before it a huge cloud that flashed with lightening and shone with brilliant color…*It seems, many times, we find stormy conditions in answer to prayer. Job 4:3-4,6 says, *In the past you have encouraged many a troubled soul to trust in God; you have supported those who are weak. Your words have strengthened the fallen; you steadied those who wavered.* Divinely inspired and motivated prayer willingly lets go, entirely surrendering the situation and outcome in His hands in prayer. Our reverence for God must give confidence. Should we not believe—trusting God will care for us and those whom we love? **Properly motivated prayer thinks and prays eternally—remembering and trusting God's unfailing love, asking God to do WHATEVER IT TAKES!**

Job 9:4-5,12-14 tells us, *God is so wise and so mighty. Who has ever challenged him successfully? Without warning, he moves the mountains, overturning them… If he sends death to snatch someone away, who can stop him? Who dares to ask him, 'What are you doing?' The mightiest forces are crushed beneath his feet. And who am I that I should try to answer God or even reason with him?* Storms of life remind us who we are and who He is, giving even further proof to our souls of the need for prayer. We are able to surrender, trusting God knows exactly what must be done to inspire repentance, restoration, renewal and revival, to inspire eternal life and divine glory from every situation.

This is why He created us to worship, enjoy and glorify Him in an intimate relationship. Christ's death proves to us our worth to Him and His desire for a relationship with us. So many Christians live the same miserable, sinful lives as nonbelievers because they miss the whole point of life and prayer. After being saved, they still live as if life is about self rather than enjoying, glorifying and worshipping God. Matthew 6:2,4 warns, *When you give a gift to someone in need, don't shout about it as the hypocrites do…to call attention to their acts of charity! I assure you, they have received all the reward they will ever get.* Sin weighs down our hearts and prayers. *Give your gifts in secret, and your Father, who knows all secrets, will reward you.* Purity enlightens the heart's inspirations to be lifted to the heavens, receiving blessing and power.

He teaches the same purity is needed for prayer in Matthew 6:5-8, *When you pray, don't be like the hypocrites who love to pray publicly… where everyone can see them. I assure you that is all the reward they will ever get. But when you pray, go away by yourself, shut the door closed behind you, and pray to your Father secretly. Then your Father, who knows all secrets, will reward you. Don't babble on and on as people of other religions do. They think their prayers are answered only by repeating their words again and again. Don't be like them, because your Father knows exactly what you need even before you ask him!* Proper motives do not want or need recognition and even stand, many times, against the crowd; but are always rewarded!

Even regarding fasting, in Matthew 6:16,18, *When you fast, don't make it obvious, as the hypocrites do…so people will admire them…I assure you, that is the only reward they will ever get.* A hypocrite is "one who deceives others by false actions." Jesus refers, here, not to the shady salesman, but to those doing false religious acts, those with selfish motivation, receiving their reward in full from people and nothing from God! *No one will know you are fasting, except your Father, who knows what you do in secret. And your Father, who knows all secrets, will reward you.* Jesus promises God rewards what is done in secret, because its motivation is purely God's glory and service to His Kingdom. Let us beware and repent where pleasing people, bringing self glory and recognition have motivated our service and prayer!

Those not spending time getting to know and love God cannot serve Him or be motivated to desire His will over self will. He commands, *Let not the wise man gloat in his wisdom, or the mighty man in his might, or the rich man in his riches. Let them boast in this alone: that they truly know me and understand that I am the LORD who is just and righteous, whose love is unfailing, and that I delight in these things* (Jeremiah 9:23-24). Doing this, we spend time praying to Him and being still before Him.

Frequently, throughout Scripture, we read of His Presence speaking to His saints: "He commanded…they did," "An angel of the Lord appeared… they fell to the ground and worshipped." Sometimes the deepest need of the heart is bowing before God, being silent and worshipping, in reverence, His holiness. The humble and loving soul will receive the blessings He promises through pure prayer.

To love and serve Him, we must first get to know Him; knowledge of God is power! We cannot enjoy God from afar, nor can we live for Him and for ourselves at the same time. We cannot give false service and worship just to make ourselves appear reverent and holy. God says to His people, *I have no complaints about your sacrifices…you constantly bring to my altar. But I want no more bulls from your barns…What I want instead is your true thanks to God; I want you to fulfill your vows to the Most High. Trust me in your times of trouble. And I will rescue you, and you will give me glory* (Psalm 50:8-9,14-15). God wants our praise of, faithfulness to and trust in Him, as He rescues, that we may bring to Him the glory due His Name as we learn to live, pray and give thanks to God whom we trust to say, "Your will be done."

God calls His children to His will, listening in prayer and living by pure motivations. He says, *Try to live in peace with everyone, and seek to live a clean and holy life, for those who are not holy will not see God.* Only holy motivations bring prayers before God. Let us come before Him in worship and praise, giving honor to Him! *You have come to the assembly of God's firstborn children, whose names are written in heaven. You have come to God himself. Who is the judge of all people. And you have come to the spirits of the redeemed in heaven…See to it that you obey God, the one who is speaking to you. For if the people of Israel did not escape when they refused to listen to Moses, the earthly messenger, how terrible our danger if we reject the One who speaks to us from heaven!* (Hebrews 12:14,23,25). We must ask and listen, surrendering to His Work and will.

Do you reject the truth of His Word when it reveals a sin or improper motivation? Prayer is holy ground, as must be the motivations, sacrifice and service we bring forth. Each person, Christian and non-Christian, is motivated in life by their desires, what they know and love, who they spend time with. Job 31:6-7 says, *Let God judge me on the scales of justice, for he knows my integrity. If I have strayed from his pathway, or if my heart has lusted for what my eyes have seen, or if I am guilty of any other sin.* Let us allow our hearts to be searched in prayer; God desires to reveal His will. When our prayers truly come from proper motives, we can willingly know, love, and surrender to God's searching. If you lack joy or strength in anything you do, your motivation is not truly holy. It is God's desire to reveal and remove all sin from our hearts, cleansing and making us holy; let us repent and surrender!

Does every prayer hindered have sin behind it? Not necessarily. There are times we wait on God's timing as He works out circumstances; prayer drawing us and others into His will. We are told to ask, seek and knock. We must, at times wait, believe, achieve and receive. There are also times He says no and changes our prayer because He has something much better planned for us; this grows our faith so that we may reach what He has in store. Many times, in prayer, He is testing, trying to remove improper motives for pure, growing love, faith and perseverance. There are times we pray and wait for others to be delivered from sin. 1 John 5:16-17 (NASB) says, *If anyone sees his brother committing a sin not leading to death, he shall ask and God will give him life,* that is, *to those who commit sin not leading to death…all unrighteousness is sin, and there is a sin not leading to death.* When we see fallen brethren, we are to pray and keep praying, knowing God's desire to redeem, restore, and revive. Those motivated by flesh find it difficult to pray for others above self; His Spirit will sustain when we ask. Proper motivations are those shared with Jesus who asks the Father, on our behalf to do "what He knew it would take," for God's glory and the sake of the church.

Let us look, too, at the lack of proper motivation in prayer when pride brings, not true prayer, but self-exultation and self-righteousness, instead of worship. Jesus teaches, *The proud Pharisee stood by himself and prayed this prayer: 'I thank you, God, that I am not a sinner like everyone else, especially like that tax collector over there! For I never cheat, I don't sin, I don't commit adultery, I fast twice a week, and I give you a tenth of all my income.' But the tax collector stood at a distance and dared not lift his eyes to heaven as he prayed. Instead, he beat his chest in sorrow, saying, 'O God, be merciful to me, for I am a sinner.' I tell you, this sinner, not the Pharisee, returned home justified before God. For the proud will be humbled, but the humble will be honored* (Luke 18:11-13). Let us examine our motivations, as well the condition of our hearts as we bow before God. Let us never close the door on our closet of prayer as a means to an end; for our time kneeling before Him, is meant to start our fellowship within. Do you humbly seek mercy for your heart and those of others? Is your heart filled with godly sorrow, seeking repentance? Do you bring judgment upon you heart by judging others, even in prayer? Holy hearts in prayer remain humble, crying out for mercy for self and others. We cannot ask for one or the other; we must give love and mercy in order to receive it and humbly receive love and mercy in order to give it.

Galatians 6:14-16 says, *As for me, God forbid that I should boast about anything except the cross of our Lord Jesus Christ. Because of that cross, my interest in this world died long ago, and the world's interest in me is also long dead. It doesn't make any difference now whether we have been circumcised or not. What counts is whether we have really been changed into new and different people. May God's mercy and peace be upon all those who live by this principle. They are the new people of God.* Paul motivated proper motivation, as new people we live and are motivated by new things.

As your interests in the physical world and self die, you will notice your prayers changing. As they become more and more for the church and its ministers, missionaries and members, you will be filled by Him with new desire and perseverance in prayer. The first ten minutes in the closet of prayer is no longer enough. The hour of prayer becomes the desire of the heart for the day. The motivations of old will be swept away, making room for the new passions of Christ, empowered by the glory and Presence of God Almighty.

EXERCISE

♦ *Prayerfully consider: when you pray, whom you wish to know about it? Who do you tell?* _____

♦ *Do you & from whom do you look for thanks?* _____
_____

♦ *Are you careful to give and leave the praise to God?* _____
_____

♦ *Why do you pray/serve?* _____
_____

♦ *Do you feel your prayers/service to be more or less important than others?*
_____

♦ *Why?* _____

♦ *Can you accept God knew exactly what He was doing when He blessed you with your gifts and talents to serve Him? Why/why not?* _____
_____

♦ *Are you using your God-given gifts & talents for God's Kingdom, or yours?*
_____

♦ **How does God want you to improve this today?** _____
_____

❖ What has God revealed to you about Himself, today?

❖ Which verse does God want you to ask Him to apply to your life today?

❖ For whom does He want you to pray this verse?

LET US PRAY

Glorious heavenly Father, full of love compassion and mercy. Lead us by Your Spirit in prayer revealing Your will to us. Oh, Lord, teach us to humbly pray with godly, not selfish motives, cleansing, redeeming, and empowering us to be holy as You are. Oh, Lord teach us to pray like You. In Jesus' powerful and precious Name we pray, Amen.

Day 35

BATTLING UNFORGIVENESS in PRAYER

||||||||||||||||||||||||||||||||||||||||||||||||||||

And when you stand praying if you hold anything
against anyone, Forgive him so that your Father
in heaven may forgive you your sins.

— MARK 11: 25 NIV —

If we are truly grateful for God's forgiveness of our many sins against Him, how can we not humbly forgive others, no matter what we believe they have done? Because we allow the pride and sins of the flesh to come in and tell us they don't deserve it. Galatians 5:1,7-9 (KJV) commands, *Stand fast therefore in the liberty wherewith Christ hath made us free, and be not entangled again with the yoke of bondage.* So many hearts struggle in prayer and Christian living- in bondage to unforgiveness. Many find it easier to believe the enemy, who says we have a choice and shouldn't forgive others. The devil knows this hinders our relationship to God, so he does his very best to divide and destroy the harmony and love in homes, friendships, churches and workplaces. *Ye did run well; who did hinder you that ye should not obey the truth? This persuasion cometh not of him that calleth you. A little leaven leaveneth the whole lump.* No matter how difficult and painful, God commands us to forgive others before He will accept our worship, praise, or prayers. A little bit of anger, unforgiveness, or other sin spoils any good intentions we may believe we have.

Instead of holding onto anger and allowing bitterness to rule, we are commanded to forgive, trusting God, and loving all others through prayer. Galatians 5:6 (KJV) says, *For in Jesus Christ neither circumcision availeth any thing...but faith which worketh by love.* The spirit of faith controlling hearts allows God's pure love to flow through, regardless of personal emotions. Emotions cannot dictate our reactions, only the Spirit and the Word give us correct responses to otherwise painful or frustrating situations. God's road is always higher and more narrow, only to be traversed with the aid of the Spirit. Matthew 7:13-14 says, *You can enter God's Kingdom only through the narrow gate. The highway to hell is broad, and its gate is wide for the many who choose the easy way. But the gateway to life is small, and the road is narrow, and only a few ever find it.* God's love is unconditional, as He yearns for ours to be, though difficult. Forgiveness brings life as it loosens us from the chains of death and the enemy.

Let us not forget the prophet's words in Isaiah 53:4-6**,** *Yet it was our weaknesses he carried; it was our sorrows that weighed him down. And we thought his troubles were a punishment from God for his own sins! But he was wounded and crushed for our sins. He was beaten that we might have peace. He was whipped, and we were healed! All of us have strayed away like sheep. We have left God's paths to follow our own. Yet the Lord laid on him the guilt and sins of us all.* We cannot judge others when we, ourselves, have sinned and been unforgiving; we all have gone astray. Christ came to heal and free; let us not choose the bondages of the enemy, but allow the Spirit to heal, freeing unconditionally. We are responsible for our own end; we must divinely forgive!

Divine love forgives and forgets without punishment; human-only forgiveness harbors bitterness and seeks revenge. The spirit of bitterness affects and kills every relationship and eats away at every facet of our lives. An unforgiving spirit stands in judgment of others, a very sinful and dangerous place to be. Remember Christ's warning to all in Matthew 7:1-2 (KJV), *Judge not, that ye be not judged. For with what judgment ye judge, ye shall be judged; and with what measure ye mete, it shall be measured to you again.* Reaping and sowing in the Kingdom is an unchangeable rule-unforgiveness sows and reaps judgment!

Remember He teaches us in prayer to forgive ourselves, also as we forgive others. Praying hearts remain focused on Christ and how He desires to use us through prayer, bringing healing to the cries of their hearts, and ours and into both our lives. When we cannot bring physical reunion, we confess in prayer, *Just say the word from where you are, and my servant will be healed! Then Jesus said to the Roman officer, Go on home. What you have believed has happened. And the young servant was healed that same hour* (Matthew 8:8,13). Yes, it hurts us when others sin against us, but they are first and foremost hurting God and themselves by sinning against Him. All sin causes death; those hurting others on the outside, inside have hurting hearts. Thank God He has brought this book into your life at "such a time as this" to show you the ways in which to be free to live in prayer; believe He wants to forgive and heal others. Will you allow Him to use you?

Our unconditionally loving, all-knowing Father understands the frustrations we may have with forgiving certain people who have wronged us; He sees and He knows both hearts. He, alone, can use forgiveness for His glory, but the healing must start with your forgiveness, leaving the rest at His throne of grace. Jesus teaches, as Peter asks, *Lord, how often should I forgive someone who sins against me? Seven times? "No!" Jesus replied, "seventy times seven!"* He wasn't actually limiting us to 77 times, but showing us—completely and continually. Then, our heavenly Teacher and Intercessor gives the parable of the unforgiving servant. He says, *For this reason, the Kingdom of Heaven can be compared to a king who decided to bring his accounts up to date with servants who had borrowed money from him* (Matthew 18:21-23). He shows mercy to a man who cannot pay, releases him and forgives the debt completely. We, too, were unable to pay our debts, which Jesus paid for us in full when he freed our souls at the cross!

How many times do we allow negative thinking to enter in, telling us we cannot forgive? God gave us our forgiveness even before we were born! *Then the king called in the man he had forgiven and said, 'You evil servant! I forgave you that tremendous debt because you pleaded with me. Shouldn't you have mercy on your fellow servant, just as I had mercy on you?'* Forgiveness frees them to be loved, freeing the forgiving heart to receive mercy, being freed from the yokes of slavery to anger, bitterness, resentment and fear. He warns further, *Then the angry king sent the man to prison until he had paid every penny. That's what my heavenly Father will do to you if you refuse to forgive your brothers and sisters in your heart* (Matthew 18:32-35). To others, we may appear as if all is well—but God sees our hearts and knows eventually pain internally will present itself externally. God's Spirit, alone, allows His unhindered, unconditional love to flow through the heart. It is not our job to judge or expect others to pay their sin debts to us. Christ freed us all from paying our debt of sin- freeing us all from prison!

If you have a broken relationship that needs to be repented of and restored, stop NOW, and do so. **God takes an unforgiving spirit very seriously; it is sin not to trust Him, putting Him before self, even pain.** Jeremiah 2:19-20 warns, *Your own wickedness will punish you. You will see what an evil, bitter thing it is to forsake the LORD your God, having no fear of him…long ago I broke your yoke and tore away the chains of your slavery, but still you would not obey me.* When we obediently seek God, He helps us forgive and forget, keeping hearts freed from the yoke of slavery. Unforgiveness eats away at the mind, heart, soul, and body like an unrelenting cancer. The medical community is continuing to find what God's Word has said for centuries, that sin kills; they now blame countless heart attacks, addictions, depression, and suicides among others on stress and unresolved anger. Exercise, vitamins, and proper sleep are all great things, but it is the Lord who truly sets us free. Hosea 1:7 promises, *I will show love to the people…I will personally free them from their enemies without any help from weapons or armies.*

Surrendering with all faith in God, we are freed, remembering God's desire is to free His children. Lamentations 3:22,25,28,30-33 promises, *The unfailing love of the LORD never ends! By his mercies we have been kept from complete destruction. The LORD is wonderfully good to those who wait for him and seek him. Let them sit alone in silence beneath the LORD's demands. Let them turn the other cheek to those who strike them. Let them accept the insults of their enemies. For the LORD does not abandon anyone forever. Though he brings grief, he also shows compassion according to the greatness of his unfailing love. For he does not enjoy hurting people or causing them sorrow.* He will not abandon you or those for whom you pray. When He seems silent, remain in prayer, trusting in His UNFAILING love—for He is working!

Accept, in faith, His forgiveness for you and another, thanking Him. Lamentations 3:23,37,40 states, *Great is His faithfulness; his mercies begin afresh each day.* For we must ask, *can anything happen without the LORD's permission? Instead, let us test and examine our ways. Let us turn again in repentance to the LORD. Let us lift our hearts and hands to God in heaven.* Know whatever hurtful situation or persons He has allowed into your life have been divinely chosen to bring forth your holiness, possibly the other's holiness, and His glory!

In all areas, God enables us—remaining in prayer, to stand firm on His promise in Romans 8:28,31 (NASB) to *Cause all things to work together for the good to those who love God, to those who are called according to His purpose.* What the enemy intends to bring about for destruction, God uses to strengthen and bring new life, new resolve, and deeper intimacy. *What then shall we say to these things? If God is for us, who is against us?* Whatever causes us to dig deeper into Him, is good! We may not immediately understand His purpose, but we must obey His command to forgive, loving others regardless. We are not justified by the love or actions of another; we are free to forgive and love by God's holy power that dwells within. Romans 8:35,37-39 asks, *Can anything ever separate from Christ's love?* When another is unloving, let us turn to Christ, our one true love. *Does it mean he no longer loves us if we have trouble or calamity, or are persecuted? No, despite all these things, overwhelming victory is ours.* Whatever calamity, whatever hurts come, God's unfailing love gives us victory! Will you walk freely in that victory today?

Has God given you someone special who is a challenge to love? Consider it a privilege; He has given an honor to you, entrusting the hurting heart of another into your praying care. We all have stories, cries of the heart that need God's love to heal! Do not wait to obey God's command to love, forgive and pray for all. Do not focus on outward appearances, but on the Cross! The feeling, the joy and freeing peace of obedience and God's love flowing through follows the action of forgiveness; we will not receive it any other way. The action must be that of obedience to God's Word, not to our worldly feelings.

For Scripture promises, *Nothing can ever separate us from his love...The angels can't, and the demons can't. Our fears for today, our worries about tomorrow, and even the powers of hell can't keep God's love away...nothing in all creation will ever be able to separate us from the love of God that is revealed in Christ Jesus our Lord.* God's love revealed in Jesus is our example of love, forgiveness, and of our reaction to hurt. True love gives up its rights and gives them to God for His glory. With this daily self-sacrifice upon the Cross of cavalry, we confess, with Jesus, *Father, forgive these people, because they don't know what they are doing.* When hurting or rejecting someone, most truly are unaware of what they are really doing to another. Daily, we say with Jesus our Teacher and Savior, *Father, I entrust my spirit into your hands!* (Luke 23:34,46).

Effective prayer depends upon forgiveness—true relationships with God and others. Broken relationships with others reflects a broken relationship with God. Being unwilling to forgive others comes from pride, disbelief, bitterness and anger, and is a very dangerous place for the Christian to be; grieving the Holy Spirit within. Where, even other Christians, may say, "You have every right…" God says, "I AM your right." Ephesians 4:26-27,29-32 (KJV) warns, *Let not the sun go down upon your wrath: neither give place to the devil.* Unforgiveness gives the devil a mighty foothold in the hearts of the hurting. Prayers from a heart not right with God or others, miss His grace and cannot come before the throne with full assurance of faith, being blocked by sin. *Let no corrupt communication proceed out of your mouth, but that which is good…that it may minister grace unto the hearers.* We are not responsible for others' actions, but our reactions.

Are our words and thoughts in prayer and speech ministers of grace or the devil's work? Do they bring life or destroy it? We cannot teach or pray what we are unwilling to live! *And grieve not the Holy Spirit of God, whereby ye are sealed unto the day of redemption. Let all bitterness, and wrath, and anger, and clamour, and evil speaking, be put away from you, with all malice: and be ye kind one to another, tenderhearted, forgiving one another, even as God for Christ's sake hath forgiven you.* Grieving the Spirit hardens a once tender, holy heart and slowly but surely drowns out His Voice, the more we refuse to listen to it. When we refuse to love, harboring unforgiveness and bitterness in our hearts, God will not forgive us. We do not lose our salvation, but our relationship with Him and eventually everyone else is hindered. Faith, love and forgiveness are all dependent upon each other. If our sins are not forgiven because we are still unrepentant and living willfully in them, God will not hear our prayers. We are to let all these things be put away from us, and remain tenderhearted!

We either yield to the Spirit or we grieve; there is no middle road of neutrality. Philippians 4:8 (NIV). exhorts, *Whatever is true, whatever is noble, whatever is right, whatever is pure, whatever is lovely, whatever is admirable—if anything is excellent or praiseworthy—think about such things.* These are the things we are to think upon, we are to feast upon the Word and drink from His life-giving waters. Harboring anger, hatred, bitterness, jealousy, and resentment—not rejecting these thoughts, grieves Christ's Spirit dwelling within, making us sick from the inside out! Job 5:2 reminds that *Resentment kills a fool, and envy slays the simple. Blessed is the man whom God corrects; so do not despise the discipline of the Almighty.*

Whether our situation is discipline or growth, either must be thankfully surrendered with joy, trusting in God. Agreeing with Paul, *I will continue to rejoice, for I know that through your prayers and the help given by the Spirit of Jesus Christ, what has happened to me will turn out for my deliverance* (Philippians 1:18-19). *Through* our *prayers...deliverance*! Remember, loving and forgiving others, His promise, *I can do all things through him who gives me strength...and my God will meet all your needs according to his glorious riches in Christ Jesus* (Philippians 4:15,19). Where it is humanly impossible to forgive and forget, it is divinely possible!

Reaping and sowing holds true in every spiritual and physical aspect of our lives. Whatever we need, we must first give away. Whatever we give away, we will receive. Whether it is love, forgiveness, anger, money, etc, we reap as we sow!

EXERCISE

Start leaving love notes around the house, in your family members' pockets, lunches, briefcases, etc.. Put an extra $10 bill in the offering plate at church this week above your regular tithes and offerings. Watch carefully and prayerfully to see what happens (you'll start doing it more often!)

- ◆ What has God revealed to you about Himself, today?
- ◆ Which verse does God want you to ask Him to apply to your life today?
- ◆ For whom does He want you to pray this verse?

LET US PRAY

Gracious, heavenly, Almighty Father. We confess all of our sins including those of allowing anger, rage, bitterness and unforgiveness into our hearts, choking out the love You have filled our hearts with. Anytime this, person/ situation(s) is brought to us, please, by Your power working in us, help us to forgive—love through us. Oh, Lord, teach us to live and pray in grace. Oh, Lord, teach us to pray...In the perfect wonderful Name of Jesus, Amen.

'Day 36

GRACE to FORGIVE in PRAYER

||||||||||||||||||||||||||||||||||||||||||||||||||

And "don't sin by letting anger gain control over you."
Don't let the sun go down while you are still angry,
for anger gives a mighty foothold to the devil.

— EPHESIANS 4:26-27 —

Refusing to forgive or accept forgiveness, as God so freely forgives, we stand in judgment of the one we refuse to forgive—sometimes ourselves. Harboring unforgiveness, allows anger to control, giving the devil a foothold, or place—an opportunity in our hearts. God doesn't say we won't get angry, but this verse reinforces how we are to react with love, and the importance of immediate, daily forgiving one another. Unforgiving spirits condemn us and others by binding hatred to both hearts, keeping us in prisons of pain, instead of in God's love.

Paul exhorts, *Do not be overcome by evil, but overcome evil with good* (Romans 12:21 NIV). Jesus makes possible the ability to overcome evil with good; we must learn and be willing to practice it! 1 Peter 2:1-3 (NASB) commands, *Putting aside all malice, all deceit, hypocrisy, envy, and all slander, like newborn babies, long for the pure milk of the Word, so that by it you may grow in respect to salvation, if you have tasted the kindness of the Lord.* Let us long for the nourishment of the Word, freeing us from all forms of sin and anger. We cannot grow in God's grace if we forever look back, holding on with all our might to those things that should be left behind. Pride and stubborn, self-righteous anger keep us from rightly seeing the hurts against us, which do not even stand in comparison to the sins we have committed against God.

Psalm 66:18 reminds, *If I had cherished sin in my heart, the LORD would not have listened.* To cherish is to "consider fondly." Evil thoughts must immediately be denied entrance to minds and hearts! If we do not choose and accept graciously, quick and complete forgiveness, we allow satan entry, leading along a bitter path away from God's tender mercy, which makes it more and more difficult for us to see we need to forgive and be forgiven. Instead, let us confess, *Your unfailing love is better to me than life itself, how I praise you!* Others, even ourselves, will fail us, but God never will. Remaining in prayer and praise, He becomes our heart's desire, and pleasing and honoring Him, our goal. *I will honor you as long as I live, lifting up my hands to you in prayer* (Psalm 63:3-4). Choosing to honor God and refusing the devil any foothold in our lives, we may approach God in prayer with clean hearts. Clench your fists right now, as long as you can; eventually it hurts and cuts of the flow of life-blood and strength in your hands. This is what "holding onto" anger, and our rights or way does to our hearts. Now release! Lifting hands in prayer is a physical sign of surrender and worship. Coming in prayer, regardless of the feeling of the heart, we "let go and let God" thanking and praising God because we know, love and trust Him.

When we allow God's love to penetrate our hearts, He removes the anger, pride, unforgiveness and bitterness. Take heed His solemn warning, *Instead of believing what they knew was the truth about God, they deliberately chose to believe lies. So they worshipped the things that God made but not the Creator himself, who is to be praised forever. When they refuse to acknowledge God, he abandoned them to their evil minds and let them do things that should never be done. Their lives became full of every kind of wickedness, sin, greed, hate, envy, murder, fighting, deception, malicious behavior, and gossip. They refuse to understand, break their promises, and are heartless and unforgiving* (Romans 1:25,28-29,31). Yes, murder is in the same camp as unforgiveness; those who refuse to understand, God considers heartless.

James 2:12 further exhorts, *So whenever you speak, or whatever you do, remember that you will be judged by the law of love, the law that set you free.* Hearts filled to overflowing with His grace and love set us free to forgive and to pray. God's love and righteous rivers will pour through our hearts and into our prayers in faith for the very ones who have hurt us. James 2:19-20 asks, *Do you think it's enough to just believe that there is one God? Well, even the demons believe this, and they tremble in terror! Fool! When will you ever learn that faith that does not result in good deeds is useless?* Holy hearts in prayer will always be tested to go forth in the action of obedience, proving faith and love. Refusing to forgive, love and obey, renders us and all the spiritual gifts God has blessed us with, useless. For my husband's favorite verse, James 4:17 reminds *It is sin to know what you ought to do and then not do it.*

Let us repent; being encouraged and patient. Things may be slow as we understand them, but not as God sees how He needs to work the answers to our prayers and the hearts freed with His forgiving, cleansing Spirit pouring upon the earth. James 5:7-9,11 (NASB) encourages us to wait with faith. *Be patient, brethren, until the coming of the Lord. The farmer waits for the precious produce of the soil, being patient... You too be patient; strengthen your hearts... Do not complain, brethren against one another, so that you yourselves may not be judged; behold, the Judge is standing right at the door. We count those blessed who endured. You have heard of the endurance of Job and have seen the outcome of the Lord's dealings, that the Lord is full of compassion and is merciful.* Let us surrender to the loving Father our hearts, and those who have betrayed, hurt and let us or others down. Let us pray, walking the path of freedom and blessing—of patient forgiveness.

Proverbs 20:22 commands, *Don't say, I will get even for this wrong. Wait for the LORD to handle this matter.* Instead of hatred, handing our hearts and matters to God, He fills us with His compassion, compelling us more and more to pray for and love them. Resisting the earthly desire for revenge, He transforms hearts which are now slow to anger and abound in love as His. Psalm 119:32 (NIV) teaches, *I run in the path of your commands, for you have set my heart free.* Through God's grace to love and pray according to His commands for these people and situations He sets our hearts free, and theirs as well.

God's special prayer promises speak of having good relationships, confirming the importance in His Heart that forgiveness plays. Jesus promises, *I tell you this, If two of you agree down here on earth concerning anything you ask, my Father in heaven will do it for you. For where two or three gather together because they are mine, I am there among them* (Matthew 18:19-20 NIV). The enemy knows there is strength in numbers; there is life and there is joy where there is Jesus!

Scripture tells us, *Two people can accomplish more than twice as much as one; they get a better return for their labor. If one person falls, the other can reach out and help. But people who are alone when they fall are in real trouble. A person standing alone can be attacked and defeated, but two can stand back to back and conquer. Three are even better, for a triple braided cord is not easily broken* (Ecclesiastes 4:9-10,12). For this reason, the devil's job wreaks division and destruction in every relationship possible, especially those in the church! Our words to others must be of love and forgiveness always, for we are asked regarding our speech, *Sometimes it praises…sometimes it breaks out into curses against those who have been made in the image of God. So blessing and cursing come pouring out of the same mouth. Surely this is not right!* (James 3:9-10). **All of our words, spoken and thought, must be holy, that our prayers may be as well.** Matthew 5:44-45 commands, *Love your enemies! Pray for those who persecute you! In that way you will be acting as true children of your Father in heaven. For he gives his sunlight to both the evil and the good, and he sends rain on the just and the unjust.* We cannot judge who deserves forgiveness or punishment (even Jesus didn't!), prayer for blessings or cursing. You can't love AND judge! We must leave all judgment in His hands; obeying Him, in return, receiving blessing.

Right relationships are required, also to claim the promise in James 5:16 (NASB), *Confess your sins to one another, and pray for one another so that you may be healed. The effective prayer of a righteous man can accomplish much.* Most have heard the latter half of this verse and try only the "earnest prayer of a righteous person" part. Gather with another believer; real encouragement, building of faith and conviction comes with unified prayer. Another is able to discern sometimes where you are not, and is able to confirm what God is talking to you about. He tells us, *If any among you strays from the truth and one turns him back, let him know that he who turns a sinner from the error of his way will save his soul from death and will cover a multitude of sins* (James 5:19 NASB). Praying for each other builds unity, love, and strength within. His love turns each of us from our wicked ways that we may be healed. When we are able to confess with our mouths to another and repent our sins, God promises we are healed, yielding the prayer of a righteous man that is powerful and effective!

EXERCISE

Prayerfully list anyone from your past or present you have trouble wholeheartedly forgiving and leave the situation totally with God. REPENT & PRAY. Maybe you have been angry with God Himself for allowing the situation? Has your joy been replaced by a quick temper; trying to personally maintain total control of situations? REPENT & PRAY. Maybe you are having trouble forgiving yourself over something, and are not accepting God's and others forgiveness? REPENT & PRAY.

Unforgiveness can take hold even when we are not truly aware of it. Ask God to reveal anywhere you may be harboring sin—ask forgiveness now for your sins; asking for His help that you may be able and willing to forgive others, leaving all circumstances in the care of our Almighty Father.

Are there any steps you need to take regarding reconciliation to those you have trouble forgiving? Romans 12:18 (NIV) says, *If it is possible, as far as it depends on you, to live at peace with everyone.* This is a command. Regardless of the contact you may or may not need to make with this person, keep them in your prayers. Do not let satan, through this situation, rob you of any more love, joy or peace. Let it no longer hinder your relationship to God, others and your privileges in prayer. Be reconciled now that we may continue our journey, leave nothing hindering your relationship with God and your prayers! This person may not ask for, acknowledge, or accept your forgiveness, but it matters not, for you are only responsible for the act of forgiving. Also note, do not put yourself or another in physical harm!

- ➻ What has God revealed to you about Himself, today?
- ➻ Which verse does God want you to ask Him to apply to your life today?
- ➻ For whom does He want you to pray this verse?

LET US PRAY

Gracious, heavenly, Almighty Father. We confess to You all of our sins including those allowing anger, rage, pride, bitterness and unforgiveness to choke out the love You have filled our hearts with, allowing the enemy an opening into our hearts. We kick him out and shut all doors to him in our lives and hearts! **Oh, Lord, live, love and pray through us.** *Oh Lord, teach us to pray…In the most beautiful Name of Jesus, Amen.*

Day 37

BATTLING DOUBT
in PRAYER

||||||||||||||||||||||||||||||||||||||||||||||||||||||||

O unbelieving and perverse generation...
— LUKE 9:41 NIV —

How does disbelief affect our prayers? Disbelief is a refusal to believe Truth, instead believing the lies of satan. There are no middle turning lanes along this highway; either we believe God or the devil. Christians are called "believers" for a reason: we must believe Christ. We must believe ALL God says in His Word about Him and us, or we do not fully believe any of it. Doubt, believing the lies, keeps us from living and praying with the faith and holy hearts necessary for answered prayers. We find the unbelief of Jerusalem causes her unfaithfulness, leaving her to receive God's cleansing punishment instead of remaining in full blessing. We shall find the same!

God says in Isaiah 1:21-22,25, *See how Jerusalem, once so faithful, has become a prostitute. Once the home of justice and righteousness...once like pure silver, you have now become worthless slag. Once so pure, you are now like watered-down wine.* Disbelief, itself, is sin, but only the beginning. All unrepented sin multiplies, killing in all areas of life. What is God's reaction when we are watered down with disbelief? *I will turn against you. I will melt down and skin off your slag. I will remove all your impurities.* The Refiner's holy fires! Maybe, some of you—like me, are feeling these fires right now, as He removes those impurities hindering our relationship with Him. This may be a difficult part of the journey, it should be—the removal of sin causes pain to the flesh. Oh, but the joy that comes in the morning!

Be of good courage. We are almost there; can you see the finish line? Take heart, the pain will have eternal gains! For we see God's Heart, *Then I will restore…after that you will be called…righteousness…faithful. Zion* (we) *will be redeemed with justice and her repentant ones with righteousness* (Isaiah 1:26-27 NASB). God doesn't want to hurt; He desires to heal, restore, redeem and bring repentance for the sake of righteousness. Because He loves, He does not leave, allowing doubt to hinder our prayers and remain in our hearts!

Many Christians lead defeated and prayerless lives because they know little of the Word and God, leaving them unsure and unable to profess Truth. Mouths with unbelieving hearts cannot confess His Word in prayer, which causes the whole being to live in uncertainty. When we refuse to believe God's Truth, what we believe and live are lies from the evil one. What have you found in God's Word the most difficult to believe? **One of the most important elements to fully comprehend and believe in a healthy life of prayer is that He hears and answers us—with His unfailing love and goodness!** Do you believe He is good? And, He actually is *waiting for* us to ask so that He *can answer*!

Let us submit our hearts to God, removing the spirit of doubt. Let us build faith by speaking aloud His Word, *He will surely be gracious to you at the sound of your cry; when He hears it, He will answer you. Although the LORD has given you the bread of privation and water of oppression, He, your Teacher will no longer hide Himself, but your eyes will behold your Teacher, Your ears will hear a word behind you, This is the way, walk in it. And you will defile your graven images…you will scatter them…and say to them, Be gone!* (Isaiah 30:19-22 NASB) Are you seeing our Teacher and beholding His glory in life and prayer? What is He helping you remove from your life, to scatter and throw out? As He cleans our hearts, so too, shall He clean our homes and lives! The shadows of doubt and despair are replaced with the mighty power of His love, goodness, and Presence, surrendering us to His holy fires pouring forth from His Heart in prayer!

Disbelief and doubt take our eyes off of God's Truth and the Cross. Instead, the enemy has us focus on seemingly overwhelming circumstances and our weaknesses. Doubt switches the focus of the eyes of our hearts onto ourselves and the little we, alone, can do, instead of what God can and will accomplish through and with us—in His Sovereign care, persevering Presence, and His unlimited power and resources. Holy hearts praying with power live and believe Psalm 68:19-20,28 which says, *Praise the LORD; praise God our savior! For each day he carries us in his arms. Our God is a God who saves! The Sovereign LORD rescues us from death.* If your heart is struggling with doubt, surrender it to Him in praise. Ask Him, *Summon your might...display your power...as you have in the past.* Is He reminding you of a time you saw His great strength from the past? This is one reason a prayer journal can be so useful. Not only do we have God's Word and Spirit to remove doubt, we have our reminders of what He has done for us in the past—where He has used our lives to display His power! Writing down prayer requests also helps us see and wait for His answers to our prayers.

The spirit of doubt always brings failure and impatience in prayer and service. Doubt arises from belief in the flesh, which always fails, versus faith in God who never fails, instead bringing the faith to persevere. Many prayers and services to God fall short for this very reason. We start strong and determined, then allow doubt and physical circumstances to come rushing in, overwhelming and overcoming our feeble hearts as they try to stay in control and figure things out logically. Confidence in prayer cannot be based on or birthed from flesh, which brings death. Most are familiar with Jesus being able to walk on the water and Peter's falling in; this is what doubt does in prayer. Just yesterday my 6 year-old, JD explained this verse to his younger siblings like this, "if you stay looking at Jesus, you can walk on water with Him. If you look down at the waves, satan can grab you and drag you down into them!" No wonder I used to be afraid of drowning!

We read of Peter, beginning strong in faith, and then failing in the flesh. *"Lord, if it's really you, tell me to come to you by walking on water".* Let us believe to Whom we pray; He listens and answers—revealing Himself, if we will only look at Him and believe! Yet, many ask, "If it's really You..." then even when He brings confirmation - shall we still refuse to believe? Is it because He answers in very unexpected ways? Do we hinder prayer not only in the how, but in how much—putting Him in a box with doubt? Doubt lets Him answer only within human reason, causing us many times to miss His power in prayer, possibly by missing the answer. *So Peter went over the side of the boat and walked on the water toward Jesus...he looked around at the high waves, he was terrified and began to sink.* I would suspect, not only taking His eyes off Jesus caused him to sink, but maybe he expected there would be no waves? *"You don't have much faith…why did you doubt me?"* (Matthew 14:28-31) Doubt lacks faith in Who Jesus is, what He says, and what He can and will do through us and for us! Do we not always expect God to take away the storm rather than giving us the courage to walk through it in spite of large waves? Doubt comes rushing into minds that have preconceived ideas of the how, when and why God answers prayer. Doubt looks only for temporal blessings; faith looks for the eternal. Doubt doesn't see Jesus walking on the waves, but only the storms, drowning our hearts in the waves of doubt sorrow, shame, and lacks the perseverance to make it any further! Faith looks at Jesus, walking with Him, as on solid, dry ground alone; asking, thanking and believing and receiving.

Let us remember our "lack of" category as well. Doubt and disbelief are a "lack of" wisdom and faith. Allowing disbelief and doubt into our minds and hearts not only hinders our ability to pray, but is treacherous for our souls as our Christian walk will become no walk at all, drowning in the floodwaters of criticism, evil, judgment, condemnation and self-righteousness. Psalm 16:1,3 says, *We can gather our thoughts, but the LORD gives the right answer.* And then goes on to encourage and promise, *Commit your work to the LORD, and then your plans will succeed.* The only work and prayers that do not succeed are not from nor are they committed to the Lord. God always gives enough faith and resources to complete all prayers and tasks empowered by Him, for His purposes, and according to His good, pleasing and perfect will.

We do not jump ahead and then ask Him to bless; we go forth with faith in and wisdom of Him and from Him, for His plans. Psalm 16:9,16,20 promises, *We can make our plans, but the LORD determines our steps.* Remaining in surrendered prayer, we are able to see where God leads us, altering our plans accordingly. *How much better to get wisdom than gold, and understanding than silver! Those who listen to instruction will prosper; those who trust the LORD will be happy.* It fills hearts in holy prayer with faith to wisely pray, receiving instruction daily from the Spirit of God. Stepping out on our own, without knowing Him, His Word, or the leading of His Spirit, yields doubts that hinder prayers. Prayer is our flashlight in the dark, lighting up the path before us. Doubt comes in when we turn off the flashlight and tune out His Spirit, leaving us with no road signs, directions, visibility or guidance.

Let us remember, our downfall was coerced by the enemy tricking Eve into doubting God's very own Words she heard with her own ears! Whenever we receive the Word, the enemy will come in and try to steal the Truth that has been revealed to us, whether it be during prayer, Scripture study or in a sermon. We read of this in Jesus' parable of the seeds and the different kinds of soil, as well in the opening to the book of James written to all the tribes scattered abroad. James 1:2-4 (NIV) says, *Consider it pure joy, whenever you face trials of many kinds, because you know that the testing of your faith develops perseverance. Perseverance must finish its work so that you may be mature and complete, not lacking anything.* This is why the spirit of thanksgiving and praise in prayer is essential. Stormy waters and huge mountains are no match for a praising, prayerful heart. However, a doubting heart that tries to fight the enemy in the flesh and argue its way against the devil is doomed! Thanking God, we see all situations, all waiting and all answers as blessing. He promises to bless the obedient who ask and believe. His blessing may not be exactly how or when we intended, but as our faith to Him is worth far more than gold, it becomes so to us, allowing us to persevere, that we will not lack anything as we become holy like Him.

Those lacking His blessing and wisdom must ask Him to remove the doubt that hinders the receiving of His blessings. James 1:5-7 (NIV) promises, *If any of you lacks wisdom, he should ask God, who gives generously to all without finding fault, and it will be given to him. But when he asks, he must believe and not doubt, because he who doubts is like a wave of the sea, blown and tossed by the wind. That man should not think he will receive anything from the Lord; he is a double-minded man, unstable in all he does.* This person receives nothing and is unstable in everything!

Let us believe and know His Word, for He promises, *I assure you, if you have faith and don't doubt, you can do things like these and much more. You can even say to the mountain, 'May God lift you up and throw you into the sea,' and it will happen. If you believe, you will receive whatever you ask for in prayer* (Matthew 21:21-22). We forget He made the mountains we need moved! Instead, we buy into satan's lies that if we can't fix it, no one can. We begin to doubt our circumstances altogether if we are not firmly grounded in Truth, wondering if God is really in control, is even listening, or really cares at all.

So, what are we to do when the enemy comes to try to steal our faith, joy, peace, patience and fruit from His Word? The most important part of the battle is to submit to God in prayer, always on the offensive. James 4:6-7 (NASB) reminds, *God gives grace to the humble. Submit therefore to God. Resist the devil and he will flee from you.* Humble reliance upon God brings grace to resist the devil; then he doesn't just leave us, he flees!

However, when we beat down the gates of hell, practically chasing him, we may feel we are on the offensive and defensive sides all at the same time and, as some say, the fires get pretty hot in enemy territory! We dig deeper into God, using the same strategy; we do not argue! **We surrender to God, praising Him while praying, speaking and living His Word!** For some reason, following really intense prayer, there is a time of testing and growing our faith, where things always "seem" to be and look the worst—right before the prayer breakthrough! Let us remember, speaking this aloud until you believe and do not doubt His requirement and promise for prayer, *For verily I say unto you, That whosoever shall say unto this mountain, Be thou removed, and be thou cast into the sea; and shall not doubt in his heart, but shall believe that those things which he saith shall come to pass; he shall have whatsoever he saith. Therefore I say unto you, What things soever ye desire, when ye pray, believe ye receive them, and ye shall have them* (Mark 11:23-24 KJV). We must not only know with the head, but we must also believe, receiving with the heart. We are engaged in warfare that has already been determined; the enemy has already been defeated. Those captives and blessings we pray for, however, are not always so easily let go as we find He is working within us first, before He can work out of us through our prayers. Doubt must be cast out of our hearts so we may believe and receive; ask and we shall have! Do not give up and do not give in; the victory is on the horizon!

EXERCISE

Check any of these lies from satan you have allowed yourself to believe, causing you to disbelieve or doubt God:

- ❑ Your prayers and problems don't matter to God.
- ❑ Prayer doesn't work, why bother?
- ❑ God is going to do whatever He wants anyway, why bother?
- ❑ That is way too much for God to change; live with it.
- ❑ Maybe God has forgotten about you; you're a waste of time.
- ❑ It's just too hard, and painful-give up!
- ❑ Things will never change…

We need to know Truth to recognize satan's lies. We need to believe Truth to pray and live it. Study God's Word—believe and pray it!

- What has God revealed to you about Himself, today?
- Which verse does God want you to ask Him to apply to your life today?
- For whom does He want you to pray this verse?

LET US PRAY

We bless Your holy Name and praise You, God Almighty the Great I AM. Forgive our lack of prayer and belief that You are who You say You are, and that we are who You say we are in You! You keep every one of Your promises. Father God, remove all sin and doubt from our hearts. Oh, Lord, teach us to pray and keep our hearts on You even through the storms of life... In the holy wonderful powerful Name of Jesus we pray, Amen.

Day 38

GRACE to BELIEVE
in PRAYER

||||||||||||||||||||||||||||||||||||||||||||||||||

*And he called the place Massah and Meribah because
the Israelites quarreled and because they tested the
LORD saying, "Is the LORD with us or not?"*

— Exodus 17:7 NIV —

What we believe in our hearts is always the path our actions follow. What we believe about God and ourselves always shows in our actions and prayers. The enemy plots and plans to get God's children to doubt His ways, His Presence, His love, and who we are in His love. When we doubt or disbelieve in prayer, it is God and His truths we doubt. He cannot answer our prayers if we do not believe in Him and what He says. We will not be spiritually able to see, accept and obey His answers if we are in disbelief of Him; this is the very origin of pride. Disbelief, doubt, and fear are all traps and ploys of the enemy to keep us from humbly relying upon and praying to God Almighty and obeying Him, which leads us to pursue the world and be "blessed" (cursed) by it.

1 Timothy 3:6-7 warns, *And the devil will use that pride to make him fall. Also, people outside the church must speak well of him so that he will not fall into the devil's trap and be disgraced.* Humility and faith bring honor to us and God; pride and doubt bring disgrace. 1 Timothy 3:13 (NIV) says, *Those who have served well gain an excellent standing and great assurance of their faith in Christ Jesus.* Being unsure of God, and who we are in Him, will make the heart

unsure in prayer, many times even unsure of its eternal standing with Christ. The KJV uses the words, *Purchase themselves a good degree and great boldness in the faith which is in Christ Jesus.* The more we are filled with and know Jesus and who we are in Him, the bolder we are in prayer and service, conquering more of enemy territory! We, first, must know satan cannot take away our salvation, however he tries continually throughout the life of a believer using tricks and traps to keep us from being effective so we don't take anyone else to heaven with us. He knows if he keeps the church from praying, he can wreak havoc in our lives and those around us. Doubt believes the enemy's lies and can't act in faith, but instead, reacts with emotion and inaction.

Doubt in God causes rebellion, whether in the form of action or inaction, by trusting in something or someone else. *Have I put my trust in money or felt secure because of my gold? Does my happiness depend on my wealth and all that I own? Have I looked at the sun shining in the skies or the moon walking down its silvery pathway, and been secretly enticed in my heart to worship them? If so, I should be punished by the judges. For it would mean I had denied the God in heaven* (Job 31:24-28). Not many admit to denying God, however, we unfortunately place so much trust in this world, we do it quite often. When we are in doubt of Who God is and how we will receive His divine provisions, He may tell us to wait and we ignore Him. He may tell us to change our ways, to live on faith by cutting up our credit cards, to leave the unbeliever we are dating, to quit a job and start a new business or simply to form relationships evenly yoked within Scriptural boundaries, giving up all worldly ways of thinking and acting. He may, too, tell us to start praying, tithing, performing services in the church, exercising, eating right, paying monthly bills, etc. Doubt will tell us we can't, freezing us in fear and denying God in our actions.

Doubt doesn't believe He will bring the needed encouragement, resources and finances necessary to obey Him. Doubt is born from lack of wisdom and faith, not resources; it is a refusal to obey God. Job 24:13 (NIV) says, *There are those who rebel against the light, who do not know its ways or stay in its paths.* Doubt and disbelief convince us our circumstances, whether they be spiritual, emotional, physical, financial, marital, educational, or mental, will never change, which causes rebellion, grumbling and further sin. Faith says, "I can do all things through Christ!"

We must remain, walking in faith and praise, that we do not falter and grumble as God rescues us. We find it hard to believe the Israelites complained after being rescued from the oppressive slavery of the Egyptians, but that is just what we all find ourselves doing today. We pray, God answers, then we allow doubt in because He does things differently than we thought. Let us focus on His Words in Exodus 9:1-2: *This is what the LORD, the God of the Hebrews, says: 'Let my people go, so they can worship me. If you continue to oppress them…'* They were definitely oppressed, as were we before God's redeeming grace. As they did, so often we complain in our deliverance instead of worshipping; forgetting Him the moment we're free—making it all about us. Instead of being grateful, moving forward into blessing and looking to Him to care for us—we look backward upon our past bondage with "rosy glasses" as if they were the "good ole days!" We doubt what God is doing because we forget who it is all about: Him. So we rebel, grumble and complain; we long for our old, comfort zone back to being oppressed by sin, and we worship ourselves and slavery!

Being filled, consumed and driven by God's holy fires, doubt will be removed, bringing the faith that moves the mountains and casts them into the sea. Faith not only lives His Word, we will love and embody it. Let us be aware each time we step out to obey, and pray those big prayers—the enemy will be lurking somewhere, waiting for the opportune time to approach us; he knows what time that is for each of us. Remember Jesus was tested and tried, tempted and confronted right before He broke out into God's purposes and plans. It may be while we flip through TV stations at midnight, walk through a mall full of sales, or are alone with a chocolate cake at lunch. **Not only does Scripture tell us to remain in prayer and praise, filled with the Spirit, but also to refrain from evil.** To pursue godliness and reach our God-ordained purposes and best plans, we must turn away from evil and our old ways which bring doubt. As God spiritually housecleans our hearts preparing us for Promise, we should do the same with our homes to help this process and remove all temptation and any evil lurking around the corner!

My husband and I had a very "heart-opening" experience when our oldest, CJ honestly asked as a teenager, "If I can't watch that why can you?" He was right! When Jesus comes in, our trash needs to be out! It is a continual process; do not take anything for granted! If it does not promote biblical values, we do not need to watch, read, listen to or have it. My husband, Donnie and CJ went through every movie and removed all rated "R" movies and even a lot of PG rated ones. I then, also threw out most of CJ's childhood books, though they seemed harmless then. Now as a Christian, I don't want to promote magic, fake powers, witches, ghosts, etc. as entertainment. I don't want the "enemy" any entrance, nor to look like a friendly cartoon character; which he defiantly would like us to do!

My four remaining children at home, now all six years old and under are impressionable to their entire environment, and Scripture commands us to teach and to train them in the ways of, whom? The world? NO! The world teaches to doubt God. We are to train them in the way they should go, not the way they should not. Scripture commands us to be innocent of the ways of evil. The problem with many is we have to be untrained now, as adults. Let us not grumble and return to our old ways of being provided for, teaching our children, relating to our spouses, family, neighbors, obeying laws, learning about God, prayer, and worship. Let us stay out of our comfort zones, that He may draw us (without waiting another 40 years) to a land flowing with milk and honey!

Many think you have to be fanatic to be holy, yet all we truly need to do is combat doubt by prayer, knowing the Word and taking it literally! God warns those who doubt His Word and His judgment, *You have no excuse...for you who judge practice the same things. But because of your stubbornness and unrepentant heart, you are storing up wrath for yourself in the day of wrath and revelation of the righteous judgment of God, who WILL RENDER TO EACH PERSON ACCORDING TO HIS DEEDS...to those who are selfishly ambitious and do not obey the truth, but obey unrighteousness, wrath, and indignation. For there is no partiality with God* (Romans 2:1,5-6,8,11 NASB). We are judged according to the revelation of Truth we are to know and understand. To some, He gives much, to others, little, but we are responsible to that which He knows we should and are able to know. Saying we are too busy and feigning ignorance is no excuse. An excuse is a lie of the devil, bringing doubt and disparity we choose to profess and believe. We are responsible to know and obey Scripture, removing doubt and increasing effectiveness in prayer.

Let us remember that it is impossible to please God without faith, therefore, we know doubt will keep us from pleasing Him, praying right or finding and fulfilling our God-given and prayer-driven eternal purposes for which we have been each created. When we are not growing and succeeding, eventually, we shall begin to falter, drift and fall; many call this backsliding.

Unfortunately for lack of prayer and listening to anointed teaching, this is the state of the majority of the church and its members. Hebrews 2:1-3 exhorts, *Listen very carefully to the truth we have heard, or we may drift away from it. The message God delivered through the angels has always proved true, and the people were punished for every violation of the law and every act of disobedience. What makes us think that we can escape if we are indifferent to this great salvation that was announced by the Lord Jesus himself?* We are all responsible to know our Teacher and His teachings, denying indifference and obeying by His grace! Ministers need to take the first responsibility by practicing and teaching the art and life of prayer, first and foremost. Scriptures preached and taught, even ministers lives lived without the power of the Spirit are fruitless. Much time in depending prayer with less time "doing" will bear much more fruit and glory for God. Romans 12:21 (NIV) says, *Do not be overcome by evil, but overcome evil with good.* The New Testament church experienced this; doubt has stolen the Holy Spirit's power we need in making disciples in the world and in our neighborhoods. Let us repent and pray!

EXERCISE

We will wrap up today by reading aloud the first time; then with a pen, circling the actions that we are commanded to take or refrain from, taking further head of God's Heart towards doubt and disbelief: *Holy brethren, partakers of a heavenly calling, consider Jesus, the Apostle and High Priest of our confession; He was faithful to Him who appointed Him....For He has been counted worthy of more glory than Moses, by just so much as the builder of the house has more honor than the house. For every house is built by someone, but the builder of all things is God...Christ was faithful as a Son over His house— whose house we are, if we hold fast our confidence and the boast of our hope firm until the end. Therefore, just as the Holy Spirit says, "TODAY IF YOU HEAR HIS VOICE, DO NOT HARDEN YOUR HEARTS AS WHEN THEY PROVOKED ME, AS IN THE DAY OF TRIAL IN THE WILDERNESS, WHERE YOUR FATHERS TRIED ME BY TESTING ME, AND SAW MY WORKS FOR FORTY YEARS. THEREFORE I WAS ANGRY WITH THIS GENERATION, AND SAID, 'THEY ALWAYS GO ASTRAY IN THEIR HEART, AND THEY DID NOT KNOW MY WAYS'; AS I SWORE IN MY WRATH, 'THEY SHALL NOT ENTER MY REST.'" Take care, brethren, that there not be in any one of you an evil, unbelieving heart that falls away from the living God. But encourage one another day after day, as long as it is still called "Today," so that none of you will be hardened by the deceitfulness of sin. For we have become partakers of Christ, if we hold fast the beginning of our assurance firm until the end, while it is said, 'TODAY IF YOU HEAR HIS VOICE, DO NOT HARDEN YOUR HEARTS, AS WHEN THEY PROVOKED ME…'So we see they were not able to enter because of unbelief* (Hebrews 3:1-4,6-15,19 NASB). We cannot partake or share in, entering into the peace, joy, patience, kindness, and passions of Christ's power and presence in holy prayers wrought from heaven through sanctified hearts in disbelief.

- ❧ What has God revealed to you about Himself, today?
- ❧ Which verse does God want you to ask Him to apply to your life today?
- ❧ For whom does He want you to pray this verse?

LET US PRAY

We bless Your holy name and praise You, God, the Great I AM, Prince of Peace, perfect Lamb, God Almighty. Lead us in Your school of prayer to know You, to trust You, to believe You and to love You with an undivided heart. Help us believe and raise up an army of intercessors, trained in Your Word- to cloth all of our pastors in prayer! Oh, Lord, teach us to believe, teach us to pray… by the power of His blood in Jesus' Name we pray, Amen.

Day 39

BATTLING DISCOURAGEMENT in PRAYER

||||||||||||||||||||||||||||||||||||||||||||||||||||

But they did not listen to him because of their
discouragement and cruel bondage.

— EXODUS 6:9 NIV —

Discouragement is one of satan's favorite deceptions for keeping Christians from being effective in all areas of service to God, especially in prayer. The definition of discouragement is "to deprive of courage or confidence, dishearten and to hinder by inspiring fear of consequences, to deter to attempt to dissuade." With discouragement comes bondage to sin and to the world of the flesh. When we lose our courage and confidence in prayer, we lack our power and ability to discern God's will, Heart and Word, lacking our persevering confidence to ask and receive.

Psalm 119:25-26,28-29 says, *I lie in the dust, completely discouraged; revive me by your Word.* God's Word and Spirit revive, bringing life. Lack of the Word and Spirit brings lack of courage, life and revival. *I told you my plans, and you answered. Now teach me your principles. I weep with grief; encourage me by your Word.* God's Word, resting within the heart and mind, allows our plans to line up with His will; the Word not resting within brings discouragement. *Keep me from lying to myself; give me the privilege of knowing your law.*

When discouragement drags our holy heart from the heights of the heavens, we have forgotten: the "W's" of our faith. When we forget His Word, Worship and Will, we lose our Way, and our hearts are filled with discouragement and despair rather than with hope, courage and faith. Discouragement comes when we forget: Who we worship and have our faith in; Who the enemy is; What our mission and God-given talents and purposes are; Where our motives are, our treasures and hearts are to be stored; When God wants us to ask, wait, listen, and act; Why we are praying and serving; and With what power and resources we are to utilize and accomplish our God-given commands and tasks.

We can all relate to the story of David and Goliath; we are home, minding our own business, we go for a quick errand and are thrown a curve ball. Suddenly, we are presented with a God-sized task He wants to use us for! Many others trained in the field have tried and been stopped. An entire army has lost its focus and courage because they say there is a giant ahead! There is an immovable mountain ahead, and God gives you the mission; are you the one for the task? Are you willing to obey when the Father says, yes, it is you! And Goliath was only the start; David was in training to be king! We are all familiar with the story of the shepherd boy who was sent to take food to his brothers in the army. God uses this boy who knows Whom he serves, What his talents and purposes are, Where his motives and success came from, When he was to act, Why he was acting, and How he had been equipped in his past experiences—to go, filled with courage when an army of trained men cowered in fear for forty days!

1 Samuel 17:26,31 says**,** *David talked to some others standing there to verify the report. "What will a man get for killing this Philistine and putting an end to his abuse of Israel?" he asked them. "Who is this pagan Philistine anyway, that he is allowed to defy the armies of the living God?"* **He was offered a reward, but that was not his motivation; it was the holy Namesake of God and God's people he fought for.** *Then David's question was reported to King Saul, and the king sent for him.* When God has a task for us, it always has a way of finding us! David did not go there to fight the giant, but when confronted with the task, he knew he could. He was obeying His father's wishes when he received God's further instructions for His divine purposes. Many times, we are asked to do a menial task, something that disrupts our day, and find ourselves receiving some of God's greatest blessings. We can be discouraged that our way is not prospering, or we can praise God and look for His purposes and

plans in every circumstance, every relationship, and every detour.

We, too, can have the spirit of remembrance and see how God has trained us for His purposes and plans, placing us in the right circumstances at the right time to receive His Word, come into His will, and receive His victory and blessing—for His people. David defends his ability to the King, in 1 Samuel 17:36-37 (NASB) *Your servant has killed both the lion and the bear; and this uncircumcised Philistine will be like one of them, since, he has taunted the armies of the living God...the LORD who delivered me from the paw of the lion and the paw of the bear, He will deliver me from the hand of this Philistine. And Saul said to David, Go, and may the LORD be with you.* David, unlike the rest of the army, was not in it for the glory or the spoils, nor did he rely upon his training alone, or another's ways (or too-large armor); he was motivated by his desire to redeem the armies of God from the enemy in the Name of God and His children.

His desire, hope and power came straight from the Heart of the living God he served and worshipped in his father's fields as he guarded the sheep. He was not off on his own, wondering if he was doing God's will, where courage is lost quickly. He did not cower as the rest, fearing what his eyes saw. His desires were from heaven, confirmed by God's preparations, purposes, placement, and blessing. When God asks us to remain in prayer, regarding a situation, or to do something in particular, it may seem impossible at the moment and many may argue, as David's brothers did, but He always sends at least one to open the doors of victory and encouragement along the way! Discouragement comes when we are not filled with heavenly passions and motivations and when we are separated from God's people, His Word, His will and His Presence.

Fear of consequences, inspires discouragement in prayer and disobedience to God. Discouragement believes what our eyes see and is swayed by what others, our feelings, and our circumstances say, rather than by the Word of God. Discouragement comes when we do not believe or when we get distracted and forget God's Will, purpose and Presence in prayer. When we lose focus on Who He is, Who we are in Him, and His unlimited, infinite love and resources we can become discouraged in life, ministry and prayer. If we put a When-time limit on God, we become discouraged, wanting things in prayer, like at Burger King, getting it our way and fast- compare it to a meal from Mom's slow cooker!

David was patient, Willing to serve God Wherever and Whenever God chose. In 1 Samuel 16:7,11,13 (NASB) the prophet has come to the house of Jesse to anoint the new king, thinking Eliab must be the one. *But the LORD said to Samuel, "Do not look at his appearance or at the height of his stature, because I have rejected him; for God sees not as man sees, for man looks at the outward appearance, but the LORD looks at the heart."* Has the enemy tried to discourage you in service and prayer by your outward appearances or circumstances, telling you "you can't..." *Samuel said to Jesse, "Are these all the children?" And he said, "There remains yet the youngest, and behold, he is tending the sheep."* Surely God would not choose the youngest, who only tended sheep, to be His anointed for service?! His own father hadn't even called him in to be consecrated and offer sacrifices with the prophet. *Then Samuel took the horn of oil and anointed him in the midst of his brothers; and the Spirit of the LORD came mightily upon David from that day forward. And Samuel arose and went to Ramah.* Here is where many, like myself are tempted to get discouraged: God's timing!

We say, "I'm anointed; let's get on with this blessing now," or, "I asked, so where is it?" God says, "Wait, watch and thank me along the way!" David was to wait to be king. He received his anointing and his purpose, but it would be fulfilled in God's Way and When; there was still much preparing to be done. David was encouraged when he stayed focused on God's promises, faithfulness of the past, and God's resources and preparations. He was intent on serving His Father, with His resources, When and Where he was, for His Father's people.

The enemy's purpose is to discourage by stealing God's blessings from us of His passion, power, and purposes in our hearts, our freedom, contentment, rest, worship, joy, love, peace, patience, gentleness, kindness, self control, baptism, teaching, responsibility, assurance, holiness, courage, repentance, prayer and hope, among others. In what ways has satan tried to discourage you, to make you forget Who God is, Why He created you, Who you are in Him, and What He has done for you? Psalm 105:37,39-41,43-45 says, *But he brought his people safely out of Egypt, loaded with silver and gold; The LORD spread out a cloud above them as a covering and gave them great fire to light the darkness. They asked for a meal, and he sent them quail; he gave them manna—bread from heaven. He opened a rock, and water gushed out to form a river through the dry and barren land. So he brought his people out of Egypt with joy, his chosen ones with rejoicing. He gave his people the lands of pagan nations and they harvested crops that others had planted. All this happened so they would follow his principles and obey his laws.* What was their reaction to these divine protections and provisions? Psalm 106:13-14,21,24-25 says, *Yet how quickly they forgot what he had done! They wouldn't wait for his counsel! In the wilderness, their desires ran wild, testing God's patience…They forgot God, their savior…The people refused to enter the pleasant land, for they wouldn't believe his promise to care for them. Instead they grumbled…and refused to obey the LORD.* Where has the devil brought disbelief, discontentment, and impatience into your heart? He knows if he keeps us from worship, prayer and service, we will disobey and be beaten by discouragement.

Courage is poured out from the throne into holy hearts in prayer, for God's will and purposes. **He will bring all you need to accomplish His God-sized tasks for you, if you will only ask and obey! I don't know about you, but I don't want to refuse the Promised land; oh, may my God even use me to lead you there!** Joshua 1:6-7,13 commands, *Be strong and courageous, for you will lead my people to possess all the land I swore to give their ancestors. Be strong and very courageous. Obey all the laws Moses gave you. Do not turn away from them, and you will be successful in everything you do. 'The LORD your God is giving you rest and has given you this land.'* God desires His rest to be within our holy hearts and our rest within His; only here do we have courage and victory. What passions, purpose or mission in prayer and service has God given you personally? Consider your talents, loves, circumstances, and contacts? What do you naturally tend toward in prayer? With whom do you favor your sympathies—who does He want to use you to lead into the Promised land?

When God makes a promise and gives a mission, the enemy tries to come in and distract, dissuade, discourage and dismay us in any way he can. Once we believe satan's lies, we doubt God is in perfect and total control, which causes disobedience, fear and frustration. Though not understanding our waiting and preparations on the way to blessing, we do know we are to obey, trusting God at all times—in and through all circumstances, knowing He is able and Sovereign. 1 Corinthians 1:25-27/16:13 remind, *This 'foolish' plan of God is far wiser that the wisest of humans plans… God's weakness is far stronger than the greatest of human strength. Remember… few of you were wise in the world's eyes, or powerful, or wealthy, when you were called. Instead, God* deliberately chose things the world considers foolish in order to shame those who think they are wise. And he chose those who are powerless to shame those who are powerful. Staying focused on Who we are in God, and not self, beats discouragement. *Be on guard. Stand true to what you believe. Be courageous. Be strong.* Staying focused on God encourages where hearts can remain thankful and filled with His peace, no matter how long we have to wait or What it takes to be trained and prepared. In 2 Corinthians 3:2-3 Paul requests prayer, *Pray too, that we will be saved from wicked and evil people, but the Lord is faithful; he will make you strong and guard you from he evil one.* Whatever we and others go through; believing in answer to prayer, His Word and protection, that He is preparing us for His work, and bringing blessing—all for eternal benefit, brings new courage, new resolve and perseverance!

EXERCISE

PRAYERFULLY consider any of these lies you have chosen to believe, noting the outcome:

- ❏ *Where is God now?*
- ❏ *Are you really going to change His mind?*
- ❏ *How could this ever do any good?*
- ❏ *Remember your past failures? Don't bother!*
- ❏ *God doesn't love you why would He do this?*
- ❏ *Do what feels good, keep everyone happy; you can compromise.*
- ❏ *You can't trust God anymore, you should be afraid.*
- ❏ *I can't believe this is the thanks you get? You/they don't deserve this!*
- ❏ *Are you really a Christian? Are you sure?*
- ❏ *Your prayers and efforts are a waste of time; He won't ever save that/them!*
- ❏ *You/they don't matter to anyone, especially God.*

Counteract satan's lies with Truth. Find a verse about your situation; proclaim it aloud.

➡ What has God revealed to you about Himself, today?

➡ Which verse does God want you to ask Him to apply to your life today?

➡ For whom does He want you to pray this verse?

LET US PRAY

Wonderful, heavenly Father, our ever present Help in trouble, our Salvation, we praise and bless Your holy Name. Father, forgive us all our sins of, doubt, fear, grumbling, and rebellion- allowing the enemy to discourage us from prayer, thankfulness, courage and obedience. Oh Lord, conform us to Your image through our trials. Oh, Lord teach us to pray In Jesus' glorious and powerful Name, Amen.

Day 40

REJOICING in SUFFERING PRAYER

||||||||||||||||||||||||||||||||||||||||||||||||||||||||||||||||||||||||||||||||||||||||||||||||||

We also rejoice in our sufferings, because
we know that suffering produces perseverance;
perseverance, character; and character, hope.

— ROMANS 5:3 NIV —

In trials and sufferings, keeping an eternal perspective allows hearts to turn from discouragement and towards hope, having thanksgiving and contentment in all circumstances. A wonderful friend of ours, and pastor, Jerry Ediger has a favorite saying that has helped all he has known and taught: His favorite saying is **"think eternally."** When we can do this in every thought, every prayer, every circumstance and every reaction, we will lead obedient, victorious lives of prayer that are glorifying to God, and empowering to His church. Thinking eternally keeps us from discouragement and keeps us in prayer and praise, with hopeful and healing hearts. Thinking eternally allows hearts, lives, prayers and actions to be those of eternal, not temporal value. For we live as those with hope, eternal hope, found in 1 Peter 1:3 (NIV), which says, *Praise be to the God and Father of our Lord Jesus Christ! In his great mercy he has given us new birth into a living hope through the resurrection of Jesus Christ from the dead.* Rejoicing in suffering brings deliverance, life from death and hope in our God and Savior. Psalm 6:2-3 asks, *Have compassion on me, LORD, for I am weak. Heal me LORD, for my body is in agony. I am sick at heart. How long, O LORD, until you restore me?* Praise, even in admitting our weakness and need for His healing—draws us to our Restorer, revealing the aliments of the heart, drawing from the compassions of heaven.

Rejoicing according to love and obedience, not according to—but in spite of painful feeling, opens the floodgates of heaven, pouring forth the spirits of repentance, refreshment, restoration, rest, and revival. Psalm 18:1-3 gives the cries of a holy heart, *I love you LORD: you are my strength. The LORD is my rock, my fortress, and my savior; my God is my rock, in whom I find protection. He is my shield, the strength of my salvation, and my stronghold. I will call on the LORD, who is worthy of praise, for he saves me from my enemies.* Praising God in afflictions brings forth the hopes of heaven and strength of song into our hearts. He then answers every prayer, making Him personal; "my God," filling every desire and bringing victory in every area of the heart and life regardless of outer circumstances.

Our past "lack of" or, spirit of poverty, is overcome and hearts replenished when we acknowledge and receive the power to know Him personally. God says, *In that day the glory of Israel will be very dim, for poverty will strike the land. Then at last the people will think of their Creator and have respect for the Holy One of Israel. They will no longer ask their idols for help or worship what their own hands have made* (Isaiah 17:4,7). Poverty is defined as a "need or destitution." When a lack of spiritual, physical, mental, emotional, relational, or financial health is present, let us praise God, turn to Him and ask for His provisions, His restoration, His eternal ways bringing healing, restoration and the richest blessings from heaven. In that day, let us acknowledge Him respectfully, knowing that He is "my" God!

Praising, repentant, restored and revived holy hearts live and pray confidently and victoriously—beating discouragement, fear, and rebellion, thinking, praying and living eternally as our heavenly Teacher. Psalm 73:24,26,28 rejoices in the blessing of suffering, confessing, *You will keep on guiding me with your counsel, leading me to a glorious destiny. My health may fail, and my spirit may grow weak, but God remains the strength of my heart; he is mine forever. But as for me, how good it is to be near God! I have made the Sovereign LORD my shelter, and I will tell everyone about the wonderful things you do.* **Much of the testimony of the Christian is the wonderful, personal things God does bring out of testing and even tragedy.**

Suffering is where we find Him—the only Strength for the broken heart, the only Hope for the weary body and soul, the only Love for the lonely, the only Destiny from which the healing, righteous rivers flowing from heaven through holy hearts, pour out, raining upon the seeds of salvation sown upon the world. When trials, temptations, pain and suffering come, the enemy tries to use them for discouragement, breeding fear and paralyzed hearts. God uses these opportunities to open the eyes of the hearts, drawing them deeper into His love, glory and holiness. He will make our pains the very platform for the watching world to see His glory, as, reacting in faith—we experience His powerful, intimate, amazing love. Ephesians 3:17-18 (NIV) is filled with God's desire for us, *I pray that you may have power to grasp how wide and long and high and deep is the love of Christ.* It is not an easy thing to know Christ. Power is required, that comes forth in answer to much persevering prayer, praise, and suffering.

To rejoice in suffering for the Kingdom and struggle in prayer for mankind is to grasp the love of Christ, sacrificing self for the glory of God; this is how Jesus lived and prayed, for the sake of our eternity and for God's glory. Psalm 85:6-9 (NIV) asks, *Will you not revive us again, that your people may rejoice in you? Show us your unfailing love, O LORD, and grant us your salvation. I will listen to what God the LORD will say; he promises peace to his people, his saints—but let them not return to folly. Surely his salvation is near to those who fear him, that his glory may dwell in our land.* That His glory may dwell in holy, praising hearts, strengthened, revived, and redeemed from the spirits of adversity, pain, and poverty! **They are only the forerunner for the glory and blessing of the Lord!**

God speaks to us through our pain, *But I will reveal my name to my people, and they will come to know its power. Then at last they will recognize that it is I who speaks to them. How beautiful on the mountains are the feet of those who bring good news of peace and salvation, the news that the God of Israel reigns! The LORD will demonstrate his holy power before the eyes of all the nations* (Isaiah 52:6-7,10). Suffering reveals God's Name, our sin, His redemption, our weakness, His strength, our disparity, His hope and our helplessness! Thinking eternally, focuses eyes on the hope of the living Word, bringing forth good news through the worst of pain and afflictions, healing the cries of the heart. Acting and praying eternally promises comfort, strength and peace for all to see, bearing witness to the world of the Name of the Lord!

Prayer does not always remove the pain, but the sting, removing our hearts out of it and into God's passionate grace, comfort and peace. Psalm 22:23-24 commands, *Praise the LORD, all you who fear him! Honor him... show him reverence...for he has not ignored the suffering of the needy. He has not turned and walked away. He has listened to their cries for help.* Remaining in prayer and His Word, filled with His Spirit, we experience His persevering Presence that fills hearts with courage, hope, peace and blessing.

Read the following aloud, prayerfully inserting your name and another's. Psalm 23, frequently read at funerals, is not about death, but our heavenly life and hope lived now and into eternity, in spite of the earthly seas of sin and death that surround, *The LORD is my shepherd; I have everything I need. He lets me rest in green meadows; he leads me beside peaceful streams. He renews my strength. He guides me along right paths, bringing honor to his name. When I walk through the valley of death, I will not be afraid, for you are close beside me. Your rod and staff they comfort me. You prepare a feast for me in the presence of my enemies. You welcome me as a guest, anointing my head with oil, my cup overflows with blessings. Surely your goodness and unfailing love will pursue me all the days of my life, and I will live forever in the house of the LORD.* Reacting in faith, assurance and filled with His peace and blessing, brings honor to His Name, ushering in eternal blessing and purposes. His Spirit pursues holy hearts until we are called home to our eternal hope, in John 14:3, *When everything is ready, I will come and get you, so that you will always be with me where I am going.*

God uses all circumstances for our growth in holiness, teaching us of His hope, love, grace, and Light, that in rebellion, we find darkness and great discouragement. In the book of Joel (read the verse aloud below), we see God's grace and mercy come flooding forth from heaven after His people have lost everything, including their hope and pride. God promises to redeem, to restore, to bring us from shame to glory, from pain to peace, from weeping to praise. Let us take literally His love, forgiveness, and desire to restore to a state—even better and holier than before; for this brings Him pleasure and glory!

The Lord calls to each of His children through suffering, *Turn ye even unto me with all your heart…and rent your heart and not your garments, and turn unto the LORD your God; for he is gracious and merciful, slow to anger, and of great kindness, And repenteth him of evil. And I will restore to you the years that the locust hath eaten. My great army that I sent among you. And ye shall eat in plenty, and be satisfied. And praise the name of the LORD your God. That hath dealt wondrously with you: And my people shall never be ashamed.* Suffering draws us unto our true Hope and Strength, that we may find "**my** God", in repentance, His peace, restoration and blessing, sharing

His holiness—finding His Heart. *So shall ye know that I am the LORD your God dwelling in Zion, my holy mountain; then shall Jerusalem be holy. And there shall no strangers pass through her any more.* The NLT of verse 17 states, *And foreign armies will never conquer her again. And it shall come to pass in that day, That the mountains shall drop down new wine, And the hills shall flow with milk, And all the rivers of Judah shall flow with waters, And a fountain shall come forth of the house of the LORD, And shall water the valley of Shittim.* (Joel 2:12-13,25/3:17-18 KJV). When holy hearts pray, we bring down mountains in the Name of Jesus; creating waves, we walk upon them united with the Spirit of power, prosperity and peace. As prayer ushers forth the mighty Breath of God, bringing storm and righteous rains to water and wash hearts and lives clean, removing the dams of sin and shame, suffering and pain, rushing holy rivers flowing freely; faith allows feet fitted with the Gospel to walk through victoriously, finding the Promised land of blessing, praising God and bringing others to follow along the way! Suffering foreruns God's blessings; trials forerun His perseverance and God's grace and Spirit forerun our hope of holiness—HIS HEART, OUR HOME OF PRAYER.

When trials, tribulations, and stormy seas come in answer to prayer, stay focused on the:

ATTRIBUTES OF GOD

EXERCISE: *Praise Him, and pray your verses aloud, for Who you need Him to be, revealed Today!*

- *Faithful (Deut 7:9,32:4).*
- *Forgiving (Neh 9:17/Isa 43:25).*
- *Who sees me (Gen 16:13).*
- *Refuge (Joel 3:16/Ps 9:9,18:2/Isa 25:4).*
- *Almighty (Gen 49:25/Ruth 1:20).*
- *Father (Isa 9:6,63:16/Matt 5:16/Col 1:2,3:17).*
- *Jealous/Avenging (Nah 1:2/Ps 18:47,94:1).*
- *Sanctuary (Isa 8:14).*
- *Shade/Shelter (Isa 25:4).*

- **Strength** *(Isa 28:6/Ps 18:2,46:2).*
- **Redeemer** *(Isa 47:4,63:16).*
- **Mighty One** *(Isa 33:21).*
- **Lord Most High** *(Ps 7:17).*
- **Provider** *(Gen 22:14).*
- **Comforter** *(Jer 8:18/Isa 66:13/2Cor1:3).*
- **Refuge** *(Ps 46:1,59:16).*
- **Rock** *(Ps 18:2,42:9,62:7,95:1).*
- **Stronghold** *(Ps 9:9,144:2/2Sam 22:3).*
- **Love** *(1Jhn 4:8).*
- **Strength of heart** *(Ps 73:26).*
- **Shield** *(Ps 33:20).*
- **Hiding place** *(Ps 32:7).*
- **Love** *(Duet 33:3).*
- **Great/mighty/powerful/awesome** *(Duet 7:21,10:17/Jer 32:18).*
- **Dwelling place** *(Ps 90:1).*
- **Helper** *(Ps 46:1,118:7/Heb 13:6).*
- **Defender** *(Ps 68:5).*
- **Hope** *(Ps 25:5,21).*
- **Truth** *(Ps 31:5).*
- **Advocate** *(Job 16:19).*
- **Heals** *(Ex 15:26).*
- **Makes holy** *(Heb 2:11).*
- **Who saves** *(Ps 88:1).*
- **Grace** *(Ex 34:6/1Pet 5:10).*
- **Peace** *(Judg 6:24/1Thes 5:23).*
- **Forms hearts** *(Ps 33:15).*
- **Helper fatherless** *(Ps 10:14,68:5).*

- **Deliverer** *(Ps 140:7).*

- **Support** *(2Sam 22:19).*

- **Compassion** *(Ex 34:6/2Cor 1:3).*

- **Architect/Builder** *(Heb 3:4,11:10).*

- **Creator** *(Gen 14:19).*

- **Maker** *(Job 35:10/Eccl 11:5/Jer 10:16).*

- **Relents sending calamity** *(Joel 2:13).*

- **Reveals His thoughts** *(Amos 4:13).*

- **Able do more all we ask/imagine** *(Eph 3:20).*

- **Holy One** *(Hos 11:9/Rev 16:5).*

- **Holy Father** *(Jhn 17:11).*

- **King** *(Ps 95:3/Jer 10:10).*

- **Tests heart/mind** *(Jer 11:20).*

- **Sustains** *(Ps 54:4).*

- **Keeps from falling** *(Jude 24).*

•◆ What has God revealed to you about Himself, today?

•◆ Which verse does God want you to ask Him to apply to your life today?

•◆ For whom does He want you to pray this verse?

GOD'S HOPE *focuses on Him*	SATAN DISCOURAGES *focusing on Us:*
His Faithfulness	Our fear/circumstance
His love	Our trial/pain
His sovereign will	Our feeling out of control
His power	Our small resources
His healing	Our physical/emotional ailments
His strength	Our physical limitations
His provisions	Our poverty
His perfect purposes	Our selfish, desired outcome
His perfect timing	Our impatience
His compassion	Our pain/instability
His grace, mercy	Our failures, sins

God didn't promise days
without pain,
Laughter without sorrow or sun
without rain.
But God did promise strength
for the day.
Comfort for the tears and light
for the way.
And for all who believe
in His Kingdom above,
He answers every prayer with
everlasting
LOVE.

— DEENA DORNBERGER-HASKIN —

(Thank you, Mom!)

LET US PRAY

Glorious, heavenly Father, Comforter, Rock eternal, teach us to think, live and pray eternally, praising You in, through, and for all circumstances. Show us through Your answers to our prayers when to persevere, when we need to change by surrendering to Your working and power, where there is sin, and help us to remember and be faithful to remaining in Your school of prayer. We thank You for Your mighty power that works within us. Oh Lord, show us Your glory— conforming us to Your image through our trials. Teach us to pray and praise You. Oh, Lord live, love and pray through us—teaching us to live Prayer! **Fill us with Your Passions, enable us with Your Power, and let us live for Your Purposes! LORD- be "my God!"** *For Jesus' precious and powerful Namesake we live and pray, Amen!*

TEACHING ME *to* PRAY

Holy heavenly, wonderful Father
Full of mercy, full of grace
Great love for me did sacrifice
Shine Your Light upon my face
Jesus wonderful perfect Prince of Peace
Comforter, Protector, Friend so rare
Powerful Teacher, Loving Intercessor
Pure I'll be in Your care
Mold me and break me
Adventuring in prayer
That only You shall I seek...
Living to pray,
You shall not lead me astray
Oh Lord, thank You!
with passion,
with power,
with purpose,
Always...teaching me to pray...